Grantville Gazette V

Baen Books by ERIC FLINT

Ring of Fire series:

1632

1633 (with David Weber)

1634: The Baltic War (with David Weber)

Ring of Fire • *Ring of Fire II*

1634: The Galileo Affair (with Andrew Dennis)

1634: The Ram Rebellion (with Virginia DeMarce et al.)

1634: The Bavarian Crisis (with Virginia DeMarce)

1635: The Cannon Law (with Andrew Dennis)

1635: The Dreeson Incident (with Virginia DeMarce)

Grantville Gazette • *Grantville Gazette II* • *Grantville Gazette III*

Grantville Gazette IV • *Grantville Gazette V*

Time Spike (with Marilyn Kosmatka)

Joe's World series:

The Philosophical Strangler

Forward the Mage (with Richard Roach)

Standalone titles:

Mother of Demons

Crown of Slaves (with David Weber)

The Course of Empire (with K.D. Wentworth)

Boundary (with Ryk E. Spoor)

With Mercedes Lackey & Dave Freer:

The Shadow of the Lion • *This Rough Magic*

With Dave Freer:

Rats, Bats & Vats • *The Rats, The Bats & The Ugly*

Pyramid Scheme • *Pyramid Power*

With David Drake:

The Tyrant

The Belisarius Series with David Drake:

An Oblique Approach • *In the Heart of Darkness*

Destiny's Shield • *Fortune's Stroke*

The Tide of Victory • *The Dance of Time*

Edited by Eric Flint:

The World Turned Upside Down (with David Drake & Jim Baen)

The Best of Jim Baen's Universe

The Best of Jim Baen's Universe II (with Mike Resnick), forthcoming

With Ryk E. Spoor:

Mountain Magic (with David Drake & Henry Kuttner)

Boundary (with Ryk E. Spoor)

Grantville Gazette V

Sequels to *1632*
Edited and Created by
ERIC FLINT

GRANTVILLE GAZETTE V

Copyright © 2009 by Eric Flint

A Baen Books Original

Baen Publishing Enterprises
P.O. Box 1403
Riverdale, NY 10471
www.baen.com

ISBN: 978-1-4391-3279-1

Cover art by Tom Kidd

First printing, August 2009

Distributed by Simon & Schuster
1230 Avenue of the Americas
New York, NY 10020

Library of Congress Cataloging-in-Publication Data

Grantville gazette V : sequels to 1632 / edited and created by Eric Flint.
    p. cm.
  ISBN 978-1-4391-3279-1
 1. Fantasy fiction, American. 2. Seventeenth century—Fiction.
3. Alternative histories (Fiction), American. 4. Science fiction, American.
I. Flint, Eric. II. Title: Grantville gazette 5.

   PS648.F3G755 2009
   813'.54—dc22

                              2009011733

10 9 8 7 6 5 4 3 2 1

Pages by Joy Freeman (www.pagesbyjoy.com)
Printed in the United States of America

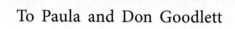

To Paula and Don Goodlett

Contents

Preface

Eric Flint

This fifth volume of the *Grantville Gazette* represents a change in the format of the *Gazettes*. Two changes, actually—one major and one whimsical.

The major change is that with this paper edition of the *Gazette* we have abandoned the formula we used for the first four volumes. That formula was straightforward: we simply took the equivalent electronic edition of the magazine, added a new story by me, and—*presto*—we had a paper edition.

For bibliophiles, collectors and completists, it was all very easy. *Gazette 1* (electronic edition) became *Gazette I* (paper edition). The only difference beyond the format was the addition of a new story by me, a new preface, and changing the Arabic number to a Roman one. Thus, *Gazette 2* became *Gazette II, 3* became *III,* and *4* became *IV.*

Alas, we can no longer continue that austere tradition. The reason is also simple, and—at least from my standpoint—represents one of those very nice problems called "problems of success."

Nice as they may be from one angle, problems of success are still problems and have to be addressed. The problem in this case is that Baen Books, the house which publishes the paper edition of the *Gazettes,* can no longer keep up with the production rate of the electronic editions.

The paper editions had already fallen badly behind at least two years ago. *Gazette III* (that's a paper edition, as is true of any of the *Gazettes* with Roman numerals) came out in hardcover in January of 2007. Four months later, in May of that year, we started publishing the electronic edition of the *Gazette* on a regular bimonthly basis—with volume *11*.

Thereafter, the situation just became hopeless, with a new electronic edition of the magazine appearing every two months. Baen is a book publisher, not a magazine publisher, and can only afford to set aside (at most) one slot per year for the *Gazette*. By the time this paper edition of *Gazette V* appears on the bookstore shelves, we will have published *Gazette 24* in electronic format. If we stayed with the one-to-one formula, it would be 2028 at the earliest before it could appear in a paper edition.

Something had to give. I discussed the problem with Toni Weisskopf, Baen's publisher, and we agreed that beginning with the fifth (paper) volume, the *Gazettes* would adopt a "best of" formula rather than being a straightforward transfer of a complete electronic magazine issue into its equivalent paper volume.

And that's what you have in your hand. The title says *Grantville Gazette V*, because there are good and practical marketing reasons that you don't want to confuse readers with too many formulas. The Ring of Fire series is already complex enough, thank you. So, we're continuing the tradition of numbering paper editions of the *Gazette* with Roman numerals. But we could just as easily and perhaps more accurately have titled it, *The Best of Grantville Gazettes 5 through 11*—because this volume contains stories that were originally published in one of those electronic editions.

That will continue to be the formula for the paper editions of the *Gazettes* from now on. They will all be "best of" volumes, incorporating stories from roughly half a dozen electronic issues. So, those of you who really want to have *every* story published in the *Gazettes* will henceforth need to buy the electronic magazine. You won't simply be able to assume that a paper edition will follow with the same contents.

I say this, you understand, in the sturdy tradition of grasping authors. The Order of Doctor Johnson, it's called. (And if you're not familiar with Doctor Johnson, see the afterword at the end of this volume.)

One thing has not changed—every paper edition of the *Gazette* will contain a new story by me that did not appear in the electronic edition, and never will. In this volume, that's my novelette "Steady Girl." And if it dawns on you that one side effect of this sturdy tradition is that a reader determined to get every *Gazette* story can't settle for just getting the electronic magazine but also has to buy each and every blasted paper edition . . .

Well, yes, that's true. I've been a faithful adherent to the Order of Doctor Johnson for many years now.

One other thing hasn't changed either, although it's undergone a transformation—and that's the whimsical change I referred to in the first paragraph of this preface.

It had always been the tradition, with paper editions of the *Gazette*, for Jim Baen to commission cover art based on a reworking of some famous painting of the 1632 era. (How much reworking? Enough to dodge modern idiotic copyright regulations. And if you're wondering how anyone can possibly claim "copyright" on images created by artists who've been dead for centuries, well, so am I.) I would then be presented with the end result, announced by a phone call from Jim—this was accompanied by what sounded suspiciously like snorting noises—and it would be up to me to figure out a story that explained the cover art.

It was a game between Jim and me that had actually started with the cover art to *1633*, one of the novels in the series I coauthored with David Weber. Jim really liked the image produced by Dru Blair of an armored seventeenth-century cavalryman staring up at a huge "ironclad." When David Weber and I complained that the warship depicted looked far more like a World War I era dreadnought than any ironclad *we* (the mere and miserable authors) had in the actual story, Jim loftily informed us that good cover art was good cover art and it was damn well our job to figure out a way to explain it in the story.

Which, indeed, we did, scribbling away in the night and muttering curses on the subject of publishers.

But the truth is, I enjoyed the game. It was fun in its own right, but it also forced me to engage in the authorial equivalent of stretching exercises. Every occupation has its hazards, and one of the hazards for storytellers is that they can easily get too obsessed with the majesty of the trade. Which, yes, certainly has its Shakespeares and Tolstoys and Flauberts to celebrate—but is ultimately a none-too-reputable craft begun tens of thousands of years ago around hunter-gatherer campfires, and continued in more civilized times by bards singing whatever the local king or baron damn well wanted to hear that night.

This is true of all arts, by the way. Joseph Haydn is today mostly remembered for his symphonies and string quartets and oratorios—but the great composer also has some two hundred baryton trios in his life's *oeuvre*. And what, you ask, is a "baryton"? It's a musical instrument that was already becoming obsolete in Haydn's day—you can think of it as grotesquely complicated violincello—but which Haydn's patron Prince Nikolaus Esterházy liked to play.

The prince wanted baryton trios, so Haydn wrote them. And while no one in their right mind considers those pieces the equal of the *London* and *Drumroll* symphonies, or *The Seasons,* still they are pleasant to the ear—and the requirement to produce them on order undoubtedly kept Haydn's creative mind nimble and flexible.

Then, in June of 2006, Jim Baen died.

I figured the game had died with him, but it's had an interesting resurrection. I was discussing the cover we'd need for *Gazette V* with Tom Kidd, the regular artist for the Ring of Fire series. In the course of the conversation, Tom mentioned that he had an idea he'd like to try. I told him to go ahead—whatever he'd like—and once he was done, I'd write a story to match the cover. An illustration of the illustration, so to speak. And that's the provenance of my lead-off story in this volume.

The trick to this exercise is to turn what is inherently a whimsical sort of tale into something that advances the overall development of the Ring of Fire series. In that regard, I'm quite pleased with "Steady Girl." First, it builds on many preexisting elements. Some of them, like Francisco Nasi's position, manifest themselves in practically every book of the series. Others, like Denise Beasley's connection to Kelly Aircraft or her relationship to Nasi, are the products of specific stories. (In the case of the first, my short novel "The Austro-Hungarian Connection" in *Ring of Fire II;* in the case of the second, the novel I recently coauthored with Virginia DeMarce, *1635: The Dreeson Incident.*)

But "Steady Girl" also goes forward, with new developments that will help lay the basis for later stories, in a number of ways.

Which ways? How?

Well, I'm afraid you'll have to wait until later books appear in the series and you can, ahem, buy them.

I told you. The Order of Doctor Johnson. Member in good standing, dues paid up and paid in full.

—Eric Flint, March 2009

Steady Girl

Eric Flint

Noelle Stull's kitchen
Grantville, capital of the State of Thuringia-Franconia
June 12, 1635

"I'm telling you, Noelle, something's wrong with Eddie," Denise Beasley insisted. She stared into the coffee cup in front of her with all the intensity of a fortune teller reading tea leaves. "He's been acting weird for weeks, now. He hardly talks to me at all any more, he's so damn obsessed with making money."

In point of fact, there were tea leaves at the bottom of the cup and Denise had drained it dry enough that they could be read. Assuming she was a fortune teller, that is, which she wasn't. Indeed, she would have heaped derision on the suggestion with all the enthusiastic energy of which her sixteen-year-old self was capable.

That was a lot of enthusiasm and energy, which made her current mood all the odder. "Glum" and "Denise Beasley" were terms that normally couldn't be found in the same room. For that matter, the same football field.

Standing at the stove where she was bringing a kettle of water to a boil, Noelle Stull looked over her shoulder at Denise. A close observer might have spotted something unusual in that look. A hint of scrutiny. A trace of amusement. Perhaps also some concern and trepidation.

5

Denise, however, missed all that. She was too intent on staring at the tea leaves in her cup. "I don't like it," she concluded. "One damn bit."

Seeing that the water had come to a boil, Noelle used a folded up towel to lift the kettle off the stove and start another pot of tea brewing.

"I've had enough," Denise said. "I don't much like tea, anyway."

"I do," said her best friend, Minnie Hugelmair, who was sitting at the far end of the kitchen table. "Even if coffee weren't so expensive, tea is better."

"And since when is tea 'cheap'?" jeered Denise. "If you want 'cheap,' drink broth. The only reason Noelle can afford tea or coffee is because she's a government bureaucrat, living off the fat of the land—fat of the taxpayer, I should say—while she makes life miserable for the hardworking folk who produce all the real wealth by making them fill out useless forms for sixteen hours a day." She took a deep breath. "Thereby draining the nation's treasury, impoverishing its spirit and threatening its very soul, because nobody has time to do any real work."

Noelle started refilling her cup and Minnie's. "Been spending time with Tino Nobili lately, I see. How in the world did that happen?"

Denise made a face. "I had to go to the pharmacy to get some medicine for Mom and I got trapped."

"Exactly how does a sixty-five-year-old reactionary pharmacist with a potbelly and a bad knee trap a sixteen-year-old in very good health who is every truant officer's personal nightmare?"

"How do you think? He musta spent half a goddam hour mixing up Mom's stuff. The over-the-counter ibuprofen's long gone, you know. I would've left except her cramps are really bad this time. By the end, though, I was figuring I might die of starvation before Tino finished, on account of how I now understood that nobody actually makes anything any longer including farmers, who are idle in their fields. And it's all on account of *you*."

"Well, yes, that's true," said Noelle. "If anybody did any actual work instead of filling out my useless paperwork—which, oddly enough, consists of specialized forms filled out by less than one percent of the population, but never mind, a good Tino Nobili rant is a thing of wonder—then my stratospheric salary might get cut down to merely ionospheric proportions. And if that happened, I might have to settle for a town mansion instead of a country estate for my retirement home."

"You've got it all wrong," Minnie said firmly. "The ionosphere is higher than the stratosphere." She began gesticulating, as if she were stacking invisible books. "At the bottom, there is the troposphere. That's where we live. It goes up about ten miles and has more than three-fourths of all the air, measured by weight. Okay, *then* there is the stratosphere. It goes from about ten miles up to about thirty miles high. After that comes the mesosphere, the thermosphere and the exosphere. The ionosphere is part of the thermosphere. *Way* higher than the stratosphere."

Denise stared at her friend as if she'd suddenly discovered that an alien moved among them. Minnie shrugged. "I pay attention in class, even if you don't. Especially science class, because it's really interesting."

"And good for you," Noelle said. "Unlike Denise, you won't wind up with a brain like Tino Nobili's."

Minnie giggled. "All shriveled up. Hard as a walnut and just about as big."

Denise gave her a disgusted look. "Fat chance." She then transferred the look of disgust onto Noelle. "It's your fault. If you didn't overwork Eddie the way you do, he'd have some time to relax."

"As it happens," Noelle said mildly, "I'm barely working him at all, these days. He asked for as much time off as I could give him, and he got it. It's to the point now where I'm skirting the edge of fraud, the way I mark him down for working full days when he's not even close. Some days he barely shows up at the office at all."

Denise frowned. "Then what's he—"

"All kinds of odd jobs he picks up," said Noelle. "Mostly from his father's connections. Down-timers with money will pay a lot to get solid advice from another down-timer who understands up-time legal practices and the way to maneuver through the bureaucracy."

"See?" said Denise triumphantly. "You just admitted it yourself. It's a bureaucracy!"

"Well, of course it is. What else would government agencies be? A sports league?"

Minni giggled again. Noelle took a sip of her tea. "Back up-time, I'd have to rein him in. Government officials are allowed to give advice to people who use their agency's services, of course, but they're not supposed to get paid for it. Down-time, though . . ."

Minnie grinned, being a down-timer herself. "Oh, come on. By today's standards, Eddie Junker is the soul of probity. He won't give anybody privy information and he won't take bribes to finagle contracts or juggle results."

"Yes, I know. That's why I look the other way."

"But *why*?" demanded Denise. "Since when did Eddie care that much about money?"

There was silence in the room. Noelle and Minnie glanced at each other.

Denise, naturally, spotted the glance. Despite the gibe, and leaving aside Denise's cavalier attitude toward formal education, there wasn't the slightest resemblance between her brain and a shriveled up walnut.

"Okay!" she said. "You guys know something! So *give*."

Noelle sighed, then drained her cup and rose from the table to return it to the sink. "He wants to learn how to fly. And he figures flying lessons are going to cost him an arm and a leg."

"Bound to," said Minnie. "The air force won't teach him unless he signs up, which he's not about to do. Eddie hasn't got a military bone in his body, even if he does shoot a gun real well. That means he's got to pay the Kellys to teach him."

Denise frowned. "How much do they charge?"

"Who knows?" said Noelle, coming back to the table and sitting down. "There are no established rules or regulations, much less standard pricing, for flying lessons. They range all the way from a half-baked 'simulation' on somebody's computer to the sort of training pilots get in the air force. And you know what Eddie's like. He's not about to do something like this half-assed. He'll want to be trained by real pros like the Kellys."

"That means Kay Kelly will call the shots," Minnie added, "and you know what *she's* like. Eddie figures she'll want the equivalent in money of the pound of flesh nearest to his heart."

Denise's expression had been growing darker by the second. "You mean to tell me that Eddie Junker's been working like a dog in order to pay the Kellys for *flying lessons*?"

"That's the gist of it," said Noelle.

"We'll see about that!" Denise exploded. And off she went, up from the table and out the back door to Noelle's apartment like the proverbial flash. A few seconds later, they heard Denise firing up her motorcycle and racing off. Doing a wheelie, by the sound of it.

She'd been in too much of a hurry to even close the door. Noelle got up and shut it, then sat down again.

"You should have told her," Minnie said accusingly.

"Told her what?"

"You know. Why Eddie's doing it. As if he just decided to start flying for no reason!"

Noelle's lips tightened. "I don't approve in the first place, Minnie. You know that perfectly well."

"So what? I probably don't approve either. Not that I don't like Eddie a lot myself, but the whole thing's just silly. In a few weeks, we won't even be living here any more. We'll be in Magdeburg. A few months after that, we'll be in Prague."

Noelle's lips tightened still further. She knew the basic parameters of the plans Minnie and Denise had made with Francisco Nasi. Now that Mike Stearns had lost the election and wasn't the prime minister any more, his intelligence chief had decided to go into private practice—in Prague, because Nasi also had some long-overdue personal matters to deal with, and Prague had the largest and most sophisticated Jewish community in Europe.

Personally, Noelle thought the man must be insane. Why in the world would he want to saddle himself with looking after two teenage girls? Especially *those* two. Either one of them was a handful and a half. Put them both together . . .

Noelle thought the wisecrack of one of the high school teachers about Denise and Minnie—*in tandem, they're the fifth horseman of the Apocalypse*—was overstating the case.

Probably.

"Who knows when we'll see Eddie again, after we move?" said Minnie. She shook her head. "That's going to be really hard on Denise. Since her father got killed, she leans a lot on Eddie even if she pretends she doesn't."

Noelle didn't say anything. Right there, she thought, was the heart of the problem. For all that there was no surface resemblance between stolid and level-headed Eddie Junker and Denise's ex-biker father, there were a lot more similarities than the average person might realize. However flamboyant Buster Beasley's reputation had been—and his death had been every bit as flamboyant—when it came to his daughter Denise, the man had been rock solid for the girl. As dependable as the tides.

There wasn't anything flamboyant about Eddie Junker. But he'd been Noelle's partner for some time now, and she knew him very well. They'd gone through the Ram Rebellion together, along with their adventure with the defectors and Janos Drugeth. If anyone had asked her to sum the man up, the first terms she would have used were "solid as a rock" and "dependable as the tides."

"Denise'll be okay, Noelle," Minnie said. "She's really smart, even if most people don't realize it because she gets bored in school and cusses like a soldier. Well, it doesn't help, probably, that she's beaten up a few boys, too. But only when they kept hitting on her after she told them to stop."

There was a lot of truth to that assessment, Noelle knew. But it still hadn't stopped Denise from . . .

Oh, let's see. Recently? Just in the last few months?

Picked a fight with an army officer. No verbal joust, either. A down home fist fight—well, Denise had gone to bar stools and salt shakers real quick—in a tavern.

Stolen an airplane.

Crashed said airplane. Well, fine, she hadn't been the pilot. Had participated in the crash of a stolen airplane.

What else of note? Noelle wasn't positive, but she was pretty sure from odd bits and pieces of data that had come her way—despite her innocuous-sounding formal title, she amounted to a secret agent for the government of the State of Thuringia-Franconia—that Denise had been centrally involved in the still mysterious episode involving Bryant Holloway's killing. The man had been "shot into doll rags," as one person who'd seen the body reported to Noelle afterward.

Could Denise Beasley shoot a man into doll rags? By all accounts, quite unlike Noelle herself, the girl was adept with firearms. So . . . yes. No doubt about it.

Would she do it, though? Knowing Denise as well as Noelle did . . .

Oh, yes, given the right situation. Noelle didn't have any doubt about that, either.

But all she said was, "I hope you're right."

The offices of Kelly Aviation
An airfield just outside of Grantville
June 12, 1635

"That's the most preposterous thing I've ever heard!" exclaimed Kay Kelly. "Ridiculous!"

She stopped striding back and forth and came to stand next to Denise, who was sitting in a chair in front of Bob Kelly's desk. Kay was a tall woman, and she loomed over the girl in a manner . . .

That might have intimidated another sixteen-year-old but affected Denise Beasley about as much as a light drizzle affects a duck.

"Oh, yeah?" sneered Denise. "You guys *bombed* him, remember? As in 'war crime.' The word 'atrocity' comes to mind, too. I know—I was there."

"You certainly were!" screeched Kay. She was starting to gesticulate a bit wildly. She had no way of knowing it, but the gestures would have seemed quite familiar to a number of high school teachers. Who had also, in the fullness of time, had cause to be exasperated by Denise Beasley.

"You certainly were!" she repeated. "That's because you were *in* that airplane! Because you'd stolen it! In fact, you were the bombardier!"

"Oh, that's pure horseshit. Lannie Yost and Keenan Wynn stole the plane. I had no idea. I thought they'd borrowed it legitimately until we were already in the air and then it was too late. What was I supposed to do? Get out and walk? As for who was the bombardier, that was Keenan. I was just the navigator."

Had Denise been committed to an anal-retentive definition of truth-telling, she would have added that, well, yes, she'd actually been the one to give the command to drop the bomb. Seeing as how Lannie and Keenan were doofuses who couldn't hit the broadside of a barn with any sort of weapon. But Denise labored under no such silly notion. Truth was an expansive sort of thing, with lots of room around the edges.

Kay had resumed pacing back and forth, and was about to start screeching again. Fortunately, her husband Bob finally spoke up.

"Oh, calm down, Kay! Let's see if we can't work out something reasonable. Truth is, Eddie Junker *was* bombed by one of our planes, even if we hadn't given anybody permission to use it.

We're all just lucky he didn't get hurt worse than a broken arm when his horse threw him."

Denise seized the moment. "Yeah, that was blind luck—as accurately as that plane of yours drops bombs, Mr. Kelly. It's no wonder the air force ordered a bunch of them."

She and Kelly exchanged big smiles. Bob was inordinately proud of his company's "Dauntless" line of aircraft—and, push come to shove, Denise had been one of the people who gave the plane its first real field test.

His wife Kay did not share in the momentary burst of good feeling. In fact, she hadn't even noticed it, as preoccupied as she'd been with her vigorous striding and gesticulating. "We're not—"

"Calm down, I said! We're not *what*? Liable?" Bob made a face. "If Eddie decides to sue us, it'll be a jury or a judge who makes that decision. You want to trust a judge or a jury? I sure don't. In fact, I'd just as soon keep the damn lawyers out of this altogether."

Kay pointed an accusing finger at Denise. "Let him sue! If he does, we'll sue *her*!"

"Oh, swell. We recoup our losses by stripping a sixteen-year-old clean of her possessions."

"Her mother—"

"Her mother? Would that be the Widder Beasley? Lemme see if I got this straight, Kay. You want us to fight it out in court with the widow and daughter of the hero Buster Beasley?" Bob shook his head. "Like I said. 'Oh, swell.' No, I don't think so."

His wife glared down at him, but the looming tactic was obviously just as useless with Bob as it had been with Denise. Kay Kelly was a rather formidable woman. But she and Bob had been married for a long time.

So Bob just ignored her and leaned forward in his chair, propping his arms on the desk and peering at Denise.

"You're sure about this? Eddie would be satisfied if we just provided him with flying lessons?"

"Yeah."

"How do you know?"

"I'm one of his best friends. Trust me. I know."

Kay hadn't quite given up. "Best friends! He's in his mid-twenties and you're way underage."

Denise looked bored. "He's twenty-three. That counts as 'early twenties,' not 'mid-twenties.' And there's no age of consent laws in the here and now and even if the seventeenth century had gotten around to that particularly stupid piece of so-called 'modern legislation,' it wouldn't matter anyway because we'd be under West Virginia law and the age of consent was sixteen. My sixteenth birthday was way, way back. Over seven months ago, now. And it's all beside the point, because Eddie and I aren't screwing each other. We're just real good friends."

Bob cleared his throat. "Kay, will you please let me handle this?"

His wife's lips tightened. But, after a moment, she went over to her own desk in the office and sat down. "Fine. Have at it."

Bob looked back at Denise. "I'm willing to bet you're doing this for Eddie, rather than him having sent you here." He held up his hand, forestalling any response on her part. "I'm not asking. Just don't think I'm a dummy, that's all."

"I never thought you were a dummy, Mr. Kelly," Denise said. That was quite true. Bob Kelly could sometimes be a walking definition of "absent minded" and he had plenty of other personal quirks and foibles. But nobody ever thought he wasn't smart. Dumb people don't design and build airplanes.

"What I'm getting at is this. If you and me reach a deal, I can assume that'll be okay with Eddie. Am I right?"

Denise nodded. "Yeah. Uh . . . Yeah. It will."

She had no doubt she was right. Given that Eddie didn't exactly know that she was doing this in the first place.

Well. Had no idea at all, if you wanted to get fussy about it.

"All right, then. I'll undertake to train Eddie Junker to be a pilot. And we'll understand that to mean that I'll train him until he's qualified for solo flight on a Dauntless." A bit stiffly: "I can't qualify him on one of Hal's aircraft, y'unnerstand?"

"Not a problem." So far as she knew, it wasn't. She had no idea why Eddie had gotten fixated on learning how to fly, but she was sure that as long as he could fly one type of plane he'd be satisfied.

And if he wasn't, well, dammit, *then* he could waste his own money on lessons.

She stuck out her hand. "It's a deal."

Kay spoke up again. "Junker pays for the fuel! Dammit, Bob, show a *little* backbone."

Denise did a quick calculation. Eddie could afford the cost of the fuel easily enough, she figured. And if she didn't leave him *something* to pay for, he was likely to go all stupid-male on her.

"Yeah, fine. Not a problem. Eddie pays for the fuel. Mr. Kelly, you drive a tough bargain. Surprised they don't call you Razorback Bob."

Rebecca Abrabanel's kitchen
Magdeburg, capital of the United States of Europe
July 2, 1635

"Does he not look splendid?" said Rebecca. The question was purely rhetorical, judging from the way her eyes were admiring her husband. Who, for his part, was standing in the middle of the large kitchen and looking uncomfortable. "Michael, stop fidgeting."

"Damn thing *itches*," Mike Stearns complained.

"Of course it itches," was his wife's unsympathetic reply. "It is made of wool. You will be glad of it, once you are on campaign. It will keep you warm in the winter and it will handle water well."

Rhetorical or not, Francisco Nasi thought it would be wise to provide a suitable answer. Hell might or might not have no fury like a woman scorned, but woe unto whichever fool neglected to praise a wife's abilities as a seamstress—or, in this case, ability to select a good seamstress.

"Oh, yes," he assured the wife in question, in tones loud enough to be heard by all occupants in the room. "Splendid, indeed."

He didn't even have to lie. Mike Stearns *did* look good in his new uniform. True, the austere design of the uniform was a bit startling to someone raised according to seventeenth-century notions of proper male costume. All the more so for Nasi, who'd been reared in the Ottoman court. But Stearns was a well-built man, and taller than average. He was still muscular and not gone to fat despite being close to forty years of age and having spent most of the last three years seated behind a desk. The severity of the uniform simply emphasized that physique.

Rebecca looked pleased, but Mike was still in a grumbling mood. "I'm starting to feel like a traitor. First, we've got a flag that from a distance looks just like a damn Confederate flag—and now *this*."

After a moment, Nasi deduced that by "this" Mike was referring to the color of the uniform. It was solid gray, shading slightly toward green. If Francisco remembered correctly, the uniform worn by the soldiers of the Confederacy in the American civil war had been that color.

But perhaps not. Nasi could hardly be expected to remember every detail of books he had read about the history of another world's future.

"Oh, hogwash, Mike," said his friend and now fellow army officer Frank Jackson. "Those uniforms were butternut."

Mike's sneer was magnificent. "Izzat so? Ever hear of 'the blue and the gray'? The 'gray,' you'll note, not 'the blue and the butternut,' which sounds downright silly."

Jackson leaned back in his chair and shrugged. "Those were just officers' uniforms. The uniforms of the grunts were butternut."

The sneer remained in place. Indeed, it expanded, as Mike pointed at a cap perched on a peg near the kitchen entrance. "See the stars there on the front of the cap? Two of 'em, no less." The accusing finger now jabbed at the insignia on his left shoulder. "Same two we've got right here. They stand for 'major general,' old buddy. Since you're apparently going senile, a major general qualifies as an officer."

Frank grinned. "Aren't we testy? Will it make you feel any better if I tell you that I happen to know just how and why the army's quartermasters settled on gray uniforms? Had absolutely nothing to do with our little American fracas, back when a couple of centuries from now. Seems they got their hands on some German history books and got swept up in a wave of future nostalgia." He pointed at Mike's tunic. "That color is officially '*feldgrau*,' fella. That means—"

"I know what it means," growled Mike. "My German is quite fluent by now, thank you. 'Field gray.' Swell. So now I find out that instead of being a damn Confederate, it seems I'm a damn storm trooper."

"Actually, feldgrau uniforms were common in the German Army way before the Nazis," Frank said. "But is there anything else you want to complain about? If so, better get it out quick, since Francisco needs a decision."

"No, I guess I'm done." Then, demonstrating that he had not lost all his senses, Mike bestowed a winning smile on his wife. "It's a nice uniform, Becky. Thank you."

He turned toward Nasi, and the smile faded a bit. "Francisco, I don't see any way you could buy one of Hal and Jesse's planes without the whole thing causing a stink."

"Hal's planes," Jesse Wood said mildly. "I got out of the business"—he looked at Nasi—"for pretty much the same reason Mike doesn't think you can buy one of the planes. Looks bad. Conflict of interest, that sort of thing."

"I am quite wealthy," said Nasi. "I assure you that I can pay the full price for one of the planes—and I am quite willing to have the figures made public. Indeed, for my purposes, the more public, the better."

Mike shook his head. "It doesn't matter, Francisco. We're just too closely associated, all of us. Me, you, Frank"—he jabbed a thumb at Jesse—"even him, though I don't know if he voted for me in the election."

"In point of fact, I didn't," said the commander in chief of the USE's little air force. "I decided I'd follow General George Marshall's practice and not vote at all. I'm pretty sure Admiral Simpson did the same thing. But getting back to the issue at hand, Francisco, all of Hal's planes are spoken for by the air force, anyway, for at least another year's worth of production."

Francisco didn't argue the matter any further. He'd expected that answer. He'd only pushed the issue at all because he was reluctant to entrust his safety to any airplane that wasn't made by Jesse's one-time partner Hal Smith.

The alternatives were either Kelly Aircraft or Markgraf and Smith Aviation. Of those alternatives, Francisco had already decided he'd approach the Kellys, assuming Mike advised him that buying one of Hal Smith's planes was not a suitable choice. For his purposes, the new Dauntless aircraft was far more suitable than the slow and heavy cargo planes made by Markgraf and Smith.

That left the problem of finding a pilot. That wouldn't have been too hard if he'd been buying one of Smith's planes. Since the Gustavs were the standard models for the air force, quite a few people by now had learned to fly them. The same was not true for aircraft produced by the Kellys. Their test pilot was a man named Lannie Yost, about whom Francisco had heard many tales from his new assistant Denise Beasley. First and foremost among them, half-amused and half-awed accounts of Yost's alcohol consumption.

No, that wouldn't do.

☆   ☆   ☆

"Piece of cake!" said Denise immediately. Her friend Minnie was vigorously nodding her head.

"You know someone?" asked Francisco.

"Eddie Junker," came the simultaneous reply from both girls.

"He's been learning how to fly from the Kellys," Denise explained. "By now, I betcha he's an expert on the Dauntless."

"He's been training for three whole weeks," concurred Minnie.

Francisco was dubious that "three whole weeks" constituted sufficient training for an aircraft pilot. He'd have to check with Jesse.

In the meantime . . .

He gave both girls a stern look. "And now, back to your lessons. I promised your mother"—that to Denise—"and Benny that I wouldn't let you slack off just because you were no longer formally enrolled in school."

Minnie was too polite to yawn, but she might as well have. Francisco had only added the name of her adoptive parent Benny Pierce in the interests of maintaining formal evenhandedness. Minnie was quite good about doing her homework. Not so Denise, to whom the comment had really been directed.

But the girl just grinned at him. Francisco, a renowned spymaster with a continental reputation, managed to keep a straight face.

Barely.

In point of fact, since moving with him to Magdeburg, Denise had been quite attentive to her studies. It seemed that being an assistant to a renowned spymaster with a continental reputation made it fascinating to study exactly the same books she had previously scorned when they were assigned to a mere student. Such is the power of status change.

"It mostly depends on the student, Francisco," said Jesse. "If they've got a knack for it, and assuming they pay attention to their instructor, a person can learn to fly a plane a lot faster than you might think. The standard training for pilots in World War II was four and half weeks. Of course, that was continuous training, which I assume Eddie Junker hasn't been able to do since he has a job. The military wanted a pilot to have two hundred hours of experience flying a specific plane before they sent him into combat. Most civilian training courses are less demanding.

They'll want a student to fly for ten to fifteen hours before they solo, and at least forty hours before they try to get a license."

That was much faster than Nasi had assumed. True, he still didn't know whether or not Eddie Junker had "the knack" for flying. But he did know that the Junker fellow was very reliable. For Francisco's purposes, a steady and reliable pilot was quite sufficient. He did not intend to fly a private plane into combat, after all.

So. Off to Grantville.

"Can we come?"

"No. You have your studies—which I promised your mother and Benny Pierce that you'd have completed before we move to Prague."

Minnie seemed unperturbed by the response. Denise scowled at him.

Noelle Stull's kitchen
Grantville, State of Thuringia-Franconia
July 9, 1635

"You bum," said Noelle Stull. For a moment, she looked as if she might snatch back the cup of tea she had placed before Francisco. "You dirty rotten bum," she qualified.

Nasi's tone was placid. "Oh, come now, Noelle. Surely you didn't expect Eddie Junker to work for you indefinitely."

"He doesn't work *for* me," Noelle snapped. "He's employed by the State of Thuringia-Franconia, same as I am. Technically, he's—excuse me, he *was*—my subordinate, but I always considered him my partner."

As heavily as possible for someone of her slender build, Noelle took a seat at the kitchen table across from Nasi. Her dark expression had not faded in the least. She still looked as if she were on the verge of snatching back the cup of tea she'd given Francisco. Even, possibly, throwing it in his face. For all the young woman's pleasant appearance—pretty, in an understated sort of way—she had a fearsome reputation.

True, her bad marksmanship was legendary. Still, she'd once managed to slay a torturer by shoving a gun under his jaw where she couldn't possibly miss—and there was always the chance that her aim with a teacup might be better than her aim with a pistol.

So, a bit hurriedly, Francisco added: "Surely you didn't think I came here simply to inform you that I'd hired Eddie Junker. He could have done that much himself, thereby saving me"—here, he gave Noelle his most winning smile—"some possible, however unlikely, unpleasantness."

"'However unlikely,'" she jeered. "I oughta—"

She broke off the sentence and frowned at him. "Then why *did* you come here?"

"I would think it obvious. Surely you didn't think I was hiring Eddie simply to be my pilot? That occupation would leave him idle most of the time, after all. No, I did some research, and by all accounts he is very good at the work he's been doing—which, when you come right down to it, is not so different from the sort of work I'd have him doing."

"'Did some research,'" Noelle jeered. "'By all accounts,'" she jeered again. "Translated into realspeak, that means you asked Denise Beasley and she praised Eddie to the skies. Based on her sixteen—count 'em, sixteen—years of life's experience."

Francisco thought it best to make no direct response. True, he had asked Denise and, true again, she had praised Eddie Junker to the skies. But the praise had been salted by quite a few astute observations, as well. Sixteen or not—sixteen and a half, Denise herself would have insisted, being of an age where half-years loom large—the girl was generally shrewd when it came to people, and exceedingly shrewd when it came to people in whom she had a particular interest.

But there was no need to get into that. "However—again, by all accounts—it seems also true that Eddie's skills at his usual work are greatly amplified when he works with you. A true partnership, indeed. My research leads me to the conclusion that the two of you, working together, are quite formidable."

He cleared his throat. "Therefore, my visit."

Judging from Noelle's change of expression, Francisco judged it was now safe to drink his tea.

It was quite good, actually.

Office of the Director of the Department of
Economic Resources
Grantville, State of Thuringia-Franconia
July 10, 1635

"You bum," said Tony Adducci. For a moment, he looked as if he might throw his chair at Francisco instead of leaning back in it. "You dirty rotten bum," he qualified.

Nasi's tone was placid. "Oh, come now, Tony. Surely you didn't expect Noelle to work for you indefinitely."

"There oughta be a law," complained the director of the Department of Economic Resources.

"Against what?" Francisco asked. "Wealthy private employers who pay generously?"

Adducci glared at him. "Conspicuous consumption."

"Ah. Sumptuary laws. Indeed, many realms in Europe have such in place." He could have added, *commonly aimed at Jews like me, in fact*, but that would have been quite unfair. There was legally no discrimination against Jews in the United States of Europe, and, at least in the State of Thuringia-Franconia if not all the USE's provinces, the law was enforced. Nor did Francisco have any reason to believe that Tony Adducci was himself a bigot.

Madder than the proverbial wet hen, yes, and the target of his ire was indeed a rich Jew. But that hardly constituted anti-Semitism, to any fair-minded person.

So all he said was: "Unfortunately for you, such laws are directed at the excessive acquisition of valuable clothing, jewelry, furniture, and such like material goods. Not," he cleared his throat, "valuable spies."

Office of the President, State of Thuringia-Franconia
Grantville
July 10, 1635

"That bum," said Tony Adducci. "That dirty rotten bum."

Ed Piazza, the president of the State of Thuringia-Franconia, leaned back in the chair in his office. He seemed quite relaxed and unflustered.

"Oh, calm down, Tony. People get hired away from government jobs into better-paying private employment all the time. Why did you think Noelle Stull and Eddie Junker would be exempt?"

"They're my best investigative team," Adducci whined.

"*Were* your best team," Piazza said. "Get over it, Tony. Your department will manage, well enough. And if you can tear yourself away for a moment from parochial concerns, you might want to contemplate the possibility that all this will work out pretty well for us in the future. Defining 'us' in admittedly factional terms."

Adducci stared at him. "Huh?"

"We're in a parliamentary system now, Tony. You *have* heard the phrase 'shadow cabinet,' haven't you?"

"Yeah, sure. The party in opposition keeps a cabinet going—in place, anyway—in case it has to step into power on short notice. What's that got to do with this headache?"

Piazza smiled. "Hasn't it dawned on you yet that what Francisco Nasi is setting up in Prague could be construed as Mike Stearns' shadow intelligence service? On the off chance, you know, that Willem Wettin's administration goes into the crapper on short notice."

"Oh."

A moment later, Adducci's sour expression cleared. Tony was another UMWA man, a former member of the mineworkers local union of which Mike had been the president before the Ring of Fire. Like most such, he was a fierce Stearns partisan.

"Well. I guess it's okay, then."

Boarding house kitchen
Magdeburg, capital of the United States of Europe
July 20, 1635

"How utterly cool is *this*?" Denise Beasley said happily. "Both Eddie and Noelle will be working for Francisco too! We'll see them all the time now."

Minnie Hugelmair nodded. "What's even better is that we'll probably wind up with Noelle as our boss. How cool is *that*?"

Denise's cheerful expression faded a bit. "Well . . . She'll be tough on us about homework."

"Tough on *you*," Minnie qualified. "I don't have a problem with homework."

"'Cause you're a suck-ass."

"Vulgar, vulgar, vulgar. You better watch out, or Noelle will wash your mouth with soap."

That was water off a duck's back. Denise Beasley's attitude toward threats of punishment could best be described as sanguine.

She jumped up from the table. "Let's go! Eddie and them should be landing soon."

Minnie looked at the clock perched on the wall of the kitchen. The landlady was inordinately proud of the thing. Personally, with tastes now heavily influenced by the Americans who had adopted her, Minnie thought it was also excessively ornate. "Baroque," the Americans often called such things, after an historical era that technically hadn't even started yet.

However, whatever she thought of the design, the clock worked perfectly well. Which meant they'd be spending at least an hour with nothing to do at the airport except look at the wind sock, as early as Denise would get them there.

But Minnie didn't argue the matter. She knew how much Denise had missed Eddie's company since they'd moved to Magdeburg this summer.

Magdeburg airfield

"That landing was pretty decent, Eddie," Denise pronounced, as soon as the pilot had clambered down to the ground. "All things considered."

Eddie Junker peeled off a flying cap, exposing a thatch of sandy-colored hair. His hazel eyes gazed down at her curiously. "All things . . . as in what?"

His tone was neither defensive nor hostile. One of the many things Denise liked about Eddie was that he was not easily flustered. His response to almost everything was careful, calm, deliberate, relaxed—in short, just about the exact opposite of her own reaction to things.

She beamed up at him. Eddie wasn't really that much taller than Denise—four inches, perhaps—but he was so wide-shouldered and stocky that he always seemed a little bigger than he really was.

"Oh, you know. Things that need to be considered. Like, Item One, you're still a tyro. Like, Item Two, you have a distaste for flamboyance—and what sort of top notch pilot isn't flamboyant?" She did an exaggerated search for some item of clothing on his person. "Like, Item Three, where's the requisite white scarf?"

Eddie shook his head. "It is quite false to say that I have a distaste for flamboyance. Far more appropriate words would be: horror, contempt and loathing. As for the scarf . . ."

He dug into the pockets of his jacket and drew forth a gray scarf. "Here it is. In case it gets too cold. Which it didn't, on this flight. It's mid-summer and I never exceeded eight thousand feet of altitude. I didn't even have to turn on the cabin's little heater."

Standing next to him, Francisco Nasi nodded. "Indeed, it was a most pleasant flight. And as for flamboyance—" He shuddered, a bit theatrically. "Imagine, if you will, my own horror, contempt and loathing for the trait. In my personal pilot, at least. I will admit that I found the quality sometimes quite charming in our former prime minister."

He shook his head. "Sometimes. But, speaking of which, I need to consult with Mike as soon as possible. Eddie, I don't think we'll be here longer than one day. Two, at the most."

Junker nodded. "I'll make sure the plane's ready to go on short notice. Where are we staying?"

"The boarding house!" piped up Minnie.

"We had the landlady hold rooms for you," Denise said proudly.

That was a slender claim to fame. Francisco had rented the rooms weeks earlier, and told the landlady he'd want them available at any time throughout the summer, whether he was present or not. But he saw no reason to correct the girl.

He looked around. "What? No fancy transportation?"

His two young female assistants showed a distressing lack of respect for their employer.

"Jeez, Mr. Nasi," said Denise, "this ain't Grantville with fancy bus lines and stuff. Besides, it's only a short ride."

She normally called him "Don Francisco." She spoke the term "Mr. Nasi" in the same manner one might speak of "the old geezer."

"They're good horses," added Minnie reassuringly. "Real mild-mannered. They probably won't throw you."

Francisco couldn't help but laugh. In point of fact, he was a better horseman than either of the two girls—if not, admittedly, in their league when it came to motorcycles.

"Lead me to these decrepit nags, then."

Boarding house kitchen
Magdeburg, capital of the United States of Europe

"So how soon are you coming back, Eddie?" Denise asked.

"More tea?" chimed in Minnie, holding up the pot.

Eddie extended his cup and Minnie refilled it. "Whenever Don Francisco wants me to bring him. Hard to say."

Denise frowned. "You're not his fucking slave, you know. Just ask him if you've got a week or two when he's not going to be needing you to fly him around. Then come up and visit us. Hell, he might even let you use the plane for that."

Junker shook his head. "Won't work, I'm afraid. I'm going to be tied up all summer."

"Huh? With what?"

"Painting lessons."

"What?" Denise was staring at him the way she might stare at a penguin which had suddenly appeared at the table.

"You heard me. Painting lessons." He starting making gestures with his hand. "Painting as in fine art. Not painting as in painting a house."

"*What?*" Denise's jaw was now sagging.

He peered at her closely. "That's odd. I don't remember you being particularly slow-witted."

Denise's jaw snapped shut. "Very funny, asswipe. There's nothing at all wrong with my wits. Unlike yours. Why the fuck do you need to take painting lessons, anyway?"

As always, Eddie was unfazed by Denise's coarse language. "In order to paint something, of course. Why else would I do it?"

Denise was practically speechless—for her, a highly unusual condition. "But—but—" The next words were almost wailed. "How many hours can you possibly spend in stupid painting classes?"

"Not very many," Eddie allowed. "No more than ten hours a week. But I need to work very hard and long hours to pay for the lessons."

Minnie had a puzzled face. "Since when does the school charge money for art classes?"

"I assume they don't. But I wanted private lessons from the best instructor I could find. And those do not come cheaply."

Denise's face looked like a pickle. As close a resemblance, at least, as was possible for such a very good-looking teenage girl. "Jesus H. Fucking Christ, Eddie! Do you have to do *everything* first class?"

Junker took another sip of tea. "I am usually rather frugal—as you know perfectly well, since your more common complaint is that I'm a tightwad and—what's that other colorful if grotesque American expression? 'Party-pooper,' I think."

"Damn right you're a party-pooper," said Denise. "You're ruining the whole summer!"

Junker and Nasi left early the next morning, flying back to Grantville. No sooner had the two girls seen them to the airfield and waved them goodbye, than Denise announced a new mission in life.

"How much does it cost to learn how to paint from a real pro, anyway?"

"How should I know?" said Minnie. "It probably depends what he wants to paint—and, in case you didn't notice, Eddie did his very best I'm-a-clam routine whenever you tried to pry it out of him."

"Well, fuck a duck. How can I find out?"

"I think Artemisia Gentileschi's in town," said Minnie. "Mrs. Simpson asked her to come up. Probably planning to parade her around the hoity-toities and maybe set up a showing. Or whatever they call it when they put up a lot of paintings on the walls and let people walk around and look at them. At least, people who are able to buy them."

Pointedly, she added: "Which excludes us."

Denise was chewing on her lower lip. "How well do you get along with the Simpson Grand Dame? I think she might still be pissed with me on account of that time I almost ran her down in Grantville because it's not my fault some people don't pay attention to traffic."

Denise Beasley's notion of "paying attention to traffic" was just as sanguine as her attitude toward threats. *She* was going about her necessary business whenever *she* was out on her motorcycle.

It followed, as night from day, that it was therefore everyone else's business to stay out of her way.

"Not too well," replied Minnie. "I think I grossed her out that one time I took out my glass eye in front of her."

Denise frowned. "So how else can we get into Gentileschi's presence?"

"Knock on the door?"

Amazingly, that worked. Mrs. Simpson wasn't home to say yea or nay, and the servant ushered them right into the artist's presence. Who, for her part, was quite pleasant and suggested a cup of tea.

Mary Simpson's kitchen
Magdeburg, capital of the United States of Europe

"Oh, I hadn't realized Eddie was a friend of yours."

Denise and Minnie stared at Artemisia Gentileschi. "*You* know him, too?" asked Denise.

"Well, of course. He's one of my private students."

On the street outside Mary Simpson's residence
Magdeburg, capital of the United States of Europe

"Well, that didn't go so well, did it?" said Denise, almost snarling.

Minnie frowned. "We were reasonably polite. And I don't think Ms. Gentileschi was mad at us. Even though we tried to pry what she called privy information out of her for probably longer than we should have. Um. Probably a lot longer."

"That's not what I meant!" That sentence *was* snarled. "I can't believe that inconsiderate fucking bum is paying *Artemisia Gentileschi* for private painting lessons."

Teenage fury gave way, in an instant, to sixteen-and-half-year-old despair. "She's *world famous*, Minnie! They even got articles about her in encyclopedias that were written hundreds of years from now. It'll take him *years* to pay her off!"

Minnie nodded. "Probably. One or two years, for sure."

"You're no help at all!"

The door to the Simpson residence opened. Hearing the sound, the two girls turned and looked up the short flight of stairs leading to the front entrance.

Artemisia Gentileschi was standing there, smiling. "It occurred to me after you charged off, young ladies, that there might be a solution to your problem."

"Rob a bank?" said Denise, perhaps a tad sarcastically.

Gentileschi chuckled. "Oh, nothing that energetic. But I always have need of models. It's especially difficult to find suitable girls, because they're either street urchins—that won't do at all—or their families insist on chaperones, and that costs still more money."

She gazed down upon them. "In your case, however, I do not think chaperones will be necessary."

"Ha!" That came from Denise.

Minnie response was more measured. "Assuming you could find any in the first place. Here in Magdeburg . . . maybe. Back in Grantville, the Babysitters Guild had Denise blacklisted by the time she was six."

"Splendid, then. I can simply deduct what I would pay you from the fee I charge young Junker. Will that suit you?"

Denise looked simultaneously ecstatic and suspicious. "Well, sure. But . . . what do we have to do? Exactly?"

"Just sit still."

Minnie shrugged. "Easy for me. I might have to hit Denise once in a while."

For her part, Denise was back to scowling. "I can't believe what I put myself through for that guy."

Prague airfield
Bohemia
August 26, 1635

"It's in much better shape than I expected," said Nasi, as Eddie Junker taxied the plane toward Prague airfield's one and only hangar. Francisco stuck his head out of the window and gazed down at the runway passing below. "It's been macadamized, I think."

"I'm sure you're right," said Eddie. He nodded toward a heavy piece of cast iron equipment parked near the hangar. "There's the roller they would have used."

Nasi looked over. "Water-bound macadam only. But knowing Wallenstein and his mania for all things modern, I won't be surprised if they make it a tarmac soon, one way or another. There must be a source of bitumen somewhere in Bohemia."

They had almost reached the hangar. There was a large welcoming party standing nearby. Morris and Judith Roth were there, along with a ferocious-looking officer whom Nasi presumed to be General Pappenheim.

Wallenstein himself had not come, of course. But Francisco didn't doubt that he'd be ushered into the king of Bohemia's presence soon enough.

Ushered again, to be precise—although, this time, the audience would be public rather than private, as had been his three previous meetings with Wallenstein. The airfield he'd just landed on had been the product of one of those meetings. Bohemia's new ruler, not surprisingly, had a keen interest in developing an aviation industry and his own air force as soon as possible. In the meantime, he and Nasi had reached a quiet mutual understanding that Nasi's ostensibly private airplane would retain all the equipment needed to make it a warplane on short notice, in the event Bohemia needed such to avert a threat.

That wouldn't be hard to do. After all, the *Dauntless* had been designed to be a warplane in the first place.

Most of the people gathered at the airfield to greet Nasi were Jews, naturally. From the looks of the throng, half the ghetto had turned out.

"Did you expect such an enormous crowd, Don Francisco?"

"Yes," he said smugly.

Eddie brought the plane to a stop. "How soon—"

"Two days. That should be enough time for you to get settled into your new quarters." Nasi smiled, a bit wickedly. "But if you wait any longer, the girl will probably strangle you. Had I realized your capacity for ruthlessness, young man, I would have hired you much sooner."

Eddie looked modest. "I've only done what was necessary, Don Francisco."

"Yes, I know. What was necessary—*all* that was necessary—and nothing more. That is the very definition of ruthlessness, you know."

It was time to climb out of the plane and greet the enthusiasts. Morris Roth was already waiting, grinning very widely.

As well he might. Were Morris a egotistical man, Francisco Nasi's arrival in Prague might have been cause for friction. Until this moment, Roth had been the preeminent Jew in the city, almost since the day he arrived. Henceforth, he would have to share much of that prestige.

But it was no matter. Francisco and Morris had had quite a few more than three private sessions, over the past few months. Theirs would be a relationship of partners, not rivals. Even friends, Francisco thought.

Eddie cleared his throat. "Uh, Don Francisco. Just to be sure—"

Nasi waved his hand. "I already said it was fine, Eddie. Indeed, I suspect it will simply add to the luster of the thing." As he started to open the door, he looked back and smiled again. "Given that the girl is a *shiksha*. Were she a Jewess . . . Oh, the scandal!"

An airfield just outside of Grantville
August 28, 1635

"Stop fidgeting, Eddie," said Artemisia Gentileschi. "I assure you I will have it done in time for your flight to Magdeburg tomorrow. Even with such a peculiar canvas."

Eddie flushed a little. "Sorry, I didn't mean . . . It's just . . ."

"Yes, I know. The girl can sometimes be the very definition of impatience. Once or twice I almost *did* order Minnie to hit her on the head to keep her still."

The artist contemplated the surface to be painted for a moment longer, and then began busying herself with her brushes and paints. "Be off, now. Shoo! Shoo!"

Eddie was back to fidgeting. "Maybe . . . I mean . . ."

"Shoo, I said! Come back just before sundown. I will show you where to place a few of the last strokes. That way, your claim to being the artist will not be entirely fabricated."

She gave him the sort of sly smile that a middle-aged woman of great experience bestows upon a young man with very little. "Not that she will ever ask."

Magdeburg airfield
August 29, 1635

"Prague is supposed to be a really pretty city," Minnie said. "I can't wait to get there."

Denise nodded, a bit absently. Most of her attention was on the airplane coming in for a landing. The same airplane that would—finally! this had to have been the longest summer on record—take them to their new home in Prague.

She glanced down at her suitcase. She and Minnie had done their best to follow the instructions Eddie had sent them concerning weight and dimensions. She thought they were well within the parameters, but . . .

With Eddie, you never knew. He could be such a damned perfectionist, sometimes.

The plane landed. Very smoothly, it looked like.

"I'll bet he's a really good pilot, even already," Minnie opined.

Denise wouldn't have taken that bet on any odds. She'd never known Eddie *not* to be good at something, if he really put his mind to it.

The plane taxied toward them. Then, as it neared the hangar, swerved to the side.

Denise's jaw dropped.

"Oh, wow," said Minnie.

There was silence, for a few seconds, until the plane came to a stop not more than ten yards away. At that distance . . .

"It's *you*," said Minnie, in what Denise judged to be the most needless statement in human history.

It sure was. Denise Beasley, in the flesh—or as close to it, anyway, as a painting on a plane's nose could possibly be.

Yeah, sure, Denise had never worn an outfit like that and never would. Not that she minded the décolletage or the amount of leg showing. What the hell, she *did* have great legs. And if her bust wasn't exactly in Playboy bunny territory, nobody had ever mistaken her for anything but a mammal since she was twelve years old.

The problem was simply that the fancy dress looked completely impractical. Denise Beasley didn't mind being scandalous but she drew the line at tripping over herself.

Still. Under the circumstances. She was not about to complain.

"Oh, wow," said Minnie. "Do you look great or what?"

Eddie was gazing down at her, now. Denise stared back up at him, not knowing what to say.

Minnie let out a whoop and clambered into the cockpit. A moment later, she reemerged, with a flyer's cap on her head and a big smile on her face and an upthrust thumb.

"There's a cap for you too!" she hollered.

Denise finally managed to speak. "Eddie, is—ah—*this* why you spent the whole summer . . . Not paying any attention to me. You know, if you wanted to impress me, you didn't have to do this."

"Sadly, that statement is quite false. Besides, I wasn't trying to 'impress' you, Denise. What good is that? I simply needed to make very clear that my intentions were . . . ah. What's the word?"

"Lustful," suggested Minnie. Again, she stuck up her thumb.

Eddie shook his head. "In part, yes. Absurd to deny it"—he leaned over and pointed down at the painting—"as I believe the illustration makes clear. But I assure you the principal thrust of my intentions are entirely what you would call 'honorable.'"

Denise stared at the painting. "Ah . . . Eddie. Is this . . . ah . . ."

"A German girl, I would simply have gotten a very nice pair of shoes to indicate my desires. Given that it was you . . ."

Again, he shook his head. "The quandary I faced. Even worse than the one Thorsten Engler faced, I think. At least Caroline Platzer considered herself an adult."

"So do I!" said Denise fiercely.

"Sadly, that statement is also false. Must be qualified, at least. Normally, it is true enough, you consider the age of sixteen—"

"Sixteen and a half!"

"I stand corrected for my grievous error. Sixteen and a half, to be well-nigh a synonym for 'maturity.' But there are other issues which cause you to flee into that tender age like a rabbit into a hole."

"Name one!"

"Me."

Denise opened her mouth, then . . .

Closed it.

What was she to say? Damn it, Eddie *was* twenty-three years old. Practically twice her age!

Well. Once and a half times, anyway. Still a cradle robber, no matter how you sliced it.

Not that she had any attachment to cradles, of course. But . . .

She realized, finally, just how high and rigid she'd made that wall. Eddie Junker, her best male buddy. Eddie Junker, whose company she enjoyed as much as Minnie's. Eddie Junker, whom she relied upon for . . . oh, so many things.

But not—but never—he was *way* older—

"Okay!" she said. "I'll admit you probably did have to do something like this."

She searched her mind and soul. Sure enough. She *still* had no attachment to cradles.

"Eddie, I'm sorry. I'm just not ready to get betrothed yet." She swallowed, then added, in a small voice: "If I was, it'd be you, for sure. But I'm just . . . not ready. I'm only sixteen. Well, okay. And a half. But still."

As usual, Eddie's reaction was imperturbable. He simply nodded and said, "I figured as much. Not a problem. I am a patient man. I simply wanted to eliminate any misconceptions."

He hopped down from the plane. Very gracefully and lightly, for such a thick-looking man. Once on the ground, he grinned at her. "Such as any notions that I simply wish to be your good friend. And have no lustful designs on your body."

Denise grinned back. Lustful designs on her body, she could handle. In fact, now that she really thought about it, she figured lust and Eddie Junker would go together about as well as bacon and eggs. As long as there were no cradles involved. Yet, anyway.

"Well, in that case. Let me explain an American custom."

After she was done with the explanation, Eddie looked back up at Minnie, who was still in the cockpit. "You will find some paints and brushes in the back. Hand them down to me, if you would."

The implements in hand, Eddie advanced upon the illustration.

"What are you doing?" asked Denise, a little alarmed. The more she looked at it, the more she really really liked that painting on the nose of the plane.

"It needs a caption."

"Oh. Yeah. Like *Memphis Belle,* you mean. Or the one on the plane that dropped the bomb on Hiroshima. *Nose Gay,* or something like that."

"I am not actually planning to destroy entire cities to demonstrate my affections, Denise. But I think this will do nicely." He went about his work.

When the caption was finished, Denise and Minnie studied it carefully.

My Steady Girl.

"Oh, wow," said Minnie. "That is just so cool."

Denise didn't say anything. Her mind was already at work, figuring the problem. Going steady, after all, had certain traditional obligations—if you insisted on using such a silly term for it.

"Can we postpone the trip to Prague? I need another day."

"I suppose," Eddie said. "Don Francisco will probably be curious, but he's a good boss. He'll accept any reasonable explanation."

He cocked his head, apparently expecting her to provide said reasonable explanation.

Which she certainly had—about as reasonable as reasonable ever gets—but she wasn't about to explain it to Eddie.

Artemisia Gentileschi, she figured. An up-timer would know more modern methods, sure. But, first, those methods were likely to be invalid before too long. And, second, they'd probably blabber. Denise and her reputation, yackety-yak-yak.

Denise thought Artemisia would keep her mouth shut. And she was sure that the artist knew what Denise needed to know. If ever a woman looked like she *really* had a reputation, it was Artemisia Gentileschi. But only had two kids to show for it. And she must be . . . what? At least forty years old, or some such astronomical age.

"Never you mind," she said. "If Don Francisco asks, I just needed to get some advice. And, uh, steady girl supplies."

She studied the illustration again. Amazing, really, how much leg he'd shown. Poor Eddie. He must have been thinking about it for months and months.

She smiled, sixteen-and-a-half going on forty. "A lot of steady girl supplies, I'm thinking."

Schwarza Falls

Douglas W. Jones

— 1 —

To: Grantville Emergency Committee.
From: John Sterling, Edgar Frost and Francis Kidwell.
Date: May 30, 1631, fifth day after the disaster.
Re: Road options around Schwarza Falls.

Yesterday, May twenty-ninth, the fourth day after the disaster, we went up Buffalo Creek to the power plant to look into how to build a road connection over the border into the lands to what is now the southwest. You asked us to tell you everything, even if we weren't certain it was important, so pardon us if we ramble a bit.

I. The Situation

The report from the power plant is correct. There's a real castle up there looking down on us. Don't imagine a fairy-tale castle. This is a deadly serious looking fortress. There's also a bit of a village there, or at least half of one. The village and the castle are both named Schwarzburg. We need to make friends with whoever runs the place, because they're guarding our southwest flank very nicely. And, if their cannon are even mediocre, I doubt there's much we could do to stop them from wiping out the power plant.

As you come around the bend in Buffalo Creek, about a mile out from Grantville, what you see is a wall of black rock, streaked with red, green and brown. This castle sits on a hill dead center on top of it, right above the power plant. The cliff has a mirror polish on it that reflects the sky when you get close enough. We guess that from the bottom of the Buffalo Creek valley up to the floor of the valley above, it must be three hundred feet. Our ridge tops are about four hundred feet above the valley floor, but the hills of the land we've been plunked into are much higher. We guess about twice as high, which means eight hundred feet up from the valley floor. The German hills aren't as chopped up as ours. They seem a bit rounder, but the valley walls are steep enough.

There's a stream in the valley we cut into. They call it the Schwarza, and where it flows over the cut edge, there's quite a waterfall. We'll call it Schwarza Falls. It's hard to guess how high it is, because it's pounding down on what was a steep slope and washing quite a bit of that slope downhill. We figure it's a clear fall of at least fifteen feet, but then it tumbles down at least two hundred feet before it flows into what used to be Spring Branch.

If it hadn't been for the fact that the Schwarza valley is offset a bit from Buffalo Creek valley, there'd be no hope of getting a road up that cliff. As things stand, though, the Schwarza had a loop to the northeast that got lopped off by the disaster. (We're starting to call it the "Ring of Fire," by the way, since that seems a pretty good description of the disaster—"RoF" for short.) The ridge to the north of Buffalo Creek just manages to come up to that part of the Schwarza's stream bed. Also, just southwest of Schwarza Falls, there's a little knob on our side that just goes up to the level of the rooftops of some houses nearby. It's all that's left of the ridge that divided Spring Branch from Buffalo Creek.

One thing is real clear. That little village at the top of the falls is in big trouble. Half the place is gone. Calling it a village may be too generous; it was a cluster of houses and barns built beside a bridge across the Schwarza. In a few places, the ground collapsed as far back as thirty feet from the edge, taking houses and barns if they happened to be there. There's quite a mound of muck and rubble along the face of the cliff below those places. There's one barn, though, that's standing right on the edge and hasn't moved an inch.

The cut-off chunk of the Schwarza northeast of the castle must have dumped its entire contents and a good part of its riverbed over the cliff in one great gush. There's a flow of debris from there down along what used to be Spring Branch Creek. It looks like what was left of Spring Branch Road inside the ring of fire was pretty well buried or washed out within a few minutes on Sunday. The culvert over Spring Branch Creek on the main road looks like it survived that first gush, but it was never intended to take the flow of the Schwarza river, so the road is acting like a dam. The water was over the road when we got there. It's a few inches deep and running fast, but the road is pretty flat so the overflow is spread over quite a distance. It's eating at the road, and we think it'll wash it out unless we dig up the culvert and put in a proper bridge.

We waded across and took a hike up what's left of the ridge that divided Buffalo Creek from Spring Branch. It's the steep but direct route into what's left of the lower Schwarzburg village. They were watching us the whole time, and there's no doubt that they were as nervous about us as we were about them. By the time we got up the hill, a guy named Franz was there to meet us, with two others who stayed back a bit and whose names we didn't get. Franz seemed to be an officer in the guard of the castle. As near as we could make out, his boss is the *graf* of Schwarzburg and a town named Rudolstadt.

Franz turned out to be a decent fellow and pretty quick witted, but he had some big pistols in his belt and a sword. We were careful not to put our hands anywhere near our holsters those first few minutes. We'd better send someone official to Schwarzburg quickly, someone who knows German!

We read Franz the message you wrote for us in German about wanting to open the road connections across the border of the "ring." After we gave him the letters you gave us, we tried to have a conversation. I wish we knew more German, but the stuff you gave us helped a lot. With lots of mistakes, hand gestures and an occasional picture on a notepad, we managed to get by.

He told us that the Ring of Fire destroyed the road from

Schwarzburg to Rudolstadt where, as near as we could make out, his boss lives most of the time. It also destroyed the road to the town of Saalfeld. As a result, it seems that we're in agreement about trying to open up a road connection.

The bridge across the Schwarza at Schwarzburg is right at the lip of the falls. It's in serious danger of collapse because of all the dirt that's been washed away from the foundations. If the bridge goes, the farmhouses that are left on the southeast side of the Schwarza will be cut off, so they're already working on a temporary wooden bridge upstream from the old one. Timber is one thing they have plenty of. The roads here are mostly grass and packed dirt, with cobblestones only where erosion is likely to be a problem.

Northeast from the falls about two hundred yards, the road is almost cut off with half of it slumped away. It looks like it was right on the riverbank there, at the southeast end of the loop of river that the Ring of Fire sliced off. Beyond that, to the northwest, the road is in good shape, with stone retaining walls in places as it takes a long switchback up the slope to the castle gate.

We didn't go into the castle, but we did go up to the square by the gate where there's a bit of an upper village. The castle sits along the crest of a knife-edge ridge with the Schwarza river wrapped around the west, south and east sides. You couldn't ask for a better defensive position, but it's not all that big. The castle must be a quarter mile long but the ridge isn't very wide anywhere.

II. Road Proposals

Franz, the officer, must have been thinking about the problem of getting a road down from Schwarzburg, because he took us to the jumping off point where a new road could connect. He pointed out the route he thought would work before we left to walk down that way. We agree with him, so we'll describe that route and forget the others.

Be aware, we're not engineers, just three guys who've had plenty of experience building and maintaining roads. We're confident that we can do this job, and do it well, but under the laws of West

Virginia, we aren't really qualified. It would be nice if there was a civil engineer to help with this project.

The road would turn north just east of the old Spring Branch road and traverse up the east side of the Spring Branch valley. This would almost follow the power company right of way once the power line gets on the same side of the creek. Then, the road would turn broadly around the head of the valley to meet the northwest end of the abandoned riverbed of the Schwarza. The climb up out of the riverbed would be short, and we'd meet the road up from the lower village about a quarter mile northwest of the waterfall.

We figure this would be about four thousand feet of road climbing three hundred feet, so the grade should be under eight percent. On the walk down, we flagged the path we followed while using a pocket clinometer to try to keep our path at seven percent. That brought us out a bit on the high side, but those flags should make charting the path back up pretty straightforward.

We figure that a crew with a medium dozer and a couple of chainsaws could carve a temporary one-lane road up to Schwarzburg along the Spring Branch route in about a day. That's about two hours at half a mile an hour for the first pass of the dozer to cut the roadbed, or about two hours, and then three more passes to shape the crown at a mile an hour, make that three hours. That's five hours of an eight hour day, but it's fair to budget the whole day to allow for the unexpected. There's some decent timber along the way we ought to try to salvage while we're at it.

There's so little watershed above our proposed route that a temporary road like that could last a few years, we think. But with another day of work to put in about five culverts, we could make a road there that would last. We think at least two of the old culverts along Spring Branch Road can be recovered with a winch and some digging, so someone should inventory culverts we can salvage from elsewhere.

With three days work and several truckloads of crushed rock, we could make the new road meet county standards for unimproved roads, which is something none of the roads we saw up on top manage to do. Two days of this would be to widen the road to two lanes, and one day would be to put down the rock and grade it nicely. If we put in the culverts soon enough, the road widening can wait until the traffic demands it.

We noticed that the power plant has a Caterpillar D6. They use it for pushing coal around. We asked about it at the front gate, and the guard there phoned the plant manager, Bill Porter. The upshot is, the power plant is willing to loan the dozer to the county for a day's work. They think that anything we can do to get the folks in that castle on our side would definitely be a good idea.

III. Defense

Finally, you asked us to say something about defending our new borders. If the folks who run Schwarzburg Castle fail to block ‣invaders, or if they decide to attack us, we could defend this end of the valley from the ridge northeast of Spring Branch. That would let us look down on our new road from about two hundred yards and we'd look across at the steeper slope down from the lower village from a distance of about four hundred yards. The castle would have an altitude advantage on us, but the ridge would offer cover and we could dig bunkers into the ridge top. You might want to put a jeep trail up to there from the valley behind the ridge.

The other defensive position would be on the ridge top across Buffalo Creek southeast of the power plant. This would look straight down our new road from a range of six to twelve hundred yards. Again, a bunker would be handy, but the castle hasn't got a good shot at this position because the chopped off hillside southeast of the castle is in the way. The big threat here is from snipers sitting right on the edge of that hillside, but the ground slopes down steeply to that cliff edge, enough so they wouldn't be able to hide behind the terrain. It looks steep enough that they'd have to worry about sliding right over the edge if they slipped.

John Sterling has the most military experience of any of us. He says he'd put mostly snipers on the ridge above Spring Branch, along with a few mortars or RPG launchers, and he'd put the light artillery on the south. Do we have any weapons heavier than hunting rifles? All in all, we agree that we'd much rather defend Grantville from Schwarzburg Castle. Seen from Schwarzburg, it looks like the cliffs do a good job of blocking all access to

Grantville for over a mile in either direction, perhaps more. The castle is the strong point that covers both paths into the valley.

IV. Other

Franz told us that there were people in some of those houses that went over the edge. We had trouble communicating about this, but I get the feeling there might be ten bodies somewhere at the bottom of the cliff. We said that he was welcome to send people down to try to find the bodies, and we said that we would try to get people to help.

— 2 —

To be delivered to Ludwig Günther, Graf of Schwarzburg Rudolstadt, or in his absence, to the head of the guard at Rudolstadt:

Your humble servant, Franz Saalfelder, officer of the guard at Schloss Schwarzburg, begs to report again on the strange events of these last few days.

I do not know that you received my first report of the events of Sunday, the fifteenth day of May, but the scout sent from Rudolstadt on that day arrived here on Tuesday, having worked his way to Schwarzburg along a very difficult route. God willing, he will have completed his circuit and returned to Rudolstadt by now with even more to report.

Sunday, the fifteenth day of May, at around noon, the very earth seemed to shake with the roar of thunder. The guards on the east-facing battlements were blinded for a moment by a wall of light that seemed brighter than the sun but as brief as a lightning flash. Fortunately, your humble servant was not looking that way at the moment, but the roar was horrible even indoors.

What devilment it was I cannot say. At first, I was sure that the very pits of Hell had opened, for all of the land to the north and east of Schwarzburg had disappeared. Where the valley of the Schwarza and the road to Rudolstadt had been, there was nothing but a pit, hundreds of feet deep, with a strange country on the bottom. Half of the houses and barns beside the Schwarza were gone in an instant, and some of the flat land beside the river fell over the edge shortly after, taking another house and two barns.

We cannot say for certain how many people were lost when the pit opened, but it cannot have been less than ten. It is fortunate that it was a Sunday and many had yet to leave the castle where they had attended chapel services that morning. Those who hurried home to fix their Sunday dinners were the victims, while the lazy who stayed to talk were saved. Fortunately, most of the refugees fleeing the mercenaries who have lately been a plague on the Saale valley have been moving on up the Schwarza into the well protected villages beyond Schwarzburg. Some of the survivors from the lower village want to go down into the pit to look for bodies so that they can have a proper burial. We can see wreckage of some of the houses that slid over the edge of the pit just after the pit opened. There may be bodies among the wreckage.

The scout you sent followed the north and west rim of the pit on his travels from Rudolstadt to Schwarzburg. He tells me that it is not entirely a pit because in some places the mountains of the strange new land within overtop our valleys. Of more import, the pit appears to be a near perfect circle, several miles in size, reaching from the edge of the valley of the Saale all the way to Schwarzburg. God willing, you will have heard his report by the time I write this.

Our chaplain cannot say whether this strange occurrence is the work of the Devil or not. His advice appears as sound as it is trite, to hope for the best while preparing for the worst. We have posted guards to report on what is within. Day and night, I have been called to the battlements or to the very edge of the pit to witness the strangest of events.

The land within the pit is occupied. There are houses of strange construction there. The strangest is a great brick building not far from the edge below Schwarzburg. At first, I thought the building was a fortress, for it is great enough to be one. Now, I believe it to be some kind of mill or forge, for they have a great pile of what looks like charcoal outside the building, and there are great smokestacks, although there is now no great amount of smoke. Immediately after the blast and blinding flash that created the pit, this fortress or mill was emitting a loud roar of noise that went on and on, loud enough to block out all else, and horrible. Great clouds of white smoke or steam rose from the mill and ceased when the noise ceased. Since then, it has been quiet, except for an occasional puff of steam and an occasional strange noise.

There are roads within the pit that look finer than any road I have ever seen. They are wide enough everywhere for two wagons to pass, smooth and well drained, with broad ditches to each side to carry away the rainwater. What is most terrifying is that they have wagons that appear to move as if by magic, sometimes faster than a horse can gallop and with nothing to pull them along. Watching from the castle and from the edge of the pit, we can see that the people within are not pleased. To them, they are within a great stone wall with few escapes, and we have seen groups of them looking up and pointing in our direction from the great mill. Their roads once went beyond the walls of the pit, perhaps. There are lines of strange towers leading away from the great mill to the north and south that support ropes made of wire. Where the Schwarza pours over the wall into the pit, it has created a new river that is flowing over one of their roads and will soon destroy it. The same new river also threatens to topple one of the strange towers.

There are two places near Schwarzburg where the hills within the pit come up to the level of the ground outside. One is just south of the bridge across the Schwarza below the castle, and one is to the northwest where the road used to turn east along the north bank of the Schwarza. We sent scouts into the pit that way with orders to stay hidden and to leave no sign of their passage. They report that there is a town several miles into the land where two valleys meet and that there are also smaller villages. There are even churches, or at least buildings that look like churches, with steeples surmounted by the symbol of the cross. This gives our chaplain some comfort.

The scouts reported many strange things. They have found twisted wire fences that must be many miles long, with sharp barbs of cut wire twisted onto the fence wire. The quality of the wire was very good, but in many places, they report that it was rusted, as if nobody ever took the time to care for it. All of the houses they spied out were very strange, constructed more of sawn wood or brick than of stone and plaster, and well painted. At night, many of the houses are lit up like daylight, with lights brighter than hundreds of candles. Even barns that are old and run-down have too many windows glazed with large panes of the most perfect glass anyone has ever seen. The towns, and even some houses outside the towns, have hellishly bright lanterns mounted on poles overhead so that people can move about at night just as freely as they do in the daylight.

Today, Thursday the nineteenth of May, three men from within the pit came up the hill. We met them at the bridge over the Schwarza, and I must report now what we learned in talking with them, or in trying to talk, for it was difficult.

These men were dressed most outlandishly. Even from the castle, even when they had not yet begun to climb, that much was evident. Each man wore a yellow helmet and an orange vest; the orange color was unnaturally bright. As they came closer, it was apparent that they wore blue pantaloons, cut very close and exceedingly well made but well worn and with the color faded. Under their orange vests, they wore well cut shirts, and each man wore a belt from which hung several things. All three men wore what must have been pistols, very small ones, but arms, nonetheless.

After we tried to talk, one of the men let me try on his helmet. It was very light compared to what I expected, not metal, but something much lighter and yet harder than leather. The helmet did not rest on the head, but was supported away from the head on a clever network of straps. I feel that a blow to the helmet would not be felt directly, not with those straps in place.

They also saw that I was curious about the implements on their belts. One of them showed me a most remarkable knife. It was small enough to fit into the palm of my hand, but it could be unfolded to reveal a knife blade, a file, a pair of pincers, and several other kinds of picks and implements, perhaps ten in all. Not only the blades, but the handle itself had the look of the finest silver, and yet it was as hard as the finest steel.

They speak English, it seems, and a little French, very little. Unfortunately, we have no English speakers in our garrison. They came prepared knowing that we spoke German, with a message written in German that they read to us and with a remarkable letter that they gave to us, which we include with this message.

There are many things we would have spoken of if we had been better able to communicate.

Their message confirmed that the town in the middle of the pit is called Grantville. My spies had reported signs within that said "Welcome to Grantville" on the roads outside the town, so this was not entirely new to me. I remain puzzled why an unprotected town would post signs saying welcome, if indeed that is what the signs say.

At first I thought the name Grantville sounded French, but their message explained that they are from a land called West Virginia in the United States of America, that they came from hundreds of years in the future, and that they have no idea how or why they are here. The message also confirmed my guess that their appearance in the pit has caused a crisis. They say they are governed by the Grantville Emergency Committee, clearly not a proper government and certainly not the government of this West Virginia or United States.

Their strange clothing and tools certainly suggest that they are not from our world, but their letter is dated Wednesday the twenty eighth of May, 1631. From this, I gather that they are using the Catholic calendar of Pope Gregory and that they have already communicated with someone on the outside of the pit.

The men's names were John Sterling, Edgar Frost and Francis Kidwell. They printed their names in Roman letters on a piece of paper that they gave to me and that I enclose with this message. Each of the men had a small book of blank sheets of paper cleverly bound with a spiral piece of wire, and each man had a pen of some strange kind that did not need an inkpot. They used them freely, drawing pictures when they did not know the words.

These men were well educated, able to read fluently even when they were reading German, a language they obviously spoke very poorly. I am being generous; they spoke almost no proper German but only some words. All three were also able to write quickly and well. This is why it took me a while to understand that they were not military men, nor were they ambassadors. Rather, they saw themselves as simple laborers, charged with but one job, that of finding the best way to build a road from the bottom of the pit up to the road at Schwarzburg. Of course, that is what their message said, but appearances can deceive and then deceive again.

I asked these men about the dead who had fallen into the pit, and this was a difficult question, both because of the language and because, I think, it was outside their authority. They said that we were welcome to send a burial party into the pit to recover the bodies, and they said that they would try to send help. I believe that they were sincerely troubled by the deaths.

Without being able to ask your leave, but knowing how important it would be to reestablish the road from Schwartzburg to Rudolstadt, we gave them permission to survey a route for connecting our roads to theirs. They will certainly not be using any new road without our leave, because Schwarzburg castle is perfectly placed to guard any road they can build. Their message did say that the road would be open to us, and that we would be welcome to use it to travel through Grantville to reach places to the north and east.

We had already been discussing the problem of a road into the pit among the guards, since we are worried about how to get food supplies up to Schwarzburg. The farmland in the Schwarza valley cannot feed the normal population of the valley, and even though most of the refugees have brought several weeks of provisions, we will face problems if we cannot reopen the roads. Bringing food in over the hills from Hildburghausen could double the cost of cartage, and it would be even more expensive to pay for cartage around the pit from Rudolstadt.

I hope I have not abused your trust! I showed these men the path into the pit that we thought would work. In showing this, I was careful to walk ahead to assure that there were no footprints visible, since our spies had crossed into the pit very near the point where I took them.

I watched the men walk back down into the pit, and I was surprised to see that they took a longer path, swinging broadly around the little valley that comes up from the pit to meet our land. They seem intent on building a road much longer than the road I would have thought of, but at a far more gentle slope. One of them had a hand-held instrument of some kind that he would occasionally use to look backward or forward along the path they were marking, while another of them would occasionally tie a strip of orange ribbon to a tree or sapling to mark the path.

I humbly beg your forgiveness if I have erred in carrying out my duties in these trying times. I will send a horseman with this letter Friday morning, with instructions to travel quickly around the pit to the north, then east to the Schaalbach road into Rudolstadt. Your scout assures me that this route should be safe, although it comes close to the pit at Rottenbach and even closer in parts of the Schaalbach valley. Until we learn that passage through Grantville is truly safe, I believe this is the best route available.

Your humble and devoted servant, Franz Saalfelder.

— 3 —

To: Grantville Emergency Committee.
From: Mark O'Reilly.
Date: Saturday May 31, 1631.
Re: Visit to Schwarzburg.

At the town meeting, you asked everyone with military experience to notify the emergency committee, and you asked everyone who knew German to notify the committee. I put in my name for both, but I never imagined that Rebecca Abrabanel would come visiting on Friday afternoon to test my German and then send me out immediately on a job. I feel that I'm in way over my head, but I guess we all are.

Ms. Abrabanel showed me a memo that some guys from the road department had just written. She asked me to read it, and then she asked me what I thought we should do. I told her we ought to send someone who knows German, someone who this officer of the guard named Franz could relate to as an equal, so that we can cut a deal with him. Then I understood it was me and I tried to back out.

Ms. Abrabanel explained that I was the best she could find on short notice. The job needed someone who spoke German, even bad German like mine. It had to be someone who had military training, and my Guard training would do. You don't send a general to make a field agreement with a captain, you send another captain, and you back him up with a couple of privates, and in this case, with a burial detail to help the Germans.

So this morning, I went up to the power plant with Pete McDougal and Ron Koch, who have mine safety experience, and Brick Bozarth and Miles Drahuta, who have UMWA training in mine rescue. We took the equipment McDougal and Koch recommended, and we ended up using most of it. We worked all day, and I'm tired. But Ms. Abrabanel said she wanted this report as soon as possible, so I'm trying to get it down on paper before I quit for the night. Thank God for computers. I wonder how long they'll last.

I. Rescue and Recovery

We found a small crew of Germans working through some wreckage at the bottom of the new Schwarza Falls. Conditions were very unsafe because the falls are cutting into the ground very quickly at the base. The Schwarzburg castle chaplain was there, Pastor Hermann Decker. I did my best to explain that we were there to help and asked what we could do.

There was one problem. These people don't usually speak the High German I learned in school. They have a regional dialect, so between that and my rusty German there were many places where we stumbled. It was a good thing I had my old English-German dictionary along, because there were lots of words that gave me trouble. Even Ron's native twentieth-century German wasn't much help.

They had already taken out four bodies. They were concentrating on the areas where wreckage showed among the rocks, sand and gravel that had come over the edge after the Ring of Fire.

The horrible thing was, if we'd known to rush out there last Sunday, right after the Ring of Fire, we'd have probably saved some lives. Some of what went over the edge fell hundreds of feet, but other stuff flowed down the slope after only a short drop. We didn't know, of course, but all of us would rather have saved people's lives than just dig up the dead.

McDougal and Koch insisted that the first thing we needed to do was to make the workplace safe, so they improvised a bridge across the foot of the falls using fallen trees and set up safety ropes. I was left to try to explain to the pastor that we were going to use a chainsaw to trim the fallen trees and that it might upset the Germans at first because it was both noisy and strange. Once the bridge was up, Ron went back to work on opening the mine, so we were without him for most of the day.

The Germans were very impressed with the chainsaw, but the simple come-along we used to winch the tree trunks together side by side was just as novel. The come-along and chainsaw helped quite a bit with digging through the building remains that had fallen over the cliff. Those houses were half-timbered, with mortise and tenon joining. Most of the joints snapped, but the timbers were very heavy and some parts of the framework that fell almost flat held together. Being able to quickly cut them apart and pull the pieces away was a real help. By noon, we recovered three more bodies. In the afternoon we recovered two more. If there are more bodies, they are likely to be deeply buried.

Some of the Germans doing the digging obviously knew the victims, because when they found bodies, they knew their names. Some of them broke down pretty badly, and Pastor Decker had his work cut out comforting them.

II. Relations with the Castle

There were observers on the cliff top overhead all the time. We saw them when we arrived in the morning, and made a point of waving to them in a friendly way before we went to meet with their work party below. They watched us pull together the temporary bridge. In midmorning, just before eleven, a delegation came down, a dozen or so. Most of them were there to join in the work, but there was also an officer and two guards.

The officer's name is Franz Saalfelder, and he's the same guy our first crew met with last Thursday. I think his last name isn't really a family name, but that it really means he's from the town of Saalfeld, the town just to our east. He's a captain of the house guard in the service of Graf Ludwig Günther. *Graf* means count, and he's the ruler of Schwarzburg-Rudolstadt. I suppose you could say that Grantville is now in the county of Schwarzburg-Rudolstadt.

One interesting thing I found is that the people in Schwarzburg all seem to refer to the Ring of Fire as "the pit." They saw the flash and heard the boom, same as we did, but to them, it was like a great pit opened up and there we were at the bottom. As near as I can figure out, the captain had the following subjects on his mind:

First, he is really worried about resupply. The Ring of Fire cut his primary supply line, and getting food in over the hills is going to be very expensive. Down in the Saale Valley they grow grain and vegetables, but up here in the hills the farming they do is mostly livestock. The economy is largely forestry and mining. I'm guessing that the Schwarza valley has always been a food importer.

Second, he is worried about refugees. We aren't the only ones worried about those raiders in the farmland to the north and east. They've driven people from their homes, and some of those have come up the Schwarza valley to the area protected by the castle. The resupply problem would be serious without the refugees, but with them, everything is worse.

And, of course, he's worried about us. I told him that we were worried about him too, since he has the high ground, but that I thought we were better off cooperating. I told him about the skirmishes we've had with the raiders, and said that we would do everything we could do to make sure that they never got through Grantville to him.

That led him to ask about our weapons. He said his scouts had been all the way around the Ring of Fire, or the pit, depending on whose words you use, and that they had heard stories about some of our skirmishes. All I had was a pistol, and I'm no great shot. I gave him a demonstration, then pulled the clip from my gun and let him handle it. He seemed fascinated by the idea of putting the bullet, powder and primer all together in one cartridge and also by the complexity of the pistol mechanism.

The captain was curious about what the power plant was, and I had no good way to explain that. He had already guessed that it was some kind of mill or forge. I told him that it was a mill, but that I didn't know how to explain what it was that we make there. All I could do is give him a name for it. So, now it is an *Electrischemühle*. I explained that when he sees bright lights at night, those lights burn the electricity they make there.

One thing the captain let slip may be of importance. The graf is away north, fighting the Catholic armies and trying to keep the Swedes out of his lands, despite the fact that they are officially on his side. So the captain is almost on his own. There is a garrison at Rudolstadt, and he's managed to reestablish communications with them.

I explained to him that the road crew would get to work Monday with his permission, to build a road up to Schwarzburg. Then I explained that it might alarm the Germans because we would use machines.

III. The Military Threat

I only went up to the castle when we took up bodies. Even then, I wanted to make sure we got the body bags back, so I didn't see that much. Yes, they have cannon, but how many I can't say. I saw only one, from a distance. It was tarnished to a brown shade that looked like brass or bronze and it had a barrel perhaps four feet long and a foot around at the breech. I couldn't see the muzzle or any cannon balls, so I don't know the caliber. It didn't seem right to be nosing into things like that, what with the job of getting the body out of the body bag and into a burial shroud.

IV. Church Relations

I don't know if anyone in Grantville has thought through what's going to happen between us and the churches of this land. I remember studying in Sunday School about the Reformation and Counter-Reformation and how hard it was for the Church to come to grips with religious diversity.

Pastor Decker didn't get to this subject right away, but you could tell from the way he asked it that the answers we gave would be important. He asked what religion we were in Grantville, after he'd noted that he understood that we were using the Gregorian calendar, which he thinks of as the Catholic calendar.

I explained that I was Catholic and so is Miles Drahuta, and then I had to ask around. Ron Koch turned out to be Lutheran,

Brick Bozarth was Church of Christ, which I had to explain was another Protestant denomination, and Pete McDougal added to the confusion by saying that his wife was Catholic but that he was more of a non-practicing Presbyterian than anything.

The pastor wondered if the fact that more of us were Catholic than any other religion was the reason that Grantville used the Gregorian calendar. I explained that the whole world switched to that calendar long before I was born, not because of religion, but because it worked better than the old one.

The pastor was very confused by the fact that we could work and live together not caring that our neighbors or coworkers had different religions. It took me a while to figure out how to answer him, but I think my answer was good. I told him that we have only to look back on the Thirty Years' War and all the other wars of religion to see how failure to tolerate religious difference can ruin entire nations.

He asked how could I, a Catholic, justify helping to properly bury Lutherans, when my church had declared that they were certain to burn in Hell. I asked him how could I, as a Christian, refuse to help properly bury another human, as all of us are made in God's image.

He needed to probe the limits of our toleration, asking if we would accept Anabaptists or Mennonites, to which I said that we would welcome them. He asked about Muscovites too, and it took me a bit to figure out that he meant Russian Orthodox. I told him that I thought that we had several Orthodox Christian families in town. Then he asked about Jews. I said that there was a Jewish family that had been in Grantville for many years, the Roths, and that the Abrabanel family had just arrived in town from Holland and already Rebecca Abrabanel is part of our government. He asked if I would tolerate the Jews if they came in numbers enough to build a synagogue, and I said of course. Then he asked about Turks, and I said that I didn't know if there were any Muslims in town but again, if they were there, they could build a mosque.

I think some of our clergy are going to have to get together with the German clergy and have some very long talks.

— 4 —

To be delivered to Martin Mühler at the Mägdleinschule, Eisfeld:

Written on this twenty-third day of May, in the year of our Lord 1631, or the second day of June in the Catholic calendar of Pope Gregory. I will explain in a moment why I mention this other date.

Martin, thank you for replying so promptly to my last letter. I wrote that letter in a state of great alarm. At the time I wrote it, I knew nothing about what had happened but what I could see with my own eyes. Now, Martin, I have actually been down in the pit and I have spoken with those who are within.

So much has happened since I last wrote. Captain Saalfelder of the castle guard has sent good men to scout around the place we at first thought might be the very pit of Hell, and even into the pit. We have found a roundabout way to get messages safely to and from Rudolstadt.

Thursday, we had visitors from within the pit, and although they spoke mostly English and had almost no German, they had a letter written to the captain in excellent German. It was a most remarkable letter, claiming to be from the Grantville Emergency Committee and asking us for permission to build a road up the wall of the pit. The captain showed me the letter, and it was remarkable even to look at. The paper was the most perfect, and it was printed, not written, using a humanist style of type. The signature was even more remarkable—it was signed by a woman, Rebecca Abrabanel. Is that name not Jewish? Also, the letter was dated using the Catholic calendar!

As I wrote before, several houses fell into the pit when it opened. It has fallen on us to give a proper burial to those who fell in those first horrible moments that Sunday noon. Our visitors said that we were welcome to come down to try to find the bodies, and they said they would try to get us help. Friday morning, one brave man, the farmer Johann Schwarz went down. His wife was one of those lost. He came back, reporting that there were bodies. More important, he came back unharmed, so Friday afternoon, six of us went down.

More of us went back Saturday. Not too long after we had started, we were joined by five men from this strange new town of Grantville. Even the names of the men were strange, Mark O'Reilly said the name was Irish, Pete McDougal has a name befitting one of the Scots mercenaries this accursed war has brought to our land, and the names Brick Bozarth and Miles Drahuta I cannot place at all. All of them were from this country called West Virginia, which is in a kingdom called the United States of America which is, indeed, in America across the ocean.

Everything about these men was remarkable. Their clothing, their tools, what they did first, how they worked, but at times, it was as if they were working miracles. This man Mark O'Reilly said that all of the others had been trained in rescue work because they were miners by trade. All of them had helmets and vests that were bright colors, so that if any of them needed to be rescued, they could be found easily.

The first thing they did was a great puzzle. Instead of joining immediately in the search they began to string ropes. Safety ropes, Mr. O'Reilly called them. Then they built a bridge across the foot of the great new waterfall the Schwarza has made where it falls into the pit. Mark explained that he did not want more people to die or be injured in searching for the dead. Indeed, these ropes and the bridge they built were a great help.

Their tools were amazing. The most fearsome was a saw. It sounds so simple to call it just a saw, because it had an engine on it that roared most unpleasantly. Although it was small enough to hold easily with two hands, it could cut through a tree as big around as a man in only minutes.

They had two of these saws and also a machine that was so simple that I believe one of our smithies could easily build one. They call it a come-along because it makes things come along. The machine had a lever, a ratchet, and a windlass drum, with cable and hooks, so that one man could lift a ton if he worked patiently with the lever and ratchet. The rope was made of steel wire, but that was the only new idea in this machine.

Their shovels were more finely forged than any shovel I have seen, but they were just shovels. By the end of the day, they had helped us recover five more bodies. Three of those would have taken days to get out without the saw and the come-along.

These men claimed special training in what they call rescue and recovery work, and they had with them two items that were horrible proof of that. They called them body bags. These were made of the finest oiled canvas, with a remarkable sliding fastener to hold each closed, and with many handles very finely sewn to the sides all around. These bags were good for only one thing, and that was for carrying the dead out of difficult places.

While I am talking about strange tools, I should say something about the engine that is even now being used to build the promised road up from the bottom of the pit to Schwarzburg. It is yellow, and the size of a small hut. For most of last week, it has sat beside a great pile of charcoal near a huge mill building not far below us, doing nothing. On Friday, though, a man came out of the mill building and climbed onto this engine, and it seemed to come to life with a rumble like distant thunder. It pushes things around. It has a great blade, like a broad shovel on the front, and it pushes with the power of many oxen. That first time we saw it used, it was put to use shaping that pile of charcoal.

Today, as I watch, there are just five men working slowly up the side of one of the mountains within the pit. They are using their marvelous saws to cut the trees in the path of the road they are building. Sometimes they use the come-along to pull the fallen trees where they want them. One of the men is working the great engine I mentioned. With this machine alone, he is doing the work of fifty or one hundred men cutting a road into the side of the mountain. I believe he will complete this road by noon, yet it must be almost a mile in length.

But, let me say more about my conversation with Mark O'Reilly. Although his German was not good, he had with him a remarkable little book, a dictionary. Part of it contained English words and their German equivalents, and part contained German words and their English equivalents, all organized by the alphabet. There was one problem with this book. His dictionary contained German as it will be spoken more than three centuries in the future. With his bad German and this dictionary, however, we spoke of some of the most remarkable things.

One curious thing came out. I have been speaking of the pit, because from Schwarzburg, it appears that Grantville lies at the bottom of a great pit that has opened up in our lands. The people from Grantville refer to what has befallen them in different terms. They call it the "Ring of Fire" because, for a fleeting moment when their town was inexplicably transported to our doorstep, they were surrounded by a strange circle of fire.

They have no understanding at all of how this happened. Whatever devilment there is behind what happened, whatever God's purpose may be in this, it is no clearer to them than it is to us. They may have wondrous tools, and they do indeed appear to come from our future, but they are afraid of the same things we are. They fear not having enough food to eat, and fear that the war that is sweeping south after the fall of Magdeburg will consume them.

The people of Grantville know of the war that plagues our lands. They call it the Thirty Years' War, because, from the point of view of their future, it lasted thirty years. Mark O'Reilly says that this war murdered one third of the population of Germany. Yes, murder is the word he used. He said that, from this and other wars of religion, the Church of his day, not just the church of the popes, but also the many Protestant churches have learned that they must tolerate each other even when they disagree deeply about doctrine.

This is the most remarkable thing of all. In this town of Grantville, there are many Protestant churches and also a Catholic church. He said that the different churches disagree on many matters of theology, but that they have been there for many years, and living in peace despite these differences. All of them have used the Catholic calendar for many years, not because of any Catholic victory, but because they have agreed that Pope Gregory's calendar is more rational than the old calendar.

Among the men from Grantville working with us, Mark O'Reilly and one other were Catholic, one was Lutheran, one was Presbyterian, which I take to be a kind of Calvinist, and one from some Protestant group called the Church of Christ. Strangely, the Presbyterian said he had a Catholic wife, but even more remarkable than this was the fact that Mark O'Reilly did not know the religions of most of the men he was working with. He had to ask, and he only thought to do so in response to my questions.

I learned that there are indeed Jews in town. One Jewish family is headed by a goldsmith who has been a respected merchant in town for many years. This Rebecca Abrabanel who signed the letter we saw last week is indeed Jewish, but she and her father are from our world, from Amsterdam. You may measure the warmth of their welcome by the fact that she seems to have taken a very high seat on this emergency committee they have established to rule their town. Mark O'Reilly did say, though, that he thought the head of this emergency committee, a man named Michael Stearns, was some kind of Protestant.

Again, note my words. He thought. It seems that he has never inquired about this matter. I am not talking about a man who lacks curiosity or judgment. This man was most curious, deeply concerned about the safety of his men and of the men from Schwarzburg, and very interested to learn what I had to say. Despite this curiosity, despite being well educated, despite the fact that he had a sharp wit, he had never inquired. I can only conclude that we will find this Grantville to be very different from any place we have ever imagined.

Mark O'Reilly said that he was no scholar of religion, but he knew far more of the Bible than the Catholic laymen I have met. When I questioned how Grantville's religions could be so tolerant, he quoted a document with which I am unfamiliar, saying that all men are made equal, but then he showed how this follows from the book of Genesis, since we are all descended from Adam and Adam himself was created in God's image. The logic of this argument is very compelling. If indeed every man is an image of God himself, not in the idolatrous sense but because that is indeed how God made us, then indeed, it would be disrespectful of God himself for us to treat each other with anything less than respect, even when we may disagree deeply.

Martin, as a brother in Christ, as my roommate of many years when we studied together in seminary, I beg your help in trying to digest what has happened here.

I write as your most humble and troubled friend, Hermann Decker.

Recycling

Philip Schillawski and John Rigby

"Hey! Watch it with that broom." Officer Preston Richards hastily pulled his feet back away from the stiff bristles that threatened the shine of his newly polished shoes. He glanced up from the night sheets he was going over, and looked at the unprepossessing figure before him. The small gray-haired woman in dumpy clothes, with her flesh hanging from her thin frame, was a far cry from the well-dressed matron he had met the day of the Ring of Fire. Then she had been a hard-bodied exercise maven. Now the only thing hard about her was her eyes. But he'd kept his eyes on her for too long.

"Don't you look at me like I'm some kind of white trash, Mr. Officer Preston Richards," the woman spat. "If I happen to be down on my luck, it's the damned Ring of Fire that took away Joseph and my boys."

Richards recalled the frantic figure he had tried to help on that day the world had been split apart. She had been in town checking out retirement homes, and had been left with only her car and the clothes she had with her. She was desperately attempting to contact her family. Now he tried for a soothing reply. "I've never thought you were trash, Mrs. Sanderlin. I just keep hoping that you'll stop staying with us on such a regular basis."

He glanced back down at the night sheets. He hadn't made it through to the petty crimes section yet, but if LeeAnn was sweeping floors in the station this morning, he knew he'd find her usual entry: "Public Drunkenness, LeeAnn Sanderlin, Drunk Tank." Sentencing for nonviolent public drunkenness had become so routine by now that most of the regulars and semiregulars didn't even go before the associate judge any more. Not unless they demanded a hearing, and most were smart enough to realize that they wouldn't get a lighter sentence by going that route. Instead they were allowed to sleep it off on the thin foam-rubber mats in the drunk tank. The next morning they were given a good breakfast by Carolyn Atkins, then put to work at odd jobs around the station or downtown until released. LeeAnn, like most of the regulars and semiregulars, didn't even need much supervision on her morning's work.

"Well, if a person needs to take a drink or two sometimes to warm the coldness inside, and doesn't hurt anybody by it, then there's no harm done, Preston Richards." LeeAnn pushed harder with the broom. "I don't mind sweeping your floors or cleaning out your cells to repay your hospitality when you bring me in, so we're square there. I don't need charity from anybody. I pay my debts."

"Are you sure you wouldn't like to talk to someone who might be able to help?" He'd tried hard to get her counseling and other help when she started to come apart. But nothing he'd tried had worked. He knew from experience that there wasn't much hope for LeeAnn unless she worked out the problems that caused her drinking binges. But that just stiffened his resolve to continue to try to help.

"No. I don't need to talk to any more experts. None of them know what they're doing, anyway, and nothing they do helps. I can get by on my own."

Richards shook his head as LeeAnn moved off. The sagging flesh at the back of her arms wobbled as she worked the broom. He went back to the night sheets, only to be interrupted again by a raised voice from the next table.

"Whoa! Karl, you nearly took my eye out with that thing!" Officer Ralph Onofrio was rubbing his forehead. "Can't you ever get that pen back together without launching the spring across the room?"

Karl Maurer, one of the newer down-timers on the force, grinned sheepishly. "Sorry, I was just checking to see how much ink is left. I do not want to run out while we are on shift." LeeAnn reached past him to place the offending spring on the table in front of him.

Onofrio shook his head. "Well, be more careful with it. We still have plenty of refill cartridges left, but if you lose that spring, the pen is useless. We don't have any replacement springs."

Maurer carefully reassembled the pen. "Why can you not simply make another one? It seems so simple a task for your technology."

"I'm not sure why not," Onofrio answered. "I've just been told that coil springs aren't doable."

"Well, it is good then that a pen spring is not critical." Maurer put the pen back in his pocket.

Richards glanced at the revolver Officer Maurer was wearing. He hadn't been intensively trained on semiautos, then. He decided to interrupt. "Pen springs aren't critical, no. But since it seems we don't have the resources to do anything about making new springs, we'll have to get by without. That means being careful with all the springs we do have." The officer nodded gravely. Richards picked up the night sheets and left the room, passing LeeAnn who was still working her broom by the door.

Guenther Wendel stopped LeeAnn as she walked toward the women's locker room at the Public Works Department Recycling Center. "Herr Officer Richards called and said you would be in after noon today. He is concerned about you. I also am growing concerned with your mornings off. You need to be more careful with yourself."

LeeAnn scowled at her supervisor. *Arrogant little German twerp*, she thought. The coldness started to grow inside her again—memories of her comfortable, fulfilled life before the Ring of Fire warred with the bleakness of her current condition. The last thing she needed was to have to deal with one of the Germans she associated with the change. "I haven't used up all my sick days yet. Until I do, you have no cause to complain. I'm still the best sorter you've got."

She pushed past Wendel into the locker room, where he couldn't follow. As she changed into her work clothes, she was still muttering. "They don't pay me enough to put up with this crap. Even the damn Germans leave here as soon as they can. I need to find some angle and get out." Her words ran up against the memories of all those jobs she'd lost when she fell apart in the year after Joe and the boys were taken. She licked her lips, wishing for some liquid warmth as the cold inside her grew some more.

LeeAnn threw herself into sorting. If she thought of it as a big treasure hunt, it sometimes could be interesting enough to take her mind off other things. There was a large pile to work through. Since the Ring of Fire, all metals, plastics, synthetic fabrics, rubber and glass were required to be separated from other trash and set out for recycling. "Strategic Materials" they now were, not just trash anymore. The announcements had been clear: *'You don't have to get rid of anything you want to keep, but if you put them on the curb, Strategic Materials MUST be in the recycle pile.'*

Hmm, this may be promising, LeeAnn thought. She pulled out a ripped and tattered piece of nylon luggage. *Yes!* It was one of those bags capable of being used as a backpack. The zippers were all popped, and the rips made it unsuitable for further use as a backpack. But the contour bars were still there. She felt the two flat bars that ran under the nylon on the side of the bag the shoulder straps were on. She easily bent the bars with her hands. She sliced open the nylon and removed the precious aluminum.

She dropped the aluminum bars into the aluminum bin. *Not much here,* she thought. Now that most people knew they could get good money from various scrap dealers for any aluminum articles they didn't need, they didn't send them off in the recycling for free. She glanced over as Berta Hess dropped some bent tubing taken from a camp chair into the bin. LeeAnn pulled out one of the tubes. It felt too heavy to her.

"Berta!" The German woman turned. "You can't just assume that any silvery metal is aluminum. You have to check." LeeAnn pulled out her magnet and nodded as it went "clack" and clung to one of the legs. "See, plated steel tubing."

Berta nodded shamefacedly. LeeAnn shook her head. *They need to train these people more,* she thought. *Berta isn't dumb, she just doesn't have the training or experience to recognize the difference.* LeeAnn glanced over to where Herr Wendel was sitting, filling out paperwork. *I do more supervising around here than he does. Instead of training people to do their jobs right, and watching to make sure they do, he just sits around.* She turned as Berta moved past her, carrying the tubing toward the steel scrap bin. *Arrgh . . .*

Shaking her head again, LeeAnn stepped over to Berta and

redirected her. "Remember, Berta. Tubing is on the Special List because it's so difficult to reproduce. It goes into the Special List bin." The tubing would be evaluated further on to see if it could be reused in its current form. If not, the plating would be stripped off and the steel itself would probably end up on the scrap heap to be melted into new steel.

LeeAnn collected the remains of the backpack suitcase and dropped the nylon in with the other synthetics. At some point, "when the budget allows," all the collected synthetic cloth would be further evaluated for possible reuse.

A broken brass candlestick was next. It went into the brass bin along with a bunch of spent .22 caliber cases. All of that went for military use, to make the bases of new shotgun shells for the army.

Her next find made her flinty eyes narrow. She nodded to herself in complete satisfaction; it was too heavy for aluminum. "So Herr Wendel wants to give me trouble, does he? I'm the only one here who knows enough to recognize this for what it is. He won't dare push things and try to get me fired." LeeAnn weighed the heavy pot-metal ornaments in her hands as she carried them to the zinc bin. The experts were still pushing hard for zinc from any source, again for military production. Even now, the zinc was still carefully stripped off from any unusable galvanized steel. Later date American pennies had gone out of circulation quickly once the "experts" finally twigged to the fact that they were mostly zinc and worth far more than their one-cent face value. The one who finally figured that out was awarded the Strategic Materials Prize. "I sure could do with the cash that comes with one of those," LeeAnn muttered.

LeeAnn luxuriated under the hot shower after work. The oil, grease, food and beverage residues on the recycled trash made for a messy job. The showers the department provided as a result were one of the best benefits of working there. LeeAnn used them every day after work, even when she was running short on soap or shampoo. Today was one of those days. Her shampoo bottle was almost empty, and her binge last night meant that the budget couldn't handle a refill until next payday. So she used soap today to cut the grease on her hair, and only a little shampoo after. That meant her hair would be dry and frizzy when it dried, but she was the only one now who cared how she looked, so that was okay.

As she dried herself, she finally identified part of what had been bothering her all through work that afternoon. Something Preston Richards had said had been nagging at her ever since. And she thought she knew who might have some answers for her. She hurried to dress so she could catch him when he left work.

Ed Barger, the equipment procurement specialist at the Department of Transportation, stopped warily as the bag lady stepped in front of him on his way down the walk from the department offices. "Uh . . . hello . . ."

"I'm LeeAnn Sanderlin," the bag lady said. "I work over at the recycling center. You're Ed Barger, right? I have some questions for you."

Okay, Ed thought, *I have seen her over at Public Works before. So she's not really a bag lady.* Still, her worn and stained coat, the shapeless knit hat covering her frizzy hair, and the big roller bag she was pulling sure made her look the part. Ed couldn't help reacting to her that way. "I . . . uh . . . I really don't have any time right now."

"This won't take long," the bag lady said, moving in closer. "I just have some questions about springs, and I remember reading what you told the paper when you-all were pushing for people to turn in their cars for tax deductions, about how the springs and things were needed for the railroad and other equipment." Ed had been moving back away from her as she spoke, but she kept moving forward after him, and now he was trapped against the wall. He glanced quickly to both sides, but couldn't see a way to escape.

"Now," the bag lady continued, grinning up at him, "I heard this morning that we couldn't make coil springs anymore, and I want to know why."

Maybe if I humor her, she'll go away, Ed thought. *It's that or call for a cop.* "Uh . . . well. It's not that we couldn't make them if we had the steel to do it with. It's easy to draw the wire and wind the coils. Heck, Europeans were drawing and winding iron wire for centuries before the Ring of Fire dropped us on them; it's how they made chain mail." It looked like the bag lady understood, because she asked an intelligent question.

"But we're starting to make good steel now. I know that Public Works sells some of the steel we get at the recycling center to be remelted. Why don't they make coil springs out of that?"

"Some crucible steel is being produced. But . . . uh . . . that's just high carbon steel at best, and even wire made from that won't work for coil springs. It weakens quickly and the spring becomes useless. You need a special kind of alloy for reliable coil springs. It will be years before we can get the elements for the alloys in large enough quantities to be able to produce much of it. That's why we needed the cars—most all the coil springs from their suspensions can be used as-is for all the equipment and railroad suspension elements where coil springs are critical."

The bag lady thought that over for a bit. "What else are coil springs critical for?"

"Uh . . . let's see. Lots of things, I guess. I think I heard that some medical equipment uses them. I don't know much about that. But, I know that modern gun designs use coil springs a lot. They power the firing pins and return the bolt after ejecting the empty case in semiautomatic pistols and rifles. And they make the tubular magazines in shotguns work. We can't duplicate any of those kinds of guns until we're able to make reliable springs."

"Thanks. I appreciate your time," she said.

Ed sighed with relief as the bag lady ended the interrogation and moved off. He continued on his way home, shaking his head about the difference between her appearance and her apparent intelligence.

Walking back home under the low overcast, the cold and rainy spring weather made LeeAnn feel every one of her sixty-seven years. And something was still bothering her—she couldn't quite pin it down—something about this whole spring thing just didn't make sense, and she couldn't get it out of her mind. She trundled her work clothes and towels along behind her in her priceless roller bag. She needed to swap them out for a clean set tomorrow, and get to the Laundromat before the end of the week. She looked up in disgust as she passed the Hoffman house two doors down from hers. The brats were out again.

The four Hoffman children were all in the front yard, and all concentrating on her. They stared at her the whole time she walked by, waving their hands and fingers at her in hex signs, and all the time jabbering on in high-pitched German. LeeAnn sighed in relief as their mother came to the door and shooed them inside, then she stiffened as the other woman sniffed loudly and tossed her chin as she followed her children through the door.

"Damn arrogant foreigners," LeeAnn mumbled as she turned up the driveway toward her rented room in her landlord's garage. "Herr Hoffman thinks he's a big man just because the army gave him some training and now they're moving him up to a better job. And of course, Frau Hoffman thinks she's better than me just because they can rent a house. Damn Germans taking jobs and houses, and they can't even speak *English*." The coldness, and the thirst, were growing inside her.

LeeAnn dumped the dirty work clothes and towels from the roller bag into the hamper and replaced them with a clean set. Then she sighed and looked around her small portion of the garage. Before the Ring of Fire, her section had been set up as an office, partially partitioned off from the main part of the garage, with a small bathroom with sink and toilet off one wall. Now it was home, for which her landlord charged exorbitant rent. Still, it had the bathroom. No shower, but she had that at work. And it was heated. Thank God natural gas supply wasn't a problem in Grantville. The heater was on now, and handled the coldness, at least that on the outside.

LeeAnn looked up as someone knocked on the garage door. "Come in," she said, but her landlord had already pushed through the door, holding a cardboard carton in his arms.

"Evenin', LeeAnn," Rafael Ugolini said. He carried the carton into the main section of the garage and placed it on a new stack of similar ones. The label on this one declared its contents to be: "*Catalogs: Reagan Years.*" He turned back to LeeAnn. "I hope you'll be on time with the rent this month."

"I'll be on time with my rent as always," LeeAnn answered. "And you've got no call to suggest anything different."

"Well, yes. But I'm going to need the money regular-like now that the new baby's coming."

"You'll get it."

"Whatever. For right now, though, I need you to be sure you keep all your stuff in your section. I'm cleaning out the back room of the house for the nursery, and I'll need all of the space up here."

LeeAnn looked over the front section of the garage. That section was filled with what—her nose wrinkled in irony at the thought—was trash. Many of the garages in Grantville were that way now. "Why don't you just recycle this stuff? Then you won't have to move it again later."

"Hah. Just 'cause you work for the recycle place that's all you think about. Well, I recycled my car when the gov'ment asked. I only got the little tax deduction for a regular car though. If I'd a bought that SUV back in '99, I could have gotten the big money for it, and the army would have another armored car sometime down the line."

"There's a lot of stuff here that should be recycled. It's not worth anything." LeeAnn gestured at the broken bed leaning over in the corner by the big door. The side rail of the frame was splintered, and shredded cotton batting was hanging out of big rips in the mattress. She moved over and nudged a twisted mass of wire and plastic clothes hangers with her toe.

"Hey, this is all twentieth-century stuff," Ugolini protested. "It's worth a lot. We can't make any of it anymore."

LeeAnn raised her eyebrows at this. She knew he was wrong about the wire hangers, anyway. She glanced significantly again at the bedraggled bed.

"Well, maybe I could put that thing on the curb. I'll probably need the space before I'm done."

After her landlord left, LeeAnn sat at her card table on a wooden folding chair and ate the bread and cheese she had brought home for dinner. Berta at work was always nagging her about her food. LeeAnn snorted. "Like I need some foreigner telling me about 'nuut-ree-shun.' I made it through two winters here, so I guess I know what I need to get by." She sighed. It sure would be nice to get some more meat once in a while, and more vegetables. But even when the harvests were just in, those were expensive because transportation was so difficult. Now they were dear. LeeAnn shrugged. She looked at the two wizened apples she'd bought for desert, but decided she was full. She licked her lips, wishing she had something to warm her growing inner chill.

She thought some more about what had been bothering her today. She still couldn't pin it down, and it was truly annoying her.

The light was fading when LeeAnn changed into the velour

running suit she used for sleeping and moved to the recliner she used for a bed. The landlord supplied electricity, but he didn't supply light bulbs, and LeeAnn couldn't afford them. *Won't let me use candles or a gas jet either*, she thought with disgust. *Afraid I'll burn the place down.* So it was to bed with the twilight and up with the dawn. When the days finally got longer, she could read after dinner. *I really miss being able to read.*

The recliner had seen better days, but it was hers. She held the covering quilt up and flopped herself down. She was rewarded with a metallic "click" and a poke in her left rear. She cursed, levered herself up, and glared at the offending chair. "Now what am I going to use to pad...

"The 'experts' can't possibly have been that *stupid,* could they?" LeeAnn muttered as she manhandled the recliner over onto its side. She peered into its innards. "Hmm, not exactly what I thought, but close enough." She went to get a set of cutters. A few careful snips removed the item she needed. She got the heavy chair back upright, then stood holding her prize and gazing off into the gloom of the garage. "Yes, they really can be that stupid. They really screwed up this one." She licked her lips, but not from thirst for booze, this time.

Her gaze fixed on the torn mattress in the corner. Her eyes narrowed. She strode over and peered in through the torn cover. *Yep. More in there.* She pulled the mattress forward and checked the object behind it. *There too ... duh, of course.* Her eyes narrowed even more, then she glanced up into the corner by the big door, and started to laugh. She slept peacefully that night in her saggy recliner, her prize clutched in her hand, warm both inside and out for the first time in ages.

As LeeAnn walked to work the next morning, Frau Hoffman was sweeping her front steps. LeeAnn gave her a radiant smile, then laughed at the look of surprised confusion her smile caused on the German woman's face. LeeAnn bypassed the recycling center and entered the main office of the Public Works Department, pulling her roller bag behind her. She marched up to the well-fed down-timer secretary outside the director's door, and stated, "Tell Garland Franklin that LeeAnn Sanderlin is here to see him. It's vitally important that I see him about Strategic Materials. And tell him that I'm applying for the Strategic Materials prize."

The secretary looked up at LeeAnn with mild disdain. "I'm afraid Herr Franklin is quite busy this morning. You will have to make an appointment."

"I don't think so. *Mister* Franklin always says he has an open-door policy to his employees, especially when they have valuable suggestions. So you march right in there and tell him I'm here. He will definitely thank you once I let him know that his 'experts' have been sitting on their fat butts on a Strategic Material for years now, and didn't even know it."

Garland Franklin was sent, quite frankly, into a state of shock when his secretary ushered LeeAnn into the conference nook in his office and she placed a football-shaped coil spring in his hand. "Ed Barger over at the Department of Transportation told me that coil springs are required for a lot of important things, especially modern gun designs. He said they are a special steel alloy that we can't make here-and-now. I got this from under the seat of my recliner. There were five of these smaller ones and four big ones," LeeAnn stated. Franklin understood the importance of that immediately. "There are probably thousands like them all over town." Franklin just nodded. "And there are thousands of other coil springs, with different size wire, in box-springs and mattresses also." Franklin couldn't do anything but nod some more. "And there are two great big coil springs on most every garage door inside the Ring of Fire. Most folks don't use their garage doors much anymore. If they knew how important they were, and were offered a reasonable price, they probably wouldn't mind selling the springs to the government. I bet you could make an awful lot of gun springs from just one of those big overhead door models.

"But one thing has been troubling me. If coil springs are so important and can't be reproduced, why aren't they on the Special List at the recycling center? I'm sure now that I remember coil springs coming through in recycled items before. I bet there have been many that just got tossed in with the regular steel scrap and a lot have probably been melted down by now. If I didn't know they were special until I overheard something that made me drag it out of Ed Barger, it's a sure bet that none of the down-timers did."

"Public Works doesn't make up the Special List." Franklin wasn't so much in shock that his bureaucrat's CYA instincts didn't immediately kick in. "That comes down to us from higher up.

My department only got stuck with recycling because it didn't seem to fit in anywhere else. And even though the administration gives recycling a lot of lip service, and makes a big deal out of the Strategic Materials prize, they never really put much behind it come budget time."

Now that Garland had recovered himself by getting back on familiar ground, he shook his head and chuckled ruefully. "I still just can't believe that all this spring steel has been there all this time right under our noses."

LeeAnn gave a wicked laugh. "It wasn't under your nose, Garland. It was under your rear end." Garland sank back into the old-fashioned overstuffed chair he favored, now actually noticing the springs creak as he did so, and laughed along with her.

LeeAnn clutched the Strategic Materials prize certificate in both hands after the award ceremony at the Fourth of July celebration. She'd already tucked the $1,000.00 cash prize into the pocket of her new slacks. Guenther Wendel was one of the first to congratulate her. He was actually beaming with pride for her as he shook her hand. *He's not such a bad guy after all,* LeeAnn thought. The breeze blew a lock of her carefully brushed hair into her eyes. She smoothed it back into place.

Preston Richards also came up to congratulate her. "You've done a very important thing for all of us, LeeAnn. It's amazing how we can all miss the obvious for so long. I'm glad to see you looking better now. I haven't seen you partake of our 'hospitality' at the jail for a while now either. That makes me even more happy."

LeeAnn glanced down at the beautiful calligraphy on the certificate once more. She had thought the cash prize would be the big thing to come from her discovery, but she was finding that having other people looking at her with approval was much bigger. She was amazed at how much her outlook had changed in the months since she had found the springs, and how good it felt to smile again. Each smile put more warmth into her fight against the inner cold than the booze ever had. "Thanks, Preston. And thank you for trying to help even when I was throwing myself away. I guess this means that you can find something to recycle in every sort of trash."

A Question of Faith

Anette Pedersen

Grantville, June 1633

"Could I have a word with you, Father Johannes?"

Johannes Grunwald jumped up from the table with a gasp and spun around quickly, sending several maps and notes to the floor. "Sorry, I wasn't expecting anybody. It's rather late." He looked at the elegant young man in the doorway, and relaxed slightly. He had met Don Francisco Nasi only in passing, but, while the head of the Abrabanel financial network in Germany might not be the most reassuring person to make an unexpected appearance close to midnight, the young Jew wasn't likely to be a personal threat either. Johannes looked down on the maps and floor plans on the table. "Please sit down, Don Francisco, I don't suppose you have much need to know the layout of Fulda's main buildings?"

"Not much, no. But my apology for startling you, Father Johannes. I suppose you are preparing something for the NUS team in Fulda?" Francisco Nasi closed the door and sat down at the table in the high-school classroom, considering the German priest. Father Johannes had been one of the foremost painters of propaganda broadsheets for the Holy Roman Empire until the atrocities at Magdeburg had made him revolt, flee and finally—a year and a half ago—seek refuge in Grantville. He had easily been worth his stipend as a teacher, not so much for his knowledge of

71

languages and paints, as because after two decades of painting for both clerical and secular rulers all over Germany, his knowledge of people, towns, and buildings was without equal among the new citizens in Grantville. "I was wondering, Father Johannes, if you'd heard anything from the Inquisition?"

"No. Nothing." Johannes sat down at the table too, and fiddled with his pen. "Father Mazzare's contacts within the Church tell of several people asking for Father Johannes the painter, but those asking are seemingly just interested in having me come to paint for them. I am told you head a vast network of all kinds of contacts, Don Francisco. Have you heard anything?"

"Oh no, nothing about you from the Inquisition," Don Francisco smiled. "Do you worry about an abduction? Or perhaps a formal request for you?"

"I don't think those I personally insulted at Magdeburg have enough power for either. My main value to anybody seems to be the paintings I make. I would like that, if only people wanted their beauty rather than their propaganda value." Johannes shrugged. "Frankly, the most likely thing to happen is an attempt to make me go back to making propaganda for the Church—willingly or under threat from the Inquisition. If I refuse that, but keep a low profile, I may be excommunicated or I may just be ignored. Only if I'm seen to work against the Church—or its political interests—do I expect any serious force to be brought against me. In which case an assassination may be easier to arrange than an abduction, at least in the areas where the Americans keep order."

"I see." Don Francisco leaned back in the chair and steepled his hands. "As I said, I've heard nothing about you in connection with the Inquisition. But I was wondering if you might be willing to leave Grantville. Perhaps to accept a few commissions from some of the more open-minded and politically neutral of your old patrons?"

"And?" Father Johannes too leaned back and looked straight at the polished young man across the table.

Don Francisco shrugged. "Look out for opportunities. Keep your options open, I think the Americans call it."

Johannes kept looking. "Please excuse my rudeness, Don Francisco, but why are you taking an interest in this? Are you asking me to report to you?"

"If you so wish. You haven't been excommunicated, so you're

still a Catholic priest. And a man. With loyalties to whomever or whatever you are loyal to."

"And just what, Don Francisco, are you loyal to?"

"Primarily my family and my faith. Is that so different from you?"

"No. Different family and different faith, of course, but that's not my problem. Where do the Americans enter your loyalties?"

"The Americans? Not the NUS or CPE?"

Johannes nodded. "Ideas and ideals, not politics and compromises."

Don Francisco raised his eyebrows and looked up at the ceiling, "What the Americans have begun may well be the best chance for prosperity and security in Europe today, for my family as well as for my faith. We realize that they are just a small town and risk drowning in the greater political picture. So I—and my family—try to aid them. Help them help themselves and thus ourselves." He looked back again to Johannes. "You have, since your arrival here, been giving the American leaders quite a lot of help yourself, Father Johannes, with your lessons in Contemporary Social and Political Studies."

Johannes laughed a little, "Oh yes. Everything I Know About the Present Political Situation—its Players and Powers. Still, my family and I owe the Americans a debt for helping little Johann, the son of my nephew Herr Martin Grunwald."

"And that debt is the only reason for your help? You don't agree with the American goals?"

Johannes shrugged. "Both yes and no. Aside from teaching and painting I've spent just about every spare waking moment reading the American books of history and philosophy. I think I've got a good idea of what they are and what they are trying to do. On the whole I'm fairly certain I approve. What still bothers me is that all these important new ideas come from people who seemingly fear neither God nor the Devil. How about you, Don Francisco? Do you fear God and do you fear the Devil?"

"I'm a Jew, Father Johannes. Our faith is different. Personally I hope God will have mercy on my human frailty, and think that the Devil—if such exists—does his work on Earth and among the living." Don Francisco rose from his chair. "But please consider my words, Father Johannes. The Americans' alliance with the Swedish king has made them a power to consider. It would be well to know how this is viewed among the clerical nobility."

"I'll think about it." Johannes started gathering his papers, but Don Francisco remained by the table watching him.

"You have been supplying the American leaders with all kinds of information, Father Johannes. And by now the Americans are being taken very seriously by both the Catholic Church and the secular powers. Do think—carefully."

Grantville, August 1633

The Thuringen Gardens was filled almost to capacity in the warm and dusty afternoon, but Johannes steered his friend, Frank Erbst, to a quiet corner. Frank was a big, strong, red-haired bear of a man, with a warm smile and an ever-ready interest in the world around him. He and Johannes had grown up together on Grunwald-an-der-Saale, the estate Frank now managed for Johannes' older brother Marcus Grunwald, professor of theology at the University in Jena. Ever since his arrival in Grantville, Johannes had been sending seeds and information about American farming to Frank. Despite Marcus' dislike of everything connected with the Americans, Frank had—with great enthusiasm—put the new crops and ideas to use at the estate. And despite the drought, the tomatoes and long beans had been running rampant during the summer on the sunny hillsides along the Saale River. Now, just before the main harvest was about to start, Frank had come to Grantville—the best market for the new crops—to make arrangements with several traders.

With their second tankards half-drained, the two old friends were now catching up on family news.

"Have you heard from Martin recently, Johannes? Your nephew was scuttling around like a woodcock on his new crutches, when I went to Jena last spring. He also wanted me to write to him about growing the new crops. He seemed to be doing some kind of *avisa*."

Johannes laughed, "It's not an *avisa*, Frank. I sent Martin some copies I'd made of the Americans' magazines, especially one in German called *Simplicissimus*. Martin has become the publisher of a monthly newspaper magazine—with his wife, Louisa, handling the legwork and the practical arrangements. Marcus helped with getting the permissions before he saw just what Martin and Louisa intend to publish."

"I've seen such before." Frank shrugged. "Why would Marcus object to council decisions posted on tavern walls?"

"*Simplicissimus* is different, Frank. The Americans are every bit as good at this as they are at farming. What Martin offers for public subscription, and delivers by post every month—soon every two weeks—is a mixture of information and entertainment. There's the latest political news, along with detailed explanations about the persons and places mentioned. There are colored plates with the latest fashions, printed with new American methods. There are pictures and descriptions of beautiful homes, and recipes for the most fashionable food. And most of all: there are illustrated jokes and gossip about court scandals and political mistakes. I've made quite a lot of those illustrations for the new magazine. I promise you, it's like nothing you've seen before. I'll give you some copies to take home."

"Sounds odd to me, but I can well imagine my wife and her sisters with their heads together over such a thing."

"Yes. And taverns, public libraries, noble households, city councils, discussion groups and students. They are all buying it for the political news, you see. Never dreaming of reading the gossip."

"Becoming a cynic, Johannes?"

The whimsy faded from Johannes' eyes, and he called for two more beers before continuing in an entirely different voice. "The Americans genuinely want to stop things like war, plague, and poverty, and they see democracy and education as some of the most important steps towards that goal. Judging from their history, they are right. Martin is promoting these ideas—spreading them among the gossip and jokes in his new magazine. I have helped him do that, but . . ."

"But now you regret that?"

"No. And I'll also go on making those pro-democracy cartoons." Johannes drank deeply from his beer. "It's just that . . . There is nothing among the American ideas to encourage people to bow to God's will or trust his priests."

Frank sat silently for a while, doodling in the wet circles on the table. Bowing to God's will was something you occasionally were forced to do, when no other choices existed. And trusting a priest? That damned well depended on the priest! Frank had no objection to trusting a trustworthy man who happened also to be a priest. But then that went for tinkers and horse traders as well. Still, even after all his fellow priests had done to him, Johannes saw things differently, and in the end Frank said slowly, "I remember a letter you wrote before taking your vows, Johannes. About how some of your fellow students held long discussions about exactly how many imps were around in the world, and the precise rank of the various kinds of angels in Heaven. These discussions irritated you, since the truth could not be known. Unless you've been having divine visions on the sly, you cannot know the future, and I'd say you should just follow your heart."

"Well, my heart tells me that however they got here, the Americans are not here for evil. Their lack of respect for the Lord still bothers me, but you are right—I cannot know the future. And it's about time that I decided what I personally should do—with or without the Americans—instead of hiding here." Johannes smiled wryly into his beer. "I used to be such a self-absorbed little artist, ignoring everything but my paintings, even when reality kicked my arse. Well, Magdeburg definitely did more than just kick, and after my stay here in Grantville, it's certain I'll never go back to what I was."

"Do you plan to leave? You wrote that you felt safe here, but you could go to Jena—or with me back to the estate?"

"I'm probably safer with the Americans than anywhere else. The Inquisition has no power here in Grantville, and Father Mazzare has assured me that I have committed no crime as the Americans see it. In Jena I know Marcus would try to protect me—his pride if nothing else would see to that—but he might not be able to. The Inquisition has no power there. Catholics accusing me of heresy or excommunicating me would not cause trouble with the Protestants. More probably, it would delight them. But blasphemy is an entirely different matter."

"Blasphemy! You?" Frank laughed.

"That depends on how you define blasphemy, Frank. I was much too upset about Magdeburg to weigh my words. But no, I don't think I'll stay here much longer. Perhaps for the winter. It's safe and pleasant, but I'm tired of hiding, and I don't really feel at home among the Americans." Johannes smiled again. "When I first arrived, I actually went around asking people: 'Do you fear God, and do you fear the Devil?' Father Mazzare answered that he did fear the Devil, not as a physical figure but as the evil in mankind. The Lord, he did not fear, as the love was too great to leave room for any fear."

"I like that."

"Me too. I finally stopped asking after a young American woman answered: 'Of course not, God is good, and once you know the Devil, you can just avoid him.'" Johannes shook his head. "Such arrogance."

"And after such a wise counsel, you too decided to trust that God is good and put your faith in Him? You know, " said Frank, chuckling, "that's just the kind of thing Louisa's late sister, Anna, could have said." Then he went on, still smiling. "I've always wondered if you were not at least a little in love with Anna?"

"Don't be silly. Anna was a frivolous little featherhead."

"And?"

"And she was also a married woman, and I am a Catholic priest."

Frank laughed at his friend. "I've long felt that you needed to do something like falling in love with a married woman. In fact, do anything that would make you forget your paintings and pay some more attention to the people around you. But seriously, what are you planning to do?"

"There's a man here in Grantville, a Jew named Francisco Nasi. He has suggested accepting a few commissions from some of my old patrons. Keeping my options open, the Americans call it." Johannes looked into his beer and smiled.

"Well, I can think of a few other things to call that." Frank's smile turned into a scowl. "Can't you think of anything better to do with your life?"

"Oh yes. I haven't been excommunicated, so I'm still a priest. I've been helping Father Mazzare at St. Mary's here in Grantville, but I never was a parish priest and don't plan to make a living from that. Instead I'm becoming what the Americans call a middleman for a while."

"An *entremeteur*? Well, you did tell me some Americans called priests 'God-pimps.'" Frank laughed until he nearly fell off the chair.

"Don't be vulgar. It's perfectly respectable. And I better go find some food; it's not small beer we've been drinking." Johannes walked off in a huff.

Even with platters of bread, cheese, pickles and sausage in front of him, Frank kept chuckling, and, as the food reached his stomach, Johannes started smiling, too.

"All right Frank, you won that one. But it's actually a very interesting project. And if it works, even the middleman's share is likely to be more money than either of us has ever seen."

"Sounds very interesting." Frank was suddenly very serious. "With two years of drought, the water in the Saale River is too low for even the rafts to float, and most of the profit from the estate is used to pay for transporting the goods overland. If it hadn't been for the American crops, there would have been nothing left for your brother's household in Jena. He's paid by the university, so it's not that big a problem for him, but two of my brothers-in-law are forced to look for paying work this winter. With grain yields as low as two to one, they'll be forced to eat the seed grain, and buy new come spring."

"That bad? Tell them to come here to Grantville. People used to working with wood or metal are badly needed. And they could learn about the new farming methods from Herr Willie Ray Hudson in the evenings. I'll introduce you to Herr Hudson, and you can write letters of recommendation. And if any adult female can be spared from the households, they can come too; many of the things the Americans do don't need large muscles."

"My sister Felicia is almost as strong as I am, but it's a very good idea. Thank you. But what is this project of yours?"

"You know porcelain, that beautiful white ceramic imported from China? My mother was so proud of the two porcelain figurines she used to decorate her table at formal dinners along with the more common figures modeled in that sugar paste called *tragant*. But my first hostess here in Grantville, Frau Kindred, has two big cupboards full of porcelain, including an entire formal dinner set for twelve persons, and a less ornate set, which the family eats from every day. The children too."

"I don't believe that."

"It's true. What her grandchildren are not allowed to touch are those beautiful bowls, vases and figurines kept in a glass-fronted cabinet. The oldest, and very finest, are called Meissen."

"Meissen? In Saxony? On the river Elbe near Dresden?"

"Yes. There are people here in Grantville already working on producing porcelain from local clays. But Grantville is not a good place for a large-scale production. It's just too far from the main routes of transportation. We would need to move the best clay here from Saxony, get the fuel for the big ovens, and then transport the finished products along the roads. That is just not practical." Johannes stopped to work his fingers and loosen the joints. "I want to work with painting some of the items myself; Frau Kindred's figurines made my fingers itch to try something similar."

"Where do you plan to build the factory? Jena?"

"No. The Saale River is not really big enough for transportation above Halle. We need a place near a reliable river connection. We are financing the project by selling shares. And since every royal and noble household in Europe has been paying their weight in gold for the imports, we are having no problems getting all the money we want. The Grantville Council and the Swedish administration have already brought large shares, as have various people in Saxony. Most of the Saxon investors want the new factories in Dresden, while the Americans—and I—want Magdeburg."

"To help heal what happened there?"

"Yes. And if I go back to painting, the way Don Francisco suggests, I could sell shares where I went. I get a percentage of each sale—in shares of course."

"You've certainly connected with the real world, Johannes."

"Yes. Did you ever hear the story about what the sailor said to the nun? And let us have another beer. Remembering Magdeburg still makes me angry."

Early the following morning, Johannes and Frank walked through the sunny streets from their lodgings to the Grange. Despite the early hour, someone was repairing one of the American machines for working in the fields in the parking lot and several horses were tied to the wooden posts erected along one side. In the hall inside the building they found old Willie Ray talking to a delicately built, dark-haired young man whose outfit proclaimed him a cavalry officer, and a big tow-haired man, who was dressed like a servant but had the hands and sunburn of a farmer.

"Good morning, Father Johannes." Willie Ray nodded to Johannes and turned back to his young visitor. "You asked about the crops painted on the walls here, and here is the painter himself. Father Johannes please meet Prince Ulrik of Denmark. Officially, of course, he is a visiting Danish nobleman, but there's not much point in trying to pretend with you. You know too many people. Well, then. If the two of you will excuse me I'll go find our pamphlets about dairy farming."

The young man stepped forward and shook hands with Johannes, while Frank bowed and went to talk with the prince's big companion.

Prince Ulrik was the youngest of three sons King Christian IV of Denmark had sired on his queen. Johannes knew that the Swedish king Gustavus Adolphus—whom the young prince had once served as a officer—considered Ulrik to be by far the best of the Danish king's many children. He was certainly the brightest and most virtuous. Johannes had read a short pamphlet, *Castigation of the Vices*, that Prince Ulrik had written a few years ago. He met the lively, dark eyes of the intellectual young prince with delight.

"Your Royal Highness." Johannes followed the young prince's handshake with a deep bow. "I am honored to meet you. Would you care for some refreshment? I know the contents of the jugs on the table are available to visitors."

"Yes, please. Wine if possible." Prince Ulrik smiled, and gestured for Johannes to take a seat on the other chair beside the open window.

"So, you do drink alcohol?" Faced with the friendly smile, Johannes relaxed and dropped most of his formality. Some nobles, even when they were officially traveling incognito, took offense if even the least title or obeisance were omitted, but clearly Prince Ulrik did not. Not to mention that his own stay in Grantville had made him rather impatient with such. "I took the greatest pleasure in reading your treatise on the vices last year." He handed the prince a rather coarse mug of red wine.

"Thank you." Prince Ulrik smiled wryly. "At the time I really had nothing to do except writing and doing a few paintings. But it is the lack of moderation in man, rather than the innocent wine I'm opposed to. After all, even Our Lord Jesus created wine." He sipped the wine and raised his eyebrows in surprise. "An excellent quality. But your works are known to me too, Father Johannes. At least I do suppose that the JIGI, who draws those political satires in the *Simplicissimus Magazine*, is the same Father Johannes, whose paintings I admired at the Jesuit school in Würzburg?"

"It is, but I had no idea the similarity was that obvious."

"It's not. But I have seen your broadsheets too, and even copied your way of creating shades during my own meager attempts at the art." Prince Ulrik's smile flashed in his narrow, sunburned face. "I have no intention of mentioning this to anyone, as your use of a pseudonym indicates a wish to be incognito. In fact, I have been pondering possible additional benefits of going incognito myself."

"Oh?"

"His Swedish Majesty, King Gustavus Adolphus, has always shown me the greatest kindness," the prince said with a pensive frown. "Last year I had intended to take service in Saxony with relatives of my late mother, but His Majesty wrote to me in his own hand, warning me not to do so. Instead I was to come to him as soon as my duties to my royal father permitted this. The American books had warned, not only when and where King Gustavus would die, but also that I would be assassinated while in Saxon service this very year. His Majesty wanted me to enter his service again, but my royal father forbade that. Instead I have been traveling on my father's behalf." Prince Ulrik shook his head. "Questioning farmers about breeding cows is not beneath my dignity—and Lars was sent with me to ensure I asked the right questions—but the increasing tension between King Gustavus and my royal father has given me a better appreciation of anonymity. Not to mention the problems between his Swedish majesty and my late mother's family in Brandenburg and Mecklenburg." Prince Ulrik smiled again. "Still, it's not yet bad enough to make me abandon my duties and renounce my family and title." He then turned serious. "I'd planned to stay in Grantville for a while, Father Johannes, to indulge myself in some studying before returning to Denmark. But Grantville is a republic, and I'm not certain a royal prince would be welcome here. You have lived here for years, Father Johannes, would you expect my royal connection to be a problem?"

"Your Highness, I have absolutely no idea." Johannes looked toward where Frank and Lars had been joined by Willie Ray, who was showing the two farmers something in the papers he was holding. "The Americans pay little attention to formal rank, and are very devoted to the idea of democracy. Calling them republicans is a bit like calling the pope a Catholic. On the other hand they have no problem—mostly—with accepting King Gustavus Adolphus as their Captain-General, and welcome him quite warmly. That your royal connections are Danish might in fact be more of a problem." Johannes frowned. "The American attitude towards enemies is different from what I would have expected, but I cannot quite pinpoint the nature of the difference. The propaganda against the Holy Roman Empire is almost absent here in Grantville, and the Catholic Church seems quite welcome, but if the recent tension became war?" Johannes shrugged. "I just don't know."

Grantville, September 1633

The weather had suddenly changed to autumn. A cold gale roamed the streets but seemed to have no effect on the activities going on. Johannes kept close to the tall brick buildings to avoid getting jostled. The smooth black surface beneath his boots was slippery with wet leaves as he walked towards his lodgings in the Heinzerlings' house next to St. Mary's Catholic Church. He was looking forward to a few quiet hours making drawings of the English king's latest antics.

"Father Johannes, come inside, *bitte*." As he passed the neighbor's house, the door opened and Gertrude Wiegert waved at him. A pretty young girl from the poorest part of Jena, she had been destined for a life of prostitution like the older women in her family until Gretchen and Jeff Higgins had brought her to study in Grantville.

In the cozy living room a young man sat with a mug of warm beer in his hands, but rose when Johannes entered. "Father Johannes please meet Oswald Weisshaus. He's a friend of my family from Jena, and also a friend of Gretchen and Herr Jeff Higgins. He would like to speak with you. Would you like a mulled beer?"

Johannes accepted and sat down.

"Good evening, Father," said Oswald Weisshaus as he resumed his seat. "I think Gretchen and Herr Jeff Higgins mentioned you during one of their visits. You are Professor Marcus Grunwald's younger brother, and don't share his dislike of Americans and new ideas, yes?"

"That is right, Herr Weisshaus. I'm sure Gretchen also told you that I don't fully agree with her either."

"She did." The young man suddenly grinned, making Johannes

wonder just what Gretchen had said about him. "Still," Oswald went on more seriously, "the man asking questions about the younger Grunwald brother was no friend of anyone."

"When was this, and who did he claim to be?" Johannes asked, suddenly alert.

"He didn't give a name, and it was a week ago tomorrow."

Gertrude interrupted, putting a warm mug on the table. "He was a real creep. He made himself so obnoxious that Oswald and the others threw him out of the new Freedom Arches."

"Yes," said Oswald. "But we've kept an eye on him, and he's staying in the Golden Star."

"That takes money. Any sign of soldiers with him?" If the Inquisition had send a single man to Protestant Jena, this might be the contact attempt Johannes had been waiting for. Though from what Gertrude had said, there wasn't much chance for an agreement with this man.

"None. Are you in trouble?"

"Probably," Johannes smiled, "but how much I just cannot figure out. Nor with whom. Thanks for the warning. Any other news from Jena?"

Jena, September 1633

The Grunwald house in Jena had been changed in the eight years since Johannes' previous visit. Not on the outside; that was still a big, sprawling construct built about a hundred years ago, shortly before the nearby Dominican monastery had been converted into the Jena University. The house had come into the family as a part of his grandmother's dower, and Johannes had lived there for several months of every year when he was a child. The small court behind the gates had been decorated with flowers in summer and small evergreen trees in winter when Marcus' wife, Catharina, had still been alive; now it was swept and clean but with no decorations. The main building was directly across the court, fronted by an imposing modern staircase built when Marcus had become professor of theology, but Johannes turned right to a door separated from the ground by only a single step. As the only son of the house, Martin had once had a spacious apartment on the second floor of the main house, but after the loss of one leg from the knee down at Magdeburg, he and his small family had moved to a place with fewer steps for him to climb.

"Uncle Johannes." Martin looked up and smiled. "Louisa told me you'd gone out very early this morning. Weren't you tired after arriving so late last night?"

"Yes, but I slept like a log and woke early." Johannes sat down and stretched out his legs. "It's been a long day, though."

"Did you accomplish what you set out to do?"

"More or less. I had a few surprises." Johannes scowled. "Elector John George of Saxony has donated the Castle Albrechtsburg in Meissen to the porcelain project, on the condition that the porcelain produced is called Meissen also in this world. The vote among the holders of the porcelain shares are now in favor of Meissen over Magdeburg."

"Frankly, Uncle Johannes, it makes sense to me. Sure, gas ovens would make the production much easier, but you told me they cannot be built yet. In Meissen you'll have the materials nearby, and the wood from the Saxon forests can float down the river to almost outside the factory door. It worked in the American world."

"Actually the clay is not near Meissen. It's from a place near Aue on the river Mulde. If it could be transported on the rivers it actually would be easier getting it downriver to Magdeburg than upriver to Meissen. Unfortunately the Mulde is as unreliable for transportation as the Saale, and overland the easiest track to the river Elbe goes by Dresden and Meissen." Johannes looked up at the big map on the wall behind Martin with the postal routes drawn in red ink and the rivers in blue. "I would have preferred not to put the factory in an area controlled by John George of Saxony. What tipped the scale, however, had little to do with logic. The shareholders liked the notion that in the isolated Albrechtsburg the 'secret' could be kept. Which in my opinion is pure nonsense, as the 'secret' is freely for sale in the books from Grantville. Sure, a lot of practical problems must be solved before anyone else can start production, but those solutions we must first discover too. With the work already going on in Grantville, we may have a head start on, for example, the French, but how to make porcelain is no longer a secret." Johannes sighed. "I finally got a consensus on the project starting in Meissen—presumably next summer, but with a second factory to open later in Magdeburg. Albrechtsburg Meissen will specialize in casting dinner sets and the simpler shapes and also do some stoneware. Magdeburg Meissen will experiment with glazing and do the finely detailed figures once the gas ovens are ready."

"A most Solomonic solution."

"Machiavellian too; porcelain glazes have all kinds of military uses. John George of Saxony doesn't know that." Johannes smiled at his nephew. It really didn't seem possible that the gentle and scholastic Martin had been a mercenary officer, and now wanted to become a *novellante*—well sort of. "But how about the magazine? Last night you just said it was going well."

"It is." Martin tried to look serious, but couldn't hold back a big grin. "The number of subscribers to *Simplicissimus* has now reached ten thousand, and we have direct deliveries to all major German towns, except in Bavaria, where we are on the edge of being banned."

"That's wonderful! But how did it grow so big so soon? I advised you to make a big first printing and spread them around for free to show people what you were making. That seems to be the way the Americans do it when they want to sell something new."

"Yes, but I also used every single connection we have: family, scholars, bankers, merchants. Every one. Even the Committee of Correspondence, Mother's family and *Grandmère's* family in France. Asking for news, information, etc. And a quite surprising number send back money for a subscription; apparently everybody wants to keep track of what is going on around the Americans. It truly is wonderful. But what now for you? Are you going to Saxony?"

Johannes looked at Martin; aside from Frank Erbst, there really wasn't anyone he cared more about or trusted more. And besides, Martin might see something Johannes didn't. "About a week ago I met a man in Grantville, Herr Oswald Weisshaus, a student here in Jena. He told me of a man asking questions about me around Jena."

"The Inquisition?"

"Sort of, only not quite. The man is staying at The Golden Star, and I went to see him today. Turned out he was working for Franz von Hatzfeldt, the prince-bishop of Würzburg, whose diocese is now, since the autumn of 1632, administered by Grantville under the Swedes' agreement with Herr Stearns. Bishop Hatzfeldt is in Bonn, and he wants his land back."

"I thought Bishop Hatzfeldt had gone to the family estate east of Cologne." Martin made a note on a piece of paper. "But never mind that. Just how do you—and the Inquisition—enter into that?"

"I met the bishop in 1627, while I was doing some paintings at the *collegium* in Bamberg, and he was the leader of their diplomatic corps. The bishop of Bamberg, Johann Georg Fuchs von Dornheim had just gifted Hatzfeldt with the administration of Vizedans in Carinthia, and Hatzfeldt wanted some decorations for his new house there. Now Hatzfeldt has offered to 'arrange' a total pardon for my behavior at Magdeburg. You know: high-strung artist, cracking under the strain, etc."

"And in return for what?"

"Just me telling him about the Americans, so he can approach them properly, and convince them—and King Gustavus Adolphus—to give him back his bishopric."

"Double agent. Don't go there, Johannes."

"Who knows? The Americans *might* do for him what they have done for the abbot of Fulda. Give him back all of the work but none of the income, while they assign a 'liaison' to watch him closely." Father Johannes smiled grimly. "But I've changed a lot from that naive, little painter Hatzfeldt knew. The old Johannes would have taken that bait, while now I want to think about it. And talk with a man named Francisco Nasi in Grantville."

Martin took a round, dark bottle and two glasses from the cupboard behind him, filled the glasses with the thick, golden liquid, and pushed one towards Johannes. "Between the war and the Americans, I wonder either of us knows who he is or what he believes in any more. In fact, I wonder how anybody could."

Grantville, Early October 1633

The news about the Danish attack on Wismar had reached Jena just as Johannes was about to leave. As he rode through the misty drizzle into Grantville the following evening, the usual hustle and bustle of the town was subdued. People stood talking quietly in small groups instead of hurrying in all directions, and even the Thuringen Gardens was almost silent in the hazy twilight.

Johannes returned the borrowed horse to the stable behind the Heinzerlings' house and went to knock on the door to the main house. He was renting two rooms in one of the converted out-buildings, but although he was wet, sore and tired after the long ride, it seemed better to hear the news as soon as possible.

After telling Johannes about the battle, and the death of the young men, in his usual profane version of the German language, Father Heinzerling mentioned that Don Francisco had sent a message asking for Johannes to come visit at his earliest convenience, so—after sending a longing thought to his waiting bed—Johannes went off again.

"You asked to see me, Don Francisco?" Johannes had found the young Jew still in his office.

"Ah! Yes. Please sit down, Father Johannes. I understand you are acquainted with Prince Ulrik of Denmark?"

"Yes. Has there been trouble? I've heard about the battle."

"Denmark is now officially at war with the CPE—or the United States of Europe as I understand that it will soon be named. The town was most upset about the death of Hans Richter and the young American officers. Prince Ulrik's identity is not publicly known, of course, but he did not conceal that he was Danish. A visiting Danish nobleman. Some of the town's more unruly elements, although they did not dare to threaten an armed man who could be expected to have a fair amount of skill at close-in fighting, attacked his servants while they were working in the stables, unarmed. They beat one of them rather badly before the police arrived."

"And the prince?"

Don Francisco's smile didn't quite reach his eyes. "The prince is safe, although he found the attack on Lars unexpectedly upsetting. He wishes to talk with you before making a decision. Prince Ulrik is a cavalry officer by profession. His primary loyalty must be expected to be to his royal father, King Christian of Denmark. Even so, King Gustavus Adolphus has sent a message asking for his young relative to give parole and travel to him with an escort of Swedish soldiers. But as I said, the prince wished to talk with you first."

☆　　☆　　☆

Prince Ulrik was standing with his back to the room, gazing out the window at the lights from the town flickering in the darkness, when Johannes entered. After a brief glance over his shoulder, the young man returned to his view.

Johannes considered a formal greeting, but decided to just stand and wait.

"Do you remember who wrote that democracy was just another word for the rule of the mob?" Prince Ulrik's voice was devoid of emotion, as if he were inquiring about a minor philosophical point of no particular importance.

"No, but I think he was British."

"That . . . That sounds likely." Prince Ulrik took a deep breath. "Any ideas why they attacked my servants?"

"It could be because they consider a servant as important as a prince. Still, the attackers did not know that you were a prince and, thanks to the prudence of the Grantville police, still do not know it. They only knew that you are the subject of what they call an 'enemy nation.' So I consider it more likely that they simply were so cowardly that they preferred to attack the unarmed. The men attacking your servants would hardly be considered upstanding citizens. Surely you've seen soldiers run amok and turn into a mob after a battle?"

"Yes." Prince Ulrik sighed and leaned his head against the window. "I suppose it was foolish of me to expect the Americans to be more civilized than that."

"People are people, and when they are hurt, they bite. I suppose being civilized is really just a question of having the self control to bite only those who hurt you, rather than whoever is near."

"I have read several pamphlets from a group called the Committee of Correspondence. Do you think they are behind this?"

"No. The committee might include the most radical and revolutionary of both Germans and Americans, but they are not stupid and they are not ruled by their emotions. This attack on you had to be based entirely on emotions."

"The American books do not tell why I was assassinated in the American world—or by whom."

"No." Johannes smiled. "But since you were in Saxon service, I'd say you should seek the reason in that court. Or rather that you should stay away from it."

"The corruption there makes me sick! All my mother's family . . . And the drunkenness in my father's . . ." Prince Ulrik fell silent for a moment. "I never said that, Father Johannes."

"*Sub rosa*, Prince Ulrik. And that you are Protestant does not change that for me." Johannes smiled again as Prince Ulrik turned. "None of us get to choose our relatives, and the command to honor our parents does not mean we must approve of everything they do; only that we should take their best qualities and copy them in ourselves." Johannes filled the fine glass on the table with wine and pushed it towards the prince, who drank and sat down.

"The quality was actually better at the Grange." Prince Ulrik sighed and leaned his head back against the wall, the sparkle returning to his eyes. "My father takes his duties as king very seriously, and has done his best to see that my brothers and I do the same. But my father isn't Denmark, and while I could never go to war against him, I also no longer feel any obligation to fight in his service."

"If you could follow your heart, what would you do?"

"Go to Schwerin. My father saw to it that I was made the Lutheran prince-bishop of Schwerin, and while I only held the office briefly, that is where I feel I belong. It's been conquered by Gustavus Adolphus, and while His Majesty naturally takes care of all his subjects, I am deeply concerned about the people of Schwerin. They have suffered much, and really need the stability of a permanent leadership."

"And if you went to the king of Sweden and gave parole, as he has requested, would he entrust you with the administration of Schwerin?"

"Probably. Chancellor Oxenstierna has hinted at such a possibility." Prince Ulrik sat for a while sipping his wine and looking towards the dark window. "The problem really comes down to the fact that the person I admire the most and want to resemble is at war with all the rest of my family. And so it seems I must either choose one or the other. Betray my family or betray myself."

"Or turn your back—at least partly—upon both. A separate peace, I believe the Americans call it." At Johannes' words, Prince Ulrik turned abruptly towards him.

"What are you talking about? Changing my name and setting myself up as an incognito mercenary captain?"

"Not unless you feel that is the right thing for you to do." Johannes smiled. "Schwerin, I suspect, would be adequately neutral. I've been doing a lot of thinking lately about things like obligations and honor, faith and betrayal. I cannot claim to have found the absolute truth, but it seems to me that logic, reason, and the things you ought to do can only take you so far. Sooner or later you get to the point where all that can guide you is your heart and your faith." Johannes looked down on his hands, rubbing them to ease the stiffness caused by holding the reins all day. "I've felt caught between my church wanting me to do what I felt was wrong and the Americans wanting me to embrace ideas that I could only partly support. So, I'm partly turning my back upon both and refusing to work for either. I'll aid the Americans only as far as I feel comfortable with, while the Church may hold my heart but not the use of my skills. I'll take my life into my own hands, work my painting as I choose, and try to right what I see as wrong."

"Are you advising me to do something similar?"

"Only mentioning the possibility of choosing a third option, when the two obvious ones leave you paralyzed and incapable of action. If Schwerin feels like the place you belong, for now at least, this might be God's way of telling you where he wants you to go. If your loyalty toward your father keeps you from giving King Gustavus Adolphus the oaths that would let you return there as prince-bishop . . . ?" Johannes shrugged. "It might still be the right place for you to be as a traveling Danish nobleman. And if your admiration for King Gustavus makes you reluctant to take action against him on your father's behalf? Then place your faith in God, and trust your heart to guide you."

Prince Ulrik's lips quirked. "Perhaps, as was done so expediently in Rudolstadt last spring, I should adopt the words of a writer of times between now and then. 'Trust not in princes. They are but mortal. Earth born they are and soon decay.' I'll think about this." He rose and went to stand by the window again. "My thanks for your time and counsel, Father Johannes."

Two weeks later Johannes once again looked up from a table filled with maps to see Don Francisco standing in the door to the school room.

"You left a message for me, Father Johannes?"

"Only to see you at your convenience, Don Francisco. There is no hurry."

"I wasn't doing anything that couldn't wait. I take it you are curious about Prince Ulrik?"

"If you have news, I am of course interested." Johannes smiled. "But I also expect the prince to find his own destiny without any help from me."

"I see. Well, the prince has reached Magdeburg without mishaps, and is presently negotiating with Chancellor Oxenstierna concerning Schwerin. Rumor has it that the prince and Prime Minister Stearns yelled at each other for a while. The prime minister felt that Prince Ulrik might be of more use as a diplomatic bridge—a negotiator—than as a bishop. But an agreement is expected." Don Francisco sat down at the table and looked inquiringly at Johannes. "But what did you want to see me about?"

"I've been considering your suggestion, Don Francisco. I'll be leaving for Cologne at the end of April, to accept a commission from the Hatzfeldt family."

"I see. Any particular reason for you to accept this particular commission?" Don Francisco looked down on the map of Kronach.

"Several reasons: some personal, some artistic, and some I'm sure would interest you."

Francisco looked at Johannes. "Any connection with your visits to the Grantville Hotel these past few weeks?"

"Yes. I've been 'playing cloak and dagger' as the Americans call it, with a Herr Otto Tweimal from Würzburg. A greasy little creep working for Bishop Franz von Hatzfeldt." Johannes smiled wryly. "He made me an offer I could not refuse."

"I've heard of him."

"Archbishop Ferdinand of Cologne's cousin, Maria Maximilane von Wartenburg, is to take up residence in the Hatzfeldt's newly acquired house in Cologne, along with most of the distaff part of the Hatzfeldt family. The property is several old houses—all of which are worn and drab—so officially I'm hired to paint murals for the ladies and advise on the restoration and decorations. Nice job and well paid. Unofficially, Hatzfeldt wants me to tell him about the Americans in return for a pardon—signed by Archbishop Ferdinand—for my behavior at Magdeburg. Herr Tweimal didn't actually mention negotiating with the Americans or King Gustavus, but also didn't hide that the bishop wants his bishopric back."

"Hmm! And Archbishop Ferdinand?"

"It was indicated that the archbishop was not to know that anything more than painting was going on."

"Bishop Hatzfeldt is an old patron of yours, Father Johannes. Do you believe he is planning a double deal behind the archbishop's back?"

Johannes shrugged. "Could be. When I met Franz von Hatzfeldt, he was a full member of the episcopal chapter administration of Bamberg as well as Würzburg. He had proved himself an excellent diplomat in negotiations with Tilly, and had slowly gained more and more influence until he was elected bishop of Würzburg just a few months before the Protestant conquest of that diocese. I'd say he is a most pragmatic man, ambitious, but very tolerant of other faiths. He definitely does care about his subjects—may actually be worrying about them—and takes his responsibilities very seriously. He'll be coming to Cologne from time to time, to see his family and to follow my progress with the house."

"And where are you planning to stay, Father Johannes?"

"I'm invited to live in the Hatzfeldt family's house there, but must of course leave it from time to time. I plan to buy materials from the merchant Beauville, but must also make arrangements with other traders and craftsmen."

"Herr Beauville is well known to me." Don Francisco smiled. "Before the collapse in the woad trade, my family dealt with him from time to time. This would be a good time to reestablish the connection. I expect this to make for a steady correspondence between Beauville and myself, and I would be most interested in any letters you'd care to send that way. But you mentioned a personal aspect to this offer?"

"Yes, but it's just that—personal."

Don Francisco didn't seem offended by the rudeness, just smiled a little and said softly, "I might be able to help, Father Johannes."

Johannes sat for a while playing with his pen. "Does the name Paul Moreau mean anything to you?"

"No, I'm afraid not."

"A fellow painter. His mother was a friend of my mother. He got into trouble with the Church. Shortly before Magdeburg, I found out that not only had he been tortured by the Inquisition, but it was also absolutely certain that the charges were—or at least the evidence against him was—false. I didn't do anything at the time but this may offer me a chance to do something to help him. At least find out what happened."

"Father Johannes, you have been hiding from the Inquisition for almost two years, and now you plan to challenge them?"

"Hiding from the Inquisition or hiding from myself?"

Don Francisco shook his head. "Perhaps I should now ask you: do you fear God and do you fear the Devil?"

"I no longer have an answer, Don Francisco."

Got My Buck

Barry C. Swift

Herman sat at the fire, obviously enjoying its heat. When Wili sat beside him, he looked over at his friend. "What's tomorrow going to be like, I wonder. I hear these Swedes have some help from that Grantville place."

Wili twisted the stick he was holding. "I once met a man who claimed he'd been in Grantville. Don't remember his name; called him 'New Guy' the way we did everyone 'til they survived a couple of fights. Horst brought him over; said they'd been together with Tilly at Breitenfeld; that he was 'solid.' Do you remember Horst? With him that was as much praise as you could hope for, so we made room at our fire. He seemed to know what he was doing; claimed a space for his blanket and went to work on his pike. Don't remember him saying much 'til someone said that the Swedes we'd be facing the next day came from somewhere called Grantville. It was the first I ever heard of the cursed place."

Herman took a sip of beer, then dunked a piece of bread in his stew. "So, what did this 'New Guy' have to say about the place? I've heard all sorts of rumors."

Wili shrugged. "He didn't say anything, at first, not 'til it was certain that the rest of us knew nothing about 'em. Then he said, 'I've been there. They may be fighting for the Swede, but they're not Swedish; they're some kind of English or Scots, but the town is in Thuringia.'"

Lucas, who was doing his usual imitation of a log on the other side of the firewood, interrupted. "I don't believe those stories about them being wizards. And who cares if they're Scot dogs or Saxon pigs? Is this a mercenary unit? How good are they? Where have they fought?"

Wili shrugged again, even though it was impossible for Lucas to see it. "We figured that it was a good thing when he told us that, to his memory, they didn't hire mercenaries. After all, no town militia was going to stand up to a veteran unit like ours. But he disagreed. He claimed to have been the last survivor of a screw up when the squad he was in got separated from the rest of his company."

Wili sat up straighter and his voice took on a higher pitch. "'There I was, alone with nothing but my wits and my knife. Fortunately, I'm good enough with the knife that I don't need more wits than I have. I set off, trying to get back to a friendly district and doing pretty well after a few days. I thought I was being careful until I got swept up by a scouting party from this Grantville. I'd wandered into their territory without knowing anything about them. I was angry with myself for getting careless, but was told later that they were more alert than most towns. I don't have much English, and that's what they mostly speak there, so I didn't understand much of what I saw.'"

Herman looked over at him. "Wili, was this just before Horst's last battle? Did this guy talk like a priest, you know, someone who did a lot of reading?"

"Yeah, Herman. Why?"

"Because I remember him now. Horst tried to give him to us but Ludwig wouldn't have him. Horst said that this guy had stood beside him in the hedgehog at Breitenfeld after a Swedish cannon broke Horst's pike and killed the three men next to him. Ludwig didn't want anyone under him who sounded like an officer, though."

Wili gave his habitual shrug. "That's more than Horst ever said to me. But then, he didn't have to. If he said a man was solid, that was enough for me."

From behind the woodpile, Lucas could be clearly heard grumbling. "So what? Who cares about this ponce? How good are these guys we're going to kill tomorrow?"

Herman threw a bone from his stew over the woodpile. It missed Lucas, but a dog jumped over the barrier, and chased it.

Wili snorted. "Shut up, Lucas. I'm getting to it." Once again his voice took on a higher pitch as he recited a story that had dominated his thoughts for much of this campaign. "'The place is strange in ways I can't describe. I got lucky when the scouts brought me in. I must have given the right answers because their questioning didn't even start to get nasty. They had some strange notions though: they laundered my clothes for me and separated me from my lice and fleas. Then, since I had some coin, they sent me to this miser's house. At least, I think he must have been a miser because he was certainly rich enough not to need to rent rooms. On the other hand, the meal he served was better than I would expect from a miser, so what do I know?'"

Wili knew he was a good mimic and once again sent a quick prayer of thanks for the teachers he had hated as a child. He had realized years ago that remembering things by rote was a potentially lifesaving skill. *Potentially, nothing,* he thought. *It did save my hide when I was chosen for the 'dangerous' job of taking a message from that suicidal idiot to headquarters.* Well, maybe not suicidal, it was his men who died, not him.

He roused himself from his musing and resumed his story, "Anyway, the new guy claimed he didn't have much English and that the Grantviller had less German but there was this other boarder who was able to help a bit and they wanted to talk about the place. Which was fortunate for us, eh, Lucas?"

"Not that I can tell," came back from the other side of the woodpile. "Although, it's boring enough to be a good bedtime story."

Wili took the posture and tone that his teachers had beat into him as appropriate for recitation. "'There was an interesting display on the wall: two fancy hats, a couple of swords, and several pistols, all hung on nails. I said that I'd only seen arrays of weapons like that in noble's houses. He got out a very small musket that he called a "twenty-two" and said that it was the only weapon he owned; those were "trophies." When I didn't understand, he told me a story about how he had been given this "twenty-two" when he was a child. It seems that the city guards ran an athletic program for the children of the town where he grew up, including teaching them to shoot. What's more, he claimed that his older sister had learned to shoot when she was ten years old, just as he had, and that this had been her musket. I thought he was joking; this "twenty-two" he was holding must have been some kind of toy musket that they used for training these girls. I tell you, the bore was no bigger than a writing quill and it had neither matchlock nor that fancy French flintlock. But he insisted that it was a real weapon.'"

Wili stopped and threw the stick he'd been fiddling with in the direction of Lucas' bedroll. "This the part you care about, so quit pretending to snore, you ignorant sot. That bit about the 'twenty-two' is one of the best descriptions I've heard about these quick-firing muskets that the Swedes are supposed to have. That Grantviller didn't consider the swords or pistols 'real weapons,' but the little musket with a bore your ramrod wouldn't fit down, was."

The stick came back over the woodpile. "So what? It isn't the weapon, but the man who wields it," Lucas said. "And that was a weapon for a girl, anyway."

"You are as stupid as you are doomed, Lucas. But I will continue this story in the hope that Herman, here, will benefit." Again, Wili resumed his recitation. "'The Grantville nobles had an interesting scheme. Each year they sold their commoners the right to try to shoot a deer. City men and peasants both could pay a fee and be allowed to tromp through the woods until a week was up or they shot a deer. It was a point of pride for them to "get their buck." My host would go out with friends who would loan him a full-sized musket for the hunt. He went every year but never succeeded. I thought of this city man thrashing through the brush and could think of many reasons why he'd never see a deer; it wouldn't matter how good a shot he was.'

"'The reason I got caught was that they had more patrols out than usual because there had been a raid recently. They claimed a couple thousand Croats had come through while their militia were off destroying a couple of Spanish tercios outside a neighboring town. That last was true. I met some of the men captured from the Spanish before I left the town. But it's not the whole truth. You remember the thrashing those Swabians got near Suhl? They were routed by a third part of the Grantville militia while the rest were dealing with the Spaniards.'"

Once again, Herman interrupted. "Too bad, since Lucas is asleep, he missed out on how easy it will be for him to kill these men tomorrow."

Wili forged on with his story. Having started a recitation, it always felt wrong not to finish it. "'Anyway, that left the town's women and burghers to handle the Croats. I didn't believe that there had been any two thousand Croats. After all, the town was still standing, but I wasn't going to call my host a liar. Good thing too, because the next day my translator friend showed me a cemetery with a couple hundred Croat graves.'

" 'So I'm glad I kept silent while that burgher sat there, stroking his tiny toy musket, looking at those hats and weapons, saying, "*Ja*, those Croats came and I finally got my buck." ' "

Resuming his usual growl, Wili asked, "Okay, Lucas, does that satisfy you? The Grantviller's women are good enough to handle Croats. Do you think their men might give you a morning to remember?

"Anyway, the next morning, the New Guy's pike was there, but that craven whoreson and his gear were gone. I was going to talk to Horst about it, but didn't get a chance before the battle. And he didn't survive the day, so that was that. Since none of us who survived got within seventy-five yards of the Grantville Swedes, I guess an extra pike really wouldn't have mattered. From what you say, Herman, about how he handled himself at Breitenfeld, maybe the New Guy wasn't so craven. Maybe he was just smarter than he looked."

Wili noticed that neither of the other men said anything. Maybe they thought so, too.

The Dalai Lama's Electric Buddha

Victor Klimov

"Respectful greetings from His Majesty Gegen Setsen Khan to Your Holiness, Kundün," said the emissary. It was not really warm in the library, but the atmosphere felt warm and friendly. "Let me present you this surprise from the Western lands."

Dalai Lama V Ngawang Lobsang Gyatso, who—in another universe—would later be called "The Great Fifth," respectfully put his hands together to greet the image of the Victorious One. The little statue looked unusual. It was made from material like ivory but was obviously much lighter and it was pink in color. The Victorious One was meditating.

"If I press this knob . . ."

The image lit up with a steady internal light. It looked a little bit like a colored lantern, but the light was not flickering. The emissary pressed the knob again and the light disappeared.

"Thank His Majesty Gegen Setsen Khan and thank you, Dr. Luvsan," said Dalai Lama and accepted the holy image. Ngawang Lobsang was fascinated. The statue was light, but not so light as it looked. The weight seemed concentrated in the base under the lotus seat. The texture of the surface felt smooth, somewhat like smooth wood but not quite.

Dalai Lama pressed the knob. The statue lit up. He looked at the emissary, lifting an eyebrow. "What causes this?"

"Kundün, as far as we know there seems to be a kind of prana energy concentrated in the base of the statue. . . ."

"Ah. That's why it feels heavy there."

"Probably, Kundün. And the trader it was bought from warned that the prana in the statue should somehow be replenished after a while. But it seemed he did not know how. He said that if it were used sparingly it should last a couple of years."

Dalai Lama switched the light off. He looked at the statue, then at the emissary. "What do your yogis say?"

"They feel the prana but they are not sure whether they succeeded in replenishing it."

"Very well." The Dalai Lama nodded slowly. "We'll try here, too. But tell me please the history of the statue. How did His Majesty acquire it? You said it came from the West?"

The emissary nodded. "Yes, Kundün. The Khan of Dörvn Öörd [Kalmyk] sent it to His Majesty. The Khan bought it from a trader from Phe-rang [Europe] for one hundred horses. The trader said that the holy statue miraculously appeared in the center of a great circular mandala, which also contained a whole town."

Dr. Luvsan moved his hand in a graceful gesture in the direction of hundreds of volumes wrapped in brocades and silks. "Naturally, the trader did not know the relevant terminology. What I'm telling now is what the Khan's advisers were able to get out of the trader. He didn't see himself the holy mandala. He only heard about it from the person who sold him the relic. His description of the town in the mandala corresponds somewhat with descriptions in the Kalachakra tantra.

"It appears very probable that the town came from another dimension. The trader was very sure that nobody has ever seen anything like this before. And the people of the town appear to be mighty warriors. The trader was sure about that. And they also ride iron horses. I don't know if one could believe that."

"Hmm . . ." The Dalai Lama stared into space for some time. "Why would a Shambhala town manifest in Phe-rang? Well . . . one never knows. The compassion of the Victorious One is infinite. We must investigate this story. We must find out whether there was indeed a mandala manifestation. And also we should find out how to replenish the light producing prana." Dalai Lama smiled.

"Yes, Kundün."

Afterword:

Kundün: an honorific referring specifically to the Dalai Lama.

Prana: in yoga, the breath seen as one of the life-giving energies or forces of the universe.

Dörvn Öörd—"The Allied Four" also referred to as Oyirad or Kalmyk people. They were the dominant group from Turkey to the Gobi Desert from the thirteenth through to the eighteenth century.

A mandala graphically depicts a landscape of the Buddha land or the enlightened vision of a Buddha. Mandalas are commonly used by Hindu and Buddhist monks as an aid to meditation.

Kalachakra is a term used in tantric Buddhism that means "time-wheel" or "time-cycles." The Kalachakra tradition, which is described in the Kalachakra Tantra (which is a book, a collection of Buddhist writings), revolves around the concept of time and cycles: from the cycles of the planets, to the cycles of our breath and the practice of controlling the most subtle energies within one's body on the path to enlightenment. The Kalachakra deity represents a Buddha and thus omniscience. Everything is under the influence of time, he is time and therefore knows all. Similarly, the wheel is beginningless and endless.

A kalachakra mandala is pictured at http://www.exoticindiaart.com/product/TF75/

In Tibetan Buddhist tradition, Shambhala (or Shambala) is a mystical kingdom hidden somewhere beyond the snow peaks of the Himalayas. It is mentioned in various ancient texts including the Kalachakra and the ancient texts of the Zhang Zhung culture which pre-dated Tibetan Buddhism in western Tibet. The Bon scriptures speak of a closely related land called Olmolungring.

The Kalachakra indicates that when the world declines into war and greed, and all is lost, a King of Shambhala will emerge from the secret city with a huge army to conquer evil and herald the Golden Age. Some suggest this king may be Kalki, a similar figure.

The myths of Shambala were part of the inspiration for the tale of Shangri-La told in the popular book *Lost Horizon,* and thus some people even refer to Shambala improperly as if it were a Shangri-La. Shambala's location and nature remains a subject of much dispute, and several traditions have arisen as to where it is, or will be, including those that emphasize it as a nonphysical realm that one can approach only through the mind.

Canst Thou Send Lightnings

Rick Boatright

*In like manner the lightning when it breaketh forth is
easy to be seen; and after the same manner
the wind bloweth in every country.*
—Deuterocanonical Apocrypha,
The Epistle of Jeremiah:61

To: *The Provincial of the Society of Jesus in Rome*
From: *Adolph Wise S.J., University of Eichstaett*

*Enclosed with this letter you will find an example of
the "Crystal Radio" that is being distributed throughout
Thuringia. I enclose also instructions for the construction
of more of these Radios as distributed by the American
government.*

*I testify, of my own knowledge, further attested by the
witnesses signatures hereto affixed and sealed, that anywhere within fifty miles of Grantville on most evenings,
when you place your ear next to the opening in the box,
you can hear voices and music and other sounds which
originate miles away in Grantville. These voices are sent
through the air itself by the lightnings into the wires of
the Radio. The Radio is delicate and fails to function
with the least misadjustment. However, when adjusted*

properly, at the correct time of day anyone can hear the Voice of America sent forth from the great stone tower of the Radio Station in Grantville.

No one that I have spoken with here in the university can begin to understand how this works. The Americans insist that this is nothing but another of their mechanical arts, related to the "electricity" of which I wrote in an earlier letter. They maintain that there is nothing more involved than the proper arrangement and composition of mundane physical materials. If so, then, as with so many other devices to be found in and around Grantville, it is the knowledge they possess that is important.

I have spoken with the local clergy, and they inform me that the Radios are being built mostly by jewelers and others who are used to working with fine wires and small detail work. There are others who are working on the equipment to send the lightnings from the great tower to the Radios. Again, the local clergy tell me that this equipment, although considerably more robust than the Radios, is still remarkably delicate in some ways and requires the deft touch of jewelers and similar folk.

The Americans insist that they welcome students. They also are training workers to assist in building their next "Radio Station," which they plan to locate in Magdeburg. When completed, it will be placed at Gustav Adolphus' disposal. It is said that he intends to use this voice to promote Lutheranism.

I beg of you to find within our ranks a young man, skilled in the jeweler's arts and firm in the Church, and send him to us. Some one of us must take this training, in order that we may first gain the knowledge of how this art works, and second, perhaps in some way delay or prevent the establishment of Gustavus Adolphus' Voice of Luther. Simultaneously, we must work to produce a Radio Station that can bring to the people the saving grace of the Holy Mother Church.

Signed
Adolph Wise S.J.
(and 12 other witnesses)

Father Nicholas Smithson lowered the letter, and looked at Father Andrew White, his superior in the Society of Jesus. "Do you believe this, Father Andrew?"

"It does not matter what I believe, Nicholas. The father general of the Society may or may not believe it, but he has indicated it shall be treated as fact until it is proved otherwise."

"So be it. What the father general orders shall be done." Nicholas nodded, then pursed his lips. "This is all very interesting, Father, but why is this letter here in London, and why are you discussing it with a humble parish priest?"

Father Andrew smiled. "Read the letter again. Paying particular attention to the skills of the workmen and the request made by Father Adolph."

When Nicholas set the letter down again, he was stunned. He could feel that his eyes were wide. He opened his mouth a time or two, but nothing came out. Finally, he coughed. "They have chosen me?"

"Aye, Nicholas." Father Andrew was sympathetic. "You are the son of a jeweler, trained in his craft, who is also a Jesuit. You are the very man that Father Adolph has called for."

"But . . . but what of my parish? Who will serve Mass, and catechism, and the rites to those hidden members of the true church if I leave?"

"My son." Father Andrew stood and walked to the window to stare out at the busy evening London street scene. "The situation in London—indeed, in all England—grows ever grimmer. Despite the fact that King Charles at one time did seem disposed to provide some little relief to those who follow Rome, since the advent of Grantville he is of no mind to tolerate dissent of any kind, even from priests. I am afraid he sees gunpowder under every chair. It may well be that we are returning to the dark times we walked under during Elizabeth's reign."

Turning back to the room, the older priest leaned against the window sill. "Nicholas, I do not doubt your courage. I am aware that if a martyr's crown called, you would respond willingly. The society has many brave, fervent men who can and will serve as priests in the darkness of London, perhaps to become martyrs if God so wills. But you, you are best suited to another task. You are called to a different work."

Nicholas sat quietly, staring at the hands folded in his lap. There was only one decision he could make, as much as he might desire otherwise. When he accepted that, peace descended. When he finally raised his head to look at Father Andrew, he felt calm.

"*Adsum, Domine.* Here am I, Lord."

> *For when the lightning lightens, the thunder utters its voice,*
> *and the spirit enforces a pause during the peal.*
> —Apocrypha, The Book of Enoch 60:15

John Grover, head of Voice of America and de facto head of radio communications in the USE, rubbed his eyes and massaged his aching temples. This week's staff meeting hadn't gone any better than the previous meetings had gone. Oh, they were making progress on the mundane stuff, things that just needed the application of some brute force and some material, like putting up lightning arresters and lightning rods in various locations in town. Likewise, those issues that just required the application of money were going pretty well; witness the report of the purchase of two more video cameras and the completion of the second studio setup.

Even the weekly Murphy report, detailing the things that had gone inexplicably wrong—such as the episode where someone took a glass of water into the studio and inadvertently poured it into the primary beta recorder, or the Marine radio man who for some unknown-but-very-stupid reason elected to save his rifle and powder instead of the radio when he fell into a creek—wasn't too bad. Every Murphy incident caused rules and procedures to either be amended or created. But the ability of people and situations to act outside of those rules and procedures was ever astonishing.

John rubbed his eyes again.

Bottom line—the local cable TV team, the communications team and the Voice of America team all had enough up-time resources to keep going for a few years, more or less, unless a major disaster occurred. The problem was preparing for what would happen when those up-time resources began to burn up, blow up, or otherwise quit functioning and the spares were used up.

John fingered the screwdriver he kept in his shirt pocket, thinking hard. Everything depended on tubes. Everything. The sniping and the infighting at the staff meetings was starting to move from sarcastic to vitriolic. If they didn't make some real progress soon, he didn't know what he was going to do, especially since his only real tube-head, Gayle Mason, was stuck in the Tower of London.

Opening a drawer, John rooted around until he found his aspirin. Dry swallowing three of them, he looked at the clock on his desk. Six p.m. Time to leave. Maybe something would happen tomorrow . . . correction, maybe something *good* would happen tomorrow.

Canst thou lift up thy voice to the clouds,
that abundance of waters may cover thee?
Canst thou send lightnings, that they may go
and say unto thee, Here we are?
—King James Bible, Job 38:34-35

Claude Yardley had been a power plant operator for a lot of years. He had torn apart his share of alternators and put the pieces back together. But he had never seen anything like this. He pushed back from the paper- and debris-covered table. "I'd say Murphy got to you again, John."

John snorted. "Yeah. He really got behind us on this one. This design should have been a non-starter. Look at this stuff." John gestured. "Wires stretched beyond their breaking points, coils ripped from their armatures, and we got what? 1000 Hz out of it?"

"Something like that." Claude looked at his notes. "3600 RPM router feeding a sixteen lobe alternator gives 960 Hz."

"We need seventy-five times more."

Claude pointed at what was left of the radio team's latest creation. "You won't get it this way. I understand why you came to me. Bill Porter and I probably know more about alternators than anyone else in the world at this point." He chuckled. "Not that that's saying much. But you need something like no alternator we've ever heard of. I think it was fictional."

John pushed the photo of the Brant Rock installation across the table.

Claude shook his head. "I don't care, John. Look, walk through it with me one more time. That thing is what? Five feet across?"

Nod.

"Okay. That makes it fifteen feet eight inches around. Times twelve is a hundred eighty-eight inches. Assume one-inch coils around the rim. There's no way to modulate the coil less than its full width, so if you assume that they alternate north and south, then you have eighty-four sine waves per rotation."

Nod.

"So, to get eighty thousand waves per second, you have to rotate the thing a thousand times per second, or sixty thousand RPM."

Nod.

"So, any one coil is going around a fifteen foot circumference a thousand times a second, or traveling fifteen thousand feet per second, or call it three miles a second, or something in the neighborhood of eleven thousand miles an hour. Just under mach twenty, in other words. And they say it was done in 1906?"

Nod.

"It's impossible." Claude shook his head. "It must have been a fake."

John pushed the photo across the table again.

"I don't care. I don't believe they had materials that would handle those stresses, and we definitely don't."

The room was quiet.

"John, I'm sorry," Claude said gently, "but I'm fresh out of ideas. I'm going home."

> *His lightnings enlightened the world:*
> *the earth saw, and trembled.*
> —King James Bible, Psalms 97:4

Father Athanasius Kircher watched as John Grover wandered from one empty table to the next. For once, it wasn't that crowded in the Thuringen Gardens. John banged each table with his pewter mug. Curious, Father Athanasius began following him. Once he got close enough, he heard John mutter, "Too hard."

Now Father Athanasius was really intrigued. Most of the tables in the Thuringen Gardens were quite new, solidly built against the general gaiety of a popular tavern. Sturdy was not a description that did them justice.

John hadn't noticed the priest. He drained his mug and looked around the Gardens. "There!" He headed for a table in one of the back corners. Father Athanasius trailed behind.

The table was one of the up-time folding tables, matched up with metal folding chairs that were also up-time in origin. Having been around Grantville for some little time now, Father Athanasius was certain that they represented an unauthorized loan from a school, or church, or one of the "civic organizations" of Grantville.

John sat carefully in a chair and banged his mug against the table top. The priest saw that it was that strange woodlike substance called "masonite." Unlike the other tables in the room, it was not sturdy, and when struck by the mug, it flexed and boomed.

"Perfect." John carefully set his cup down on the floor, and centered his chair on the table. He pressed the center of the table firmly with the heel of his hand. It flexed.

"Yes." John leaned forward, and banged his head against the center of the table.

Shocked, Father Athanasius stepped forward and grabbed John by the shoulder. John stopped in mid-bang. "No, John!"

John looked up at him. "Oh, hi, Father A."

"Let me buy you another round, John." Father Athanasius sat down across from John. "We'll talk it through. Whatever the problem is, it should not drive you to self abuse."

"I've been beating my head against a wall at work," John said, somewhat truculently. "I might as well do it here as well. Maybe it will break an idea loose." Father Athanasius reserved comment, and just looked steadily at one of the men he thought of as a friend.

John slumped a little. His voice grew quieter. "You're a good man, Father." He sighed and his hand crept toward his shirt pocket. He started stroking the screwdriver he kept there. "But you can't bring Gayle back from the damned Tower of London, you can't bring all those jewelers back from Prague, and you can't push skills I don't have into these hands."

There was a moment of quiet. John shook his head. "It isn't Mike Stearns' fault. Gayle Mason is the best QRP CW operator in the world. I agreed that she had to go to London. But that means that the best source of knowledge about radio tubes is hundreds of miles away."

Father Athanasius picked up John's mug, and waved at a waitress.

"It isn't Morris Roth's fault that every jeweler in the world wants to be near the world's only source of knowledge about faceted gems. But that means that the people with skills in working with very small wires and parts that I need don't come to Grantville anymore.

"It isn't my fault that I have an associate's degree in business, not a masters in electronic engineering. I'm the best available for running VOA, but I don't know the background of the history and development of radio. No one in Grantville does."

The waitress arrived with two fresh mugs. John took his without even noticing it.

"It's nobody's fault. But you put it all together, and Murphy has arranged the world so that we cannot get Gustav's radio station on the air. And I have to. Mike is counting on me."

"We have talked about this Murphy before, John," the priest said gently. "Most would blame Satan when faced with such adversity."

John shook his head. "It isn't evil I'm dealing with, Father. It's just perversity. It's like the bread always falling butter side down. If things can go wrong, they will. Wasn't that true when you built your water organs?"

Father Kircher nodded firmly. "It was. It is." He thought back to those days, and grimaced. "Everything that could go wrong did. Indeed. We just did not express it so compactly."

"Imps, daemons, gremlins . . . name them as you will, Father. But Murphy acts in the world as sure as God does. But he isn't evil." John took a swallow from his mug. "The best decisions have been made. I know that. Gayle being in London, Morris being in Prague, are absolutely for the best. Godly. But Murphy arranges that the Godly best causes something else to go wrong. We have the Voice of America running, but we can't make the tubes for Gustav's station."

Father Kircher nodded. "I know. The station manager has asked each religious leader in town to give the morning invocation before the dawn news broadcast. Yesterday was my turn! It is amazing to have your words carried by the lightnings across the heavens to say, 'Here I am!'"

John smiled at the nod to Job. He remembered using the line himself when defending his interest in getting his Ham license to his Baptist pastor thirty years earlier. *My sword,* John thought.

John heaved a big sigh. He took his screwdriver out of his pocket and fidgeted with it. "The worst is the alternator."

"Alternator?" Father Kircher prompted gently.

"That's the most perverse of all, Father. It's a tease. We know that Reginald Fessenden and Ernst Alexanderson built an RF alternator in 1906. We *know* they broadcast voice to crystal radios without tubes. We *know* they were heard over a hundred miles away. We know all that. We even have a picture. A poor, dark, grainy picture, but a picture nonetheless. We can look at that picture of Fessenden's alternator at Brant Rock, Massachusetts. But that's all. We have no idea what was inside that round case. Just that it was 'an alternator.' I can't build a photo. It's a tease. We have to invent an alternator. And so I started, thinking, 'Gee, we have all the alternators out at the power plant, every car has an alternator, how hard can it be?'" John looked back towards the folding table. He looked back at Father Kircher. "So we pulled most of the people off Gunter's team, since working on tubes without Gayle was very slow going, and started in on the alternator. I know now how hard it can be. It can be very hard."

Father Kircher's hand made the beginnings of a gesture that he knew would be of no comfort to his Protestant friend. "I know, John. I will think on it. Perhaps we can find someone to help. Perhaps we can find a way to put Murphy behind us."

John shuddered. "No! Never behind you, Father. You always have to keep Murphy in front of you. Dead in your sights, never allowing him a moment to screw anything up. Out of sight, out of mind. We need a way to keep Murphy before us."

"A talisman, then. Something to help you remember to focus on the possibilities both good and bad, to keep at the work."

"Yes, exactly. Well, that and a jeweler with an interest in radio who can help with the wire and the forms and the work on the damned alternator."

"I will think on it, John, and I will pray."

"No one can ask more, Father." John drained his cup and stood. "Thanks for listening."

"You're welcome." Father Athanasius' "my son" was unspoken, but heard nonetheless.

> *The vision of dreams is the resemblance of one thing*
> *to another, even as the likeness of a face to a face.*
> —Deuterocanonical Apocrypha, 3 Sirach

"Nick? Is that you?"

Nicholas Smithson froze. God in Heaven, how could this happen? How could it be that there would be someone in Grantville who knew him?

"Nick? Nicholas Smithson!" The voice was insistent. Nick slowly turned around, and almost groaned. Of all people. Father Augustus Heinzerling. What was Heinzerling doing here, and why hadn't that information been given to him? There was no possible way that he could convince Augustus that he was someone other than Nick Smithson. They had spent too much time together at the English college in Rome.

"Hello, Gus."

"It is you!" Heinzerling looked delighted, but then suspicion began to creep across his face. "It is you. What are you doing here?"

"I . . ." Nick hesitated, torn between telling the truth and concealing his mission. "I cannot tell you that, Gus."

Now Heinzerling's face took on the appearance of a thunder cloud. "What do you mean, you cannot tell me?"

"I have orders."

Heinzerling's jaw tightened. He took a firm hold of Nick's arm. "You will come with me and explain yourself to Father Mazzare, then." He started off, and Nick perforce went with him. Father Gus in a mood was no one to trifle with.

Father Lawrence Mazzare looked at the young man accompanying his curate with some confusion. Father Kircher watched from the back of the room. "Okay, Augustus. What exactly is your problem again?"

"Where do I start?" Father Heinzerling ran his hands through his hair. "I see this man at the radio station this morning asking for work. I knew him when he was at the English College of the Society in Rome studying. We spent many hours together in Rome attempting to find an Italian who knew how to brew beer. I thought he was my friend." Heinzerling glared at the young man.

"Go on."

"I greet him as brother of the Society and as a friend, calling him by his name, and he refuses to tell me what he is doing. He is dressed in common garb, had not come to see you. I say he's a spy for the Jesuits!" Heinzerling looked confused for a moment, then surged on. "Or a spy at least for someone in the Society. I am the official spy for the Society in Grantville, not some upstart impudent Englishman!" His frown was truly impressive.

Larry repressed a grin. No wonder Gus had looked confused. He turned to the young man. "And you are?"

Nicholas looked at this up-time priest, Father Lawrence Mazzare. What little he had been able to find out on his way to Grantville indicated the man was very well educated, and could give lessons to a saint in propriety, probity and rectitude. However, no one had mentioned his gaze—that calm, straight gaze that seemed as though it could see through four inches of oak, much less his own flimsy pretenses. It reminded him very strongly of the father general of the Society. Nicholas abandoned all hope of dissembling; forthrightness was the only course with a man like this.

"I am Father Nicholas Smithson of the Society of Jesus, late of London."

"'Nicholas?' Are you named after Father Christmas or Saint Nicholas Owen then?" Larry calculated in his head. "You look a little old for it."

"*Saint* Nicholas Owen?" Nicholas exclaimed.

Larry walked over to the bookshelf and took down a volume of the Catholic Encyclopedia. "Here." Turning the pages, he found Saint Nicholas' entry. "In 1970, Nicholas Owen was, umm, will be, umm," Larry made that vague hand gesture that had come to indicate the other world. "Would have been canonized by Pope Paul VI among the Forty Martyrs of England and Wales. Their joint feast day is kept on October twenty-fifth."

He handed the volume to Nicholas who looked it over with astonishment, reading of the events and the names that rang with meaning to English recusants. Margaret Clitherow, Edmund Campion, Henry Walpole, and then . . . "Edward Ambrose Barlow? But I know Edward! We were at St. Gregory's in Douai together. He's alive. Or at least he was three months ago, chaplain to the Tyldesleys in Leigh."

Father Mazzare laughed. "Yes. Things like that happen a lot here. Remind me later to tell you the story of the name of this church." He put the book back on the shelf, then resumed his seat.

"But we were talking about you," Mazzare continued. "Are you named after Saint Nicholas Owen, then? And what are you doing in Grantville?"

"I am named after 'Saint' Nicholas Owen. I suppose I will have to change my feast day." Nick smiled. "My mother was reluctant to name me after a dwarf, but father insisted that Nicholas Owen did the work of three normal men and was a great champion of God. He met Owen while he was building some of his secret rooms at homes of customers of my father."

Larry lifted an eyebrow. "And your father was?"

"James Smithson. He is a jeweler, a specialist in fine metal work and elaborate braided wire pieces. He trained me and my brothers to follow in his craft." Nick shrugged. "That is why the Society sent me to Grantville. We have heard of the call for jewelers and metalworkers to work on the Radio. And we know that this Radio is planned for King Gustav's use, for his 'Voice of Luther.' Thus my disguise. It is highly unlikely that a Lutheran king would want a Jesuit learning the secrets of his Radio."

"Nicholas, you have a lot to learn about Grantville, and not just our list of saints. Father Kircher will introduce you to John Grover, the head of Voice of America. Unless I miss my guess, he will be absolutely delighted to meet you. If you can make the coils he needs, no one here will care about your religion.

"You can also resume your priestly functions. Fathers Heinzerling and Kircher and I can use the help. You can stay here, and in return you will take your turn for the morning and evening masses.

"Father Athanasius will introduce you to the director of the radio project in the morning. For now, let Augustus find you a place to put your things, show you around the church, and you can try the local beer. It's not English ale, but I suspect it's better than anything available in Rome."

Father Mazzare stood and held out his hand. "Welcome to St. Mary's."

Yet a man is risen to pursue thee, and to seek thy soul:
but the soul of my lord shall be bound in the bundle of life
with the LORD thy God; and the souls of thine enemies,
them shall he sling out, as out of the middle of a sling.
—King James Bible, 1 Kings 25:29

John presided over this week's staff meeting in a much better frame of mind than last week. The interminable list of reports didn't faze him. Even the bickering between Ken Butcher, Andrew Rogers and Jennifer Hansen didn't bother him. The final report was from Gunter Klein, the only down-time team head.

"The vacuum pump works, but is not yet good enough. We get a glow, we get a pretty light bulb, we do not get a tube. It is slow, but each week is better. You will have tubes before you need them. I swear it."

Ken opened his mouth to say something, but John forestalled him. "Drop it, Ken. They're doing the best they can, especially with Gayle gone." Ken sat back, and sullenly nodded.

"One last item. I need to introduce a new staff member this morning. This is Father Nicholas Smithson. He is not our new chaplain. Father Nick is a trained jeweler specializing in fine wire work. He is going to be starting on the alternator project with us immediately, so if he asks you for information or assistance, please try to make yourself and your folks available.

"That's about it for today, folks. No one ever got any engineering done sitting in a staff meeting." John stood up. "One last thought. We do have to think of everything. We're stretched way too thin. We need something to help us focus. We need some way to keep in our minds that we have to bust the problems before they happen. Father Kircher said the other night that we need a talisman. I think he's right. When you have a minute, try to think of something, a talisman, a touchstone, something to keep our minds on the goal and on the nitty-gritty at the same time."

John knew his people would try. He knew he would try. Still he thought it slightly unfair that Father A had arranged for his special table to be returned to the Moose Lodge. He didn't belong.

Nicholas Smithson sat at the kitchen table in the St. Mary's parish house and looked at the collection of items spread before him. There was a coil of very fine wire, a magnet, a voltmeter, and a textbook.

He waved the magnet in front of the coil of wire. As the magnet approached the coil, the meter moved left. As the magnet retreated the meter moved back to the center and then to the right. He waved the magnet back and forth and the meter waved back and forth.

"Eighty thousand times per second. No one can move a magnet eighty thousand times a second."

He set the magnet down and picked up the coil of wire. He waved the wire over the face of the magnet. The meter waved too. He set the coil down. He picked up the magnet again and spun it in front of the coil. The meter waved back and forth as the magnet spun, right-left-right-left for each rotation.

"Eighty thousand waves per second." He looked at the piece of paper where he had done the geometry. "If I spin this forty thousand times per second, I get eighty thousand waves, and the outside of the magnet is only going"—Nick looked down—"seven thousand miles per hour. I think not."

Nick picked up the "thing" John had given him. Eight magnets soldered together in the center. He spun it in front of the coil. The meter waved, but less. John had assured him that this was because the individual magnets were smaller, and that made sense. But still, eight flicks per rotation. The outside would be going only eighteen hundred miles per hour.

"I think not."

Moving the coil, of course, was worse. Coils are fragile things. And large. Much bigger than the magnet.

"Such a simple thing. August would understand it. My mother could understand it. Magnet back and forth, make electricity. Magnet and coil move, make electricity. Magnet and coil sit there, nothing gets made."

He picked up the drawing he had made of the Brandt Rock transmitter from the photograph, and reviewed his calculations.

"Thousands of miles per hour. Murphy would destroy it."

Nick thought about John's introduction to Murphy's Law. Everything that can go wrong, will. The son of a goldsmith used to working with heat and molten metal and thin wires and fluxes and solders knew all about Murphy and his imps even if he had not named them so. He sat, spinning the magnet.

Father Kircher came in. "Hello, Nicholas. How went your first day with the radio team?"

"I learned much." Nick waved his hand over the objects on the table. "I learned why John was banging his head." He spun the magnet again. "I may have to go find this 'Moose Lodge' to borrow their special table back."

"Now, Nick. None of that! And I have news, and an idea!" Athanasius removed a book from his habit and set it in front of Nick. "Who are you named after?"

"Saint Nicholas Owen. Saint at least, here in Grantville."

Athanasius opened the book to a marked page. "And who is this?"

"Saint Elizabeth Seton, the first American saint."

Athanasius nodded. "Who will never be born, nor sainted by a pope who will never be born nor elected to the seat of Peter. And yet, here, in Grantville she is a saint."

Nicholas looked up. "So?"

Athanasius gestured to the volumes of the Catholic Encyclopedia. "What of all those other Grantville saints in their dozens or hundreds? Are they less saints because they will not live? Are they less saints because they were proclaimed so by popes who will neither live nor serve? I do not know. But I know that I have agreed that here, in St. Mary's, and in Grantville, we honor their days."

"Yes, Saint Nicholas Owen and the Forty Martyrs—a third of whom are perfectly well alive—is a mass I intend to celebrate myself."

"So, it isn't their realness that makes them saints here is it? Or who proclaimed them?"

"No . . ." Nick agreed cautiously.

"Then I offer you your talisman, and your protector for the radio team." Athanasius laid another book on the table. *The Warlock Unlocked.*

"I offer you Holy Saint Vidicon, patron saint of the Cathodean order of the church. Martyred in 2020 in service to the Church, sainted in 2030 by Pope Clement. Those of his order are dedicated to reducing the action of Murphy's imps and the control of the perversity of technology. His feast day is February twenty-ninth."

"February twenty-ninth? That's, that's . . ."

"Perverse?"

"A fictional saint?"

"A saint, who will never be born, named so by a pope who will never be born, nor elected. Read the book. Then, we will talk again. In the meantime, I offer you this as well." He handed Nicholas a wooden-handled tool.

"What is it?"

"Your talisman. The same one John carries. The same one most of the 'techs' carry. A 'little yellow screwdriver.'"

Larry Mazzare looked almost stern. "No. You may not form an order dedicated to a saint invented by a science fiction writer in 1982."

"But . . ."

"Which part of *no* didn't you understand?"

"But . . ."

"You may distribute the talismans. You may use the story from the book as the inspiration for the talisman. You should use the terminology. God knows that Murphy certainly is perverse and acts in the world. If that weren't true then several of the parishioners' cars would quit breaking for no reason."

Nicholas saw Larry's look become stern. "However, if you need to call on a saint to assist you, I urge you to look to the saint most closely related to your talisman, not some fictional construct of an unchurched Episcopalian."

"Who?"

Larry picked up one of the screwdrivers from the box. "I note the appropriateness of the cross at the tip. I'm glad you didn't get flat bladed ones." He paused. "You ought to know who I mean. He was canonized not ten years ago. A man known for his sense of humor. He ought to be able to help us laugh in the face of Murphy's perversity."

"But the talisman?"

"Oh, come now. He would have appreciated the appropriateness of it. By all accounts, he would have had the entire congregation laughing."

Nicholas just stared at Larry.

Father Mazzare opened a reference to a painting of a man. He grinned as he showed it to Nicholas. The man in the painting wore half a beard and was kicking a ball while leading a rag-tag group of people who carried household goods through a street. "Come now. The pun is even in your native tongue." He spun the book around. "Saint Phillip."

> *Thy life hast thou ordered in wisdom,*
> *and hast called understanding thy mother.*
> —Deuterocanonical Apocrypha, Esdras 2:55 (Ezra 4:55)

The hallowed halls of the Grantville National Research Library were far from Nick's idea of what a library was. First, there were far too many books. What had started out as the Grantville High School library had changed over the last months. Now, with the ceiling tiles removed and the shelves extended up to the metal ribs holding the roof, with more shelves tucked into every nook, and tables and chairs in every cranny, Nick felt that the services of his name saint would be well used. No master carpenter had designed this place.

And the books! There were more titles in this one room than existed in the rest of Europe. Books, pamphlets, magazines, broadsheets, newspapers. Surely the answer would be here.

It amazed him that the Americans had not tried this. He had asked John for the results of the library search and their notes. One page of notes, and one magazine article. It simply wasn't possible that there was not more information that that. He looked at the room again. There was a sign. Library research orientation class: 09:00. He saw someone standing in front of a small group of what appeared to be down-timers, and joined them.

"Welcome to the Grantville National Library. My name is Gladys Wood. I'm a senior researcher here. This brief orientation will help you to begin to find material in the library. We will cover several basic areas: Our fee structure, collections, indexing, annotation mechanisms, physical access . . ."

"Dictionary form. They organize information alphabetically. It is insane! Related material may be completely separated. Related people are not listed together. Related places are not listed together. It is completely arbitrary and utterly brilliant." Nicholas looked at his long list of words taken from the article he had. Dictionary form. "I can do this. It was what I was trained to do. They don't need a jeweler. They need a scholar."

Nicholas tapped his screwdriver on the table as he looked out across the desk, contemplating. "Brother Johann, Melville Dewey was a very great man."

"Yes, he was."

"The index, the 'card catalog,' was a work of genius. The subject coding, clearly the work of inspiration. But these . . ." Nicholas waved his hand over the pattern of three-by-five cards carefully arranged on the desk. "These are brilliant. Without them, glossing this library would have been the work of years. But this . . . this is wonderful. I make a note of the source, I list a topic, a comment and so on, and I can rearrange, I can move the gloss from place to place. Cross references. Dictionary Form. Brilliance."

Brother Johann nodded. "I know." He looked at the cards, with a bit of irritation showing. "I only wish the stationer we ordered them from had not been so literal when we said we wanted him to duplicate the sample we provided. The "Recipe" printed across the top, and the drawing of breads doesn't actually assist in the work. But, we have only fifteen thousand left. They'll soon be gone, and we can get more. Plain ones this time."

Nick nodded. "That will help. But it is really no matter now. I just use the plain side."

"So," Johann asked, "have you found it yet?"

"No, but we are getting closer. I can feel it. With each additional source, with each additional reference, the quarry is that much closer to us. It won't be long."

With that, the two men bent their heads back over the books they were reading, and continued in pursuit of the alternator so desperately needed by their friends.

Nick's eyes widened. He sat back in his chair with a sudden jerk, and his chair screeched on the floor.

"Those idiots." Softly whispered. Brother Johann looked up in surprise.

"Those idiots!" No whisper now, but full voice and almost yelled.

"What is it, Father Nick?"

Nick turned to his fellow researcher.

"Brother Johann, have you heard the word 'sophomore' here in Grantville?"

Johann nodded. "Of course. They use it to identify a rank of their children in school."

"The word is Greek in origin, you know." Johann nodded again. "It means 'wise fool.' And I've just decided that it should be applied to all of Grantville. To have all this wisdom and knowledge available to you," Nick waved a hand to take in the stacks of books, "and not know how to use it makes one a fool, indeed."

"You found the answer?" Johann began to show excitement.

"Yes, I found the solution to problem of the alternator. It doesn't move."

"What?"

Together they bent over a volume from the Encyclopedia Britannica 1911 edition.

☆   ☆   ☆

"So, I understand congratulations are in order." Nick looked up to see Father Larry and Father Athanasius approaching him.

"Not really, Father. I just found something they had lost, is all."

"Nonetheless, Father Athanasius tells me that John's ecstasy almost approaches hysteria. Good job. It will make a lot of people very happy. So, how long did it take you to find the answer?"

"The alternator? With Brother Johann's help, I had that in a little over two weeks. It merely took careful work, word after word from the encyclopedia, then more lists of words, and more encyclopedia articles. I cannot build them, you understand, neither the alternator nor the frequency doubler. That will take mechanics and such. But the solution was simple enough. John's team has the information and they have started building a model."

Nicholas laughed. "Saint Phillip be praised." He reached up to his breast pocket and touched his screwdriver. "The solution is both funny and perverse. It will require careful attention, and it will be difficult, but it can certainly be done. The Americans would never have thought of it."

"Why?"

"Because the secret of the alternator is in not *doing*. The alternator does not spin! It just sits there. The coils, the magnet, all of it, just sits there. It is very unAmerican. What spins is a plate of iron with holes that occasionally let the magnetic field through to the coils. The plate, unlike the coils or the magnets, can be made quite strong, and large, and can spin fast enough to make the waves many, many thousands of times per second. Alexanderson was very clever. And the irony is, the Americans will not see the irony in it."

They all laughed at the joke, and the irony of the joke.

Father Mazzare surveyed the stack of papers and the mass of note cards scattered over the surface of the table. "So, what are you doing here—designing it for them?"

"No, I turned over everything we found to John a few days ago."

"So what's this, then?"

Nick waved a hand over the table. "I'm writing a guide to the study of up-time documents. A guide to the exegesis of up-time texts, and the application of their techniques to our writing and publishing. The Dewey Decimal System of course, the APA standard form for citations, the concept of 'Encyclopedia' and the differences between those and 'Dictionaries' and 'Gazetteers.' The power of organizing information. Why did we not think of it? Alphabetical organization is an insane way to arrange topics—except of course, that it works. Rules for sorting. Rules for indexing. All the tools that the up-timers have that they seemingly have not learned how to use."

Nick shook his head. "The alternator is a good example of why it is needed. The up-timers, most of them, simply do not think like scholars. Most of them, like John, tend to be doers, not thinkers. Do you know? Everything they needed for the radio alternator was in the encyclopedia. They simply didn't know how to look. They spent a half a year winding coils and breaking wires trying to spin the coils or the magnets because their first inclination when faced with a problem is to *do something*. They even have an aphorism about it. 'Those who do not know history are doomed to repeat it.' They all know this, but few of them grasp it."

"Yep." Father Larry nodded. "You missed the other saying, though. That one goes 'Don't just stand there, do something.' I wouldn't want to say that no one in Grantville understands what you're talking about. Most of the folks just have never had to learn it. They're thinkers, but not scholars. If things don't work out the way they would expect them to from their experience, they can generally figure and tinker a way out of it. Heck. *I* do that. We all do."

"And thank God for that! But it means that we who have been adopted by them will have to be their link to what they know." Nick waved his hands at the stacks again. "Even their teachers are not scholars by trade. The Americans managed to make teaching into a job separate from scholarship. I, for one, would never have believed it, but it is true."

Nick tapped the papers in front of him. "So, I have been writing a guide."

"Do you have a title, yet?"

"I am still looking for a title. I am considering," Nick coughed, *"How Not to Think Like a Redneck."*

Father Larry looked amused, but his voice was very dry. "As one who would wear half-a-beard, I'm afraid you're not authorized to use that term. You're not a member of the group."

Nick grinned, and reached into his satchel. He pulled out a yellow Cat hat, which he firmly placed on his head. "John made me an honorary redneck, and told me to go for it."

Grantville's Greatest Philosopher?

Terry Howard

Ken looked up when the door opened. When he saw the men who were entering, he moved down to the cash register. Once there, he put his hand on the sawed-off shotgun that hung in a rack on the underside of the bar. "Julio," he called.

"Yeah?" Julio Mora replied.

"Nine one one, *now!*"

"On it." Julio left the sink of dirty dishes and headed for the phone in the back room.

Three men walked through the door. Each was well dressed, one more so than the others. They were armed but that was common enough. Two of them had that air of "trouble on a short leash." Muscle, Ken thought. Bodyguards, competent, deadly, dangerous. They were also down-timers. Under the big "Club 250" sign on the door a little sign read "No Dogs and No Germans Allowed." All down-timers were "Krauts" as far as the denizens of Ken's bar were concerned.

If it had been a bit later in the day Ken would have told them to get out, knowing there was enough firepower at hand to make it stick. It was, after all, that kind of bar. At this hour, though, the "I want a drink for lunch crowd" was mostly gone. There were only three patrons left. Ken knew they were nothing but three more targets. It was time to stall and pray that the police came quickly, so Ken waited nervously for the down-timers to speak first.

After standing inside the door for half a minute the trio consulted briefly and one of the guards spoke in fairly understandable English. "We have read the sign."

Uh oh, Ken thought.

"We are not staying," the guard said.

Relief swept through the owner of the bar. Ken had never killed anyone in the bar and didn't want to start now. For that matter, he had never been killed and sure didn't want to start that now, either.

"We were told that the great philosopher, Herr Head, always had lunch here."

James Richard Shaver, Jimmy Dick, often referred to behind his back as Dick Head, a name he richly deserved for being a jerk of the first water, actually managed to blush. Ken, from long practice, managed to swallow his laughter completely. Some of his patrons were a mite touchy, especially when they were drunk.

"Herr Krieger wishes to converse with him," the guard continued. "It need not be here, where we are not allowed. Over dinner tonight, at the newly opened salon, perhaps?"

Ken let out the breath he was holding and took his moist hand off the shotgun. The tension flowed out of his muscles and evaporated without leaving any residue on the floor. Politely, he answered the trio with complete honesty. "There is no one here right now who answers to the name Herr Head. Can I ask who sent you?"

"We sought the gathering place of the local philosophical society at the . . ." The guard did not quite pause, "'front counter,' where we took lodgings. We were directed to the . . ." This time he did pause while he wrapped his tongue around a more difficult, recently learned, word phrase, "'Police Station.' They directed us to the . . ." Again a new word. "'Post office.' There we were told that the only fulltime, practicing philosopher in town was Herr, excuse me, Mister Head, and he could be found here having lunch, since there was no longer a Cracker-Barrel in town."

"Did the post office say Mister Head or dickhead?" Ken inquired.

"Yes, Dick Head is the name we were given."

The other two patrons snickered and James blushed again.

"Where are you staying?" Ken asked. "If Herr Head comes in today, I'll give him the message. And then, if the greatest of Grantville's philosophers wishes to talk to you, he can send a disciple to make arrangements."

All the while Ken spoke, Jimmy Dick was thinking hard. He was never going to live this down. He knew it. People who hadn't spoken to him in years, if ever, would hail him on the streets of Grantville at the slightest of excuse, just to have the opportunity of addressing him as "Herr Head." The more polite of them would seek the opinion of Grantville's greatest philosopher. Small towns can be quite cruel that way.

It was almost a relief when the door opened and two cops walked in.

"Is there a problem, Mister Beasley?" one of them asked.

"No. No problem at all. These gentlemen were just leaving."

One cop looked at the other and tilted his head slightly towards the door. The second nodded ever more slightly. Then Hans, the down-time cop, went out with the three strangers to make sure they didn't have any complaints that should be addressed.

Lyndon approached the bar. When he reached the cash register he asked, "What happened, Ken?" Officer Johnson was probably the only cop that ever addressed Ken Beasley by his first name. He once briefly dated Ken's stepdaughter, and Ken still thought well of him.

"Sorry about that, Lyndon," Ken said. "When three armed Krauts came through the door looking dangerous, I thought I had a problem. Turns out someone down at the post office sent them here on a wild goose chase; just to get rid of them, I suspect."

Lyndon worked so hard to swallow his laughter that he almost choked on it. "Sorry about that, Ken," Lyndon apologized. "I guess that's our fault. When the three wise men came wandering into the station looking for our philosophers so they could commune with them, the person behind the desk tried to explain that we didn't have any. She finally got rid of them by sending them to the post office. After all, they have everybody's address. Well, someone thought it was funny, I guess, to let them chase their tails all over town and called the post office and suggested Jimmy Dick."

"Thanks a hell of a lot!" James added from the sidelines.

Lyndon continued. "If the post office had given them his home address they never would have come here."

"Hey?" Jimmy Dick called out. "Hello." He waved his hand in a big "bring on the train" wave. "I'm down here. If you can't talk to me, you could at least not talk about me as if I ain't here, damn it."

"Oh, I'm sorry, Jimmy," Lyndon said. "When I didn't see you talking to them I figured you weren't here."

"Why the hell should I talk to them? And why was it funny to give them my name?" James demanded. Then before that could be answered, if indeed it could be, he also asked, "And just who do I thank for that anyway? And why would I want them poking around my house?"

Lyndon started to answer the first or second question and then bit his tongue. He didn't answer the third question either but he did reply to it. "Jeez, Jimmy, I'm not sure who made that call."

In truth, Lyndon knew exactly who made the call. He knew it had been discussed for almost three minutes and everybody in the office, including the chief, knew about it and thought it was funny.

The conversation started out with someone suggesting that they call the post office and have them send the three wise men down to the stables to look for Don.

"Don who?" someone asked.

"Donald Duck," someone else suggested.

"That would do, but I was thinking of Ma Quixote's oldest boy."

The people in the room had chuckled. Then someone had showed his age by saying, "If they want philosophy, we should send them to Ma and Pa Kettle."

"Who's that?" At least two people asked.

As he tried to explain who Ma and Pa Kettle were and then what a cracker-barrel philosopher was, the name Dick Head came up.

The truth was that they were, perhaps, just a little embarrassed that they did not have a Philosophical Society in town nor did they have anybody they considered a philosopher. So they sought to hide the embarrassment in humor. Pain turned inward is depression. Pain turned outward is anger. Pain turned sideways is humor. All three can be destructive.

"If there's no problem I'd better get back to work," Lyndon said. Ken noticed he hadn't answered the fourth question, either.

The other two patrons were out the door behind him before it shut all the way. The closing of the door seemed to trigger a wave of laughter.

"Ken, bring me a bottle of whatever you're calling whiskey these days," Jimmy Dick said. "That story is all over town by now. Looks like I'll be doing my drinking at home for a good long while."

"Shoot, Jimmy. That won't help and you know it. The only thing you can do is make it your joke on the Krauts and ride it out."

James picked up his beer and took a long slow sip and thought for a minute. You can't talk while you're drinking and you can't talk while you're thinking. Or is it you can't think while you're talking? James' mind went back to junior high school. If someone insulted you it was best to turn it back on them; it was almost as good if you could turn it on someone else, then you were doing the laughing instead of being laughed at.

"Oh, come on, Jimmy," Ken said, "why do you think I told them you'd have a disciple come to their hotel? You can have the whole town laughin' at you or you can have the town laughin' at them."

"I don't know, Ken."

"Go have a free dinner. Order two of the most expensive meals on the menu. Hand them some bullshit. Then tell everybody in town what saps the puffed up highbrow Krauts are."

"I don't know, Ken," James said, again. The answer came a bit slower this time.

Ken knew he was coming around. "Well, why not?" Ken pushed.

"That interpreter he had was hard on the ears," James said. It was lame and he knew it. He also knew that he would be taking Ken's advice. He just couldn't give in without arguing. It wasn't in his nature.

"So when you send the messenger tell 'em you're bringing your own. Better still, tell them you're bringing two, so it'll be three on three."

Julio brought half a tray of glasses to add to the stack under the bar. The only time he ever brought less than a full tray was when he wanted an excuse to come out front. "I'll get my grandson to deliver the message," he said.

"He's in school, ain't he? I want to get this over with." James said.

"I'll call over there and get him out," Julio said.

"Why don't we just call the hotel?" James asked.

"Naw! It ain't dignified enough. Grantville's greatest philosopher would send a formal note. While we're waiting for the boy, I'll call home and get a blank card. Don't just stand there, Julio," Ken said. "Call the school and get the kid over here."

☆   ☆   ☆

When Matthew got back to school he had missed one class and was late for the next. When he entered Mister Onofrio's math class he handed the teacher a note from the office. The note said simply "Matthew Bartholow was excused and may be admitted to class at this time."

After forty years of teaching, Emmanuel Onofrio knew a rat when he smelled one. "You will speak to me after class, young man. Do you have today's assignment?" It was the last class of the day and Emmanuel knew Matthew's shift as a bus boy didn't start until dinner time. The lad had tried, once, to use it as an excuse for not having his homework done.

When the room was empty except for the two of them, Mister Onofrio asked, "Just where were you, young man?" in his well practiced "I can see your soul so don't mess with me" voice.

"My grandfather sent for me to run an errand," Matthew replied.

"And what was this errand that was so important that it couldn't wait?"

"They needed a message delivered." The boy's answer sounded rather lame to the old man.

"And what was this important message, that had to be delivered, by you, before school was out?" The mathematician wanted to know. The boy blushed but did not say a word.

"Come, come," the graybeard said. He knew he was near a confession when the lad blushed. "Speak up."

"Well, they didn't tell me not to read it," Matthew said.

"So you read it. What did it say?"

"Dick Head, along with an interpreter and an associate, will be pleased to except Herr Krieger's dinner invitation tonight at seven. Please make reservations for six at Grantville Fine Foods."

At the name Dick Head, Emmanuel Onofrio started to dismiss the whole thing as a bad joke. But the name Krieger caught his full attention. "Krieger?" He almost gasped. "Not Wilhelm Krieger?"

"That's the one. I got his first name at the counter when I delivered the note," Matthew said.

"Why would he want to see that idiot Jimmy Dick?" Emmanuel asked the universe, all but forgetting that there was another person in the room.

"All I know is that the post office sent 'em lookin' for Dick Head and they found him where Grandpa works afternoons," Matthew said.

"The *post office?*" The puzzled teacher nearly yelped. "Why would they send him there?"

"I don't know."

"That will be all."

Shortly after Matthew left, Emmanuel was on his bicycle. He was heading for the post office and determined to get to the bottom of it all.

The gray haired man stepped up to the window to be promptly told, "Sorry, Emmanuel, there isn't any mail for you. I'd send it on to the school anyway."

"No, I'm not expecting anything. I was wondering though . . . Well, I heard something improbable from a student and thought I ought to check before I called him on it. You didn't see Wilhelm Krieger today did you?" Emmanuel asked.

"Not that I know of," she answered.

"Thank goodness. That's a relief. I was told you sent him looking for Jimmy Dick," he said.

"Oh! The three wise men. Yeah, I sent them to Club 250 to see the Dick, ah, Jimmy Dick." Even grown ups can be intimidated by an old teacher.

"Why?" Emmanuel practically shouted.

The post mistress must have "got her back up" at his tone of voice, at the implied criticism, and at being made to feel like a naughty little girl. "'Cause the cops called over here and told me to. If you got a problem with that go and talk to them." With those words she turned away from the window.

Shortly thereafter, Emmanuel found himself at the police station. Shortly after that, he found himself in Chief Richards' office. Oddly, it was the chief who was uncomfortable.

"Chief Richards, do you know why one of your people sent Wilhelm Krieger to speak to Jimmy Dick?"

"Well, Mister Onofrio, what can I say? It seemed like a good idea at the time."

"Chief, you just sent the biggest jerk in the whole town to

represent us to the greatest intellectual mind that Germany is likely to produce this century."

"Never heard of him," Chief Richards replied.

"He probably didn't live long enough to make it into our history books. Beyond doubt, he will be in the ones we're writing now. His published work on philosophy guarantees that, even if he never writes another word. We can't have him thinking that jackass, Jimmy Dick, represents Grantville. You've got to stop it." Chief Richards knew Emmanuel must be a very flustered academic. He wasn't just speaking forcefully, he was nearly shouting.

"I don't see what I can do about it. Having dinner isn't a crime. If you feel that strongly about it, go talk to Jimmy Dick. Now, is there anything else I can help you with before I get back to work?" Chief Richards was getting a bit annoyed. He wasn't used to being yelled at in his own office.

Emmanuel put his kickstand down outside of Club 250 within a few minutes of leaving the police station. As he read the sign, "No Dogs And No Germans Allowed," he sighed. He took a deep breath, squared his shoulders and entered the den to bait the lions.

Ken looked up as Emmanuel walked in. Emmanuel could see that Ken didn't immediately recognize him. Then he apparently decided that Emmanuel was obviously an up-timer, probably okay. The old man approached the bar and Ken asked, "What can I get ya'?"

"I'm looking for Jimmy Dick," Emmanuel said.

"He ain't here," Ken answered.

"You're Ken Beasley, right?" Emmanuel asked.

"Yeah," Ken answered.

"I'm Emmanuel Onofrio," Emmanuel said.

"Ralph's uncle?" Ken asked.

"Or his brother, depending on which Ralph you're referring to. Perhaps you can help me. I need to convince Jimmy Dick to not keep that dinner date tonight."

"Why?"

"Mister Beasley," Emmanuel started to explain but was interrupted.

"Call me Ken," Ken said. "The only people who call me Mister Beasley in here are cops here on official business."

"Ken, Jimmy Dick is the butt of a horrible joke. A joke that's in very bad taste, I might add, perpetrated by the police department."

"Manny, we knew that when we sent the note accepting the invitation," Ken said.

Emmanuel ignored being called Manny. The old man detested that nickname, but was dealing with a shock of his own at the moment. "You knew?"

"Sure," Ken said.

"Then why did he accept?"

"Well, Grantville is going to be laughing about this for years to come. We decided we'd rather have them laughing at some damned Kraut stuffed shirt than at one of our own," Ken explained.

"But, Mister Beasley, Ken, that Kraut stuffed shirt is Wilhelm Krieger. He's here to research our philosophy before he writes about it for all of Europe to read." When it came to Herr Krieger's purpose Emmanuel was guessing. Correctly, as it turned out, but still just guessing.

"Really?"

"Do you actually want all of Europe to judge us by Herr Krieger's impression of Jimmy Dick?" Emmanuel asked.

Ken looked taken aback for a moment. The stakes were a lot higher than he had realized, apparently. Still, he asked, "Do you really want Jimmy to spend the rest of his life being laughed at over this?"

Emmanuel started to speak and paused with his mouth open. He hadn't thought of that. He was angry with himself. In an argument you take the time that your opponent is speaking to plan your next point. In a discussion you listen to the other party and think about what was said before responding. He hated arguing and was annoyed with himself for having slipped into one. Still, he had to try. "Mister Beasley, this is important. Way too important to leave in the hands of Jimmy Dick Shaver."

"Well, the cops should've thought of that before they set him up to take a pratfall. Shouldn't they have?"

"I can't agree with you more. Their behavior is reprehensible. But what can you do, report them to the police?" Emmanuel asked.

Ken actually laughed. The hostility that had been building was, provisionally, set aside, though it was ready to hand and could be easily put back in play.

"Where is Jimmy Dick? Perhaps I can reason with him," Emmanuel said.

"I doubt it." Ken smiled. "His mind is pretty well made up. Have a seat and a beer on the house. Jimmy will be back shortly. He's gone out to nail down his interpreter for tonight."

That caught Emmanuel's curiosity. "Who is he getting?"

"He wants Old Joe Jenkins."

"That old hillbilly?"

"Yep." Ken nodded. "Jimmy said he heard him translatin' sermons, German to English and English to German right down to the emotional slant of the preacher and was never more than one word behind. He also said that Old Joe Jenkins was the smartest man he had ever met."

Emmanuel was shocked to find that he was angry or jealous and chided himself for it. Why should he care about the opinion of the biggest jackass in a town half full of petty, close-minded people? Besides he had never really met Jimmy Dick, so the poor man didn't really know what a smart man was. Then he chided himself for being overly proud and again for being uncharitable to the village he grew up in and had chosen to retire to.

"Who's his other second?" Emmanuel asked.

"Huh?" Ken looked confused.

"Jimmy has been challenged to a duel of wits. He's taking two seconds. One is Joe Jenkins. Who is the other one?"

"I don't think that's been settled yet," Ken said. He knew for a fact that Jimmy was assuming he would be the third member of the party. He wasn't thrilled with the idea. Fresh organic fertilizer had a way of splattering anyone close by when it hit the fan and he didn't want to deal with it. A thought grew in his mind and a smile grew on his face. "But I think it should be you."

Fritz Shuler was ecstatic. On this weeknight his struggling restaurant, Grantville Fine Foods, was booked to capacity. He hadn't had a night like this since the opening rush. The crowd was almost all up-timers, for a change. There was one reservation from a down-timer. Then the calls started trickling in. The trickle steadily increased until he was turning people away.

Fritz was frantically putting the final touches on the new policy that he hoped would be the salvation of his investment. He had researched up-time dining before he opened. He found a paper maker who would make paper plates and napkins. His niece bought plastic flatware and cups at school from anyone who would sell them.

He had set out to provide an authentic West Virginia dining experience. He featured catfish, Kentucky style chicken cooked in a very expensive "pressure cooker," and beef grilled to order, on top of a full menu. The down-timers found it charming but up-timers didn't come back.

Someone finally explained the difference between fast food and fine food. After tonight when diners arrived they would be asked, "Paper or cloth napkins?" But tonight, except for the one table, everyone would have real linen, silver flatware, fine china and glass. He hadn't planned to start that until next week but when the river floods, it's time to float the logs.

After a hard day of frantic preparations the night was not going well. People who arrived at six were lingering over coffee and wine, as if waiting for something. People who had a seven o'clock reservation were arriving early, as if they were afraid they would miss something. Customers were piling up in the waiting area. There were no open tables except for the one set for six with paper and plastic. Fritz was not going to put an up-time patron there. He gritted his teeth and started passing out free wine.

The down-timers arrived a bit early. Oddly, no one in the waiting area objected to being passed over. Fritz showed them to the table where they immediately examined the place settings in detail as was typical of a first time down-timer diner. Fritz was shocked when the rest of the party arrived and were up-timers. Well, it was too late to change things now.

Fritz showed the new arrivals to the table. Before they could seat themselves one of the down-timers stood up. Fritz was startled and just a bit worried.

In passable English the standing man said, "Herr Krieger suspects that he is being played for a fool." From the look on his face the interpreter was completely convinced of it and was more than a little pleased about it for some reason.

Emmanuel's heart dropped. He had hoped he could take the conversation into Latin, the language of scholarship, and control the night. Now the game was lost before it started. All he could think to do was apologize profusely. Before he could start Joe Jenkins spoke up.

"Why does he suspect that?" Joe asked.

It was a fair question, Emmanuel thought, but something about the way Joe said it was . . . Latin! It was Latin; accented but understandable Latin. Where did a dumb hillbilly learn Latin?

The interpreter looked perplexed. Emmanuel guessed that he didn't know Latin, just his native dialect of German and the passable English he had picked up somewhere. Herr Krieger, on the other hand, was suddenly focused completely on Joseph. He motioned for the interpreter to sit down.

"My man here claimed to have overheard a conversation leading him to believe Dick Head is not a name but an insult," he said in crisp Latin. His voice was quite tainted with suspicion and hostility.

"Well, he is right about it being no one's proper name." Joseph continued speaking in Latin, to Emmanuel's ongoing amazement. "I am Joseph Loudoun Jenkins, now commonly known as Old Joe. When I was young I was known as Low Down Jenkins. Over there is Emmanuel Onofrio, known to his students as Oman Frio, meaning Old man 'Frio. Don't look sour, Emmanuel. You know it's so. Emmanuel is otherwise known as Ralph's brother or Ralph's uncle, depending upon the age of the speaker. Your third guest is James Richard Shaver, commonly known as Jimmy Dick, sometimes called Dick Head."

"Why?" Wilhelm asked.

Joe began to answer. "Well, sir." Hearing the West Virginia accent and word choice coming out of Joseph's mouth while speaking Latin was amazing to Emmanuel. Still, somehow, it felt like Joseph was yet going to pull it out of the soup. "We came from a very busy time. Anything we could do to get things done faster we did it. Even our language was rushed. We didn't have time to say 'The United States of America,' so we said 'the U.S.A.' When I was a young man we had a 'President,' a leader named Eisenhower. He was very highly esteemed. Everyone referred to him as Ike. Later two Presidents in a row were known by initials, J.F.K. and then L.B.J." Joseph answered the question while completely ignoring what was asked.

Jimmy Dick spoke up. "Are we just goin' t' stand here or what?"

Herr Krieger's interpreter translated the question into German. Wilhelm nodded slightly and motioned to the chairs with a slight hand movement. Emmanuel realized that James was a loose cannon who was getting irate about not knowing what was going on. He started translating the Latin into English for him.

"So you shorten names for convenience. That is nothing that we do not do. But he is Dick Head. Is that not an insult?" Wilhelm asked.

"Have you studied Hebrew, Herr Krieger?" Joseph asked.

"Briefly," Wilhelm said. "There were works I wanted to read, but in the end it proved more workable to have them translated."

"I know what you mean. I tried to learn Hebrew and Greek but it was more time than I could spare back then. Knowing French helped when I decided to learn Latin six months ago," Joseph said.

"You have only been working on Latin for six months? Incredible," Wilhelm said. Emmanuel agreed.

"We Americans do things in a hurry. I thought I might need it for dealing with the Catholics, so I was motivated. As I was saying about Hebrew, you know that the word 'Rosh' can translate as 'first' or 'top' or 'head.' Dick can be used in English to mean 'penis.' But it also can mean 'any man' for obvious reasons. Like the words," he shifted to English for two words "lumberjack and steeplejack. So, yes, it can be an insult. But then, to misquote scripture, 'a philosopher is not without honor except in his own home.'"

Wilhelm smiled and started to call for wine by picking up his glass and holding it in the air. But he stopped with the red plastic cup only inches off the table. "Why are we the only ones who have these?" he asked.

"Shit," Jimmy Dick said. "They came from up-time with us and when they're gone they're gone. You're being honored." He swallowed the words, "ya dumb Kraut," because Emmanuel had impressed on him how important the dinner was. "Honored with a piece of the future. Everybody else here tonight has to make do with the here and now."

Emmanuel started translating what was said into Latin before Herr Krieger's man could give an uncensored version. People at the nearby tables seemed to be taken with sudden fits of coughing.

"Waiter, wine for my guests," Wilhelm Krieger called out. When he did it seemed as if there was a pause in conversation while he spoke. The noise level in the room unquestionably went back up when he set his glass down. "This," he waved his hand to include everything on the table, "is truly amazing, so light, yet strong." He picked up a fork and looked at it skeptically. "Can you truly eat with this? It seems as if it would break."

Emmanuel was busy translating German to English for Jimmy Dick, who was amongst the minority in Grantville who refused to learn German. So the conversation fell to Joseph, who responded in German. "They can break if you try cutting meat with them, so you use the knife. They were made to be thrown away after one use."

"Truly?" Wilhelm asked with raised eyebrows. "What of the expense?"

"You could buy a box of one hundred for less than you earned in an hour," Joseph replied. "They were not highly esteemed but it saved the time of washing up. Our thought was 'anything to save time.' We were a very busy people."

Herr Krieger's eyebrows went up again. Emmanuel could almost see him thinking that there was a fortune to be made here.

"Unfortunately, we can't make any more. Even if we had the equipment, the materials are not available. These are the last for at least ten years," Joseph said.

"Unfortunate, indeed. Do you teach at the local academy also?" Krieger asked.

"No. I don't have the credentials it takes to do that," Joseph said.

"But with your Latin . . . and you are a philosopher, surely?"

"Neither Latin nor philosophy are much regarded." Turning to Emmanuel, Joseph said, "Why don't you tell Herr Krieger about the school system."

Emmanuel set about giving a detailed account of Grantville's schools. As far as he was concerned, he was justifiably proud of them, even if they were on the low side of average up-time. Joseph translated for Jimmy this time. Ordering food interrupted the flow of Emmanuel's lecture, but he eventually concluded with, "I would put our high school graduates up against Jena's university students when it comes to general knowledge. When it comes to specialized knowledge, I would match Jena graduates with ours in the same field. Of course, we have areas of study that they do not." He was thinking drivers' ed, and then others.

The food arrived. Diners began to leave while others arrived and took seats. It didn't look like the hoped for fireworks were going to happen. No one had the Latin to follow the conversation, so why stay?

"Your colleague says Latin and philosophy are not esteemed?" Wilhelm asked.

"We offer Latin as an elective. Philosophy is covered as part of English literature," Emmanuel answered.

Herr Krieger cautiously cut at his steak with the plastic knife and was visibly surprised that it worked. The silent bodyguard tried cutting his with the fork. It broke in his hand. A staff member immediately turned up with a set of silver utensils for him, and took the knife and spoon away. Emmanuel had the chicken. It was quite good. It had been so long since he last had Kentucky fried chicken that he couldn't tell the difference. The slaw, mashed potatoes and gravy were superlative.

After his first bite Wilhelm Krieger reverted to Latin. "Herr Head, is war mankind's greatest glory or its greatest shame?"

Emmanuel translated the question.

"Hell, it's neither," Jimmy Dick Shaver answered. Joseph translated the answer.

"Neither?" Herr Krieger prompted.

"War is a great adventure," Jimmy Dick quoted. "But, an adventure is someone else havin' a hard time of it somewhere else. War is glorious when you win with an acceptable casualty rate. But no casualty rate is acceptable to the casualty. And since someone always loses, war is glorious less than half the time.

"To the men in the middle of it," Jimmy continued, "war is at best boring drudgery spiked with moments of terror. For some, it is a walking nightmare that never leaves them this side of the grave."

"Then it is our greatest shame?" Krieger asked.

"There are greater shames," Jimmy said after Emmanuel translated the question. "The holocaust comes to mind."

"Do you want me to explain that?" Joe asked.

"Might as well," Jimmy said.

"In our history, Herr Krieger," Joseph said, "in the years of the nineteen thirties and forties, a Prussian government rounded up twelve million people they did not approve of. Jews, gypsies, Poles, Slavs, and others. Then they exterminated them."

"Like Vlad the Impaler killing every beggar in the kingdom," Herr Krieger said. "But, that many?"

"It was a very full world," Joseph said. "Look it up at the library. The key words are Nazi, and Holocaust. It will surely confirm the six million Jews. You may have to dig to find the others. They are often forgotten."

Wilhelm Krieger looked at Jimmy "But, this Holocaust is surely a fluke?"

"No!" Jimmy replied. "Pol Pot, five million, Saddam, three million, Stalin . . . who knows how many millions."

"So these holocausts are man's greatest shame?" Krieger asked. The undertone of skeptical unbelief was less than perfectly hidden.

"Hell no!" Jimmy answered.

A frustrated Wilhelm finally demanded, "If it is not war and it is not slaughter then what is it?"

Emanuel translated the question. Joseph waited for the answer. Jimmy paused. His last "Hell no" was a reaction without conscious thought. Now he needed a response. "Tell him that mankind's greatest shame is running out of good whiskey. No, wait." A memory of personal pain gushed into his mind like a torrent of water from a long forgotten dam that crumbled. "Tell him our greatest shame is an uncherished child. A man's greatest glory is to love his wife and raise his children well."

Joseph translated it. Wilhelm started at him like a pole-axed steer for at least five seconds. Then he turned to Emmanuel. "Did he translate that correctly?"

"Yes," was all Emmanuel said.

Wilhelm looked back at Joseph. "Do you agree with him?"

"Well, it was my greatest joy. And yes, it is my greatest glory. So I agree with him." Joseph said.

"And you?" Herr Krieger asked, looking at Emmanuel.

Onofrio's memories flashed back through a list of unloved, bright children who faded into dull commonness or blossomed into brilliant horrors. "Yes. An uncherished child is our greatest shame."

"You people are hopeless romantics." Krieger's tone made it clear he thought the idea contemptible.

Both up-timer translators laughed. When Emmanuel explained why, Jimmy smirked.

"What is so funny?" an obviously angry Wilhelm demanded.

Joseph dried his eyes. "My wife, may she rest in peace, often told me that I was a typical male with no idea of what romance was."

Wilhelm humphed before asking, "Herr Head, how many children did you and your wife raise?"

"I ain't mankind. I'm one man. 'Nam was my greatest glory and my greatest shame. When I returned no women worth puttin' up with would have me and any women who would put up with me weren't worth havin'."

He saw no reason to tell this damned Kraut about his personal life. When Bina Rae found out their baby had "bad bones," probably from something he brought back from 'Nam—something he hadn't told her about—she moved out on him. She acted like Agent Orange was some sort of venereal disease he could have avoided. When she left he took to hitting the bottle hard and lost his job. Bina Rae wouldn't talk to him, wouldn't go to counseling and wouldn't let him see Little Merle without a big fight each and every time.

Now Merle was living in the nursing home and as long as the bills were paid he never heard from or of her. Merle would not speak to him for abandoning her. She never even heard his side of the story.

The only happy year of his miserable life crashed in 1973. Bina Rae came home from the doctor and was packed up and gone when he got home from work. He got drunk and stayed drunk. Along the way he got divorced and listed as sixty percent disabled instead of the usual thirty percent for a head case. Up to the Ring of Fire the Veteran's Administration paid for Merle out of his disability check. Now he was making do with family money off of rental properties an agent managed.

None of that was anybody's damned business, especially some damned Kraut.

"So you admit that your greatest glory and your greatest shame is war. But you would have me believe it is raising children." Herr Krieger turned to his interpreter and spoke in loud, angry, German while rising to his feet and pocketing the plastic spoon. "You are right! I am being played for a fool. Settle up with the proprietor and return to the lodgings." Then without a fare-thee-well, he and the silent bodyguard stalked out of the totally silent room.

Jimmy Dick was the first to speak. "Ya know, this catfish is really quite good."

The dining room burst into roaring laughter.

When it had mostly died down Emmanuel Onofrio stood and extended his hand to Jimmy "Dickhead" Shaver. "Mister Shaver," he said in a voice pitched to carry, "it was truly a pleasure translating for Grantville's only full-time practicing philosopher."

The Painter's Gambit

Iver P. Cooper

October 1633

Birgit's mother had warned her not to take any food or drink from boys, not to answer any of their questions, and, most especially, not to smile at them. Birgit had dutifully agreed. Unfortunately, she broke all three rules the same day.

Birgit and her friends Anna and Barbel had gone to Halberstadt to enjoy a festival. They walked arm in arm across the town square, the Domplatz, and were surprised to find several of their fellow villagers clustered around a young foreigner. He was regaling them with tales of the fabulous New World. Strange beasts. Indians. He even had drawings to show them. Drawings he had made himself.

Birgit and her companions hovered on the edge of the crowd. Suddenly, the storyteller gestured in her direction. "Now, that beautiful lass would amaze the natives. They would say that her hair was like a river, lit by the morning sun." Birgit smiled involuntarily. Then she collected herself and started to pull away. Her girlfriends pulled her right back.

"Say something to him," Anna whispered furiously.

"But he's a man!"

"That's the point, you idiot."

Birgit blushed. "Um—can you draw me?"

"Draw us all," said Barbel.

"All of you? It will endanger my health and sanity, to study so much beauty all at once. But I will attempt it." The young man took out a piece of chalk and drew rapidly in his sketchbook. "What do you think of this?"

The artist had drawn them as if they were wearing elegant gowns, and were standing on a cloud, looking down at a shepherd who looked like him.

Birgit puzzled over the scene. "It doesn't seem to be a story from the Bible."

"No, it isn't. It is the judgment of Paris. The Greek goddesses Aphrodite, Hera and Athena appeared before Paris, the prince of Troy, and asked him to choose who would be awarded a golden apple, inscribed, 'to the fairest.'"

Barbel fluttered her eyelashes. "So which of us would you choose?"

"Hmm . . . In the myth, Paris didn't even try to judge the goddesses' beauty, he just picked the one who offered him the best bribe."

Barbel giggled. "And what sort of bribe would you like?"

Birgit carefully stepped on Barbel's toes. "Would you like to share my apple?" she asked.

"I would be delighted."

Anna spoke up. "Come, Barbel, I think Max is on the other side of the square, let's go say hello."

"I am fine right here. Or I would be, if my toes weren't hurting."

"I think your toes will hurt even more if you stay. Come. Now." She turned to Birgit. "Call us if you need us."

Birgit took a bite out of her apple, and then handed it to the stranger. "I am Birgit. Birgit Wegener. I am the eldest daughter of the smith in Stroebeck."

He took a bite, too, and smacked his lips. "I am Felix Gruenfeld. My father is—was—a book printer and bookseller; he is . . . retired . . . now. I am a member of the Guild of Saint Luke's in Amsterdam. The artists' guild, that is. I was returning to that city when I discovered that it was under siege. I decided to flee to Germany."

"It is hard for me to think of Germany as a place of refuge, especially after the sack of Magdeburg," said Birgit.

"I understand, but you have the Lion of the North to defend you now. And Amsterdam has been in sorry straits since the English and French betrayed the Dutch at the Battle of Dunkirk."

Felix reached for the drinking horn at his side. "May I offer you something to drink? I am sorry, it is just small beer." Birgit took a sip, and he did the same. He scrounged up some cheese for them to share, too.

They chatted for a while. Birgit grew more and more interested in this man, so different from the others she knew. She was disappointed when he said, "Unfortunately, I need to take my leave of you. I must try to sell a few pictures in the market this afternoon. Once the festival is over, the local guild will be very hostile to any outsider trying to sell paintings in this town."

"Of course, I understand. Have you sold any pictures so far?"

"I have not been doing as well as I expected. The landscapes and natural studies which were snapped up by the burghers back home don't seem to satisfy Germanic tastes."

Birgit waved the picture of her and her friends at him. "Your sketch was very good. Perhaps you should be trying to sell portrait miniatures, instead."

Felix had a pained expression. "It is my desire to use my art to convey the reality of nature, which is God's creation. To depict the sweep of great mountains, and the delicate colors of a butterfly's wing. And to express these both beautifully and accurately. To paint portraits is to trivialize my skills."

Birgit had noticed that Felix wore clothes which, while made of a good material, had been carefully patched. She was also a practical girl. "I apologize, good sir. I had not realized that you were independently wealthy, and hence could paint and draw without catering to popular tastes."

Felix held up his hands. "*Touché!*" He paused. "Still, I can't very well paint portraits in advance, in the hopes that the sitter's father or spouse will show up at the marketplace. Portraits must be commissioned. So on one visit I look for prospects, and on the next, I deliver the portrait and get paid. Right now, I need works which will appeal to many people, and might be sold on the spot."

"You could always paint scenes from the Bible."

"There is that. Although they are difficult to sell in some towns."

"But surely an artist of your caliber can overcome the problem. You could leave out the saints' halos, for example."

Felix nodded thoughtfully. "I thank you for your advice. I will think on it." Waving goodbye to Birgit, Felix said, "I think that at the hour of vespers, I will go pray inside the Church of Saint Martin."

"That is very pious of you," said Birgit. "I am very pious myself."

Felix and Birgit's courtship progressed from there, albeit in fits and starts. Birgit could not go to Halberstadt often without arousing parental suspicions. For that matter, Halberstadt, with only ten thousand inhabitants, was not the best place for Felix to sell paintings. Still, they found opportunities to meet, even though it took some effort.

Birgit began to learn Felix's story. There were many painters in the Netherlands, and hence it was important to have a specialty in which you were the acknowledged expert. After achieving mastery, Felix had decided to make himself the expert on the New World, and had wangled a position in the entourage of the governor of New Amsterdam. He painted portraits, made maps, and so forth.

Felix returned to the Netherlands, only to find that his mother and elder brother had died of some potent disease, and that his father had abandoned himself to drinking and gambling. His life savings, which could have gone to setting himself up in his own shop, as an independent master, went instead to paying his father's debts. Felix had to make do by inking in landscape backgrounds for the portraits of others. Boring work. Felix admitted to Birgit that this might explain some of his antipathy for portraiture. Except when the subject was her, of course.

Besides his artistic activities, Felix also collected "curiosities"— plants, minerals and so forth which might interest a collector. In the Netherlands, the interest in these wonders was not limited to the nobility; many wealthy merchants had *Wunderkaemmer*. Felix's curiosities could be sold, or given, to a prospective patron.

It was while Felix was away from home, on a collecting trip, that the next disaster occurred. It was a turn for the worse in the long war with the Spanish Hapsburgs. They destroyed the Dutch fleet, seized Haarlem, and laid siege to Amsterdam. It was clearly not the best time to try selling nature art in the Netherlands. Or art of any kind, for that matter. Except perhaps Catholic altarpieces.

Since Felix was of German descent, he decided to try his luck in the Germanies. Unfortunately, most of his stock and materials were in Amsterdam, on the other side of the siege line.

"Do you play chess?" Birgit asked.

"No, I don't. Didn't you ask me that before?" Felix took a closer look at her. They were in a dark corner of the cathedral in Halberstadt, but now that his eyes were better adjusted to the gloom, he could see that she was upset. "Hey, what's wrong?"

"One of my friends was indiscreet."

"Let me guess. Barbel."

"Yes. She said something about us . . . didn't realize her mother was nearby. And her mother makes Barbel seem like a monk under a vow of silence."

"Big talker?"

"Yes. It is only a matter of time before my father finds out. Days at most."

"So perhaps I should make a preemptive strike. Tell him that we are engaged to be married. I can say that, right?" He grinned at her. She smiled for an instant, then looked grim.

"It is more complicated than that. I have put off telling you about the peculiar courtship and marriage customs of Stroebeck. If your art were selling well again, they wouldn't matter so much. But under the present circumstances—I am worried."

Felix was puzzled. "Just what are these customs?"

"Let's say that you need to learn to play chess. Right now."

"Checkmate!"

Felix Gruenfeld studied the board glumly. This was no friendly chess game. He was in the Saxon village of Stroebeck, where commoners had played chess for six centuries. In Stroebeck, the game of chess was an intimate part of the game of life.

Felix quietly tipped over his king, conceding the game. His opponent, Hans Wegener, smirked.

The mayor of Stroebeck cleared his throat. "Felix Gruenfeld, you have asked for the hand of Birgit, daughter of Hans Wegener. Under the laws and customs of Stroebeck, in order to proceed with the marriage, in spite of the opposition of Hans Wegener, you had to either defeat him at chess or pay a forfeit of twenty gulden to the village treasury. Since you have lost the game, you must either pay, or leave." Birgit was fighting back tears.

"I just don't have that kind of money right now. But if—"

Hans cut him off. "We don't need vagrants like you in Stroebeck,"

The mayor was more tactful. "I am sorry. The forfeit must be paid in cash, and on the spot."

Felix looked despairingly at Birgit. She blurted out, "You can try again in six months!"

"Hah!" said Wegener. "You are hopelessly inept. Six months or six years, you still aren't going to win against me without tutoring from a master. And how would you gain such training? If you can't pay the penalty, you can hardly pay for chess lessons. For that matter, outside of Stroebeck, chess is strictly a nobleman's game, and you can hardly expect a nobleman to agree to teach you. If one took pity on you, and gave you a few lessons, they won't make you the equal of someone who has played every day for three dozen years."

Felix looked at him stonily. "That may be, but I will be back in six months, and if I must, six months after that."

He bowed to Birgit and left the room.

Felix had realized that his chances of winning the game were not good. After his defeat, he had gone, as he and Birgit had planned, to the nearby city of Halberstadt. There, Birgit's brother, Karl, met him.

At one point, Felix had been a bit nervous about how Karl would regard the whole affair. Felix feared that Karl might be inclined to protect his little sister from undesirable suitors, and Karl was a journeyman smith. Swing a hammer all day, for years on end, and you are quite capable of flooring a mere artist. Even one who has roughed it in the New World.

However, Karl had reached that stage of life in which the son knows much more than the father. Hans' heated opposition to Felix had made Felix prime brother-in-law material, so far as Karl was concerned.

"Here, Birgit gave me these for you. This is for your stomach,"—he handed over a loaf of bread—"and this is for your heart." The second present was a small leather pouch, which contained a lock of blond hair. Felix quickly hung it around his neck, and concealed it under his blouse.

"Where are you going next?" Karl asked.

"I hear that Gustavus Adolphus is in Magdeburg. Perhaps he

has need of an artist? Or at least of a draftsman? My status would be much enhanced if I had a royal patron. If the Swede is off with his armies, I will try my luck at that Grantville we keep hearing about. Once I am settled, I will send word here. Check for messages at that tavern you are so fond of, The Roasted Pig. Now give me a moment to write a note for you to carry back to your sister."

Birgit was, indeed, a practical girl. This first became evident to her family, years before, when her mother was sick for a few weeks. Birgit went to the market, and did the shopping. And, of course, the obligatory haggling. She was a natural. After her mother recovered, it was decided to let Birgit continue in that role. She was so good that she impressed the pros. One merchant said he would have hired her on the spot, if she were a boy.

The family was less accepting when she started making suggestions as to things that her father could make in the smithy. That is to say, her father was less accepting. More to annoy him, than because of his faith in Birgit's business acumen, Karl made a few of the simpler items as journeyman projects. And was pleasantly amazed when they sold, sold very well indeed.

It was not prudent to remind her father about it, however.

Given her mental makeup, it was not surprising that, *being* a practical girl, Birgit turned to the question of how to improve the financial situation, not to mention the marital prospects, of a certain talented but slightly *im*practical artist-cum-curiosity collector.

Birgit was at her friend Anna's home. "I need to write a letter," she said.

"To Felix?" Anna mouthed. Birgit nodded. Anna quietly brought her paper, a quill pen, and an ink bottle.

"Dearest Felix," she began. "I know you are my steadfast knight. Do not despair. I am confident that you will sell your art, that you will find a great patron, and, most important of all, that we will be united.

"I was thinking about how you might more profitably practice your skills. Did you not tell me that you can make copper engravings and woodcuts? A print can be sold more cheaply than a water color. The profit on each print is small, but those profits will add up.

"Moreover, you have told me that your father was a bookseller. Do you not know the names of your father's colleagues in other towns? Can you engage them to sell your prints for a percentage of the profits? Please think upon this."

She added a few felicities, sealed the letter, and handed it to Anna. "Can you have Max take this to The Roasted Pig, in Halberstadt? Father is watching me too closely for me to dare take it there myself. And Karl can't go this week."

A bleary-eyed Felix stumbled through the door of the Inn of the Maddened Queen.

The town of Grantville was wondrous, all right . . . wondrously confusing. There was no town square, and there was no telling which shops might be on a particular street. The residents spoke English, but with terrible accents. His attempts to locate the local Guild of Saint Luke's had been greeted with polite incomprehension.

He had stayed, at first, at a large dormitory. He didn't like the looks of some of the other guests and decided to find alternative accommodations. One of the citizens of Grantville had directed him to Clarksburg Street, and the Inn of the Maddened Queen. He hurried in; it was raining heavily.

Felix went to the desk and inquired as to the cost of lodging. He winced when he heard the number, it was way out of his league.

Felix decided that he would at least get something hot to drink before he went out into the night. Perhaps he would have some of this *coffee* he had heard about. There was a menu board on one wall, and the price of a cup of coffee, at least, seemed reasonable.

The painter bit his lip when he came upon a table at which two men were playing a game of chess. He tried to find seating as far away as possible. No luck. In fact, by the time he finished his circumnavigation of the premises, the only open seat was at an adjacent table. He grimaced, and turned his chair so that his back was to the players.

"I guess you don't like chess," said the fellow facing him. He was a stocky man, with very bushy eyebrows.

"It evokes rather unpleasant memories."

"Oh?"

"I was in the Harz Mountains, and stopped in Halberstadt. It is a small city, perhaps thirty miles southwest of Magdeburg. There was a festival going on and, well, I met this girl. A real beauty, and clever, too. We saw more and more of each other, on the sly, but we weren't sly enough, I'm afraid. Her father found out.

"He said that he would refuse his consent, and she said that she wanted to have it, but didn't need his consent."

"Is that true?" Bushy Eyebrows was clearly doubtful.

"Her town, Stroebeck, is in the bishopric of Halberstadt, which is ruled directly by the Catholic prince-bishop Leopold Wilhelm von Hapsburg. So it strictly follows the canon law as proclaimed by the Council of Trent. That said that marriage does not require parental consent, and that it is anathema to assert otherwise."

"But even if that is so, cannot her father refuse to pay a dowry? Can he not disinherit her?"

"Oh, yes, and he threatened to do those things. And she avowed that she would marry me nonetheless.

"Then, he said, 'Oh my foolish and wicked daughter, I will insist on the strictest compliance with the laws of this town. By those laws, any outsider who wishes to marry a fraulein of Stroebeck must play her father, or his champion, at chess. If the prospective bridegroom loses, he must pay a forfeit to the town treasury.'

"The penalty is much higher if her father did not consent to the marriage. That wrinkle is not in conflict with canon law, because it does not formally forbid the marriage itself."

"Chess? How strange."

"Stroebeck's the *Schachdorf*, the 'chess village.' They all learn to play when they are knee-high, boys and girls alike. Unfortunately, we got caught before my Birgit could teach me much more than the pieces and their moves.

"If her father liked me, he could have appointed, say, his six-year-old son, or the village idiot, to challenge me. But he wasn't keen on having me as a son-in-law, so he took me on himself. And he'd been village champion three years running."

In the meantime, the chess players had finished their game. One of them, a solidly built man with gray hair, got up at this point. "Hi, my name is Vince Masaniello. I couldn't help but overhear you."

Felix shrugged. "That's all right. I suppose there is some cathartic relief in talking about it."

"So let me get this straight," Vince said. "There is a village out in the Harz Mountains, near Halberstadt, where the commoners play chess."

"Yes, that's right. My sweetheart told me that it all started when the bishop of Halberstadt imprisoned some prince or duke in a tower in Stroebeck. He was bored, so he drew a chessboard on the floor of his cell, and made pieces, and taught his guards how to play. They taught their friends, and the game became popular. Even the women played.

"Then some court functionary had to spend a night in Stroebeck, and was surprised when the mayor invited him to play chess. And even more surprised when the mayor beat him repeatedly.

"Word spread, and upper class Brandenburgers would make a point of stopping by to play. Not just with the mayor, but with any villager who showed an interest.

"Time came when, once a year, some bigwig would come to Stroebeck and play against their chess champion. If the Stroebecker won, well, they didn't have to pay taxes that year."

Vince snickered. "I bet that really gave a boost to chess education in Stroebeck."

"So I was told. But my problem is that if you want to marry a Stroebeck girl, you have to either beat her father's champion at chess, or pay a big fine. And I had neither the chess skills nor the cash. I am a painter without a big patron."

Vince pondered Felix's story. "The best chess player in Grantville is Joshua Modi. He held master rank in the United States Chess Federation."

"Master? There is a Chess Guild in Grantville?"

"Oh, no. It is a just a rank. The bottom rung in the UCSF is Class J. The classes go up to Class A, and then above that are Expert, Master, and Senior Master."

"And how many people are of Joshua Modi's rank?"

"Perhaps one USCF member in one hundred. And only perhaps one in fifty Americans was a member of the USCF."

"That is impressive. Do you think he would be willing to teach me?"

Vince scratched his head. "I am sure he would love to do so, but I doubt he has the time. He and Colette are spending most of their time in Essen nowadays. Greg's a fine player, too, but he is busy designing things-that-go-boom in Magdeburg. They may be able to give you a few tips before you have your rematch in Stroebeck, but that's about it."

"Can you help me?"

"Well, I am no chess master, but the knowledge of the game has advanced a lot in the four centuries since the Ring of Fire. If you are bright, I am sure I can teach you enough so that you will give your prospective father-in-law quite a shock."

"I would be very grateful." Felix bit his lip.

"What's the matter?"

"My heart is big but my purse is small."

Vince smiled. "Don't worry about that, an old man likes to have company. You will learn by playing with me and my friends." He spread out his hands, indicating the room. "The Grantville Chess Club takes over this place every Thursday night. And I am sure we can find some chess books you can borrow and study, so we don't beat you too many times in a row."

"The Grantville Chess Club?" asked Felix.

"Yes, didn't you notice the sign outside?" Felix walked over to the door and poked his head outside. The Inn's sign showed a red, four-pointed crown, with a lightning bolt over it.

"I suppose the crown is symbolic of the queen, and the lightning bolt of madness," said Felix doubtfully. "But what does that have to do with chess?"

Vince explained. The inn had been started by Joshua and Colette Modi. Its name was a chess player in-joke. The medieval chess queen had been a rather weak piece, but its role had changed over the past century. The Italian masters Lucena and Damiano popularized a new, faster form of chess, in which the bishop was allowed to move more than one space at a time, and the queen was given the powers of both the rook and the improved bishop. The new game reached Germany by 1536, where it was usually called the "rapid" or "foreign" chess game.

"And if you preferred the old game," Vince concluded, "you called it the 'chess of the maddened Queen.'"

"Is this your prayer book, sister?" asked Karl.

Birgit looked up. "Yes, it is."

"Well, don't leave it out." He handed it to her.

"I will take it to my room right now. I might read a prayer or two, while I am at it."

Birgit carefully closed the door to her bedchamber. As expected, a letter was concealed inside the book. It was from Felix. He assured her of his undying love, and announced that he had safely arrived in Grantville. Birgit was happy to learn that he had found someone to tutor him in chess. But really, he needed to find buyers for his art.

The letter ended with a story. "I must tell you about the dream I had. We were standing together on the battlements of the tower in Stroebeck, watching the sunrise. Suddenly, the tower shrunk, and we shrunk with it. The tower was now a fighting platform on the back of a great elephant, and the elephant was standing on a giant chessboard. The other pieces were there, too, and they were alive as well. The knight was on a horseback, and carried a great lance; the bishop stood, brandishing a mighty mace. For you know, dear Birgit, that the church militant cannot use edged weapons. The queen had a chariot drawn by a winged dragon, and the king sat on a throne carried by bearers. I could not see the player who controlled our movements, but his opponent was your father.

"If one piece captured another, they actually fought, the former slaying the latter. At last we were brought into play, capturing a pawn. But then your father's queen charged across the board, straight toward us, her mount breathing fire that singed us from several squares away. It was clear that we were doomed.

"Then I woke up, of course."

Clearly, her sweetheart did not have fond memories of his first chess match. Not surprising.

But Felix's dream had given Birgit an idea. At her first opportunity, Birgit visited the minister at the Church of Saint Pancratius in Stroebeck. "Reverend Sir, there is a way in which our town can draw some business from Halberstadt."

"What do you have in mind, Birgit?"

"A game of what you might call 'living chess.' The pieces are played by townspeople. The pawns are young children, the minor pieces are older ones. And perhaps the privilege of being the king, queen and rook could be sold to visitors. Captures would be presented as a mock battle. And the village champion could play a paying visitor. Or some dignitary."

"What an interesting idea, Birgit. I will tell the mayor how clever you are."

"Oh, it wasn't my idea. I am just a girl, after all. It is something that Felix thought of."

"Felix? The young artist your father disapproves of? You have been in touch with him?"

"Yes, sir. Please don't tell Father. Felix will return in six months. He deserves a fair rematch. Please don't let Father trick him into playing some crazy variant."

"Well, if he is willing to come back in six months, it says something about his character. And this 'living chess' idea of his, it speaks well for his creativity and intelligence. I will see what I can do."

On that first Thursday, Vince had taught Felix the moves of each piece, and taught him how to mate using the major pieces, the queen and rook, against a lone enemy king. He also showed him a few common chess situations: discovered check, double check, and forks. Felix was falling asleep at that point, and Vince ordered him home to get some rest.

When Felix returned, the following week, Vince announced that it was time for Felix to play an actual game. Not surprisingly, Vince won match after match.

Felix sighed. "Chess is taking so long to learn. Sketching and painting came so naturally to me."

"I hope you won't take offense, young man," said Vince, "but I think that your time could be better spent putting your artistic skills to good use, rather than learning how to play chess. If you have a livelihood, your Birgit's father will be more likely to favor the marriage, and you can afford to pay that penalty if you lose the 'engagement' game."

Felix shrugged. "In the rest of Germany, your standing in the community is primarily dependent on your ancestry, and your financial situation. But in Stroebeck, a great deal of consideration is given to how well you play chess. So yes, I need to make money, but I cannot ignore the Stroebeckers' board game obsession."

"I understand. Let me show you what you did wrong in the last game." He did so.

"Dearest Birgit," wrote Felix. "I begrudge every day I must spend here in Grantville, without you. It is purgatory.

"Nonetheless, Grantville has its compensations. First of all, there are no guilds. Can you imagine that? I can sell my work without either paying dues, or waiting for a market day.

"Moreover, my landscape drawings have drawn attention from an unexpected quarter. The school here teaches a branch of natural philosophy which they call 'geology.' It is the study of the Earth. One of the teachers walked by and noticed how accurate my depiction of what they call the 'ring wall' was. I told him about where I have traveled, and the specimens I collected, and he said that the government might be interested in my services. I could make maps, and draw illustrations of minerals, rocks and landforms for the books they are writing, and even perhaps train to be a 'field geologist.'

"Please give me your advice."

Felix entrusted the letter to a friend who had business in the Harz Mountains. In token of his appreciation, Felix sketched the friend's daughter. "Her grandparents in Braunschweig will be very happy to see how much she's grown!" the friend commented.

The response came a month later. "Dearest Felix, I hope and trust that you immediately accepted this offer. It gives you a reliable source of income, which few artists enjoy. Moreover, it moves you into government circles in which you may come to the attention of greater men, whose patronage can allow you more freedom in what you choose to portray."

Birgit gritted her teeth. She knew it wasn't proper, but she couldn't help herself. This was the third time since Felix left that a young man had been invited to her home for dinner. A young, *unmarried* man, of good family and prospects, of course.

One would-be beau was a journeyman smith, who could take over her father's smithy one day. He had been unwise enough to say that he was "just passing through Stroebeck."

"Passing through Stroebeck?" she had asked in mock surprise. "On your way to where? Paris? Venice? Vienna? Moscow? Far Cathay?" Before she was done with him, her victim wished he was in far Cathay.

Another, a clergyman's son, had bragged of having attended the University of Wittenberg. Birgit pretended to be impressed, lured him into a game of chess, and caught him in a four move Scholar's Mate. She then scornfully suggested that he return to his studies if he couldn't outplay a mere girl.

Birgit's father had sternly warned her to be polite this time. Or else. The latest pawn in her father's game of matrimony was even less promising than the first two. He was her second cousin, Johann, a merchant's clerk in Leipzig. He was handsome, but boring.

After an interminable dinner, in which he contributed such sprightly conversational tidbits as "pass the salt, cuz," Birgit suggested that they take a walk to the town square together. Her father beamed.

However, Birgit had made her plans. Once they were out of her father's sight, she said brightly, "Oh, we must stop at my friend Barbel's house. She will be so upset with me if I go to town without her." Cuz was agreeable to this detour.

They knocked, Barbel emerged, Barbel batted her eyelashes at Johann, right on schedule. As the threesome walked, Birgit contrived to fall slightly behind the other two. In town, they encountered Anna. Also on schedule.

Anna suggested that they go visit Max. Barbel demurred. "I have an idea," said Birgit. "Barbel can take our guest to see the Tower, and I will go with Anna. We will meet up at the square when we are done."

Johann politely declined. "I am here to see Birgit, I can't leave her behind."

"Don't be silly, you have seen me many times before. Like that time when I was seven years old, and I threw up on you." Birgit could see that Johann had not forgotten that incident.

"It is your duty to escort Barbel." It wasn't very logical, but Barbel was giving Johann plenty of encouragement. Which Birgit wasn't. He agreed, and they all went their separate ways.

When Johann proposed to Barbel a few weeks later, it was a surprise to Birgit's father, but definitely not to Birgit.

Birgit had removed her father's rook, bishop and pawn from play, but she needed her knight to win the game.

Felix relaxed into the booth he'd managed to acquire at Tip's Bar. He'd achieved some notoriety, as he was the first down-timer his Grantville friends had met who could say he had been in America. More precisely, who had been in what, but for the Ring of Fire, would have become the United States.

One of his new up-timer friends, Louis Giamarino, bought the first round. "So, Felix, how come you're here?"

"Here in Tip's Bar? I am celebrating the printing of the new geology pamphlet I illustrated." Felix just happened to have a copy with him, which he proudly presented to Louis. It had sketches of the rim wall, with and without the rock formations labeled, diagrams explaining how a topographic map depicted a landscape, and so on.

Louis flipped through the slim pamphlet quickly, and closed it with a snap. "Well, congratulations. But I meant, here in Grantville. I'm telling you, if I could get back to America, I'd go in a heartbeat."

Felix shook his head. "It would not be the America you remember, the America in the twentieth-century books I have been shown. It is mostly wilderness. Beautiful, but savage."

Louis spotted a buddy, Tony Masaniello, and waved him over. "Hey, Tony, c'mere. This is Felix of New York."

"New York?" said Tony. "But you didn't come through the Ring of Fire."

"No, he lived in *down-time* New York. What they call New Amsterdam. But he was born in Holland."

"Really? How'd you end up in America, then?"

Felix took a deep breath. "This is a long story, please stop me if I am telling you too much.

"You have heard of Peter Minuit, perhaps? Herr Minuit was born in Wesel. He patronized my father's bookshop because he, too, was German born.

"In 1625, the Dutch West India Company honored Herr Minuit with the appointment of Director General of New Netherland. He asked my father if he knew of an artist, skilled, yet young enough to risk the rigors of a transatlantic voyage. One who could prepare maps, as well as drawings. Drawings which might intrigue the people back home to invest in the Company, and perhaps even to settle in New Netherland.

"My father, of course, volunteered me! But in truth I was pleased by the prospect of seeing new lands and peoples, and capturing them on paper and canvas. I stayed in the New World for several years."

Felix sighed. He was approaching the painful part. "Then, unfortunately, my patron had a falling-out with his superiors. He was recalled, and I left with him. That was in early 1632.

"Then matters turned from bad to worse. Our ship, the *Unity*, was damaged by a storm, and we had to seek shelter in the British port of Plymouth. Instead of offering us aid and comfort, the English threw us into prison and seized our goods, my paintings included."

"Why did they do that?"

"The English had the nerve to claim that because Cabot landed in Newfoundland in 1497, that they thereby gained title to all of America, including New Amsterdam. And so all of our American goods belonged to them, not us."

Felix raised his voice, involuntarily. "Unbelievable! Considering that Cabot thought he was on the shores of Asia. And, of course, that he didn't properly map the territory, or land settlers."

"Easy, Felix, don't burst an artery."

"We were released, eventually, but we didn't reach Amsterdam until May of 1632. And I never saw my American paintings again." Felix shrugged. "I have heard that King Charles is fond of art. He knighted Rubens and Van Dyck, after all. I suppose that my paintings are now in good company, at least."

Felix took a long swallow. "Fortunately, the English thieves didn't think to take my sketchbooks. And, of course, I still own all the artwork that I did before I went to the New World.

"It is really too bad that so much of it is still trapped in Amsterdam. I would like to show Birgit my etchings."

All the up-timers laughed. Felix looked at them confused. What was so funny?

Hans Wegener normally had his son go to Halberstadt for supplies not available in Stroebeck, but this time he had to make the trip himself. Karl was sick in bed.

Hans had traipsed about more than he expected to; his usual supplier had been out of stock on several items. Hans passed The Roasted Pig, and decided to stop for something to eat before returning to Stroebeck.

Hans placed his order, and then noticed that the innkeeper was giving him a strange look. Hans beckoned the man over. "Am I a two-headed calf? Why do you stare at me so?"

"It is just that you look very much like someone who comes here regularly."

"A younger man? Perhaps an inch taller than me, but a similar build? Big frontal lock of hair, always askew?"

"Yes, that's the one. His name is Karl."

"That's my son. He's sick today. I am in town in his stead."

"Ah, then you'll be wanting his mail."

Mail?

Rummage, rummage. The innkeeper found what he was looking for. "Here you are." He extended his hand for a tip, and Hans grudgingly gave him a small coin.

Hans studied both sides of the letter, then held it up to the light. *Enough*, he thought. He broke the seal, and read the letter. His face purpled.

My son! My daughter! In cahoots with that artist! I'll disown them! And I'll throttle that Felix!

Wait. I have a better idea. "Are you a father?" he asked the innkeeper.

"Why, yes, I am. Why do you ask?"

"Your son, or daughter, ever do anything foolish? Despite your warnings?" Many times, the innkeeper assured him.

"Well, this letter writing, it is about something foolish. And parents must look out for each other in these situations. So what I would like you to do is this. If any other letters come in for Karl, you tell him nothing, but hold them for me. And I will come by, from time to time, and pay you a silver piece for each one. Also, if Karl has any letters to send, you accept them, but don't send them on. I will buy them back at the same price."

Whether driven by parental solidarity, or professional cupidity, the innkeeper agreed.

That's that, thought Hans. *Check!*

Vince had told Felix that he was happy to hear that the Stroebeckers had offered Felix the choice of playing either the old or the new versions of chess. That meant that when Felix returned for his rematch, he could insist on the rule of the mad queen, which in turn would mean that he would have the full benefit of several hundred years of chess analysis.

What Felix hadn't been prepared for was just how confusing those chess manuals were. Reading them was like reading Egyptian hieroglyphics. If anyone actually could read them, that is; Felix was vaguely aware that Athanasius Kircher, the famous Jesuit scholar, had been working on that project.

Hours of poring over those manuals. Hours of playing chess

at the club. The only thing that had kept Felix motivated was the thought of how much it would mean to Birgit if Felix could win her in the traditional Stroebecker fashion. Every time he read one of her letters, he felt inspired, and returned to his studies with renewed vigor.

Talking about letters . . . why hadn't she written recently? It had been . . . weeks. Had she found someone else? What could Felix do to remind her of his love?

Felix started rummaging through his room. There it was, his most precious sketchbook, the one he used in Halberstadt those few months ago. Now he needed a piece of wood. But wait. He could draw what he wanted readily enough, but he didn't have time to cut away all of the wood save for the parts he had drawn upon. Well, suppose he cut away the lines. That would print as white lines on black. Strange, but all that he could do in the time he had. Felix went to work . . .

Birgit was fretting. In a week, it would be exactly six months since Felix's ill-fated first chess match with her father. Thus, it would be the first day on which he could formally demand a rematch in order to win her hand. But she had not gotten a letter from Felix in weeks.

Will he come? He said he was doing well in Grantville. He has illustrated a book. His last letter said that he met a duke, one who writes and collects books, and wants Felix to illustrate his latest work. So Felix now has commissions. Patronage. Will he want to leave?

He must be meeting rich merchants, and noblemen. And their daughters. He also wrote that he is giving art lessons in some sort of academy. Are those daughters taking lessons from him?

Birgit had a sudden mental picture of how such a lesson might evolve. The rich merchant's daughter pleads that she doesn't know how to hold the paintbrush. Felix comes behind her, and guides her hand with his own. Urgh!

He hasn't mentioned any girls in Grantville. Is that because he hasn't met any he likes? Or is he avoiding the subject? Perhaps he doesn't want to hurt my feelings, tell me that he has found someone else.

No, that can't be. He loves me. On Saturday morning, I will climb the stairs of the Wartturm, the old tower where Bishop Arnulf imprisoned Duke Guncellin centuries ago, so I will see him as he comes up the road. And I will do it every Saturday morning, until he comes.

If he comes. He has traveled all over the world. What can he see in a girl who never traveled farther than Leipzig?

But no. He sees more than my pretty face. He enjoyed talking to me. He values my advice. He will come.

She trembled. *What will I do if he doesn't come?*

A few days later, Birgit heard a knock at the door. It was her friend, Anna. Birgit had been forbidden to go to Halberstadt, so Anna was Birgit's news source.

Her mother was out in the garden, and her father and brother were in the smithy, so they had some measure of privacy.

"Look what I have," said Anna. What she displayed was a white-on-black print, depicting three women and a man. Birgit gasped. It was virtually the same picture that Felix had drawn of Birgit, Anna, Barbel and himself, months ago. In fact, it was titled, "The Judgment of Paris."

"Where did you get this?"

"Apparently they arrived in Halberstadt a few weeks ago. Went to one of the booksellers first, and they have been circulating since then."

Birgit snatched the print out of Anna's hands.

"Hey, I'm in it, too!" Anna protested.

"You know what this means? It means that Felix hasn't forgotten me." Birgit sighed with relief. "Perhaps he *will* be here on 'The Day.'" Her voice added the capitalization.

April 1634

"So," said Hans Wegener jovially, "let's play chess. Sooner we play, sooner you lose, sooner you leave, sooner my Birgit marries someone worthy of her." Hans and Felix were in the town hall, where "marriage matches" were traditionally held. A large crowd had gathered to watch; such a match was a big event even under ordinary circumstances. But to see a rematch with an insistent suitor? One vehemently opposed by the father? Only the dead of Stroebeck were not in attendance. Felix's eyes went to Birgit, who, taking advantage of her father being turned away from her, blew Felix a kiss. Felix blushed.

Hans pulled out a chessboard, and began setting up pieces. Felix wasn't too worried. He had spent a great deal of time playing chess with up-timers and down-timers at the Modi's inn, solving chess problems in a book he had been lent, and reading books on the theory of the game. He had even been given the opportunity to spend some hours battling Josh Modi's "computer chess program."

Felix smiled at Birgit, and then mentally reviewed the opening repertoire he had been taught. He didn't pay much attention to Hans' movements until Hans leaned back in his chair.

Suddenly, Felix did a double-take. The board was too long. It was twelve squares by eight.

Hans caught Felix's look of dismay. "Haven't seen this one before? It is 'courier' chess. Very old, dates back, oh, almost to the time of Barbarossa. You don't know it? Here are the pieces, rook, knight, *alfil*, courier, *mann*, king, *fers*, *schleich*, *courier*, *alfil*, knight and rook. And twelve pawns in front. We each begin with the same four moves. Oh, no castling, assuming you know what that is." Hans smiled broadly.

"This is unfair," Felix protested. "I was given the choice of the version of chess at our first match. With the 'mad queen,' or without. And nothing was even said about this, this 'courier' chess."

Hans shrugged. "That was for a first match. For a rematch, the version is the father's choice. And this is a traditional game."

Felix appealed to the mayor. "This form of chess is not traditional where I come from. It is not fair that I have to play it."

The mayor harrumphed. "It is not played in the Low Countries, perhaps, but it is played in Germany. And most certainly in Stroebeck."

"But isn't Herr Wegener challenging me? In dueling, the challenged one has the choice of weapons, so I should have the choice of chess board and chess rules." Felix was worried. Different board, different pieces, forced opening; it undermined all his hard-won twentieth-century chess knowledge.

The crowd murmured. At this point, Birgit's quiet lobbying paid off. Her ally, the minister, said, "that seems reasonable to me." Hans scowled at the churchman. The latter added calmly, "Surely, Herr Wegener, your chess skills permit you to make this concession."

"Oh, very well." The mayor offered Hans a more modern-appearing chessboard, and Hans set up the pieces. Felix then carefully explained his assumptions as to how all the pieces moved, when and how a pawn could be promoted, and, exactly how castling was performed. Felix *had* been warned how many different castling variations were practiced in his time.

"A chess lawyer," Hans commented. Hans pulled a pair of pawns, white and black, off the board. "I don't believe that the challenged in dueling has the right to shoot first." He put the pawns behind his back, shuffled them about, then brought both fists forward. "Pick your ill-fated army."

Felix tapped Hans' left hand; Hans opened it, revealing the white pawn. Felix would move first. Felix had questioned Duke Augustus, a down-time chess author who occasionally visited the Inn of the Maddened Queen, as to what openings and defenses were favored in the seventeenth century. Felix's up-time friends had helped him pick out and study an opening repertoire which would give a down-timer a shock. But they had warned him that it would only take him so far; he had to be able to improvise if he wanted to win against a good opponent.

In quick succession, the artist and the smith each moved out their king pawns. Felix attacked with his kingside knight; Hans defended with its queenside counterpart. Felix moved out his bishop to the fourth rank.

Hans raised his eyebrows. "Well, someone has been giving you lessons. It is the Italian Game. I know it very well indeed." He, too, moved his bishop to bishop four.

Felix responded with pawn to queen knight four, offering his pawn up to capture by his opponent's bishop. It was the first move of the Evans Gambit, the darling of the great attacking players of the nineteenth century. According to all Felix's sources, it was unknown to the chess fans of the seventeenth century. Felix was nervous, however. How complete was the Grantville Chess Club's knowledge of seventeenth-century chess? They hadn't warned him about courier chess, had they? Could the Evans Gambit be well known to Hans?

"Pawn pusher!" said Hans with delight. "Didn't you see my bishop?"

Felix was also pleased, but concealed his reaction to Hans' outburst. He knew the story behind the Evans Gambit. Its inventor,

Captain Evans, spent many hours playing it against himself, and finally sprung it on the British champion, MacDonnell. Evans won; it was a great upset.

The gambit's great merit was that it allowed for powerful attacking combinations in the middle game. The problem was that if Black survived the onslaught, and held on to the gambit pawn, then he had the advantage in the endgame.

If Felix hadn't earned enough from his work in Grantville to pay the forfeit, he wouldn't have dared play the Evans Gambit. But the goal now was not really to satisfy Stroebeck traditions, but to impress Birgit's pappa. And that would more likely be achieved by bold attacking play, than by a cautious strategy.

Hans interrupted Felix's ruminations. "By the way, young man, you probably haven't heard the news. The village council, of which I have the honor to be a member, recently decided that that for a rematch, the forfeit should be double the normal one."

Felix winced. He was no longer quite so sure that the Evans Gambit was a smart strategy. "I knew nothing of this."

"I wrote to you," said Birgit. "You didn't get my letter?"

"Fancy that," said Hans. "Perhaps you used the wrong letter carrier." Birgit scowled at Karl, who spread his hands helplessly in response.

Regaining his composure, Felix returned his attention to the board. He constructed a strong pawn center, and attacked vigorously. Hans tried to counterattack, and did not deign to protect his king by castling. He soon regretted this oversight.

"Mate in three," Felix announced. He smiled at Birgit, who gave him a thumbs up.

Hans studied the board, then sent it crashing to the floor. "Why must I lose to this idiot?" he complained. Clearly, the Evans Gambit had won Birgit's hand, but not Hans' approval.

Birgit glared at her father. "That is no way to speak about my fiancée."

"That was an interesting game," the mayor commented. "I wish we had a way of reconstructing it."

Felix saw an opportunity to earn a few brownie points. "Actually, there is a method. In Grantville, where I am working now, the chess players have recorded thousands of chess games. I could teach the people of Stroebeck how to read these records, and how to notate their own games."

"Thousands of chess games? The commoners play chess in Grantville, too?"

"Anyone can play chess in Grantville. And they have records of chess games from hundreds of years of play." He looked slyly at Hans Wegener. "I could bring one of their chess books for you, Herr Wegener. It is the sort of thing that a dutiful son-in-law would do."

"That is . . . thoughtful of you," said Hans. He paused. "I would like to have a few minutes to speak to my daughter alone."

"Of course," said Felix. He was confident that nothing Hans could say could diminish Birgit's love, or persuade her not to marry him, now that Felix had broken down the barrier set by Stroebeck tradition. His only fear was that Hans might do something foolish, like try to carry Birgit off against her will.

Hans and Birgit went into an alcove, and Hans addressed his daughter. "I still don't like the idea of your marrying a painter. Yes, I know a few are honored and rewarded beyond measure by princes. But how many die forgotten, in poverty?"

Birgit stared at her father. "I have seen his work. It is very good. And it has been well received in this town of Grantville, which stands high in the regard of Gustavus Adolphus. True, he is poor right now. But he has good prospects of advancement. And, here in Stroebeck, we have a name for taking a reasonable risk, don't we? It is playing a *gambit*, yes?"

Her father nodded, slowly.

The Minstrel Boy

John Zeek

Saturday morning, February 1634

"Well, that's that." Bill Frank lowered the hood of the new rail engine. "Though I have no idea how we're going to deliver it."

Hagen Filss, who had been handing him tools, responded, "Maybe when Sergeant Hatfield and Private Schultz get back they will know, Herr Frank."

Warrant Officer Frank looked over at the young soldier. "Hagen, first off you should remember that *Mister* Hatfield is no longer a sergeant, but a warrant officer. And second, there's nothing that says he's going to stop here in Grantville. He might go straight to Wismar to join the rest of the company." Then, seeing the lost look in Hagen's eyes, he added, "I know, son. You think you can talk him and Corporal Rau into taking you with them. Face it, Hagen. You're only seventeen years old. This war is going to last a while, so there's no sense in you rushing into it. You should have let the major send you to school."

"Herr Frank." Hagen drew himself to his full height. "I can read and write. I speak two languages and I know my numbers. What more does a soldier need to know? And I am a soldier."

Bill realized Hagen was trying to convince himself as much as anyone else. It was hard to be the only regular from the train crew to be left behind. Hagen might be seventeen, but he was smaller than the average rail trooper. To top it off, Hagen had the type of face that was going to look boyish into his forties.

After studying Hagen for a while longer, Bill šimply nodded his head. "Okay, Private Filss. As a soldier you should know enough to obey orders. And your orders were to work here at the company shop. Is that understood?"

"*Ja*, Herr Frank."

"Okay. I have a couple of errands for you to run. First I want you to run over to the communications office and have them send this message to the major."

"*Ja*, Herr Frank. Does that message contain my request to rejoin the train crew?"

Bill suppressed a sigh. "Yes, Private Filss, it includes your transfer request, but the main purpose is to tell her that this engine is ready to go. Second, I want you to go out to Henry Johnson's place and check with Dora Schultz about the coveralls."

"Is there anything else, Herr Frank?"

"Not today. When you finish with those errands you can have the rest of the day off. Relax, take a walk, talk to a pretty girl, or better yet take a pretty girl for a walk. I don't want to see you until quitting time this evening or, better yet, tomorrow morning."

Bill watched Hagen walk to the rack next to the door of the shop, take down his pistol belt and buckle it around his waist. He shook his head. It had taken a direct order to make Hagen hang his pistol on the rack when he was working in the shop. The boy still wore the circle of red cloth on his left sleeve that was the mark of the train crew and not the green square that the shop crew had decided on. *Damn,* Bill thought, *it's going to break that boy's heart if he doesn't find a way to get back on a train crew.*

Hagen followed the original test track from the engine shop on his way to the communications office. It was here that he had first seen a TacRail train. It was just the engine and one flat car, but he had stood and stared, amazed that it was moving without horses pulling it. His first friend, Jim Cooper, had explained it to him. Jim hadn't cared that Hagen was short and scrawny and too young. The first person to treat him as an equal, Jim had even convinced Sergeant Hatfield to allow him to enlist.

Thinking about Jim made him think about the other men of the crew. Sergeant Hatfield, who had taught him how to shoot, and Corporal Toeffel, who had sold him his first pistol; Private Schultz, who had trained him to be a brakeman. He missed them, even Corporal Rau, who had always teased him about his age, calling him "*Der Bub*," but had also showed him how to use a dagger in a fight and how to walk quietly.

Now they were all gone. Gone to war. Even Anton Busch, who was the closest to Hagen's age. No one had thought of leaving Anton or Jim behind, but Corporal Toeffel had ordered Hagen to stay and help in the engine shop. It wasn't fair. He was as good a rail trooper as the rest. Sergeant Hatfield had to take him.

With a jerk, Hagen realized he been so lost in thought that he had almost passed the building he needed and had to backtrack half a block to the front entrance.

Katharina Stuetzing was seated at the desk, acting as a receptionist. For some reason Hagen remembered Herr Frank's last comment about taking a pretty girl for a walk. Katharina definitely was a pretty girl, but just looking at her made Hagen blush and stammer. Besides, he still had the second errand to run.

"G-g-good morning, Private Stuetzing. I have a message from Herr Frank at the engine shop. Can it go out in this morning's radio traffic?"

"*Ja*, Private Filss. Give it to me and I will see that it goes to the radio room." Katharina smiled. Her smile just made Hagen blush all the more. And what was worse he knew he was blushing.

"*Danke*. Uh-uh . . ."

"Was there something else, Hagen?"

Hagen was stunned. She knew his name. He hadn't thought she even knew he existed. "Uh, has there been any news about Sergeant Hatfield's party and when they will be returning from Suhl?"

Katharina leaned across the desk and lowered her voice. "One of the radio operators told me that a message came in from Lieutenant Ivarsson. He and Herr Hatfield left Suhl two days ago. Where they are going and if they are coming here, she didn't know. I asked. I knew you wanted to know. After all, you've asked every day for the past week."

"*Danke*, Private Stuetzing."

"Hagen, you can call me Katharina."

Hearing her tell him to use her first name made Hagen blush even harder. He was barely able to say "*Danke*, Katharina," before he turned and walked into the closed door, giving his nose a rather nasty bump.

"Are you all right?" Katharina started to get up from behind the desk.

"I am fine." Hagen finally found the door knob. "I have to run more errands for Herr Frank." Hagen blushed even harder when he heard her laughter through the closed office door. *Why? I am a trained soldier. I am ready to face men in battle. Why do I blush and lose my wits when I talk to a girl?* Hagen straightened his shoulders and stood erect. *A soldier should always walk proud.*

Walking to the tram stop he thought about the changes he had seen in the short time he had been in Grantville. Even the tramway was new. The city had taken over the right-of-way cleared by the rail company and replaced the light portable track with permanent track. Now horse-drawn and motorized tram-cars provided transportation into town from the outlying areas. When the car stopped, he pointed to the train crew patch on his shoulder to indicate he was on military business and should be allowed to ride free.

The driver waved Hagen to a seat as the car started to move. Looking up Hagen could see the notice painted on the front of the car over the driver's head. "Tramcar #4, Built by the 141st Rail Company" below the neatly printed notice was piece of paper with the names of the crew who had built it. Hagen was proud to see his own name at the bottom of the list. This was one of the last tramcars the old crew had built before the orders came sending them to Magdeburg.

Just as the tram was leaving town, Hagen's attention was caught by a sign beside the tracks:

Elizabeth's Railway,
Built by the 141st Railway Company, NUS Army.
We Build Them Anywhere—*Wir bauen sie überall*

The day they had put up that sign, General Jackson had just activated the company. The up-time sergeants, Hatfield, Plotz and Torbert, had insisted they needed to commemorate the occasion. First Sergeant Plotz had picked Hagen to break a bottle of beer on the tracks to mark the launching of the then new company. Hagen wanted to rejoin the company more than anything else in his life.

He was pulled out of his thoughts by the tram coming to a stop near the training camp for the Committee of Correspondence-raised regiment. The regiment was gone now, off to war along with the rail company, but apparently the camp was still being used. Hagen saw three people waiting for the tram. At first he thought they were soldiers, from their tie-dyed camouflage coats and rifles, but then he recognized Wendel and Gerd, Private Schultz's sons, and their cousin, Susanna Eckhardt. All three were in the Junior ROTC.

"Allo Wendel, allo Gerd, allo Suse," Hagen called. Then he had to return their salutes as they all saluted him. "Why are you saluting me? I am a private, no one salutes privates."

"We salute privates," Gerd answered. "We salute everyone in uniform."

"*Ja*," his older brother added. "*Onkel* Henry just finished a lesson in military courtesy, when we are in our ROTC uniforms we are to salute everyone in the military. Army, Navy, Air Force or Marines, it doesn't matter."

"Oh, I see." In the back of his mind, Hagen was pleased. This was the first time he had been saluted. "Why the rifles? Is the ROTC doing guard duty now?"

"*Nein*, though we could. We had target practice on the rifle range in the training camp. " Suse sat down next to Hagen. "Want to see our targets?"

"She just wants to show off." Wendel seated himself on Hagen's other side. "Suse, Hagen knows you are the best shot in the family. *Onkel* Henry tells everyone."

Gerd sat down on the facing seat. "Not just in the family, but the best shot in the whole ROTC, though if we traded rifles I can come close to matching her."

Gerd's comment caused Hagen to look at Suse's rifle. Where both of the boys were carrying large bore muzzle loaders, Suse's rifle had a bore smaller than his little finger. It made sense. Wendel and Gerd both took after their father and were stocky with wide shoulders. Suse, while she was not a small girl, wasn't close to their size.

"Hagen," Suse asked, "when are you going to start going to

school? I know *Onkel* Henry could have you made an assistant instructor for the Junior ROTC and you would still be in the army."

"Where did you hear I was going to go to school? I have been trying to get back to the train crew. Why would I want to go to school?"

"I heard *Onkel* Henry talking to *Onkel* Anse and *Onkel* Wili before they left for Suhl. They said Major Beth was going to offer you the chance to go to school here in Grantville."

It all became clear to Hagen. *Onkel* Henry was Henry Johnson, the instructor for the Junior ROTC program. *Onkel* Anse was Warrant Officer Hatfield and *Onkel* Wili was Private Schultz, Wendel and Gerd's father. Major Beth had to be Major Elizabeth Pitre, the commander of the 141st Rail Company. Major Pitre had offered to send him to school but he had turned her down, thinking he would be allowed to go with the company.

"I don't need to go to school. I know all a soldier needs to know already," Hagen answered.

"Oh, come on. There is always something new to learn," Wendel commented. "Besides, if you went to school you could finish up in two years with me and we could both go to OCS. Wouldn't it be better to be officers instead of privates?"

"Not me," Gerd interjected. "I am going to study mechanics and become a warrant officer like *Onkel* Anse."

"Hush, Gerd." Suse frowned at him. "We're talking about Hagen's future, not yours. Besides warrant officers are all people who know how to do something. You'll have to study a lot harder than you do now to become one." She turned to look at Hagen. "And you do need to finish school. There is a lot more than being a soldier. The war will not last forever. What will you do when it is over?"

"I am going to become an engine driver," Hagen asserted. "After the war is over I will work for the railroads they are building, and drive an engine hauling people and cargo. Besides your *Onkel* Henry says it is going to be a long war. I want to rejoin the train crew to help make it shorter."

"Well, we can talk about it later. Here is our stop." Suse signaled the driver to stop the tram.

"Where are you going?" Wendel asked when Hagen rose to join them.

"I am on my way to see your mother. I am supposed to pick up the coveralls she made."

The two Schultz boys walked on ahead toward the house, but Suse walked beside Hagen. "I hope you are not mad because I think you should go to school. But you should think about it."

"I am not mad, Suse. You're saying what you think. I just don't agree with you."

"Hello, Hagen. Are you getting enough to eat? You look skinnier every time I see you." Dora Schultz looked Hagen up and down. It reminded him of the way a mother would look at her child.

"*Ja*, Frau Schultz. I have been eating at the Thuringen Gardens."

"Bah, you should have come out here to eat and saved your money. With Wili and Anse gone, we have room at the table."

"*Ja*, you should stay for dinner," Suse said.

"*Danke*, Frau Schultz, Suse, but I have to take those coveralls back to the train shop before I can take time off."

"Tomorrow, then," Dora said in a tone that allowed no excuses. "Wili and Anse will be back tonight and we will have a big dinner tomorrow. Now come with me and I'll get the sample coveralls for you."

Hagen followed her toward the back of the house. "Frau Schultz, you said Private Schultz and Herr Hatfield would be home tonight. Are you sure?"

"*Ja*, Lieutenant Ivarsson came by to tell me just before you got here. They will be here sometime before nightfall."

Hagen felt a burst of hope. With a new engine that had to be delivered and Herr Hatfield coming back to Grantville tonight there was a good chance he could rejoin the train crew. Herr Hatfield was going to need help with the engine. "Are you sure it will be no problem if I come to dinner tomorrow? It sounds like you'll have a house full."

Dora turned to face him. "Hagen, with seven *Kinder* in the house, we always have a full house. Ursula and I like to cook and we like to see people eat what we cook. You will come to dinner and you will eat. Besides, he doesn't know it yet but Wili is now a corporal; the letter came today. So we will be celebrating. As the wife of a corporal, I order you to come to dinner."

"Yes, ma'am, Frau Corporal Schultz." Hagen smiled as he came to attention.

"Ach, you are teasing. Here are the samples for you to take to Herr Frank. Run fast and you can catch the tramcar on its return trip to town."

Hagen only took time for a quick wave to the Schultz boys and Suse before he headed for the tram tracks. The tram car was just visible as it made its way back to town. He had missed it. It was supposed to wait for ten minutes after going around the loop at the end of the line. And the driver was also supposed to top up the natural gas in the tram's fuel tank at the large tank there before heading back. That should have taken another ten minutes. *Surely I wasn't in the house that long.* Hagen started to trot back to town.

He had only taken a few steps when he heard a voice from behind. "Look, Anse, Wili. '*Der Bub*' came out to meet us. But looks like he got bored and is going home."

Hagen stopped and turned around. Herr Hatfield, Corporal Rau, and Private Schultz were halfway down the slope that marked the edge of the Ring of Fire. Schultz and Hatfield were riding in a wagon and Rau was riding a horse just in front of them. Hagen felt his hopes rise. Here was his chance to return to the train crew, if he could just make them listen to him.

"Hello, Herr Hatfield, Corporal Rau," Hagen called. "And a special hello to *Corporal* Schultz. I just heard the news from your wife."

Hatfield slapped Schultz on the back. "There you go, Wili, you're a corporal. I bet Dora already has the stripes sewn on your coveralls."

The door of the house flew open and the entire Schultz family erupted from the house. Dora was in the lead, followed closely by the two Schultz daughters, Talle and Esther. Only politeness kept Gerd and Wendel from pushing their way to the front, but they were close behind.

Watching the reunion of the Schultz family, Hagen was happy for his friends, but was very aware that he was the odd man out. He was an only child and his mother and father had died in Badenberg, when it had been held by Hoffmann's mercenaries.

Rau dismounted and stepped up beside him. "Hagen, walk with me to take this horse over to the shed. We're just in the way here."

"I should be going back to the train shop. I was not really waiting on you. I was supposed to take these to Herr Frank." Hagen held up the package he carried.

"I'm glad to see Bill Frank has got you hard at work." Hatfield stepped up to them. "We're going to take the wagon in and unload it at the shop. So drop your package in the back and come on up to the house. We'll ride into town and you can help unload the toys we bought for the company. Wili can stay here with the family."

Hagen saluted and went to put his package in the wagon. He knew that when Hatfield said "toys" he had to mean weapons. Sure enough, the back of the wagon held a number of long bundles that had to be rifles or smoothbores. Seeing them piled in the wagon gave the thought of joining the rail company a new meaning. There was a good chance his friends would be fighting a war soon. Hagen became even more determined not to be left behind.

Hagen started to get in the back, but Hatfield waved him to the seat. "Come up here. I want you to drive. We've been taking turns pushing these nags the whole way from Suhl and I, for one, am tired of horses."

"*Ja*, let *der Bub* drive." Rau jumped up to sit on the tailgate.

Hatfield settled onto the seat. "Okay, Hagen. Now is as good a time as any for you to tell me what has been going on while we were away."

Hagen started to tell about the orders coming for the rail company to deploy to Magdeburg and then to Wismar. But Hatfield interrupted, "Skip that. We got a radio message from the major while we were in Suhl. What I want to know is what has happened since the company left."

So Hagen told him about the new engine and the two flat cars that the shop crew had ready to go. And about the delivery problem that Herr Frank foresaw developing.

Hatfield shook his head. "Delivery is no problem. We'll load them on a couple of flatcars and haul them to a barge. The barge will carry us to Magdeburg. They're the major's problem from there. What I really want to hear is what you have been doing. I know Major Pitre was going to talk to you about going to school. So why is Private Hagen Filss not following his major's wishes and going to school?"

"Uh, er, H-h-herr Hatfield, it was not an order. The major asked me if I wanted to go to school. When I said no, she said it was all right. I would not have disobeyed an order."

"You're lawyering me, son. You knew she wanted you to go to school. Would you have been willing if you knew I was the one who asked her to leave you behind to go to school? I might make it an order and if I do, you will go to school and you will work hard."

Hagen was stunned. He had thought that Herr Hatfield would be the one to save him from being left behind. His shoulders slumped, and he worked to hold back a sigh of disappointment.

"Sir, is that what you are going to do? Are you going to order me to go to school?"

"I don't know. Right now I think that it would be the best thing for you. Not just the best for you, but the best for TacRail. We need trained men, men who can become mechanics. You did a good job working with Jim Cooper, and now you have experience working for Bill Frank, so you seem to be the one to pick. After all, you'll be taking mostly classes in mechanics."

"All I did was hand Jim his tools, and all Herr Frank has me doing is running errands. Anyone could do what I do."

Hatfield reached over and took Hagen's sleeve between his fingers. "You're still wearing a rail crew patch. The rail crew needs trained mechanics. What am I going to do about you? If you go to school, I promise there will be a spot open for you with the company when you finish. Maybe with a nice promotion. How does that sound?"

"I am happy being a private. I feel like I am letting my friends down. I should be with them, not here safe in Grantville." Hagen tried very hard not to beg or sound like a child.

Hagen brought the wagon to a stop and Hatfield hopped down and went inside the building. He felt Rau moving up to stand behind him. "It's a hard road isn't it, young Filss? You have been getting a man's portion and now you think you are being asked to go back to being a child."

"*Ja*, but more than that. What if my friends need me? I should be doing something."

"And you feel that you might miss the great adventure of your life." Rau laughed. "I know, *Bub*. Remember I went for a soldier when I was about your age. Of course, the city fathers of Jena and the night watch helped make my choice for me." Rau patted Hagen's shoulder. "I'll talk to him; maybe I can convince Anse you should go."

"Thank you, Sergeant Rau."

"For that I will be at my most persuasive. I like the sound of Sergeant Rau. It looks like there are going to be three train crews, now that we have three engines. If I get a crew, I'll ask for you as a loader or brakeman."

"Thank you again, Sergeant."

"It is nothing. All you need is a little seasoning. Now head up, act proud, look like a soldier. Here comes Anse."

With all the men working it didn't take long to empty the wagon and fill the store room. When they were done Herr Frank locked the door and handed the key to Hatfield. "There you go. Don't lose that. If you do, we'll have to break the door down. That's the only key."

Hatfield stuck the key on the chain of his pocket watch. "Safe as a bank, I have never lost a key. Bill, why don't you and your wife come by the house tomorrow? Dora is having a special dinner to celebrate Wili's promotion to corporal."

"Sorry, but I'll have to turn you down. Our church is having a business meeting after services, and I have to attend since I'm on the trustees."

"Well, some other time, then." Hatfield pointed his finger at Hagen. "You will come to the dinner, Private Filss. Dora gave me special orders to make sure you were coming."

"Yes sir, Chief Hatfield." Hagen came to attention.

Hatfield wet his finger and drew an imaginary line in the air, "One point for remembering to call me chief." Then he turned and walked out of the shop.

"Filss, it's still two hours until quitting time. So get out of here. I gave you the day off." Herr Frank pointed at the door.

As Hagen was leaving the church the next morning, he was surprised to realize he had no idea what the sermon had been about. He had spent the entire service lost in thought over how he was going to convince Herr Hatfield not to send him to school. Sergeant Rau was his only hope.

As if thinking about him had conjured him, Hagen saw Rau waiting at the tram stop. Unlike Hagen, Rau was dressed in civilian clothing, rather a mixed style with blue jeans tucked into knee high boots of local manufacture. He had topped off his outfit with a long green coat, worn open to show the lace of his shirt collar that covered the top of his red vest.

Rau waved. "Ah, you make your appearance. Dora Schultz will not have to send us to hunt for *der Bub*. But you don't have to wear your uniform. This is just a dinner with friends, not an inspection."

Hagen thought about making an excuse, but decided that Rau would understand. "Sergeant, all I have to wear to dinner is my coveralls. All my clothing from before I joined the army is worn out."

"Not to worry, young Filss. Come on, here comes the tram."

Dinner at the Johnson house was interesting. With the four Schultz children, the three Eckhardt children and the four adults left in the household it was already a full table. Adding Hagen and Rau as guests made even the large Johnson dining room feel small.

After dinner Hagen sat for a while and talked with the Schultz and Eckhardt children. Then, getting bored with watching Henry Johnson's efforts to teach Gerd how to play chess, Hagen started to wonder where the railroaders had gone. He wandered into the kitchen where Suse, her mother Ursula, and Dora were just finishing the clean up.

"Hungry again, already? There is some chicken left and a little pie," Dora said.

"*Nein, Danke.* I could not eat another bite. I was just looking for Chief Hatfield."

Dora pointed out the back window of the kitchen. "He took Wili and Jochen Rau out to the garage. They are talking railroad business."

Hagen headed for the door. As he approached the open garage door he could hear the three men talking inside. What had to be the voice of Chief Hatfield said, "Okay, I don't know for sure what the major has planned, but if we bring her a complete crew to go with the new engine I bet she will keep it together."

"*Ja*," Hagen heard Sergeant Rau answer. "You will have an

engine, Toeffel will have an engine and who will command the new one?"

"Shoot, Jochen," Hatfield answered, "she just made you a sergeant. Who do you think Major Beth will give the engine to?"

"*Ja*, Jochen, *und* I will pick from the best brakemen in the company to get you a chief brakeman," Wili rumbled.

Hagen was about to walk away. He didn't want to be accused of eavesdropping. But then he heard his name mentioned.

"I want Filss for one of my brakemen," Sergeant Rau said. "You know he is going to volunteer."

"Jochen, do you really want him? He's awful young," Hatfield answered.

"He was old enough for you to have Wili train him to be a brakeman."

"Yes, but . . ."

"*Und* he is a good brakeman, for someone his size," Wili interrupted. "If Jochen is going to have a lot of recruits he is going to need a trained man. I say take him with us."

"I still think he's too young. Would you say the same thing if he was one of your sons? Would you take Wendel?" Hatfield asked.

"*Ja*. I would watch over him, but Wendel I would let go to war if he was as trained as Filss."

"Anse, I was younger when I became a soldier," Rau added. "And I would bet Wili was even younger when he joined his village militia."

"*Ja*, fourteen. I was big as a boy," Schultz said.

There was a long pause and Hagen thought that was the end of the conversation. Then Hatfield spoke again. "Okay. I'll talk to Filss. But if he goes, I want him to stay with you. Wili, I'll want you to take good care of him."

Hagen started to back away from the door. There was a chance he might be allowed to join the company! He stumbled over the wood that was piled under the eaves of the garage. The noise caused Chief Hatfield to call from inside. "Who's there?"

"It is me, Chief."

"Come on in, Filss. We were just talking about you."

When Hagen entered the garage he discovered that the three were seated on stools around a stove. Each had a bottle of Herr Johnson's home brewed beer, and a small cooler was set nearby that had to contain more.

"Pull up a stool, Hagen. Grab a beer if you like. I want to talk to you," Hatfield said.

Hagen realized this was going to be like juggling one of the grenades Sergeant Rau was so fond of. If he said the wrong thing, Hatfield would order him stay and to go to school. "Chief Hatfield, I don't drink very much beer. I had two glasses at dinner. That's enough for me."

"Probably a wise choice. Hank's brew is not your usual small beer." Hatfield took a sip. "How long were you outside before I heard you?"

Hagen knew only total honesty would work. If he was caught lying, who knew what Hatfield would do to him? "Sir, I was there long enough to know the three of you were talking about me and if I was going with you to Magdeburg. I was not spying, but when I heard my name I had to listen."

Hatfield spoke to the other two men. "Guys, I want to talk to Filss in private. Do you mind stepping up to the house to give us some room? I think we've covered all the bases and we'll be ready to start work tomorrow." Wili and Jochen both made noises of consent and left the garage.

Hatfield turned to face Hagen. "Okay, Filss. I want you to answer a couple of questions and then I'm going to decide if you go with us or go to school. If you're not happy with my decision, I'll cut you loose and you can enlist in one of the regiments the CoC is raising."

Hagen got a lump in his throat at the thought of leaving TacRail. "*Nein*, Chief, I don't want to leave the railroad company. If I must go to school to stay, I will go to school. I am a rail trooper."

"Filss, why are you so set on going with us? It's going to be a long war. Why is it so important to you to get into it right now?"

Hagen sat and thought. Then he gave an almost honest answer. "Chief Hatfield, I want to do my part. My friends are all going to be in danger. I would feel like a coward, like I was letting them down if I was not with them."

Hatfield looked at him for a moment then asked, "Hagen, you lost your family when Hoffmann was in Badenburg didn't you? You know how war can be? Do you want to go to war because of that?"

"Not to get revenge or anything like that, but to prevent it from happening again. So yes, what happened to my family is one reason I joined the rail company to start with. Mostly, though, it is just wanting to help my friends. To do what I should be doing."

Hatfield leaned back against the workbench. "Son, if I sent you to school you would still be helping, maybe more than if I make you a brakeman right now. In a couple of years you'd be more valuable to TacRail than as a brakeman. You'd still be doing your part. Hagen, I wanted to send you to school to help you."

Hagen studied his boots for a moment. "Chief Hatfield, if you send me to school I will work hard, but I am not sure I would ever become a mechanic. But I am a brakeman now. Corporal Schultz has taught me a lot and I'll do a good job."

"Hagen, tell me the truth. How old are you really? I know you and Jim Cooper lied about your age when you joined up last year. I went along with it and I shouldn't have, but I felt sorry for you. And to be perfectly honest I needed an extra pair of hands. The major jumped me about you a couple of times, and I told her you were small for your age."

"I was seventeen last month. I was fifteen when I joined."

Hatfield stood up and walked around the garage. "Hagen, seventeen is too young to be thrown into what we might face. But if I leave you behind I'll feel like I am punishing you. If I take you will you promise to stay close to Wili or Jochen?"

"*Ja*. And I will do everything they say." Hagen could feel hope building inside him. *Please let it happen, he prayed silently. Please.*

Hatfield took another walk around the room. "Okay. Report to the shop Monday morning; you're going with us, so you might as well help plan the move. The major is going to skin my butt when she sees you, but I'm not leaving you behind." With that, Hatfield walked out the door and headed for the house.

Hagen watched him go. Then, in a voice only he could hear, he said, "Thank you, *Onkel* Anse. The rail company is my family. You, Wili, and Jochen are my *Onkels*. Jim Cooper is my brother. Thank you for letting me go with my family."

A Taste of Home

Chris Racciato

It was raining. Daphne Pridmore was getting thoroughly sick of the rain. It meant that she had to stay inside for the most part. Going out to check on the hives was pointless. If they could use the truck, it might be worthwhile, but they'd decided to save the wear and tear on their only truck for emergencies. As much as she hated to admit it, cabin fever wasn't a real emergency. If she really wanted to go out, it would mean getting the horses hitched to the wagon. And driving the team in the rain. And dealing with very agitated bees, who would be less than amused at the stupid human who wanted to bother them when they were all snug in their hives. Even the bees knew when to stay inside.

Noises occasionally filtered up from the basement. Ikey, her husband, was no doubt puttering down there with one of his many projects. Everybody else was gone for the day. The kids were at school, both hers and those of the families living with them. If the rain didn't let up between now and the time they got out of school, the kids would end up going to her brother-in-law's house for the night. She missed having Zeke and Evie living with them, but it was nice to have a place closer to town for the kids to stop in at. Several of their down-time boarders were out on a route collecting honey in the caravan and wouldn't be back for a few more days. The caravans had been built with exactly this kind of situation in mind. The large wagons held all the comforts of home and enough supplies for a couple of weeks.

The seventeenth-century version of an RV. She listened to the rumbling thunder and hoped they were all okay.

She wandered around the house looking for something to do. Eventually she ended up in one of the smaller upstairs bedrooms. At one time it had been Ikey's grandmother's sewing room. Now it was the repository for all of the oddball projects that they had worked on over the years. There were scraps of leather in various states of being tooled or made into different items. Boxes of fabric were bulging out of the closet, often spilling their multihued contents over the ones below. A lone spinning wheel sat abandoned in the corner, covered with dust and strewn with pairs of hand-dipped candles. In short, it looked like a craft store had been caught in a tornado and then had all of its contents dumped in the tiny room. Daphne spotted one of their project books peeking out from under a macramé plant hanger. She picked it up and thumbed through it. It listed all of the things on their "To Do" list, month by month. This one was from a year before the Ring of Fire. She smiled as she read it to herself. So much had changed.

1. Clean fireplace
2. Clean out car
3. Finish spring quilt
4. Go shopping for groceries
5. Drop Mariah with Grandma Mamie and have movie night . . .

The more she read, the more homesick she became. Here was her life, written down on paper. The week by week retelling of what had been an ordinary life in a small town. She thumbed a few pages ahead. It was the same. Some of the items were different, but there was so much that they couldn't do now. Tears welled up in her eyes as she went through page after page of what they had considered important enough to write down at the time. So much of it was meaningless to her daily life now. How could she worry about getting oil for her car when there was no gas to run it? Or go to a Renaissance Faire, when they were living in a time that was scant decades from when Shakespeare wrote his plays? The tears started rolling down her cheeks as she went through May, June, July . . .

A small note in the end of July caught her attention. It was scrawled in Ikey's handwriting "Check on peppers, add salt if needed." It took her a moment to figure out what he was writing about. Then it hit her. That was the summer they had grown so many peppers that they didn't know what to do with them all. They had found an article talking about Tabasco sauce, and decided that it would be fun to try. They had filled up one of Ikey's wooden five gallon barrels with the pepper and salt mixture. Then they had put it away to ferment. It was right before Ikey's dad had been in a car accident. Daphne quickly flipped through the remaining pages. There was no mention of them bottling the sauce. Nor could she remember ever finishing them. That meant they might still be around someplace, assuming that Ikey hadn't thrown them out.

It had been over a year since the last of their Tabasco had run out. Many of their other up-time spices were gone as well. There were many other things that they could get down-time. Herbs were the easiest, either from their garden, the local markets, or trading with another up-timer who was growing something they didn't already have. Even bay leaves and several kinds of ginger could be found if you knew where to look or who to ask. Salt was easy to find as well. And there were many new things that she would have never considered as spices, like juniper berries and rue. But when it came to adding heat and flavor to dishes, they were severely limited. Curry powder was unheard of. Black pepper could be found, at exorbitant prices. True, they had plenty of chili peppers, but every time she had used them when it was her turn to cook, the down-timers complained about the food being too hot. She put them on her own food, but for the most part they added more heat than flavor. The mere thought of Tabasco sauce was enough to make her mouth water. She tossed the book back on the corner of the table and headed for the basement. If the peppers were still around, Ikey would know where they were. He had barrels of stuff stashed all over the place from brewing and was notorious for not putting labels on anything, so the only way to track them down was to go find him. She wiped away the tears and hurried off. She was a woman on a mission. Her day was looking up.

Locating Ikey wasn't an overly difficult task. One simply had to go down the stairs and follow the sound of banging. That usually meant he was at his workbench tinkering with one of his gun projects from the store. This time was no different. He had his back to the door, and was prying on something with a large wrench. Daphne paused for a moment to consider the best way to approach him.

"Honey, dearest, snookums?" she asked sweetly.

"Uh-oh." He turned cautiously. "What am I going to be doing for you this time?"

"Oh, nothing major, dear. I just need you to help me find something."

"Uh huh," he said noncommittally. Daphne knew he was trying to figure out the best way to escape from the basement. Fortunately, she was between him and the stairs. And there was no way for him to make a dash for the storm doors without being incredibly obvious. There was no helping it, he was well and truly trapped. "Ummm . . . What do you need me to find?"

"Do you remember the barrel of peppers we were going to make hot sauce out of a few years ago?" When he nodded, she continued. "Do you have any idea where that might be?"

The relief on his face was almost comical. "No problem. It's up the hill at the old house. I think I put it in the basement next to some mead and cysers. Why?"

"We are completely out of Tabasco sauce. I figure I have time today, and it's probably ready by now. I wanted to finish it up. Could you go up and get it for me?"

"But it's still raining."

"I know, but the golf cart has a roof. And it won't take you that long, will it?" she asked innocently.

"Aww crap. I guess I'm running up to the old house, huh?"

"You don't have to, dear . . . I could do it by myself." She smiled. "If you don't feel up to it."

He rolled his eyes. "Yeah, like I'm going to fall for that one."

"How do I get myself into these situations?" Ikey said to himself as he drove up the hill through the pelting rain. True, the cart had a fabric roof. But when the rain was coming in almost horizontally, that didn't help much. The ancient golf cart worked its way up the muddy track that led to the small modular home at the top of the hill. It had been Ikey and Daphne's house, a gift from his family shortly after their wedding. It had a barn and a small corral for their livestock, now moved down the hill to his grandparents' farm. Weeds grew in the front yard, and the whole place had an abandoned air to it. One day soon they would have to come up here and clean all of their stuff out. There was no point in keeping it vacant. With as tight as housing was in Grantville, there were bound to be people willing to live there despite its relatively remote location. But that would be a project for a later day. Preferably one that was a bit drier. In the meantime, he had a job to do. He pushed the button on the garage door opener and pulled in out of the rain.

Finding the barrel he was looking for only took a few minutes. Getting it out of the stack was another matter entirely. It was buried under several years worth of brewing projects. Forty-five minutes later he had the barrel of peppers free and several dozen other barrels and demijohns sorted into several groups. The "Finished" stack was the largest, followed by the "Still Aging" stack, the "I-don't-know-what-it-is" stack, and finally the "Oh-my-god-I-think-it's-evolving" stack. He would definitely have to wander back up here soon to finish sorting it all out. And possibly come armed, judging by the looks of some of the murkier mystery containers. He loaded up the peppers and two other barrels, and locked up. No point in leaving that much alcohol lying around unattended. Or possibly unleashing some fermented creature loose on the unsuspecting countryside. There was a lull in the rain, so the trip back down the hill was both uneventful and drier. But only slightly.

Daphne smiled at her drenched, muddy husband. "I was beginning to think we needed to send out a rescue party."

"No, no, dear, I'm fine. I was just going through what's still up there. You'd be amazed. I brought down a few other things I thought we might enjoy," he said, while standing in the entryway dripping.

"Like what?"

"Oh, I don't know . . . I found that pear mead we made a few years back. And some mulling spices. I figured some hot spiced mead might help you warm up after you finished drying off."

Daphne looked at her husband quizzically. "Drying off? You're the only one who's soaked."

"Not for long!" He lunged at her. She squealed and tried to

jump out of his reach, to no avail. He caught her up in a bear hug. Shaking his head like a dog drying off, he sent water and mud flying everywhere. In a matter of moments, she was nearly as wet as he was.

"Brat!" She swatted him as she broke free. "Look at this." She spread her arms to display her now dampened clothing. "I just washed all of this, and you got mud everywhere. What am I supposed to do now?"

"I don't know." He grinned. "Take a hot shower?"

"Oh . . ." She paused for a moment. There was nobody else in the house for a change. "Race you!" And with that, she ran down the hall, stripping as she went. Ikey followed on her heels, shedding clothes almost as fast as she was.

Several hours later, they lay in front of the fireplace in their bedroom, sipping hot mead from mugs. Outside the wind howled and drove the rain against the windows.

"I have enough distilled vinegar to make a gallon or two. After that I'll have to hit one of the stores in town. Last time I was there I think I saw some stuff that should be pretty close. I'm not sure how concentrated it will be though."

"Well, honey." He rolled on his side to face her. "I guess we'll just have to play it by ear. We just have to get it in large batches and mix it to taste. I don't think people will care if it ain't exact. Close enough will work. And we will have to start aging more peppers if you plan on making more than a few gallons."

"That's a good thing. I have tons of them growing. I was expecting to sell a lot more of them, but I just couldn't get that many people here to eat them. We could probably get several bushels of them by the end of summer, and still have enough for seeds for next year. I could also make a batch with the habaneros and ornamental peppers."

"What? Why? I thought that chemical weapons had been banned from production."

Daphne calmly transferred her mug from one hand to the other and then proceeded to slap the back of his head. "Wuss. I'm sure we can find people who'd want it."

"Aside from the Inquisition, you mean?"

She didn't even bother to dignify that comment. "You know how it is. I like venison and pork as much as anybody, but the spices here leave a lot to be desired. And when some of these people get their hands on them, well, you remember the dinner party at the Metzgers' place?"

Ikey shuddered. How could he forget? One of their first business dinners outside of Grantville had been at the house of an affluent brewer in Badenburg. Just about everything served that night had been liberally doused in ground black pepper or nutmeg. Even the wine had pepper in it. They found out later that it was a way of displaying how wealthy the Metzgers were. Black pepper was expensive. So was nutmeg. Both of them had to be imported from Asia. Having lots of both to put in everything meant that you had cash to burn. It also meant one of the worst meals either of the Pridmores had ever been to.

"Okay, granted. We'll see if anybody wants it. I'll see if I can dig up some little bottles and labels. I think there are some glass blowers who set up around here recently. They might be interested in a small contract." He sipped some mead from his mug. "And one of the brewers will probably have the corks. Maybe I'll go ask Herr Metzger."

"Don't you want to wait and see how it tastes?"

"Nah, I gave up trying to second guess you and Evie about business stuff years ago. I got sick of eating my words again and again. Besides, I smelled the mash when I was opening it up to check on it. It was good enough to make me drool."

"How could you tell? You drool all over yourself all of the time. . . ." Daphne quickly rolled out of the way of a playful swat aimed at some of her more well-padded regions. The first one missed. The second one didn't. Things went down hill from there, resulting in several more hours of playful recreation.

A month and a half later the first batch was finished. The Germans sat around the breakfast table and watched in fascinated horror as Ikey and Daphne splashed the fiery red concoction all over their scrambled eggs.

"Ohhh . . ." Ikey moaned. "God, I missed that."

"Mmmm." Daphne rolled her eyes. "Even if we don't sell a single bottle, it was worth it."

"I don't think I want to sell any of this stuff. I don't want to run out again. And this took years to age."

"We have gallons of it, honey. We won't run out anytime soon.

We also don't have to age it that long. The only reason we did this time was because we forgot about it. We can start picking more peppers today. It's not fair to keep this all to ourselves. Let's rack some of it into the bottles and put it on the shelves down at the market."

"All right. But only because I already have the bottles and labels. If we run out though, you are getting a major I-told-you-so."

The local market agreed to carry the sauce. Since the Pridmores already had a contract for supplying honey and mead, it was no trouble to add another item to their display area. The debate as to whether or not it would sell was put to rest by the end of the first day. All fifty bottles were gone in just over an hour. People were calling the farm to find out when more would be ready. The next morning Ikey brought the rest of the bottles in and he barely made it through the front door of the store. The biggest buyer was one of the managers from the Thuringen Gardens. He bought forty bottles. And had he not brought two of his larger bouncers with him, it would have been unlikely that he could have gotten out of the store with all of them. Another big buyer was a woman in TacRail coveralls who was accompanied by a trio of men who made the bouncers look like friendly puppies. She said it was a surprise for a friend of theirs. They bought almost twenty bottles, and left the store with significantly fewer dirty looks than the Gardens' manager.

When Ikey went to settle accounts with Jim Garrett, the grocery store manager, he was surprised. His percentage worked out to nearly twice what he had expected. When he asked about it, Jim merely shrugged his shoulders and said, "I upped the price after yesterday. You said it would take you a few months to make another batch. After the comments I heard at the Gardens last night, I knew people would be willing to pay more for it." He grinned at Ikey. "It also didn't hurt when I mentioned that it would be awhile before you could make more to my wife. Rather loudly. In the restaurant."

"You doubled the price?!" Ikey blurted, aghast.

"Nah. But I did give you a bit more of a cut than we normally do. All of those extra people in the store waiting for you to get here bought a ton more stuff today. It was the biggest Wednesday sales we've had in a long time. Just keep me in mind the next time a batch is ready. If you can give me a few days of lead time, we'll have them lined up around the store by opening time in the morning."

"It's that hot of an item?"

"How many things do we have that remind us of home like that? Sure it's good stuff. But in case you didn't notice, nearly all of the people that bought it today were like you and me. Up-timers. Or they were getting it for up-timer friends. It reminds us of what we left behind. Where we came from. Something that nobody else on this continent would even think of making. It is something that is uniquely ours. By the time your next batch is ready, you'll have plenty of German customers, I'm sure. Especially now that they have it at the Gardens. But for now, it's for us."

"I knew Daphne and I missed it. I just didn't think of it that way. I figured we might get a few of the diehard fire eaters and chili fanatics. And maybe a few others." Ikey paused. "I guess it's just a taste of home."

N.C.I.S.: Young Love Lost

Jose J. Clavell

People sleep peaceably in their beds at night only because
rough men stand ready to do violence on their behalf.
—George Orwell

I rode to the crime scene in the early morning calm of Magdeburg's streets. It was not difficult to find. The area, surrounded by the flickering light of torches, oil storm lamps, and at least one up-time flashlight, was in one of the worst-looking parts of town, and in a city that has been subjected to sacking and burning, that says a lot. The flashlight—one of the very few still left with some battery power—was being used sparingly, but it gave me a good idea of my goal. That was very fortunate because this area was far from our usual security rounds haunts around the riverside navy yard. I dismounted and left the reins of my "horse pool" mount in the care of one of the Marine military policemen who formed the outer cordon of the scene.

Some members of the city watch leaned on their pikes nearby, observing us, talking and joking in low murmurs, apparently without a care in the world. Their common seventeenth-century finery looked—now, to me—too ornate, especially contrasted with the simple subdued style of the up-time uniforms, armbands and weapons of the MPs and navy masters-at-arms who were present. Their disrespectful attitude towards the dead also bothered me but showed clearly that whoever was inside the area was no longer their concern. That made it one less turf fight for me. The young military policeman, on the other hand, was having problems dealing with their carefree stance and his clenched jaw and stern face failed to hide his contempt. In situations like this one, relations between military personnel and civilians tend to fray rather quickly, which, apart from the late hour, explained the absence of curious bystanders.

I nodded to the MP and murmured my thanks, purposely ignoring the watchmen as I entered the cordoned-off area. I saw more MPs and masters-at-arms and sensed the air of contained fury that emanated from them. I braced myself for what was waiting. I could now see two bodies on the ground and, long before I got close enough to see them properly, I smelled the coppery odor of blood mixed with the pungent smell of feces and urine, the ultimate indignity of death. Finally, I came close enough to make out the full details. A woman in a modest civilian dress lay facedown across the body of a man; she looked vaguely familiar. I racked my brain trying to place her. The man was in the undress greens of an enlisted Marine, a private first class by the single red chevron on his sleeve, and a stranger to me. Both were barely in their twenties, just children really; a young couple out on an evening stroll, not unlike dozens of others, and who, now, would never grow old. The scene filled me with sadness at the unnecessary waste of young lives and anger at the unknown killers. The area around their bodies had been blocked off with staked cords. It had helped to keep it mostly undisturbed but it still didn't answer my first question of the night. What the hell were they doing out here, so far away from the yard?

The owner of the up-time flashlight joined me and stood quietly by my side as I pondered that and many other questions, taking in the scene. Brunhilde Spitzer is a few years younger than I am, a comrade and more, from our Committee of Correspondence days. Brunhilde was not really her given birth name either; once she had been a camp follower and prostitute before heeding the message of Gretchen Richter, changing her name and starting a new life. Like Gretchen, you don't stand in her way. Perhaps that explained why she adopted the name of one of the Valkyrie warriors of the old tales; I have never inquired. I knew firsthand the power of that message; it had also changed my life, although in my case I got to keep my old name. When Admiral Simpson asked me to join and later lead what would become the Naval Criminal Investigative Service, I, too, followed Gretchen Richter's message and, emboldened by the love of a good woman, accepted and embraced the opportunity for a fresh start away from the petty thievery of my old life.

"Special Agent Spitzer," I said finally.

"Director Schlosser, I am sorry that I had to call you all the way out here this early in the morning. But I want a second opinion. You did much better than me at the crime scene investigation classes and I could use your advice. The night watch commander told me that they are our people, so this is our mess, sir." She addressed me in a formal manner that still barely contained her anger. There were too many non-NCIS personnel within hearing range, so we could not speak candidly. It was for the best; our exact opinion of the city watch and their officers was not for outsiders. Besides, we needed to maintain the professionalism that Dan Frost had drilled into us, and set an example for the young MPs and MAAs present. So I simply nodded in understanding.

The crime scene belonged to us now; it was our first major murder case.

When Admiral Simpson had put his group of civilian agents together, our primary mission had been to provide for up-time and naval personnel security as bodyguards—in naval parlance, force protection. In the beginning, Committee of Correspondence members had provided that service to the navy, by orders of Joachim Thierbach, the local committee chairman and who was assisted by Gunther Achterhof, my mentor. Even then, it was under my direction; that position had first brought me to Simpson's attention. You could say that the good admiral had a personal interest in the subject, since French agents had tried to kill him shortly after his arrival in Magdeburg. In the maelstrom of the political scene of our newly formed nation, the United States of Europe, the navy could not afford to be associated too closely with one of the political factions. So the CoC was out and Simpson had approached me with a job offer. It had seemed simple enough: do the same thing for him that I had done for the committee, but now for pay. That was an offer that I could hardly refuse. Revolutionary fervor can go only so far in providing sustenance to the body or a roof over one's head, especially now that I had other responsibilities.

Our scope of responsibility continued to expand, in what I now knew to call mission creep. There was money to be made out of the business generated by the needs of a burgeoning navy and Marine Corps and the works of the shipyard, lots of it. Some parties were none too scrupulous in its acquisition. The local authorities were uncooperative at times and some were outright on the take. That was not news to me; I had similar experiences in my CoC days, but it caught Admiral Simpson by surprise, and he told me to take care of it. So, we found ourselves dealing with corruption, fraud, shoddy materials, and theft.

Naturally, a case could be made that putting me and mine in charge of those investigations had been akin to letting the fox guard the henhouse. After all, most of our agents had lived very interesting lives before joining, and not always on the right side of the law. I prefer to think that we possessed hard-won expertise on the subject matter that makes us very difficult to fool. Owing our loyalty to the navy that had given us a second chance; we could not be easily bought, either. It showed in the success of our efforts. I have to confess that there is some truth to the rumors that a visit from me or mine could ruin your whole day. The admiral had once commented that our idea of law enforcement would have given apoplexy to any up-time cop. I reminded him that he was no longer living there; besides, our growing notoriety meant that no one now dared to cut corners on materials or services bought by either the navy or the Corps.

Despite the best efforts of pastors, priests, and rabbis, the men and women who had suddenly found themselves as new citizens of the USE had not suddenly metamorphosed into angels, either. The naval services had gotten their fair share of bad apples. We were tasked with cleaning them out. By this time, recognizing that we were now far from the bodyguards that he had originally envisioned, and needing a permanent solution, Admiral Simpson had bowed to the inevitable and created NCIS with our original men at its core. I mean, *re*created NCIS. His twentieth-century navy had a similar outfit, almost certainly for much the same reasons. Now officially the naval law enforcement organization, our mandate put us in charge of the entire navy- and Marine Corps-related criminal matters and, to prevent jurisdiction conflicts, also contained an imperial warrant from his majesty, Gustav Adolph II, that extended our reach through the whole USE and its territories.

The admiral had also taken steps to standardize and improve our training to keep us on par with the rest of the new technologically savvy naval service that he was busily building. He had hired the former chief of the Grantville Police, Dan Frost, to advise and orient us in the acquisition of those skills that the job now required. Chief Frost must have found it amusing to work with men that he would have once thrown into the slammer without a second thought. I know we did. He trained us and we then trained the military police and masters-at-arms, establishing the pecking order for naval law enforcement. It was during this period that "Brunhilde" joined us.

Of course, I was initially strongly opposed. Bodyguard work demanded big and muscled men. You either deter an attack with your sole presence or need to be able to fend it off on your principal's behalf. No women needed apply, I thought—sentiments that even my early exposure to Gretchen and her CoC ideals were unable to override. Once more, Simpson reminded me that we were no longer exclusively in that line of business, and then ordered me to hire her. She didn't remain our only female recruit for long. Since that time, I have very reluctantly come around to his point of view. Working for him and the navy, I was exposed to many women in nontraditional roles. Now, I know that they can be as capable, brave, dedicated, and, on several occasions with female miscreants, as malicious as any man. However, it was the internalization of Chief Frost's teachings that forced me to finally turn the corner on my beliefs. I learned that women could be invaluable on police investigative and undercover work, especially when the society in which they operated tended to make them invisible. That had also given me insight into how the up-timers see us. It was not a flattering portrait.

Brunhilde had taken to this line of work with an ability that was frightening in its single-mindedness. I suspect that her prior occupation and her life experiences had prepared her well for it. Regardless of my feelings, and despite our preexisting relationship, she progressed quickly through the ranks through sheer competence. In Frost's seminar on crime scene investigation, she had come in a very close second in class standing. I was first. Like me, she had discovered within herself an unexpected ability to solve criminal riddles and I was proud of her. She had been the senior agent of the criminal division on watch when she sent for me tonight, getting me out of my lonely but warm bed.

I stooped to get a different view of the bodies. Apart from the senselessness of it all, death did not bother me. I had seen too much of it already, and even inflicted it on others.

The girl's face once more caught my attention with its familiarity. I felt Brunhilde beside me, opening her always-present notepad, and waited for the mystery of her identity to be solved. "Herr Director, the female is Seaman Apprentice Wilhelmina Bischel. She was . . . assigned to the health clinic."

I heard the sudden grief-stricken catch in her voice as it hit me like a punch in the belly. We both knew her as Willie, a friendly girl with a sunny disposition and constant smile that allowed her to deal with all sorts of difficult people, like an embarrassed and suffering NCIS Director, whose worried wife had forced him to seek care for a recurring ailment. I closed my eyes and muttered a short prayer for her soul. I felt ashamed for not recognizing her. The last time I had seen her, she had been full of life and happiness; her friends at the clinic had been teasing her mercilessly about her new beau. It had sounded serious and I had been happy for her.

"The male is Private First Class Wilhelm Hafner. He was a rifleman with Second Platoon, Bravo Company, First Battalion."

I nodded and assumed that he was the beau in question. I stood and walked around them before stooping again. This investigation had suddenly become very personal to me.

Chief Frost had started his seminar by giving us a lecture on all the technology that was no longer available to him and that now waited to be rediscovered again. It had been sobering. He had concluded by declaring that, despite these losses, the most important pieces of equipment had come through without any problem and were easily available to each of us: the brain, ears, and eyes of a trained investigator. The rest of the course had concentrated on helping us hone those innate abilities. Still, at moments like this, I would give my hoped-for first-born to have photographic equipment available. I had heard of some research in that direction, but I was not holding my breath. Maybe I could try to hire a sketch artist like they had done in Grantville. I have to look into that. I stood up again, deep in thought, and looked at Brunhilde. I knew that she had already formed an opinion, but appreciated the way she was letting me make up my own mind. "Who put the cord around them? It seems that someone was paying attention when we gave the class to the MPs and MAAs about preserving scenes."

Brunhilde usually has a well-developed sense of humor that I enjoy deeply but tonight she was all business. "Petty Officer Leiss and his partner, Private First Class Schuhmacher, were first on the scene, sir." She indicated the two individuals who held their horses in the shadows.

I walked towards them and Brunhilde followed. Leiss was in his late thirties, a riverboat man by the look of him. He was composed but wary. His partner, Schuhmacher, seemed younger than the deceased. Her face, even in the darkness, looked extremely pale although it also had a mixture of anger and grief. I pegged her for a farm girl with little experience with violent human death until tonight, and having chosen military law enforcement as her career, obviously made of sterner stuff than her appearance indicated. I gave her credit for that. Sadly as both a Marine and an MP, this would not be her last confrontation with the aftermath of violence. "Leiss, Special Agent Spitzer tells me that you and your partner were the first on the scene. I appreciate the care that you took with it. Can you tell me anything else?"

"Not much, Herr Director. Me and Schuhmacher were returning back to our rounds, after we made a stop at my home. My wife is expecting our third child and I like to check on her during my shift. It had been cleared with my tour commander. When we heard the whistles of the city watch, we responded with the intention of providing backup. But when we arrived, the watchmen immediately handed primary control of the scene to us and backed off. It surprised the hell out of me, sir. That is, until I saw his uniform and Schuhmacher identified the young woman as navy personnel. We cordoned off the area and sent out for backup and NCIS support."

"You did very well, Leiss. I'll see to it that you two are commended for your quick thinking. " I made a mental note to keep an eye on the man. We were always on the lookout for more qualified personnel to join our ranks. I looked at his partner. "Schuhmacher, I am presuming that you knew Seaman Bischel."

The woman came to attention. Grief stricken or not, she was still a Marine. "Yes, sir. We both were billeted at Frau Muir's guesthouse. She lives on the same floor, two doors from me, but we seldom talked. Different shifts, you know. I knew that she was seeing Hafner; heck, the whole house knew it. She was head over heels in love. The scuttlebutt was that they were planning to marry as soon as he made corporal, sir."

I nodded. Her information dovetailed well with the little that I knew about Bischel. Still, she had been in contact longer with the deceased. I decided to follow my instincts. "Stand at ease, Marine. Did she ever mention anything to you about having enemies or problems with other men?"

She frowned. "Herr Director, the only thing that I can recall is that one of the girls once mentioned to me in passing that one of her cousins was not happy about her joining the navy or seeing Hafner. She and Hafner were from different religious backgrounds, but I thought that it sounded more like jealousy."

I considered her information for a moment. There was something there. Call it a hunch; according to Chief Frost, it was the other invaluable weapon in the experienced investigator's arsenal. "Thank you. Leiss, I would appreciate it if the two of you could stick around for a while."

"Aye, aye, sir," he said.

I returned to the bodies, a silent Brunhilde in tow. My attention was momentarily diverted by the arrival of more naval personnel from the yard. When I had been summoned to the scene, I had also sent out for others whose assistance could be useful in the investigation.

I turned back to Brunhilde and whispered, "Okay, Brunei, this is what I am thinking. This was not a robbery attempt gone wrong."

She looked down at the bodies. "No, it was not, Gunther. She still has her money belt, although I don't see any of their daggers. My gut feeling is telling me to look into that cousin."

My gut was telling me the same thing. "Agreed. By the footprints, I believe that there were multiple attackers, so he had accomplices. It looks like a well thought-out ambush."

Brunhilde looked carefully at the footprints by the light of her flashlight. "At least six, and the kids fought back. I don't believe that all this blood belongs to them."

It was a small consolation in the whole sordid affair that they had not gone meekly into the good night. I just wished that their efforts had been more successful or help closer.

I turned to greet the new arrivals. Senior Chief Hospital Corpsman David Dorrman, an up-timer, was the navy's most senior medical tech. He was accompanied by two litter teams. All of them now stood thunderstruck; they had no problem identifying Seaman Bischel. She had been both popular and well-loved in their ranks. The senior chief let loose a long streak of swearing, half of which was neither English nor German. I let him get it out of his system; I needed him with a clear head.

Finally, he turned toward me. "Director Schlosser, do you know who did this?"

I looked him straight in the eyes. "We have some ideas, but we would like you to examine the bodies and provide us with as much information as you can."

"Here, Director? I can't properly examine them with this little light." He put on his gloves.

"Sorry, but time is of the essence. My gut feeling is that the attackers didn't go too far."

He nodded and turned to his team. "Okay, folks. I need some help here. Help me get Willie on the litter." Carefully, almost with reverence, they picked up Bischel's body and placed her atop the waiting stretcher. Her face looked placid but tear-streaked; her eyes were open. At his command, his corpsmen opened several ponchos and, without being told, turned around as they held them open around her. I was sure that if she could, Bischel would have been grateful for the high regard that they held for her modesty. I wished that I could do the same, but my duty required that I examine the evidence first-hand.

I watched as Dorrman used large scissors to cut away her upper garments, revealing one stab wound on her left side. Brunhilde pointed at the multiple stab wounds on her forearms. We exchanged a knowing look. Her death now seemed accidental, although she had been in the thick of the fight. Dorrman closed her eyes, covered her with a blanket and looked up at me with tears in his eyes. "She didn't die immediately, Director. I'm not a coroner or a physician but I suspect a pneumothorax. Even if I had gotten here in time, I doubt that I would have been able to do too much for her."

I nodded. By the position of the bodies, I surmised that she had had just enough time to drag herself to where her lover had fallen. Brunhilde wiped a single tear away with her hand, her face impassive. There would be time to mourn them later. We watched as Dorrman moved to Hafner's body and, with his corpsmen's assistance, moved him to the second waiting stretcher. In seconds, his upper body had been bared. Unlike Bischel, he had multiple knife wounds on his chest, abdomen and arms, making it likely that he would have bled to death even if you didn't take into account the fatal stab wound under his sternum. Dorrman looked up at me without comment. There was no need; the scenario was now clear in my mind. I exchanged a look with Brunhilde and saw agreement in her eyes.

I moved to the second group that I had summoned that night.

I had requested a squad of scout-snipers and was pleased but not completely surprised to see Gunnery Sergeant Hans Hoffman, the head of the scout-sniper school, at its head. If I hadn't been looking for them, I would have missed them completely in the darkness with their camouflage battle dress uniforms and that unnatural stillness that was the mark of the trained sniper. I had requested their assistance because most scout-snipers had prior backgrounds as game wardens and were adept at following trails and tracking wounded prey. Their eyes were on the two blanket-covered bodies and their faces seemed carved in granite.

"Gunny, we think that their killers were wounded in the attack and may not have gotten too far. Do you think that your men can attempt to pick up their trail?"

He looked once more at the bodies and then back at me. "We will try, Herr Director . . . we will try really hard," he said, before starting to issue his orders. The squad split into two-man teams and spread around the site in a circular search pattern, starting from the cordoned-off area. I knew that they were going to have to earn their pay tonight.

The area around the bodies and outside the corded area was muddled with footprints. I blamed our good friends from the city watch. Our agents, MPs and MAAs are trained to walk the same patches and not add confusion to crime scenes. The watchmen didn't have the benefits of future forensics knowledge and most didn't care to learn. We'd offered them training but they had been unwilling to accept lessons from people that they still considered thieves, thugs and prostitutes.

It was fifteen long minutes before one of the teams found a trail. Hafner and Bischel's bodies had been carried to the waiting ambulance and were now on the way back to the infirmary at the yard. Dorrman and all the male corpsmen had stayed behind and were now checking their personal weapons. Although navy, Fleet Marine Force corpsmen tend to reflect the same aggressive outlook of their usual companions.

The lucky team's bird call signaled their success. Immediately, Hoffman and the rest converged on them, examined the signs, and proceeded to follow the trail. I held everyone else back to give them space to maneuver until they were ahead of us by at least five hundred meters, then we followed. There was no thought of involving the city watch; for what we needed to do, they were practically worthless. We needed live perpetrators, not more dead bodies. Besides, it was a matter of naval honor.

We moved as silently as possible with frequent stops and starts for over half an hour before one of the scouts appeared at my side. Brunhilde, surprised, had to strangle a cry. I followed the scout back to where Hoffman waited. Our quarry seemed to be holed up in a dilapidated shack on the outskirts of Magdeburg.

"Herr Director, the trail ends there and we think that they are all inside. How do you want to do this?" he murmured in my ear. I looked at the house and then at the horizon, where the faint light of dawn had started to appear. If we delayed too long, darkness and the element of surprise would disappear. I decided that the rules of hot pursuit applied here and returned, trailed by Hoffman, to where the main group waited. I quickly sketched my plan on the ground and explained it to everyone, my voice pitched low.

The second wagon had brought weapons and Marine-issue breastplates and helmets. The scout-snipers quickly suited up. They were trained in ship-boarding maneuvers and that made them suitable to act as an improvised up-time-style special weapons and tactics team. Maybe it was overkill for a group of killers that had not shown too much enterprise in covering their tracks, but I was not in the mood to play fair. I donned a spare breastplate and helmet, intending to be part of the takedown, until I saw Brunhilde doing the same. I was momentarily flabbergasted but held my tongue.

She looked directly into my eyes, and I was able to easily read her determination. I could have ordered her to stay behind, and my instincts screamed at me to do so, but I could not do it. She has earned her place here. So, I shrugged my shoulders instead and made sure that my NCIS gold badge was pinned firmly to the front of my breastplate. Brunhilde did the same. At my signal, everyone moved into place. The military police and masters-at-arms, reinforced by Dorrman and his corpsmen, surrounded the house at a distance. I had Leiss and Schuhmacher keep a discreet eye on Dorrman; he was still extremely pissed off and I didn't want it to interfere with the matter at hand. I wanted the bastards alive.

The scout-sniper squad split in two; half went towards the back where they would attempt a rear entry. Brunhilde and I joined the group led by Hoffman with our handguns drawn. I made sure that Brunhilde was behind me, where they would have to go through me to get to her. We tiptoed toward the front entrance, using cover as much as possible, until we got to the door. The house seemed eerily quiet. I waited until Hoffman gave me the agreed "all ready" sign. I counted to three and then, with all the force in my lungs, shouted clearly for all to hear.

"IMPERIAL AGENTS. OPEN UP."

Legalities served, Hoffman and the rear entry team leader used almost simultaneous shotgun blasts to force open both doors. I followed my group into the house but by the time I entered it was all over except for the paperwork. Our suspects were being tied up even as they were waking up. If the thought of putting up a fight had crossed their minds, it had quickly died in the presence of the many armored and expressionless scout-snipers. They surrendered peacefully while still claiming their innocence. Well, not all of them. One was found dead on his bed. The notorious cousin and the rest of his accomplices were worse for wear, too. Our young couple had sold their lives dearly. We found their naval issue daggers on top of one of the tables.

Even without a confession, the circumstantial evidence against them looked strong. In a clear voice that dripped with contempt, Brunhilde read them their rights as we frog marched the cousin out of the shack. Although I once considered such things to be quaint up-time customs, both the admiral and Chief Frost had convinced me that we needed to set a higher standard than was commonplace—standards that hopefully one day would set the example for a whole nation—even the Magdeburg city watch. Besides, we were naval law enforcement professionals now, and we wouldn't take a second place to anyone.

Disappointed that no one had tried to escape custody, Dorrman had to be satisfied with providing our captives with medical care. I wanted to ensure that they would stay healthy long enough to make their almost-certain appointment with the executioner. However, first they were bound to have a long interview session with me. The results would be presented to the city prosecutor and magistrates. Confession was good for the soul.

I was so looking forward to that.

The slow cadence of a muffled drum set the pace of the funeral procession, the sound echoing along the packed streets of Magdeburg where its citizens stood respectfully. I had unconsciously fallen into step as we followed the two caissons that, side by side, were taking the flag-draped coffins of Corporal Hafner and Petty Officer Bischel—both promoted posthumously—to their final resting place. The pallbearers taking them there were a mixture of Marine and navy personnel extracted from the ranks of corpsmen, sniper-scouts, MPs, MAAs, and members of Hafner's platoon under the direction of Senior Chief Dorrman and Gunnery Sergeant Hoffman. Bravo Company, in dress blues and with fixed bayonets provided the escort.

Brunhilde and I walked behind the kids' grieving families. Admiral Simpson and the Marine commandant were at the head of the NCIS delegation, practically all of our agents who were off duty. Our gold badges had a thin black band across them, providing a shiny contrast against our subdued mourning clothes and set us apart from the rest. Behind us, military dependants, civilian clerks, shipyard workers and their families, off duty navy and Marine ranks and any others that could lay claim to membership in our close-knit service family, followed. Still, the funeral was considered an unofficial activity and I was glad that Brunhilde's hand was firmly grasped in mine. She was here today as my wife and not as a fellow agent—another working couple in this strange naval community of ours, just like the two youngsters in the coffins would never be. I thought that, on a day like today, we needed each other's support in our mutual grief for two lovers who could have easily been us.

But I was also grimly satisfied; their killers would have their own appointments with death, in the form of the hangman's noose, in a week. They had confessed to setting the ambush with the purpose of roughing up Hafner on her cousin's instigation. Of course, they failed to take into account the mettle of the individuals who volunteered to join the naval service and the situation had escalated beyond their control. Now, they'd had their day in court, and the case was closed.

On a more personal and happier note, this morning Brunhilde had given me the news that we had hoped to hear for so long. On a day of mourning over young lives lost, it was nice to know that another young life was just beginning, although the determined mother insisted on remaining on the job. Reluctantly—very reluctantly, I might add—I agreed. Me and mine would stand guard over them to protect and serve as we do with the rest of the naval community.

After all, we are the Naval Criminal Investigative Service—that's both our mission and our great honor.

The Prepared Mind

Kim Mackey

Chance favors the prepared mind.
—Louis Pasteur

Grantville, May 1632

When Amy Kubiak walked into the biology classroom, Lori Fleming had her head on her desk. Amy smiled. Pete Farmer had been a good biology teacher when Amy had had him in high school. But now that she was working to become a teacher herself, she knew that she would have had trouble if Pete was her colleague. He had been so patronizing to his female students, unlike Greg Ferrara. Lori, on the other hand, wasn't patronizing at all, and her experience in the USDA helped her make her biology lessons more connected to reality, unlike Pete's mania for microbiology.

"Lori, you okay?"

Lori raised her head slowly. "I'm fine. Just another long meeting last night with the Ag group. I swear, men say that women are the gossipers, but you get J.D. and Gordon and Willie Ray together . . ."

Amy laughed. "I was wondering why Alexandra was looking so bushed. When did the meeting finally break up?"

"Midnight. Again." Lori grimaced. "But at least I have tonight free. Once we get Tony's little job done."

Amy grimaced herself. "Nice how we got 'volunteered' for it.

Ever notice when cleaning work needs to get done that Tony always seems to find other things he has to do?"

Lori got up from her desk and stretched. "I noticed. I just wish he was less of a bureaucrat and more of a leader. He may be head of the science department, but that doesn't mean he can't, or shouldn't, get his hands dirty along with the rest of us."

"Speaking of hands, he better start keeping them to himself in the future. I like teaching, especially chemistry, but now that I've got other options . . ."

Lori tilted her head quizzically. "Other options?"

Amy nodded. "My roommate, Nicki Jo, has been hired by Colette Modi to get the ball rolling on a chemical company that will be set up in Essen. She's cutting back to half-time at the methanol plant so she can spend more time with the chem team doing research. She said if I ever need work, she could use me in a heartbeat. And now that the Modis are flush with cash from Louis de Geer, it would pay pretty well."

Amy paused and smiled at Lori. "We're procrastinating, aren't we?"

Lori laughed. "Yeah, we might as well bite the bullet and get it done. Onward!"

Together the two women left the classroom and headed down the hall.

"Oh God!"

Amy laughed as she pulled on her latex gloves. "That bad?"

Lori looked into the open door of the science department's refrigerator and shuddered. "Worse than bad. Horrid. Smelly. And there are . . . things growing on the walls!"

Amy looked around the corner of the refrigerator door and shook her head. "Want me to go get some sulfuric acid? Or a flame thrower?"

"No, I think the hot water and bleach will do. But this looks like it's going to take awhile. You still up for it? It's my responsibility, according to Tony."

"Yeah, well, too bad he didn't tell you that last fall. Or that it was stuffed with Pete Farmer's bacteria and fungi supplies. You could have used them."

Lori shook her head. "Probably not. This first year I was just happy to stay a chapter ahead of the kids in the textbook. I was too scared to try any labs beyond some basics with plants and animals. Not to mention I had no time outside of school to think about labs what with all the extra work helping with the agricultural stuff."

She sighed. "Well, let's get started. If we find anything we want, we can put it in the cooler to stay fresh."

It was fifteen minutes later when they found the paper bag labeled "Kwik-Stiks."

"Kwik-Stiks?" Amy asked, opening the bag. "What are Kwik-Stiks?"

"I don't know," Lori said. "Cultures of some kind? Let me see."

Amy pulled several silver packages from the paper bag along with a product sheet that she handed to Lori. Lori nodded as she read the sheet. She pointed to the first few lines.

"See? I was right. 'Lyophilized reference stock cultures.'"

"Lyophilized?" asked Amy.

"Freeze-dried, essentially. Keeps microorganisms in good condition for awhile. So what have we got?"

"This one sounds interesting. *Clostridium sporogenes*. Putrid odor. Yummy."

Lori took the package, marked "Microbiologics" on the label, and looked more closely. "Yeah, but notice the expiration date. October 2000. Which would have been last October. Way out of date. Anything else?"

Amy rummaged through the paper bag and pulled out another Kwik-Stik. "How about this one? *Penicillium roqueforti*. Even more yummy. Roquefort cheese organism. And can't we use this to get penicillin?"

Lori shook her head. "No, you need a particular strain of penicillium, not just any strain. I forget the exact species. As I recall, Alexander Fleming, the guy who discovered penicillin, had his cultures contaminated by accident. Besides, this one has an October 2000 expiration date as well."

While Lori had been talking Amy had been rummaging in the bag and she pulled out the next package in triumph. "Bingo! expiration June 2001!"

"*Penicillium italicum*, causes blue mold of citrus fruits." Lori smiled. "Closer, but still not the right one."

With a flourish Amy pulled another package from the bag. "Next to last one. Ring a bell?"

"*Penicillium notatum*. High yield. Expiration March 2001. A little out of date, but it still might be viable. Expiration dates are generally conservative. This is the stuff we want."

"Cool!" Amy said. Moving quickly the two women searched through the remaining paper bags in the refrigerator. Most of the Kwik-Stiks they found were far out of date or of organisms that didn't seem important. Only three were *Penicillium notatum*, two labeled "low yield," with expiration dates of June 2001, and the one labeled "high yield." They transferred the penicillium Kwik-Stiks to the cooler while they finished cleaning the refrigerator, then transferred them back.

"So what should we do with the Kwik-Stiks?" Amy asked.

Lori shrugged. "I'm not sure. I do know that the chem team took some stuff last fall, so they may already have some penicillium cultured up. Ask Nicki Jo tonight when you see her. If they can use them, I bet Len Trout would be happy to give them up. And they probably won't be viable for much longer."

That night at the Modi house Amy told her boyfriend, Franz Dubois, and Nicki Jo Prickett about the Kwik-Stiks.

"*Penicillium notatum*? Oh yeah, the chem team already has some of that cultured." Nicki Jo said. "But it's good to have more. Given the expiration date, I bet the school district will let us have it for free. Use it or lose it, and it's probably too close to the end of the current classes to use it in a high school lab experiment."

Franz Dubois looked puzzled. A second cousin of Colette Modi, he had arrived in Grantville in December 1631 from Hanau near Frankfurt. Always fascinated by chemistry, he had found himself spending many hours talking with Amy Kubiak. Within a month he had discovered that he was fascinated with Amy Kubiak as well.

"*Penicillium notatum*? Used to produce penicillin?"

Nicki Jo nodded. "Yup. But penicillin isn't really that much of a priority right now. We're in the seventeenth century, not the early twentieth. We need stuff that is going to prevent or cure the major epidemic-type diseases we might see, like typhus, bubonic plague and smallpox. That's why the chem team is concentrating on things like DDT and chloramphenicol and the medical people are working on smallpox vaccinations. Oh, we'll be making some other antibiotics, mainly the sulfalike drugs, which aren't that difficult if you have the ingredients. Sulfanilamide is even in one of my organic chem books. But synthesizing pure penicillin in sufficient quantities is pretty difficult, according to the sources we have. That'll have to wait a few years. In the meantime, we're sending out cultures of *Pencillium notatum*, along with instructions, to various hospitals and universities around Germany as we get visitors headed in the right direction."

"But if we can't really make penicillin right now, what good is it to send out the cultures?" Amy asked.

"I think the rationale is not to have all your eggs in just the Grantville basket," Nicki Jo said. "If something happens to us, the people in charge wanted to make sure there are plenty of the right penicillium species available for the day when someone *can* manufacture it. It probably took a decade of intense effort uptime to mutate the original Fleming strain into even the lower yielding strains we have cultured right now."

Amy looked over at Franz. "What about those two men from Cologne you're translating for? Aren't they physicians or something?"

"No," Franz said. "One, Gerhard Eichhorn, is a surgeon, and the other, Matthias Wagener, is the praeceptor of a hospitaller order in Cologne, the Antonites. They're leaving for home next week though."

"What's a praeceptor?" Amy asked.

"Essentially just the head monk," Franz said. "But with responsibility for overseeing all the hospitals the order administers in Cologne and interacting with the city council to ensure things run smoothly."

Nicki Jo nodded. "Well, check with them to see if they'd like some of the penicillium. The Kwik-Stiks would be more convenient to transport than the actual cultures. I'll check with Greg to get the okay and he can arrange for permission from Len Trout."

Matthias Wagener turned one last time to look back at Grantville before urging his horse into a canter to catch up with Gerhard Eichhorn.

"An interesting six weeks, wouldn't you say, my friend?" Matthias said when his horse came level with Gerhard's.

Gerhard snorted. "You've always had a gift for understatement, Matthias. Do you finally believe they are really from the future?"

Matthias shrugged. "Of course. Or from some future. But the philosophical questions are the most fascinating. Why did God decide to send them here? And why now?"

Gerhard smiled. "So you don't subscribe to the opinion of some of the Protestants we met? That God sent Grantville back in time to punish Catholics for Tilly's sack of Magdeburg? The timing would certainly indicate a correlation of some kind."

Matthias waved his hand in dismissal. "Highly unlikely, Gerhard, in my opinion. God is not so petty. If anything, God sent them back for the children. Think of how many children will be saved now that we know more about disease and the reasons for early mortality."

Matthias shook his head. "And not just children. Now that we know about the importance of sanitation, we can focus on building better sewage systems."

"Well, I will help when I can. But your position as praeceptor of the Antonites should be sufficient to enlist the city council behind the changes that need to take place."

"Easier said than done, my friend." Matthias shook his head again. "Too many will resist the changes because the Americans are starting to ally themselves with Gustavus Adolphus. Others because they will see no economic benefit, just expense. Still others will say it is good that so many children die young, rather than to grow up into misery and pain and starve to death.

"As for you, Gerhard," Matthias continued, "I would be very careful if I were you with the knowledge you've gained in Grantville. Franz Wilwartz is always looking for ways to make your life more miserable."

Gerhard grimaced. It was true. Franz Wilwartz, like many barber-surgeons in Cologne, was more barber than surgeon. He had always been jealous of Gerhard's skill in treating wounds and other ailments. Twice in the past five years he had threatened to file a complaint against Gerhard with the *Beleidmeister* about not following guild regulations. And now that his daughter had married one of the more prominent physicians in Cologne . . .

"Oh, I'll be careful, Matthias. I just hope I can convince the guild of the need to change some of their regulations. I'll need your help in that, of course."

"You'll have it, Gerhard." Matthias said. "So what did you do with the *Penicillium notatum* the Americans gave you?"

Gerhard turned and slapped the box tied to his saddle. "On ice, as the Americans would say. Hopefully I can keep it relatively cool until we can get back to Cologne. And yours?"

Matthias smiled. "Given the fact that the package was already out of date, I decided it was important to get it back to Cologne as soon as possible, so I hired a special courier. Gysbert should have it in four days, at the most, God willing."

"Gysbert Schotten? The herbalist?"

Matthias nodded and smiled again. "The greenest thumb in Cologne. If anyone can get the mold to grow, he can. I just wish I could see his face when the package arrives."

Insane, thought Gysbert Schotten, *Matthias Wagener has been driven insane.*

How else to explain this enigmatic package on his desk and the fact that it had been delivered by special courier?

For weeks he had been receiving letters and manuscripts from the praeceptor. His enthusiasm for the "new science" had been contagious. But this . . .

Gysbert shook his head. He had done what he could to prepare a room for experimentation. But the documents he had received indicated that he would have to take extensive precautions to keep the cultures from being contaminated, and how was that going to be possible? He had no autoclaves, although perhaps a regular oven might work. Dry heat instead of steam. He had no microscopes, no thermometers, nothing.

"Father, should we begin?"

Gysbert looked at his assistant, Wolfram Muysgin. Wolf was a good boy. Eager, enthusiastic. Good instincts for many things. But now those instincts would have to be retrained for an environment very different from what they had assumed. No more "humors" or blood that was "too hot" or "too cold." Oh no. Disease caused by small animals called "bacteria." Or even smaller ones called "viruses." And a constant . . . what was the word? Ah yes, a constant "evolutionary" war fought between bacteria, yeasts, molds and fungi. An ongoing, ever-present need to keep things as sterile as possible. What was the phrase the praeceptor had stressed so emphatically? Ah, yes. "Cleanliness is next to Godliness."

"Father?"

Gysbert shook himself. "We'll start in a minute, Wolf. But first,

I think we need to pray to God for success. If He has truly sent Grantville here from the future for benevolent reasons, perhaps He will bless our work if we ask him. Let us pray."

Together Father Gysbert and Wolf Muysgin bowed their heads and prayed.

Imperial Free City of Cologne, July 1633

Wolf Muysgin stopped once again to consider his new workplace. The new laboratory for the hospital was a two-story brick and stone building that had been built next to the Antonite's herbal garden. The laboratory had been built at an angle so that the winter sun would light up the windowed rooms of the second story as much as possible.

Once inside Wolf removed his shoes and slipped on a pair of wool socks, then added a pair made of linen. He followed up with a fresh lab coat that stretched to his knees. He waved to the laundress, Frau Hessler, as he entered the stairs leading to the second floor. The first floor of the laboratory was given over to the laundry and experiments that did not require the same decontamination protocols as the second story. There were two doors on the stairs, and after passing through the second he was surprised to find Father Schotten in the hallway.

"Father, you're back! How was your trip to Grantville?"

Gysbert smiled and motioned Wolf into his office.

"Wonderful, Wolf. But also frustrating. And disappointing in some ways."

"Wonderful I can understand, after all the stories the praeceptor told us. But frustrating and disappointing?"

Gysbert nodded. "Frustrating because the Americans we have heard so much about are terribly busy, Wolf. They have little time for visitors with difficult questions. Doctor Nichols was especially busy dealing with outbreaks of disease. Nothing too serious, mostly dysentery and flu. But he was not very helpful."

Gysbert sighed and sat back in his chair. "My search of their books and encyclopedias was the disappointing part. Essentially nothing beyond what we were already told."

"So we are on our own, Father?"

Gysbert nodded. "Yes, I'm afraid so Wolf. If we want a medium to produce higher levels of penicillin, we will have to experiment ourselves. Corn steep liquor of the type and purity suggested in the literature is too expensive for us. So let's investigate various kinds of vegetable extracts, I think. You can start working on that. For myself, I will attempt to find an answer to the contamination problem. It does us no good to produce penicillin in quantity if it lasts only a few days because of bacterial or other contamination."

Gysbert suddenly smiled. "But enough of that. Frau Hessler seems to think you have made a breakthrough with your yeast cultures. True?"

Wolf nodded enthusiastically. The brewers' and bakers' guilds of Cologne had helped finance the Antonite laboratory when they had been told about the possibility of improved strains of yeast. "True Father. Come, let me show you!"

Imperial Free City of Cologne, April 1634

To Gerhard Eichhorn, the gloom in Steel Mountain House was as palpable as a cold north wind along the Rhine.

Deservedly so, he thought, when the family's only son is about to die. For four days Simon von Hardenrat had become weaker and sicker. Gerhard had been called in on the second day when the family became alarmed at Simon's high fever. Nothing Gerhard had attempted had seemed to work, despite the new medical knowledge he had gained thanks to his trip to Grantville in 1632.

What good is knowledge if it only informs your own helplessness?

"Any change?" Gerhard asked as he entered Simon's bedroom. Peter von Hardenrat, Simon's father, shook his head wearily. Peter had relieved his wife at his son's sickbed sometime in the early morning.

"No major change, Herr Eichhorn. The fever is no worse, but no better, either. We keep bathing him with cool distilled water, as per your instructions. But I fear the infection is spreading. And his neck is starting to bulge."

Gerhard Eichhorn sighed. "It is as I feared. He may have either diphtheria or a very severe bacterial infection. Something the Americans called *Staphylococcus aureus*."

Peter nodded. "Is there anything we can do? Besides pray?"

Was it time to try again? thought Gerhard.

The first experiments had not been very successful, leading Gerhard to suspect that the Americans had been right about the need for purification. But the Antonite monks had been working for almost two years with the *Penicillium notatum* cultures. Maybe they had had better fortune.

"Perhaps." Gerhard said. "How well do you know the praeceptor of the Antonites in the hospital on Schildergasse?"

"Surely you're jesting, Father. Could it really be that simple?"

Gysbert nodded. "It seems so, Wolf. Borax is the solution to our contamination problem. And not only does it limit most contaminants at only two-tenths of one percent, but in combination with the pressed pea juice you discovered as a medium, the yields are thirty to forty percent above baseline. Clearly borax not only lowers contaminant levels. It also acts like a fertilizer to improve production. We can start thinking about experiments with people soon."

Wolf cocked his head. "Is that wise, Father? I thought the literature said the penicillin had to be purified to be effective."

Gysbert smiled. "I think the literature may be wrong, Wolf. Remember that cut I had last week? It became a bit infected. So I decided to do a little experimentation on myself. What do you think?" Gysbert held up his finger for inspection. Clearly the cut had healed well, with no sign of redness.

"But . . . I thought the Americans said . . ."

Gysbert smiled again. "Perhaps the Americans don't know everything, Wolf."

"Father Gysbert?"

Gysbert and Wolf looked at the door. Dietrich Tils, the praeceptor's secretary, was standing in the doorway.

"Yes, Dietrich?"

"The praeceptor wishes to see you. Immediately."

"And if Hardenrat's son dies, Gerhard, what then?"

Gerhard shrugged. "He is a fair man, Gysbert. And one of Cologne's most prominent citizens. If you save his son, the Antonites will gain a powerful friend indeed. Isn't that so, Praeceptor?"

Matthias Wagener nodded. "And he is indeed a fair man, Gysbert. If we try and do not save his son, he will not hold it against us. But if he discovers we could have done something and did not try..."

"Fine. Let us try then. But we must remember that penicillin leaves the body very quickly. The boy will have to have additional doses of the juice every three hours. How should we administer it?"

"As throat and nose drops, I think," Gerhard said. "Do you have enough?"

Gysbert nodded. "Just enough for ten days, I think. If he isn't cured by then... may God have mercy on his soul."

Magdeburg, January 1635

"Holy crap, James, is this for real?"

James Nichols nodded at Mike Stearns. "As real as it gets, Mike. This hospital in Cologne is saving lives using homemade penicillin." He smiled. "I told you sending out those cultures would pay off."

"But I thought we needed some high tech to make penicillin."

"Well, you do to make pure penicillin. But this stuff is pretty crude. Turns out this monk, an Antonite named Gysbert Schotten, is a pretty decent jack-leg biochemist. So through a bit of luck and a lot of hard work he was able to make enough crude penicillin to start supplying most of the hospitals and physicians in Cologne. It won't be enough for a nation of millions, but it's certainly enough to take care of a city of forty thousand."

"So, should we start making this stuff?"

James smiled. "We already have." He shook his head. "Who would have believed it? Pea juice and borax to improve the yield. One of those 'duh' moments, like Greg Ferrara had. It might not be as effective as pure penicillin, but if we need an antibiotic that we can use topically, it should work in a high percentage of cases. And the nice thing is, we can spread this around to a lot more places than sulfanilamide or chloramphenicol. We just need to try to make sure that people use it wisely. Back in the Fifties they were putting penicillin in everything from toothpaste to lipstick."

When James had left Mike walked to the window of his office. Pea juice and borax. Not something that had been in any of the books in Grantville, that was for sure. Synergism. Up-time ideas fusing with down-time hard work and perseverance.

Smiling, Mike Stearns turned back to his desk.

Capacity for Harm

Richard Evans

Belfort, Franche Comté, 1633

"So, Herr Doctor Lebenenergie. You designed this yourself?"

"Not exactly, Commissioner Vaden." Tomas cursed himself for ever thinking that coming to Belfort would be profitable. He knew that Franche Comté was rife with witch hunts again, but he just needed some extra copper wire and plates for his second machine. Those could be made in Franche Comté.

"I met with some Americans a couple of years ago. I studied their books on electricity. While I was there, I saw them use a device that made that power available to them with a press of a button. They shocked a farmer back to life."

"Sorcery!"

"So I thought at first, sir. But it was nothing but a machine. I hied myself to this town they said they came from and just walked into their library and asked about these machines. I spent two months there." Tomas tried to sit up straighter but the bindings prevented it. "I watched their doctors use similar machines and finally came up with the theory that applying this power in varying amounts to the proper locations of the body, one could rebalance the ichors within and cure maladies. This was proved to me when I saw a movie called 'Frankenstein.' They laughed and called it 'fiction' and said it was a moral lesson about a man's *hubris*. The machines in that movie were well within what we could make right now.

"So I did." Tomas knew now what that movie had been trying to teach him, but now it was too late. His only recourse was to make himself useful to these witch hunters. Somehow. "I built my *Elektrischer Generator* from parts I found near Geneva and Upper Genoa. The lodestone was the most expensive piece."

"Lodestone? Explain." Someone just out of sight asked. Tomas felt someone moving up behind him.

"Continue, Herr Eichemann." The other Vaden waved the questioner back.

"Certain stones, when hung from a string or wire, will always have one side point to the North."

"Yes, those I know of," the elder Vaden interjected. "They are how the compasses on the ships work, gentlemen." He shook his head. "We know that is not sorcery. Nor are we here for that reason. I believe this is much simpler. Continue." The elder Vaden's cold, dead eyes compelled Tomas to obey.

Tomas Eichemann took time to gather his thoughts. He wasn't sure exactly what the two witch commissioners wanted with him. No one he knew of had accused him of being a warlock—that he knew of. The two men had just ridden out to his camp and invited him to attend them back in town. Invited him. With their guards present.

He should have left earlier in the day when he'd heard that there were people asking for the whereabouts of the traveling doctor and his magical device, the *Elektrischer Generator*. It was always safer to leave when people started asking questions. Twice before he had managed to flee other towns just ahead of the authorities. Small towns were the worst; nowhere to really hide. Especially to those who had good clean clothing, their own wagon with many strange devices hanging from its side, too. Jealousy or suspicion always resulted in the same thing. Someone had sold the information to someone else who knew someone who was in a position of authority.

But the smith had promised him that the copper plates for his capacitor and the wires for his two inductor coils would be ready that afternoon, no sooner. *I should have gone to Geneva instead. No one would have cared about one more traveling merchant there.*

The smith had delivered them as promised. Tomas had just

managed to get a couple miles out of town and make camp when the two men with the wide-brimmed black hats and cloaks of official witch commissioners had appeared out of the dark. They hadn't been alone. Twenty guards on horse were with them. All were wearing the colors of the bishop of Strassburg. They had called him by name. The invitation hadn't been one he could have refused and lived. The four mercenaries he'd hired to see him safely through the battle lines had laughed when he ordered them to protect him. Then the sorry bastards had faded into the nearby woods. Their laughs mocked him even now.

"Continue, Tomas Eichemann. Yes, we know your real name." The elder Vaden sneered at him. "But we will get back to why you have given yourself the new title and name, later. Tell us more about why you needed a lodestone."

"The stones have a power inside them that can push something called electrons. Those are particles that are too small to see. But when they are present in great numbers, we can see their results during a summer storm."

"This box makes lightnings?" The younger Vaden's eyebrows rose in disbelief.

"Of a sort. Water?" The heads shook from side to side. There would be no comforts until all their questions were answered. Tomas licked his dry lips. "When spun inside a coil of copper wire covered in lac, the lodestone—the magnet, as the Americans call it—pushes the particles in one direction. That creates flow of power. It acts like a water wheel in reverse, pushing electrons through the copper as if it were a channel. Or you could think of it as a pump pushing water through the pipe.

"When spun at the right speed it creates enough power in a small coil to make it magnetic, like the lodestone. The coil pulls a metal cylinder bound to a small spring and makes a contact under the lid. Just like a lodestone attracts metal filings or that nail that your brother has been playing with. This opens the circuit to let power flow from the smaller generator to a larger coil deeper inside the box. If the device is working, the two silver studs under that glass lid will throw small lightnings at each other. Then you throw that small lac-covered lever there next to it to close a second circuit.

"This lets the small power created by the hand crank form a larger, more powerful, magnet to spin off the same gears, so you produce more energy for the same amount of work. This is because the second coil has more magnets, many pumps, or many water wheels, working together. These iron core magnets don't really spin this time though. This time it is the coils that spin." The older Vaden nodded his head and then looked to his younger brother who was standing by the box.

"Close the box, Brother." He turned back to Tomas. "Continue if you would, please." The friendly smile wasn't forced at all and that scared him deeply. Tomas suddenly recalled prayers that he'd hadn't spoken in many a year.

"There are two taps, links to the coils, copper brushes that spin along the circular plates shown on the drawing. That lets the power go towards charging two plates of copper that have sheets of glass between them. They call that a capacitor. It stores the power until needed. To that is connected another coil, this time heavier copper wire wrapped around another iron core. This is hooked up to the lac-covered wires that are attached to the proper locations of the body with clamps or leather cuffs with the contacts sewn into them, so that power can be applied. How much is dependent on how fast you spin the gear handle and how long you press the red button."

"I see. Like this?"

Tomas screamed. His body jerked against the leather straps binding him to the heavy wooden chair.

"Yes. Yes. But you shouldn't spin the handle so fast. Too much power will harm the patient." Tomas gasped a bit. "Too much power can burn them from the inside. If the patient has a weak heart, it can kill him. If the lightnings under the glass are large and constant, you can back off spinning it so fast." Tomas felt his voice break from his adopted instructor and doctor's persona. He knew it sounded like the desperate pleadings of a condemned man.

The two brothers looked at each other and smiled. "Indeed?"

Tomas grasped at a straw. "I have the body charts and shock tables in that map case. It's over by my pack. On the table." Tomas tried to nod, but could only flick his eyes in the proper direction.

"Ah. We shall study it most thoroughly, Dr. Lebenenergie. Most thoroughly, indeed." The Vaden brothers had the most spine chilling smiles that Tomas had ever seen.

The older brother smiled again. He leaned forward and whispered into Tomas's ear. "Yes. I must thank you. With such a device, I do believe we can process more voluntary confessions per day. And we won't even leave a mark upon our charges. So the priests who feel that we are beating confessions out of the accused will have no grounds at all." The smile chilled Tomas to the core. "No grounds at all."

"That was most efficient, Commissioner Vaden. Very well done." Tomas' eyes darted over to see who had spoken and locked his eyes on those of a local magistrate. "I told you, Antoine, these men are efficient in their work. The two best lawyers I've ever met."

"Truly," answered another magistrate. Tomas couldn't quite identify him in the dim lighting. "Though I am more concerned that we got down all the pertinent details about the device. I believe that is the most important thing here."

From behind him Tomas Eichemann heard another voice, this one higher pitched. "I've got the information, sir."

Sweat began to roll down his forehead. What was really going on here? There were at least four other silent figures in the room. Tomas gathered his breath and looked up at them. "Am I to be charged as a warlock, then? Or am I free to go? I helped you as I said I would. I have done everything in my power to show you how to build your own *Elektrischer Generator*. I'll even help you build your own. As many as you need! But I don't see how a healing machine can help you in your Holy cause, commissioners. It is a machine to shock the body back into working right. I have many affidavits, witnessed and sealed, of patients who've been cured by my machine."

"Yes. That you have. And we thank you so much for the neat lists of names you gave us. Many of them are very rich indeed. You sold them smaller versions for their own use, I see."

"Yes. But those won't last like this one. The magnetics will fail eventually, as will the soft metal gears. They only make minor shocks that stimulate the muscles and circulation. They will need me for full revitalizations, as they don't know how to do that. It is very good money. I could share it with you, make you partners perhaps?" Bribing commissioners was risky, but commonly accepted as necessary. Many of them were in the business more for the money than any real desire to do Holy work.

The younger Vaden turned to the small crowd behind him.

"Gentlemen, he has voluntarily admitted that he's sold devices to many unsuspecting clients. Devices designed to fail."

The older Vaden smiled. Grimly. "As for the donations . . . That won't be necessary, Tomas. Though we do thank you for your donation . . ." Someone behind them coughed politely. ". . . offer."

The younger Vaden chuckled. "Yes, indeed. We can both use new boots. The roads here are simply atrocious, wouldn't you say, Brother?" Someone else chuckled.

"Yes." The older Vaden leaned down over Tomas and smiled. "As for your release . . . not just yet. We do need to see the full capacity of this machine, after all. As well . . ." He smiled. "We need to see which is stronger. The guilty soul of a self-proclaimed doctor and admitted charlatan or that of a machine." He waved his hand to the hooded man who stood by the machine. The crank began to spin.

"I do believe you will find a comfortable place in Heaven, Tomas. Eventually."

The black gloved hand pressed the red button. And held it down.

Little Angel

Kerryn Offord

Grantville, January 1634

Maria Helena Kolb slowly searched the line of trees. Somewhere, hidden in the shadows, she was sure Benji Matheny was hiding in ambush. *Time to send in the cannon fodder.* "Daisy, Regina: when I give you the word, I want you to run around that tree over there and, if you find Benji, throw your snowballs at him." Maria Helena smiled at the younger girls. "Do you understand?"

Both girls held up their hands, each holding a carefully crafted snowball, and nodded.

"Right, then wait a moment for me to make some more snowballs."

Daisy and Regina waited impatiently while Maria Helena finished shaping some snowballs. "Are you ready yet, Maria?" Daisy asked.

Maria Helena checked her access to her ammunition, then, taking a snowball in each hand, nodded.

Daisy and Regina burst out from behind cover and ran for the tree Maria Helena had indicated.

Benji stood up and opened fire on them. Maria Helena, still behind cover, was presented with Benji's back as a target. She, quite naturally, took full advantage of the exposed target, and opened fire.

It was a massacre. Three to one odds, even if two of the three were barely four years old, were enough to completely trounce eight year old Benji.

Totally outgunned, and short of ammunition, Benji took to his heels, the girls in pursuit.

"Where do you think you're going, young man?"

Benji threw a look over his shoulder. The girls were close now. He ran up to his Great Grandma Aggie and took shelter behind her. Peeking round from behind her he could see Maria Helena idly tossing a snowball in her right hand. *It wasn't right that a girl should be able to throw as well as she could.* "They ganged up on me, Granny Aggie. It's not fair." Benji noted that Maria Helena was patiently waiting for him to make a break for the house. "Granny, tell Maria Helena to drop that snow ball."

Aggie Beckworth smiled at Maria Helena. "Okay, girls, you've had your fun. You can drop that snowball you're tossing, Maria Helena."

Maria Helena looked from the snowball in her right hand to Benji, who was making faces at her from the protection of Granny Aggie. With a sigh she gave it one last toss and let it fall to the ground.

Benji slid out from behind Granny Aggie and . . .

Thwak!

The snowball Maria Helena had been hiding behind her back was in flight almost before Benji stepped clear of Aggie. It hit him flush in the face. The snowball Benji had been in the act of throwing went wide.

Aggie Beckworth struggled for breath as she laughed at the shock and surprise on Benji's face. She hastily grabbed a handkerchief from a cuff and coughed into it. It took a few minutes for the coughing spasm to come to an end. Short of breath, Aggie looked down at the anxious faces. "It's all right, children. Just a bad cough. Now get inside where it's warm. We don't want you catching a cold."

Benji, Daisy and Regina ran up to the house, shaking the snow from their clothes before going indoors. Maria Helena gave Aggie a searching look before walking back to the house. Every few steps she looked back to make sure Aggie was following.

☆   ☆   ☆

Lora Matheny looked from the blouse in her hands to her daughter. "Look at this blouse, it's filthy. How did you get it so dirty?"

Scuffing her feet, Daisy looked up at Lora through her eyelashes. "Me, Regina and Maria Helena had a snowball fight with Benji."

Lora sighed. She had a pile of washing to do, and she was sure her washing machine was on its last legs. The weather was lousy for drying clothes, so she had washing draped all around the house drying. The laundry door was sticking, and with her husband Jeff still working in Nürnberg, she'd asked her father if he could fix it. He'd promised to come in after work, and that meant she'd probably have an extra for dinner. Two, if he brought Uncle Stu along to help.

"Go and play with Regina and Maria Helena then, and try to stay clean."

"Yes, Mommy." Daisy slipped away.

Lora walked over to her favorite chair and slumped into it. She was exhausted. It wasn't that the kids were a real problem. They could be trouble, but that, as Jeff always said, was in the design specifications. It was *everything* that was getting her down. Yesterday she'd visited her mother at the assisted living center. If you could call what her mother was doing living. Her half-sister Karrie was just as bad. The rental income from Mom's home was contributing to their care, but things were tight, so tight that Grandma Aggie had moved in so that her place could be rented out. It made for a crowded household, but she wouldn't have it any other way. Family was important. If only the sun would shine so she could get the washing dry.

A few days later

Dell Beckworth lowered his pack to the ground. Then, rifle in hand, he joined his brother at the edge of the ring wall. Together they looked out at the scene below. "Any idea why our bit of hunting ground is suddenly worth twenty percent more than last year?"

"Nope." Stu kicked away a bit more of the unstable cliff edge. The brothers watched the loose soil and rocks fall to the ground a couple of hundred feet below. "The way we're losing bits of it over the ring wall, I'm surprised anybody wants to buy it."

"Yeah, but the letter came from someone." Dell reached into his jacket pocket and pulled out the offending letter and reread it. "Yep. It still says Joachim Schmidt wants to buy our bit of dirt. Any idea who Joachim Schmidt is?"

Stu shook his head. "Nope, and Mrs. G. doesn't know who he is either."

Dell raised his eyebrows at that little tidbit. In his admittedly limited experience, Mrs. Gundelfinger knew everybody and everything that was happening in Grantville. "What? Something the marvelous Mrs. G. doesn't know? That's a first."

"Hey, don't knock her information network, Dell. It saved us a hell of an embarrassing interview when you dropped that letter of credit from the Mehlis City Council right under her feet."

Dell shuddered. That had been a bad moment. "Don't remind me. The way she picked it up. Looked at it, then smiled up at us, and casually asked if we'd bought a bridge recently still gives me the heebie-jeebies."

"Yeah, that was a nasty moment. But things got better when she asked us into her office. Hell, she even paid us something for the information the Mehlis City Council had Derek Modi designing their new bridge. I'd say having Mrs. G. accepting us as clients is the first bit of good luck we've had in years."

Dell folded up the letter and put it away. "Yeah, lucky. From the latest financial report she gave us, we could be out of debt inside ten years." He spat over the edge of the ring wall. "Shit, I'm fifty-five this year. I want to be more than just out of debt in ten years' time."

"Ain't that the truth? Still, if we accept that offer for our bit of hunting ground we could give it to Mrs. G. to invest."

Dell paused to survey what he could see of their land. It was typical West Virginia hill country. Wooded hills that looked like inverted ice-cream cones. "Yeah, except she gave us a 'don't sell' warning even before that letter arrived."

"Makes you wonder what she knows that we don't? But I bet Mr. Too Big For His Britches has the same information."

Dell grinned at the name they had for one of the more successful opportunists in Grantville. Both of them hoped to one day see Mr. Too Big have a Too Big fall. "Yeah, as an ex-county commissioner he'll have the contacts. You think Joachim Schmidt's a front for him?"

"Yeah, I'd bet money, if I had any. It's unusual for the bastard to offer over the odds though. That means he must be in a hurry to close the deal." He cast a curious gaze over their acreage. "I can't think what could raise the value though. You can't build on it. You can't really harvest the timber. It's too much trouble to selectively log, and if you did any clear felling, the hill would slide out from under you." He looked down the slope, towards a rocky outcrop. "The only thing I can think of is that that seam of coal."

Both of them looked in the direction of the dog-hole mine where they'd harvested coal to heat the hunting hut that was now lost up-time. Stu shook his head. "But Mrs. G. says we don't own the coal. The mineral rights on most of our land were owned by the coal company, and they escheated to the government."

"Most of the mineral rights?"

Stu sighed. "Yeah, most. Great-grandfather John Beckworth didn't sell the rights on the piece he bought way back when he first settled in the area."

"Don't tell me. That bit was left up-time."

Stu nodded. "An accurate survey might show some of the bit left behind still holds its mineral rights, but I wouldn't bet on it."

"Shit, our luck stinks," Dell said. "Come on. We've seen all there is to see. We might as well head home. Just keep an eye out for dinner."

"Hurry up and finish your breakfast, Daisy. You don't want to be late."

Daisy struggled to swallow. She shook her head. "No, Mommy." Toddler Haven was a fun place to go, but Mom only let her go one morning a week. She wished it could be more often since most of her friends went there. Daisy rubbed her jaw. It hurt. She looked at the remains of her breakfast. She didn't think she could eat any more, so she slipped from her chair and ran over to give her mother a hug.

Lora hugged her back. Then she helped Daisy and her adopted sister, Regina, into their winter jackets and helped them put on their mittens. Once the girls were dressed for the elements, Lora put on her heavy coat and they set out for Toddler Haven.

☆   ☆   ☆

"Mrs. Matheny, Gaby McPherson calling from Toddler Haven . . ."

"Hi, Gaby. I hope Daisy and Regina are behaving themselves."

"Actually, it's about Daisy that I'm calling, Mrs. Matheny. Mrs. Beckworth has taken Daisy to the hospital. She said to tell you to get there as soon as you can. Regina is still here at Toddler Haven, but Mary Moran says she'll take her home with her."

Lora gulped for air. "Can you give me any idea of what's wrong with Daisy, Gaby?"

"Not really, Mrs. Matheny. Daisy complained of neck pains and a sore jaw. And she's wet herself. She was awfully embarrassed about that and the fuss Mrs. Linder and Mary were making. It might just be a bug that's going around, Mrs. Matheny, but Mrs. Linder insisted Daisy should see a doctor."

"Right. Thank you for calling, Gaby, and thank Mary for me. Bye."

Lora hung up the phone and stood staring into the distance.

Aggie placed a hand on her shoulder. "Is something the matter, Lora?"

"They've sent Daisy to the hospital, Gran."

"Come on, we'll have to pack a bag for Daisy in case they want to keep her overnight, and something for you. You'll want to stay with Daisy. Don't worry about Tommy, I'll take care of him." Aggie hesitated. "I'll give your father a call. You don't want to be alone at a time like this."

Dr. Susannah Shipley was nearing the end of her shift in the emergency room when Daisy Matheny was brought in by a panicky Heather Beckworth. By the time Heather finished her description of Daisy's symptoms she was already fearful of the probable diagnosis. Susannah tried to put Daisy at ease while she did a quick examination. She paid special attention to the jaw and abdomen. Next, she asked Daisy whether she had hurt herself recently. Daisy showed Susannah the sore finger she had scraped while picking up snow during a snowball fight. It had happened three days ago. Susannah made a quick mental calculation and came to a shocking conclusion. This little girl was probably going to die. But she wasn't going to give up without a fight.

"Nurse, find me a critical care bed for Daisy Matheny and admit her immediately. I need to call the pharmacy."

Nurse Annette Salerno grabbed a phone and started to make arrangements to admit Daisy.

Susannah used another phone to call the pharmacy. "Raymond? I've got an emergency. Do we have any plasma in stock from someone we know had a tetanus booster shot? The more recent the better."

"What sort of emergency, Susannah?" Raymond Little asked.

"A four-year-old girl with acute tetanus poisoning. I know the patient. She hasn't had any vaccinations against tetanus. She should have had her first DTaP shot just before the Ring of Fire, but she was ill."

"Oh shit! Right. Just a moment and I'll check."

Susannah waited impatiently for Raymond to come back to the phone.

"We've running low, but I can send you a couple of units. The antibody counts might not be very high though. It's been almost four years since the donors had their booster shots."

"That's better than I expected, Raymond. It'll have to do, since it's all we've got."

Dell Beckworth left Lora at Daisy's bedside and made his way to Dr. Shipley's office. "Can you tell me what's wrong with Daisy, Doctor?"

Dr. Susannah Shipley was tired. She tried to sit up straight in her chair. "I'd rather talk to Daisy's mother or father, Mr. Beckworth."

"Well, that'll be a trick. Lora's in there crying over Daisy, and her father's miles away down in Nürnberg."

Susannah slumped a little. "Can you get a message to her father?"

"Oh, shit! It's that bad?"

"We think Daisy has tetanus."

"Tetanus? But surely you can treat that. There're vaccines . . . aren't there?"

Susannah shook her head slowly. "Up-time, there were vaccines and antitoxins and we could always get more. I'm sorry, Dell, but we've run out. We've used what we brought back with us on neonatal cases. We're doing the best we can using plasma taken from some of the last people to get a tetanus shot up-time, but I don't think it'll make much difference in Daisy's case."

"What the hell do you mean you don't think it'll make much difference in Daisy's case?" Dell yelled.

"Everything is happening too fast, Mr. Beckworth. Even if we had the antitoxin, I don't think we could do anything for Daisy. Even up-time, when someone wasn't immunized, tetanus was a very dangerous disease. It's caused by a toxin that kills in extremely low doses. Daisy, from what we can tell, has had more than a lethal amount." Susannah rested her hands on her desk. "I'm sorry, Mr. Beckworth, but I think you should prepare yourself for the fact Daisy isn't going to get better."

"Not get better?" Dell shot to his feet, the chair went flying backwards. "You mean she's going to die? She's too young to die. Daisy's only fucking four years old."

"I'm sorry Mr. Beckworth, but we've doing everything we can. In Daisy's case, I don't think it's going to be enough."

"How much time, Doctor?"

"The speed it's been working, a couple of days, if that."

"Shit!" Dell buried his head in his hands. He sniffed, and pulled out a handkerchief, blew his nose and mopped his eyes. "I better see about getting a message to Lora's husband."

Susannah remained seated. She grabbed a handkerchief and blotted her eyes. Sometimes she really hated her job.

"Hi, Mary. I've come to take Regina home. How is she?"

Mary Moran opened the door to let Stu inside. "She's sleeping just now. But what's happening with Daisy? We were all worried about her at work."

Stu stared blankly at Mary and shook his head.

"Oh, how's Lora coping?"

Stu sighed. "Not very well. Look, I'm sorry, but could you just get Regina, please. Mom's home alone with Lora's kids, and she's not very well herself."

Stu started to worry as he turned to walk up the drive. Lora's house was dark. There should have been lights on. It wasn't that late, and anyway, surely his mother would stay up until she got news of Daisy.

When he arrived at the door he became even more worried. The sound of a child crying could be heard. It sounded as if Tommy had been crying for a long time. It wasn't like his mother to let a child cry like that. He rushed inside.

The sight before him made him jerk. For a moment, in the

first flash of light, he'd mistaken the blanket-covered toys on the floor for a body.

Tommy had never been able to settle without his blanket as long as Stu had known him. He picked up the blanket to give it to the baby, but the odor made Stu back off. It smelled as though Tommy hadn't been changed for a while.

Stu was worried about his mother now. There was no way she would let a baby stay wet. He headed for his mother's room, but she wasn't there, either.

Stu paused. The sleeping weight of Regina was somehow comforting, but she was starting to feel heavy. *Best to put her to bed before searching for Mom.* He headed for the girls' bedroom, then froze. His mother lay curled up on Daisy's bed, some of Daisy's favorite toys gathered in her arms. Beside her, holding her hand, sat Maria Helena.

Maria Helena carefully slipped her hand out of Aggie's and walked over to Regina's bed. She opened the bed covers and gestured to Stu.

The look of calm acceptance in Maria Helena's eyes almost caused him to throw up. He placed Regina on her bed and left her in Maria Helena's capable hands. Then he moved to check his mother. She looked peaceful, too peaceful. He touched her hand. It felt cold. He felt for a pulse. He couldn't find one. Finally, he took her spectacles and held them close to her mouth. No sign of water vapor.

Stu swallowed and turned to check on Maria Helena and Regina. Regina appeared to be sound asleep. Maria Helena met his gaze. Blinking and breaking eye contact he looked around the room before returning to look at Maria Helena. "Benji?" he asked.

Maria Helena pointed up the hall.

"Will you be all right, Maria Helena?"

She nodded.

Feeling guilty for leaving her in the room with a dead body, Stu walked over to Benji's room. Benji was curled up in bed and Stu had to make sure that Benji was just sleeping. He was.

Quietly Stu slipped out of Benji's room, closing the door behind him. He looked at the bed where Maria Helena sat beside her sister. He couldn't leave the two girls in the same room as a dead body. It just didn't seem right, but first things first. He had to get Tommy cleaned up and properly settled.

Nürnberg, two days later

Jeff Matheny looked at the radiogram with dread. The look Tom Johnson, the radio operator, had given him when he passed it over promised bad news. The fact that the radiogram was folded and sealed suggested the worst of bad news. With great trepidation he broke the seal. He looked to the bottom first, to see who it was from. "Dell." *Shit, the only Dell he knew was his father-in-law. Why was his father-in-law sending him a radiogram.* He moved his eyes to the main text.

> DAISY DYING STOP
> TETANUS STOP
> GET HERE ASAP STOP

Jeff swallowed. His daughter was sick, and he hadn't known. He looked at the header of the radiogram to see when it had come in. *Oh, shit. It's two days old. My daughter may have died without me at her side. And hell, Lora. My family needs me.* Jeff set off to tell his boss he was heading for Grantville.

After the funeral

Stu Beckworth stopped walking to turn and look back at his niece's home where friends and family were still gathered to comfort the family. He spat at the ground. "The sooner that bastard goes back to Nürnberg the better."

Dell nodded his agreement. Lora's husband had arrived in Grantville barely in time for the funeral. There might have been some excuse for that, but there was no excuse for the way he ignored the two girls in favor of his sons. "Yeah! The sooner the better. For a moment there, I thought you were going to thump him."

"Believe me, Dell, if you hadn't dragged me away from there I would have done more than thump the bastard. Maria Helena went from excited and animated that her 'father' was coming home to totally lifeless as he walked right past her, and her sister was reduced to tears. I could have killed him there and then."

"Yeah, well, then it was a good thing I dragged you away. There's been enough death in the family for now."

Stu shoved his hands in his jacket pocket and started walking again. Dell fell in beside him. They walked another half mile before Dell broke the silence.

"Why the hell isn't the government doing something to protect the children, Stu? Okay, so they got that smallpox immunization program up and running, but what about tetanus?" Dell stared at the setting sun. "I asked Dr. Shipley after Daisy died. She said she hadn't heard anything. You got any idea what it takes to make a vaccine?"

"No. Do you?"

"No. Dr. Shipley suggested I talk to Dr. Ellis. He was part of the team responsible for the smallpox vaccination. I think I'll drop in after work tomorrow and ask him. You want to come along?"

Stu looked torn. He hesitated, and then shook his head. "I think I'd better hang around Maria Helena and her sister. Maybe the bastard will spend a bit of time with them before he goes back, but just in case he doesn't, I want to be around to let the girls know that they're important."

The Home of Dr. Emery Ellis, M.D. (retired)

"Sorry about what happened to Daisy. A real shame that." Dr. Ellis shook his head.

"It's Daisy I wanted to talk to you about."

Dr. Ellis stepped back from the door. "Come on in, Dell. But I have to tell you, I've spoken with Dr. Shipley about Daisy's case, and there was nothing more she could have done."

"Yeah, that's what she told me. But that's not what I want to talk about. I want to talk about what it takes to make a vaccine."

Dr. Ellis guided him to a seat before sitting down himself. "I guess you really want to know about a tetanus vaccine, don't you? Well, generally speaking, once you can reproduce the bacteria in the laboratory, making a tetanus vaccine becomes a possibility. The trouble is, the bacteria are anaerobic, meaning that they live under conditions without oxygen. It's damn near impossible to culture the bacteria without developing some special equipment first. I hear Les Blocker is trying to do that, but he's not making a lot of progress."

"The vet? Any idea why he's not making much progress?"

Dr. Ellis shook his head. "Yes, the vet. Veterinarians actually know a lot about vaccines, Dell. The big problem is the lack of trained staff. There just aren't enough trained laboratory technicians. Come into the study and I'll show you what I have on vaccines and vaccinations."

Dr. Blocker's Veterinary Clinic

"Hi, Dell. Dr. Blocker's fallen a bit behind. If you'll just wait in the waiting room, he'll see you as soon as he's free."

Dell glanced over towards the waiting area. The first thing he saw was the young girl. He froze for a moment. She looked so much like little Daisy. Backing away from the waiting area he turned to June. "If you don't mind, I'd prefer to wait outside."

Outside the surgery Dell leaned against the wall. The sight of the girl had brought back memories of that night spent beside Daisy's bed praying for a miracle that didn't come. When his breathing returned to normal, he pushed off from the wall and started to look around. The animals in the paddock beside the surgery attracted his attention. He'd always had a bit of a soft spot for the llamas. Or were they alpacas? He'd never really been sure of the difference.

He lean against the fence and he watched one of the animals approach. It didn't appear threatening, so he stood his ground until the llama started to gently butt its head against his chest.

"He wants you to scratch under the halter."

"Dr. Blocker?" Dell asked.

Les leaned forward and scratched the llama. "Call me Les. You're Dell, aren't you? Dr. Ellis told me you might come around asking about vaccines."

"Yeah, I'm Dell. Dr. Ellis told me you were working on a tetanus vaccine. Can I ask how far you've got?"

Les shook his head. "Not very far at all. In fact, we've basically shelved it as too difficult. We just don't have the trained staff. I'm spending half my days trying to train some new veterinarians and the other half tending to animals."

"What will it take to get you back working on a tetanus vaccine?"

The vet pushed away the llama and gave Dell a wry grin. "More than twenty-four hours in every day would be a great place to start. Come on, let's go for a walk. If I hang around the surgery, I'm bound to be called away."

The office of Helene Gundelfinger

Mrs. G. looked across her desk at the two up-timers who had asked for an urgent appointment. "Herr Beckworth, Herr Beckworth, how may I help you?"

"We want to sell everything we have. We need to raise as much money as we can."

Helene gently tapped a pencil on her desk. "I can't recommend that. Can you tell me why you need the money? There are a number of investments I've recently made that should make a fine return in time."

"We don't have time. Hell, too much time has already been wasted."

"Easy, Dell. Mrs. Gundelfinger deserves to know why we want the money." Stu turned to Helene. "I'm sorry about Dell, Mrs. Gundelfinger. My grandniece, Dell's granddaughter, died last week. She shouldn't have. If she'd been vaccinated, she wouldn't have died. We want to underwrite a research program to produce vaccines like they had up-time."

"Children die, Herr Beckworth, are you sure your research program will do any good?"

"Yeah, I know children die, Mrs. Gundelfinger, but not my grandkids, and not from such a fucking lousy way as tetanus. Not when a simple vaccination can prevent it," Dell answered.

"Tetanus?"

"You probably know it better as lockjaw."

Helene thought a moment. She had seen people die of lockjaw. It wasn't a pretty way to die. She glanced up at the ceiling. Above her office her daughter was taking her nap. She would do anything to prevent her daughter suffering that fate. "You might not need to sell all of your investments, Herr Beckworth. If you can gather people capable of developing such a vaccine, I will help raise the money. Would I be correct in assuming you want the vaccine to be available to the greatest number of people and not just the well-to-do?"

Dell nodded. "Especially the children."

Daisy Matheny BioLab, Grantville, a few months later

Dr. Emery Ellis surveyed his domain. He had come out of retirement to serve as the first director of research at Daisy Matheny BioLab, the company named after the first up-timer to die of tetanus. Whereas most new businesses struggled to raise capital, Daisy Matheny Biolab hadn't even had a true public offering. Shares had been offered only to selected individuals. People who would rather see affordable health care for all, instead of more money in the bank. There had been a few rumbles from people who hadn't been invited to participate. Emery grinned when he considered the possible social implications of not being a shareholder in Daisy Matheny Biolab. He and his wife were safe. They held a hundred shares.

Lora stood with Tommy in her arms watching the nurse give the children their shots. It wasn't the tetanus vaccine. They weren't even thinking of human trials of that vaccine yet. Maybe next year. Instead, she and the children were being vaccinated against typhoid. It was a double vaccine, a needle and an oral vaccine embedded in a sugar cube.

Maria Helena volunteered to go first. There was no sign of emotion on her young face as she sat quietly waiting for the nurse to finish. Then she stood up and walked over to Stu. Lora bit her lips when their hands met. She was sure money changed hands. She'd have to have words with Uncle Stu about the evils of bribing the children.

Then she watched Benji approach the nurse. Lora braced herself for a repeat of the fuss he'd made for the smallpox vaccination. But Benji surprised her. He couldn't carry "stoic" like Maria Helena, but the expected fuss failed to materialize.

The smile that passed between Uncle Stu and Maria Helena caught her attention. Then she grinned. Of course, that was why

Maria Helena had gone first. There was no way Benji was going to appear less brave than a girl.

His dose administered, Benji retreated as far away from the nurse as he could get. He slowly sucked on his sugar cube while he rubbed his arm. That left Regina next in line. Maria Helena moved closer to her sister and held her hand. Regina didn't cry out, but she did give the nurse an accusing "that hurt" look.

That left just Tommy to go. Sucking on his sugar cube, a rare treat given the price of sugar, he kept his face buried in Lora's shoulder through the whole operation.

Benji and Regina ran on ahead, but Uncle Stu was dragged along by Maria Helena pulling at his hand. Lora smiled at the happy picture they made. There had been a special closeness between the two since the night Grandmother Aggie died. These days Maria Helena was almost a typical happy-go-lucky nine-year-old.

Lora had worried about her father. He had felt badly about his inability to do anything to help Daisy and had been the real driving force behind the Daisy Matheny Biolab. Once the biolab was up and running he'd been lost. In the end, he'd taken advantage of some of the contacts he'd developed lobbying for the biolab and gone into business with a gun maker in distant Melis. He was finally showing signs of being over his guilt at not being able to save Daisy. Reading between the lines in his latest letter, Lora was sure he'd found a new woman friend. *Well, good luck to him.*

Dr. Ellis caught her standing under Prudentia Gentileschi's magnificent portrait of Daisy.

"The artist did an incredible job, Lora. But how did she know what Daisy looked like?"

"Jeff was missing the kids, so we shot some videos and sent them to him in Nürnberg. When Prudentia asked about any pictures we might have of Daisy, Dad sent Jeff a radiogram asking for the tapes. She really caught Daisy."

Dr. Ellis nodded. "Yes. A marvelous memorial for a life lost so young." He gently made to lead Lora away from the painting. "Come, I'm sure your family is wondering what happened to you."

Lora gave the painting one last look before letting Dr. Ellis lead her away.

None So Blind

David Carrico

Magdeburg
January 1635

The slap knocked Willi sprawling, eyes watering with pain. He had to bite his lip hard to keep from crying out.

"Five nothings!" Willi felt Uncle's hand grab the back of his rags and haul him up. The hand shook him so hard he felt like a pea rattling in a cup. "You spend all day on the streets and all you bring me are three pins and two worthless quartered Halle coins!"

Willi dropped to the floor again. His head was spinning, but his hand had fallen across his stick. He instinctively grasped it, then pulled it to his side. It took a moment to rise to all fours. As soon as his head settled some, he pulled himself up on the stick.

"I'm sorry, Uncle, but the place where I was, not many people put coins in my bowl." He hesitated. "And . . . and I think someone took money from my bowl. It kind of sounded like it."

"What? Did you see who it was? Why didn't you stop . . ." Uncle's voice died away as he realized that no, Willi did not see who the culprit was and therefore could not stop him. "Hmm. Well . . . I guess that might not be your fault. But you'll have to do better in the future. Here." Something thumped into Willi's chest and dropped to the floor. "That's all you've earned today."

Willi knelt down again and felt around the dirty floor. Within a moment his fingers encountered what he expected to find—a dried hunk of bread. It was more than he had expected. When Uncle felt he had been cheated, those in his family were more apt to receive curses and blows than blessings and food. Willi gathered the bread up. He would go hungry tonight, he knew, for it wasn't much more than a crust.

It took Willi a moment to peer around and figure out from the play of light and dark which way his corner was. It took some time to make his way there, stepping with care and feeling his way with his stick. At least none of the family was in a mood to push things or plant feet in his way in the hope he would trip tonight. In the last four years, he had provided that entertainment many times, often falling helplessly to the ground with cruel laughter ringing in his ears.

Willi's blanket was still where he had left it, wadded up behind an old trunk so that no one would notice it. Threadbare and full of holes though it was, he did feel warmer with it wrapped around his shoulders. The winter was not even half over, and he felt like he hadn't been warm since forever.

He ate the bread slowly, one small bite at a time; partly because it was so dry and hard that it took a lot of chewing to make it possible to swallow, and partly to make it last longer. It would at least give Willi the illusion of having enjoyed a full meal—a most uncommon experience in his short life.

Willi was swallowing the last bit as he heard someone coming toward him amidst the noise of the other children chattering and yelling. He cocked his head to one side, then smiled as he recognized the step. "Erna," he said.

"How do you know that?" the girl demanded as she took his hand and with care set a small pottery cup in it. "How do you always know it's me?"

"You walk different." Willi sipped the water in the cup.

"But even when I try to sneak up on you, you still know it's me."

Willi held his hands out and shrugged. That caused water drops to splash out of the cup, and he licked them from his hand. "I don't know how. I just do."

He felt her plop down beside him. "So where were you today?" she asked.

"By the cathedral."

"The cathedral? No wonder you were so late getting back. You'd better not let Uncle know you went there. He's told us more than once to stay away."

"Well, I won't tell him, so if you stay quiet he won't hear, now will he?"

Erna swatted his arm. "Why did you walk so far? Weren't you afraid of getting lost?"

"I've heard Fritz and Möritz talk about it, so I knew the way there. I hoped the folk coming out of the church would give alms, but they were as cold as the building itself. And what they did give, someone else took."

"That really happened?" Erna leaned close.

"Yeah. Someone tossed a coin in and then someone else snatched it back out before it stopped ringing. It was so fast I felt nothing, saw only a dart of shadow." It wasn't the first time that Willi had cursed his ruined sight. It wouldn't be the last.

"Well, next time take someone with you, to watch over you."

"Who? You?"

Willi was knocked sideways by her punch on his shoulder. "Yes, me. I can watch from a ways away and make sure nobody robs or cheats you."

Willi shrugged. "If you want to. But how will you earn your bread if you're near me?"

"Uncle's been teaching me some new stuff. I'll manage."

Willi wanted to ask what new stuff, but just then Uncle called out, "Lights out." As usual, his stinginess with lamp oil was getting the lamp blown out at the earliest moment.

Erna left amid the sound of scurrying around. A moment later she was back. "Lie down and I'll cover us." Willi curled up on his left side facing the old trunk, wrapped his arms around his stick and hugged it to his body. He felt the weight of first his blanket, then hers, covering him. Erna wiggled under the blankets and put her back against his.

The two of them were too small to gain a space close to the fireplace and its few coals—Uncle not being any less stingy with the firewood. Those went to the older, harder children; older than Willi's eight years. Forced into the outer part of the room, they had learned that if they shared their blankets they stayed warmer than if they slept alone. Even so, there were many nights that they shivered together as the cold cut through the meager coverings.

Erna went to sleep as soon as she stopped wiggling to find the right position. Willi was kept awake by his growling stomach for some time, but at length he drifted off.

The next morning Erna ripped the covers off of Willi. "Come on! It's daylight. If we don't get out there, we won't get anything." She barely let him use the chamber pot, and then they were in the street. "So, where to this morning?"

"Not near the cathedral, that's for sure." Willi pondered. "How about Zenzi's? I haven't been there in a few days."

"Zenzi's it is. C'mon." And so, stick in one hand and Erna tugging on the other, Willi was towed to one of his favorite places, a bakery that was several blocks away.

"Here we are," Erna announced in triumph. "You want your usual spot?"

"I can find it." Willi pulled his hand away and reached out to touch the front of the building, then walked along the front to where a beam jutted out. He put his back to that bit of corner and settled to the ground with a sigh. Reaching inside his ragged jacket, he pulled his bowl out and set it on the ground in front of him. He leaned back against the corner, set his stick against his shoulder, settled to wait for opportunity.

Erna crouched in front of him. "Lean forward."

"What?" Willi was confused.

"Lean forward, I said."

Willi did so. He felt a band of cloth cross his eyes and get tied behind his head. "What did you do that for?" His hand fumbled at the cloth, only to get slapped.

"Leave that alone." Erna leaned close enough that he could feel her breath on his face. "Willi, you can't see. But the people can't tell that unless they get a really good look at your eyes. This way they can tell right away and you'll most likely get something from them."

"But I can see!" Willi's voice broke, to his embarrassment.

"Willi." Erna's voice was full of pity, which only deepened his embarrassment. "It's been almost four years. You only see light and shadow. You try to see more, and all you get is more falls and more of those bad headaches. Just wear the rag. You'll feel better, and you'll make more coin, too." Willi heard her sit back. "I'll be up and down the street, doing my thing and keeping an eye out. Won't nobody dip into your bowl without my seeing it."

"All . . . all right," Willi choked out, feeling as if he was giving up on his dreams to see again.

Erna patted his cheek, for all the world like she was the mother he could hardly remember instead of a slip of a girl not much older than him. "That's my Willi. I'll keep watch." He heard her stand and walk away.

Willi sat in his darkness. The rag soaked up his tears.

Magdeburg
February 1635

The two men with sergeant stripes on their sleeves marched into Frank Jackson's office, stopped in front of his desk, then saluted smartly—or as smartly as a couple of West Virginia hillbillies with no military service could manage.

"Cut it out," Frank said in a weary tone. "Bill, shut the door. Siddown, both of you." He looked at Bill Reilly and Byron Chieske. "We," Frank emphasized that word, "have a problem. You guys are going to help solve it. You know who Otto Gericke is?"

The two men looked at each other. Byron shrugged. Bill turned back to Frank. "He's some kind of mucky-muck here in Magdeburg, right? Burgomeister, or something like that?"

"Yep, he is; one of several. He's also the engineer appointed by Gustavus to rebuild Magdeburg. And a more thankless task I can't imagine." The other two men nodded in agreement. "But when he's wearing his burgomeister hat, he's the only one of the city council who can pour water out of a boot even when the directions are written on the heel. As a consequence, he's the one who's in charge of anything important, including the city night watch. And he's asked for help in upgrading them into something resembling a police force."

Bill looked to Byron again. Byron looked puzzled. "So why doesn't he approach the admiral for some help from that investigative unit he set up?" Although there had been pretty widespread deprecation of the "NCIS" unit at first, after a few successes in investigating some crimes, including a bloody double murder, no one thought they were a joke now.

Frank grimaced. "There's been one too many exchanges of insults. That wouldn't stop the navy guys from working at it—the admiral keeps them on a pretty short leash. The city boys, though, have been 'insulted,' they claim. They refuse to work with the navy.

"Mike's pretty pissed about it. He doesn't need extra trouble right now, and for a squabble to boil up between the navy and the civilian government is just not a good thing in more than one way. I wasn't in the room, but my understanding is that he more or less told the admiral that if his investigators couldn't keep from talking trash, he'd better muzzle them. Oh, it was a little more polite than that, but the message got across." Frank grinned an evil grin. "I also heard that the admiral's subsequent talk to his crew chief was a bit . . . ah, blunt." He sobered. "But the city watch still won't have anything to do with them."

Frank folded his hands on his desk. "Bill, I know you were about done with your degree. What was your major again?"

"I was in my last semester for a degree in Business Admin, with a concentration in business law and contracts."

"Right. And you worked for that security firm in Fairmont for a while, right?" Bill nodded.

Frank turned to Byron. "And I know you were majoring in criminology and had just qualified to serve as a reserve officer for the county sheriff. Correct?" Byron nodded. "I checked with Dan. He said something about you doing some ride-alongs."

"Yeah, some for Dan and some with the sheriff's deputies."

"Were you bucking to join the Grantville PD?"

"State Trooper."

"Ah. Well, that's all water under the bridge. Dan Frost's partner, Dennis Grady, is based here in Magdeburg, so by rights this job ought to go to them. Building police forces is what they do. The city council is too cheap to pay their consultancy fees, though, so Mike told me to handle this problem.

"Here's how it is. You two have more experience in law and law enforcement than anyone else I can lay my hands on, so you're it. As of now, you are no longer part of the transportation detachment. You're seconded to the USE Department of Justice. You'll have to find out where it's at and who's in it—I don't have a clue. Your first assignment, straight from the prime minister, is to shape the Magdeburg city watch into something more than a good-ole-boy's club that walks around at night with torches."

The two of them looked at each other wide-eyed for a moment, then turned equally horrified glances on the army chief. Frank stared at them for a moment longer, then grinned. "You're both officers now—Reilly, you're a captain, and Chieske, you're a lieutenant. Carve up the work however you want, but one of you needs to work with Gericke and try to get the organization and procedures laid out. The other one needs to start working with some of the watch, so they can get used to the idea of us Grantvillers poking our nose in their business."

Frank focused on Byron alone. "Chieske, you're probably going to end up with the second job. I think you can do it. But there's one thing you won't do. You take the strong and silent type to an extreme. You make Calvin Coolidge look like a town gossip. I haven't figured out yet if you just don't like to talk, or if you caught on at an early age if you kept your mouth shut you'd stay out of trouble. I don't care, actually. But you will knock it off with the city watch."

The general directed a stern look at him. "I don't mean you should turn into a smart-aleck motor-mouth. But you will talk to these men, using reasonably complete sentences. You will instruct them. You will correct them. You will even, God help you, discipline them if you have to. You're not one of those street corner white-faced clowns. You're an officer in the army, my army, and you will do your job to the best of your ability, no matter how much it makes you uncomfortable. Is that clear?"

Byron nodded.

"I said, is that clear?" Frank's voice was frostier in tone.

"Yes, sir."

"Good."

Byron shivered a little. Frank sometimes had that effect on people.

General Jackson smiled again. "Who knows? If you play your cards right, Gustav Adolph might draft you. You could end up in the history books as the first two agents of the Imperial Bureau of Investigation. Or maybe the first two USE Marshals." He stood and shook hands with them. "Odogar has got your rank insignia and badges in his desk in the outer office.

"Get to work."

Magdeburg
March 1635

Frank's thoughts were right. They divided the work so that Bill Reilly—Captain Reilly, now—worked with the burgomeister. That left Byron to work with the men of the watch themselves.

A few days after trying to work with all of them, Byron had decided that it was going to be tough to get through to the watch as a group. Despite the fact that many of them were close to his own age, or even older in a couple of cases, they reminded him of nothing more than a group of high school jocks. He knew they weren't stupid—these were the cream of the patrician and merchant families, after all—but they had adopted a uniform "We don't need to know anything you have to show us" attitude. Byron had muttered a few words about the NCIS to Bill, who sympathized with him. They both knew that there was plenty of pride and arrogance to go around. The watch had almost certainly given as good as they got in the insult arena, but that didn't make the results any easier to deal with. Byron had gone to Otto Gericke and asked the burgomeister to designate one member of the watch—one who might be a little more open or reasonable than the others—to partner with him.

The result was Gotthilf Hoch, one of the youngest members of the group and from a minor patrician family. Byron watched him as he squirmed a little in his chair. He had been sizing Gotthilf up for the last day or so. He thought he could work with him. No time like the present, he supposed, so he had asked the young man to step into his office.

"So, why did you join the watch?"

Gotthilf's eyes widened in surprise. "The statue speaks!"

Byron grinned. "I'm not that bad, am I?"

Gotthilf returned the grin uncertainly, as if he didn't know how Byron would react. "Nay, but there are those who have wagered you would only speak when spoken to or when ordered to. Coin changes hand tonight when I tell them of this."

"All right, so I don't talk a lot, unlike some others I could name." The grins returned at the thought of a few of the members of the watch. "So, why did you join?"

Gotthilf flushed a little. "After . . . after Tilly's men destroyed the city, I thought to help protect it again."

"And?"

"And . . . I thought it would be good to be seen as a member of the watch." That all came out in a rush.

"Aha. You liked the idea of wearing the sash and carrying a musket or torch around at night with a bunch of other guys." Byron glanced at the younger man, only to catch his profile as he stared down the street in his turn. "That sounds like the ambition of a fifteen-year-old boy." Gotthilf's flush increased. "But the idea of protecting your city, now . . . that's a goal worthy of a man."

Gotthilf turned to stare at Byron.

"Yep, that's an ambition I can respect," Byron continued. "Thing is, it doesn't go far enough."

Gotthilf's stare turned puzzled.

"You were thinking of protecting Magdeburg and your family from outsiders. What about protecting Magdeburg and its citizens from assault from within?" Byron pointed out the window to the street. "These people have the same desire for peace that you do. Shouldn't they be given your protection? From theft and murder and rape, not by soldiers but by those who are just stronger and more vicious?"

Gotthilf's eyes followed Byron's finger. For long moments he stared out the window. When he turned back to Byron, his jaw was set firm. "The talk is that you Grantvillers come to overturn our laws and create anarchy, that you are all but lawless yourselves. Look at how your admiral insulted the city by raising those outside the law to enforce it in his precious NCIS."

"The rumors have it wrong, as usual. We believe in laws, but we believe in moral laws; laws that are based on reason and logic, not on custom and ritual. And the admiral has his reasons—after all, sometimes you have to set a thief to catch a thief. But that has nothing to do with protecting your people." Byron smiled at Gotthilf's surprise. "You already have the tools you need to reach your desire. Eyes to see, ears to hear, and a mind to reason. If you have those, all you need to know is how to use them."

The young man was still thinking about that when Byron ended the discussion with, "Meet me tomorrow morning here. Leave your sash at home. In fact, dress in something old and worn, something that looks like it's been used for more than sitting for a portrait." His grin was fully as evil as Frank Jackson's. "And wear your most comfortable shoes or boots. We're going to be doing a lot of walking."

☆   ☆   ☆

Gotthilf Hoch, stalwart member of the Magdeburg city watch—in his own opinion, anyway—was walking as escort today for Lieutenant Byron Chieske of the USE Army. At least that was how he thought of it. He knew that Byron referred to him as his partner, but that implied an equality that Gotthilf didn't feel. As a member of a patrician family in the city, he wasn't sure he should be forced to work with this up-timer. However, Burgomeister Gericke had made it very clear he expected Gotthilf to do so, so here he was.

He looked up at Byron as they walked down the busy streets of Magdeburg. This wasn't the first day they'd been walking the streets. When he questioned Byron about why, he got a response that he was still mulling over, trying to understand: "I need to learn the city—learn it the way the people know it . . . not from horseback, or with a group of the watch or a company of friends, but up close and personal. And if I've got to be out there, you're going to be out there with me." That devil-may-care smile was on his craggy face as he finished.

It was a fair distance to look up at Byron—he was on the tall side, even for an up-timer, whereas Gotthilf was short, even for one born before the Ring of Fire brought Grantville to these times. In fact, on those few occasions when Gotthilf was being honest, he would admit that he almost bordered on being a dwarf. That made the contrast with Byron even stronger.

Byron glanced down at him and raised an eyebrow. The man was a walking definition of laconic, Gotthilf decided. He could talk, but at times his facial muscles did most of his talking for him. In any event, it wasn't difficult to interpret this question.

"Yes, we're almost there." He stepped around a steaming pile of dung left just moments before by a horse. "Another block, I think." Byron nodded and continued walking.

They were well away from the docks, in an area of Magdeburg that was very much still in a state of transition. The sack of the city in 1631 by Tilly's army had burned most of it to the ground. Almost four years later, the city was still in recovery. Money was flowing in because of Magdeburg becoming the capital of the USE, from the naval yards and from many of the new up-timer inspired businesses. Nevertheless, much of the city was still a mess.

Take this street, for instance. It must have served as a fire break, since most of the buildings on the west side of the street showed no evidence of flames. The east side buildings were, for the most part, ash and a poor grade of charcoal. Many of the former building sites had been cleared, with a few of them even showing evidence of reconstruction. The west side buildings hadn't totally escaped damage, however, as doorway after doorway showed evidence of having been forced or kicked open by Tilly's marauding troops.

The area was busy, though. Enterprising vendors brought wagons, carts, or even packs full of anything that would sell, and set up in the open spaces created by the fire. These weren't the big merchants; they were peddlers, small farmers from outside the city, itinerant craftsmen. Withered or dried fruits and vegetables; firewood that was more twigs and small branches than solid wood; cloth scraps and ribbons and old clothes; odds and ends of plates and cups and knives; pins and needles; even a portable butcher shop—bring your own meat; all could be found down this street. It was even whispered sometimes that some of these folk were those who would also perhaps purchase items without inquiring too much into whether the seller was the rightful owner.

A rangy dog ran by, splashing them both with liquid from a rather noisome puddle. Gotthilf cursed as the smell reached his nose. His immediate reaction was to look and see how badly his clothing was soiled, resentment boiling in his mind. It took the visual reminder that he was wearing old clothes from one of the servants for him to relax. His best tunic and culottes were still hanging in the wardrobe at home. For once he was glad that this inscrutable Grantviller had made him wear something other than his finest clothes. Only then did it dawn on him that his servant's opinion might not be the same as his.

Byron's clothes were equally scruffy and unremarkable, Gotthilf noted. In fairness, he had to admit—with reluctance—that the lieutenant hadn't asked him to do anything he wasn't willing to do himself. There were enough up-timers in Magdeburg these days, and enough down-timers starting to dress like up-timers, that his worn clothing attracted nothing more than the occasional calculating stare that assessed the value, then caught sight of Byron's face and looked away.

Although it was broad daylight, Gotthilf caught glimpses of women sidling up to men on the fringes of the crowd, offering themselves as they pursued the wherewithal to buy enough food to stay alive—or enough beer or spirits to stay drunk all night would be more like it. Young though he was, he had seen enough of the streets to have the cynical attitude of one who had observed the worst that mankind could do to itself. He had no illusions as to whether the raddled harridan he was watching at the moment would choose food or drink when darkness came.

Gotthilf's head turned forward again as another cross-street was reached. Byron stopped, which caused Gotthilf to halt as well. "This the area?" the up-timer asked.

"Yes, Lieutenant." The up-timer's abruptness irritated Gotthilf again, but he didn't let that interfere with his responsibilities. "The people of these streets have little love for the town watch, but such complaints of theft as have made their ways to our ears seem to center near this street."

"And no one has seen anything?"

"Not that we have heard."

"Hmm." Without speaking, the American moved to the west side of the street and leaned against the front of a building, hands in pockets.

After a moment, Gotthilf followed. "The building is in no danger of falling, you know. We don't need to prop it up." Byron's mouth formed a fleeting grin, but his eyes remained focused down the street. "What are you doing?"

"Watching."

"For what?"

"Don't know. I'll let you know when I see it, though."

Gotthilf shook his head, wondering if all the Grantvillers were this crazy.

Willi settled into his corner in front of Zenzi's with a sigh. Erna hadn't come with him. She'd said something about Uncle wanting her to do some work somewhere else today and left before he did. The way had seemed longer than usual without her chattering beside him. He'd had to go slower, as well, but he'd walked the route often enough that his feet automatically took him to Zenzi's.

The rag across his eyes was securely in place, or so his testing fingers told him. Willi pulled his bowl out of his coat, salted it with the couple of quartered Halle pfennigs like Uncle had told him to do and set it in front of him. He leaned back against the corner and propped his stick against his shoulder, settling in for the day. Pursing his lips, he began to whistle.

Byron felt the pressure of the wall on his shoulder blades as he stared down the street. He watched Gotthilf out of the corner of his eye as the youth looked around in imitation of what Byron had been doing the last few days. His gaze was slow, but Byron thought he was actually starting to observe what he was seeing.

Gotthilf looked back to him. "This is some more of that pattern stuff again, isn't it?"

"Yep. That's what I'm trying to do here, today. Start understanding how this street works. Once we can see that, then we can start looking for the thief, because he'll stick out like one of the emperor's Finns at one of Mary Simpson's parties."

That got a laugh from the young watchman.

Willi heard steps coming from the door of the bakery toward him. He cocked his head for a moment, then smiled. "Frau Zenzi." He gave a nod. "Good morning to you."

From the sound of her steps, Frau Kreszentia Traugottin verw. Ostermann—known as Zenzi to one and all—was not a small woman. Her husband, Anselm, was the baker for *Das Haus Des Brotes*, but she was the one the buyers dealt with. She held her own in exchanges that sometimes were impassioned and occasionally vituperative. Willi had overheard descriptions of ancestry, personal appearance and habits that, if true, were incredible. And more than once he had heard her take up the hardwood oven paddle and use it to chase would-be thieves or extortionists from the bakery. Swung edgewise by someone who knew how to use it—which Zenzi did—the paddle could break bones and crack skulls.

For all that, however, Frau Zenzi had been nothing but kind to Willi from the first day that he hunkered down outside her shop. Whether it was his age or size or affliction, she had always had a kind word to say to him and would often slip him a piece of warm bread with butter. Once she had placed a sweet roll in his hands. Willi's mouth watered whenever he thought of that day, when he'd had a taste of heaven.

"So, Willi, how are you today?" Willi liked Frau Zenzi's voice. It was deep and warm and furry sounding, but would never be mistaken for a man's voice.

"Today I am fine, Frau Zenzi. And how is your business today?"

"Eh, well, it is not as good as I would like, but it is good enough. God provides." Willi heard her clothes rustle as she bent down. "Hold out your hand, Willi."

He did so, and felt a cup placed in it. The tang of buttermilk came to him as he sipped.

"It's not much," she said. "I would have more, but the bread sold out early today, even the rolls that were burned on the bottom."

Willi licked his lips, feeling the thick coating of the buttermilk on them. He lifted the empty cup and felt it taken from his hands. "Thank you, Frau Zenzi. It was good." He hesitated. "Frau Zenzi? Why do you give this—the bread, the milk—why do you give them to me?"

He felt her kneel down in front of him, then her hand touched his head. "Do you not know, young Willi?" He shook his head. "'Inasmuch as you have done it unto the least of these, my brethren, you have done it unto me.' Those are the very words of Jesu Christus. I don't understand many things about the Bible, or about the words of Luther or Calvin, but these words of Jesu I understand. To the least, I will give. And you, young Willi, are among the least."

She patted his head gently, then stood. Willi's throat felt swollen from the emotion he was feeling that moment. To think that someone did care for him even a little fueled a warmth in his belly that made him forget the cool day.

"Uff." Frau Zenzi sounded disgusted. "Here comes that Dürr woman again, wanting us to bake something for her. If ever a name was fitting it is hers, for she is as thin and dry as an old stick."

"She sounds mean," Willi ventured.

"Ha! That's because she is mean, Willi my lad, for all her trying to sound sweet. Well, I'd best go deal with her. Soonest begun, soonest done."

Willi heard her steps move off. He sat quietly in his darkness for a moment, feeling the warmth inside, then resumed his whistling.

Byron pushed away from the wall of the building. "Come on. Let's go for a walk." Gotthilf was beside him as he started down the street.

The pace was more of an amble than a walk. Byron kept his

hands tucked into his jacket pockets as he looked around. He decided that most of these folks would have been right at home at an up-time flea market either as buyers or sellers. The energy, the conversations, the raised voices, even some of the gestures were all the same. If the people had been speaking English instead of German, this could have been the Saturday morning meeting at the old drive-in theater over by Fairmont.

One trade in particular caught Byron's attention. He was looking the right way to see several silver coins exchange hands for a single table knife, fork and spoon setting of stainless steel flatware. The vendor looked nervous when he saw Byron staring at him after the exchange was made.

"Don't look now," Byron said after they were several steps past that point, "but the fellow in the faded green coat may be dealing in stolen merchandise. *Don't* look," without changing expression as Gotthilf started to turn.

"Why aren't you confronting him?" Gotthilf was scowling.

"Because I can't prove it . . . or at least not yet."

"But you saw something back there."

"Yep. I saw him sell something that could only have come from Grantville." Gotthilf started to turn again, and Byron grabbed him by the arm. "*But* . . . that doesn't mean it's stolen. Only that it might be."

Gotthilf settled beside him again. "So, you just ignore it?"

"No. Because it might be stolen. So it's our responsibility to look into it. We'll ask some questions in Grantville about what I saw. We'll ask some questions around here about this fellow. We'll start putting the pieces of the puzzle together, and depending on what picture we get we may arrest the guy."

Gotthilf stopped. "Pieces? Puzzle? Picture? What are you talking about? And what does that have to do with stolen property?"

Byron's jaw dropped for a moment. "Um . . . I think we just tripped over an up-time thing." He spent some time describing jigsaw puzzles, until Gotthilf understood the concept. "So, police work is a lot like that process, except we have to make the pieces ourselves."

"I understand . . . I think. But it seems like a lot of work when we could just arrest him now and have done with it. You saw it, you think the items were stolen, the magistrates would probably be satisfied with that."

Byron wanted to smack his forehead. "Gotthilf, it's about the truth. It's about what I can prove, not what I think." He reached into his inside pocket and brought out a piece of paper. "Listen, this is even in the Bible. From Deuteronomy chapter seventeen, verse six: 'At the mouth of two witnesses, or three witnesses, shall he that is worthy of death be put to death; but at the mouth of one witness he shall not be put to death.' That's basically establishing that justice will be based on more than one man's opinion."

Gotthilf still looked stubborn. Byron was glad that he had talked to Lenny Washaw about this stuff. He had had a feeling that having something from the Bible that would support his teachings would impress at least some of the down-timers. He wasn't much of a church-goer himself, but he knew Lenny through his wife Jonni and her sister Marla. Lenny was a Methodist deacon, so he knew more Bible than Byron did, that's for sure. Once he had explained his need, Lenny had come up with several passages for him.

"Listen, Gotthilf, have you ever read the story of Susannah and the Elders?"

"No."

"It's in your Bible. Read it. You'll see what I'm talking about."

They continued strolling down the street. Byron had quit talking and was just looking around. Gotthilf was trying to see what the up-timer was looking at, but he saw nothing noteworthy.

His feelings ran through a cycle of confused, irritated and frustrated, over and over again. He thought he understood what Lieutenant Chieske was saying, but it just didn't make any sense. If you thought something was wrong and you knew who did it, everything in him said you should do something about it. It didn't make sense that you should just talk to people.

Gotthilf shook his head, walking two steps past the up-timer before he realized he had stopped. He turned and stepped back to where Byron had his head cocked to one side. "What is it now?"

"Listen."

After a moment Gotthilf could hear it; someone was whistling. Someone was whistling well, although he didn't recognize the tune. Byron had caught the direction and headed toward the sound. Gotthilf trailed in his wake, shaking his head again. Now the madman wanted to see someone whistling.

Byron stopped so suddenly that Gotthilf almost trod on his heels. The whistling was in front of them. He stepped around the up-timer, only to see nothing—nothing, that is, until he looked down to see a small boy seated in front of a bakery, whistling.

Gotthilf had to admit the boy was good. For a moment, he stood there and listened. He didn't think he knew the tune, but something about it . . . He shook it off when Byron knelt before the boy.

"Hello." Byron's voice was light, but his expression was serious. "My name is Byron. What's yours?"

Gotthilf noted the dirty rag tied around the boy's eyes and the wooden bowl with several coppers in it sitting on the ground in front of him. A beggar. His mouth twisted in distaste.

"Willi." The blindfolded head turned to look up at Byron, as if the boy could see. "You sound funny. Are you from Jena?"

Gotthilf was ready to wager there was nothing wrong with his eyes.

"No," Byron responded, "I'm from a lot farther away than that."

"Mainz?" Willi was obviously trying to think of someplace far away.

"No," Byron laughed. "I'm from Grantville."

Willi's mouth made an O. He started asking excited questions, which Byron answered patiently, one after another. When the boy ran down, Byron asked his own question.

"Do you know the name of the song you were whistling?" When the boy shook his head, Byron said, "It's called 'The Rising of the Moon.' My wife's sister sings it a lot at the Green Horse tavern."

"Oh, I never heard the name. That's pretty. I just heard the song when Un . . . when someone I know would hum it."

Gotthilf snorted and nudged Byron with his foot. When the up-timer looked up with a frown, he said, "We have work to do, or so you told me, yet you sit here talking to a beggar who can probably see as well as you can."

The boy's mouth set in a hard line. He reached up to pull off the bandage, then raised his face to them. Gotthilf swallowed a curse as he stepped back from the sight of the scarred and cloudy eyes.

Byron took Willi's face between his hands, tilting it this way and that to let the light shine upon it. "Can you see anything at all?" The question was asked in a tone that matched his gentle hands.

"Some light, some dark." Willi's voice was low.

"Has it gotten worse?"

Willi nodded.

"When did it start?"

"When the soldiers came." The boy started putting his bandage back on to hide his eyes.

Byron looked up to Gotthilf. The sack of Magdeburg—four years ago. Gotthilf swallowed in sudden nausea. "Where's your mother and father?"

"Soldiers killed them." Willi's voice was now almost inaudible.

"I'm sorry." Byron rested a hand on the boy's hair for a moment. "Who do you live with now?"

"Uncle."

"What is his . . ."

"Willi! It's time to go." Byron was interrupted by another boy running up to Willi's side. "Come on, you know Uncle doesn't like us to be late." The boy helped Willi pick up the bowl and put the coins in his pocket. "Come on!"

"Wait." Byron reached in his pocket and pressed something into the boy's hand. "Goodbye, Willi. Nice talking to you."

Gotthilf stood beside Byron as the two boys hurried down the street, Willi being led by the other.

"You know when I said I'd let you know when I found what I was looking for?"

"Yes."

"I think I just found it."

"The boy?"

"Yep. Boy that size shouldn't be begging, blind or not. On my watch, you don't abuse or take advantage of kids. Someone's not taking proper care of him, and I think I'll find out who."

"But he's just a beggar." Gotthilf was astounded at the up-timer's thoughts. Astonishment fled in the next instant, however, as Byron turned to him with a transformed face. His eyes were cold. His face was still, as if engraved in stone, except for a muscle tic in his left cheek.

" 'We hold these truths to be self-evident' . . ." Byron's voice, cold enough to match his eyes, was obviously quoting something.

". . . 'that all men are created equal, that they are endowed by their Creator with certain unalienable Rights, that among these are Life, Liberty and the pursuit of Happiness.'" After a moment, he continued. "That's from the American Declaration of Independence. It expresses our belief that all men are created of equal worth. And that includes Willi."

Byron's hands snaked out and grabbed the front of Gotthilf's jerkin. He suddenly found himself nose to nose with the taller man, feet dangling inches above the ground. "That boy is a victim." The up-timer's voice was, if possible, even icier than before. "And no victim is ever going to be dismissed as 'just' anything. Not on my watch. If you don't learn anything else today, learn that."

The up-timer released his grip. Gotthilf landed hard on his heels with a jar that brought a *clack* from his teeth and set his head spinning. He looked up to be transfixed again by the cold glare from Byron's eyes.

"You've got some Bible reading to do. While you're doing that, I'm going to do some research."

Still a little wobbly, Gotthilf watched the back of the tall up-timer recede down the street.

Willi was two streets over before he was able to dig in his heels. "Erna!" He wrenched his arm out of her grasp. "What are you doing?"

"Getting you out of trouble," she hissed in his ear. "One of those men was an up-timer."

"I know that. His name is Byron. He was nice."

"Well, I think the man he was with was one of the city watch. He looked like one I saw wearing the sash a week or two ago."

Willi swallowed. "He wasn't nice."

"That's right. And you just remember that. We're going to have to tell Uncle, and he's not going to like it. Now come on."

"Wait." Willi held out his hand. "Byron gave me this. What is it?" He heard the sound of breath sucked in. "Well?"

"It's a silver pfennig. Uncle will like that for sure. Now put it away and come on."

As it turned out, it was two days before Gotthilf saw Byron again. He spent a frustrating morning trying to locate the Bible passage he had been directed to read. Finally he gave it up and went to visit his pastor. The ensuing reading and discussion lasted most of the day. Verse by verse the old scholar walked him through the account, in the process showing him the wisdom and knowledge owned by Daniel, the hero of the tale.

"It is a cautionary tale from several aspects," the pastor concluded. "First, to those who are in positions of authority: it says to guard themselves against temptation, and warns them that if they do succumb to temptation, nothing they can do will hide their sin. They will be found out."

He turned a page. "Second, to the community: to not be quick to judge without first carefully weighing the facts. Things such as this must be diligently examined, and even the highest ranked involved should be questioned carefully.

"Third," and here he gave a direct look to Gotthilf, "to those charged with these examinations: to be diligent to look for the facts, and not be swayed by opinions or statements from others. It is reprehensible to allow someone to be falsely accused and convicted of a crime."

"That's what he said," Gotthilf muttered.

"He?" the pastor asked.

"Byron Chieske, the Grantville lieutenant I'm supposed to be working with."

This led to a discussion of the events of the previous day. Somehow it didn't surprise Gotthilf to find that his pastor agreed with the up-timer.

"He sounds as if he is a man of wisdom, integrity and insight. I suggest, young Gotthilf, that you listen to him."

Gotthilf sighed. "Yes, sir."

The following morning Gotthilf tried to apologize to Byron for not showing up the previous day.

"Don't mention it," Byron waved it off. "I was up to my eyebrows in looking for an orphanage."

"Orphanage?"

"Yeah. A place where kids who lose their parents and don't have kinfolk go to live."

Gotthilf struggled to absorb another new up-time idea. "We have no such things."

"That's what I found out." Byron shrugged. "So then I asked what happened to the kids whose parents were killed in the sack."

"And?"

"Most of them were placed with kin. If no kin was found, older children were placed as apprentices and younger children were placed with families who would care for them until they were of an age to be apprenticed." Byron looked satisfied, to Gotthilf's eye. "The church kept records, they did. When I explained my concern about Willi they not only opened those records, they gave me a clerk to read them. And here," he reached in his pocket and drew out a notebook which he threw open, "is a list of families who accepted young boys into their foster care about that time."

Gotthilf reacted to Byron's smile with an uncertain smile of his own. "Let me guess: we go to talk to these people."

"Right. Here's the addresses. Let's go."

They turned away from the next to the last address on their list. "All children accounted for and healthy," Gotthilf muttered as he pulled the address list out one last time. "We're down to one Lubbold Vogler."

"It's called the process of elimination," Byron assured him. "You work through all the possibilities until you arrive at the one that fits. So, we've eliminated all the others, we should get our answers from Herr Vogler at this last address."

But the face that opened the door at their knock disappointed them. "No, no Vogler here."

"Did he live here before you, do you know?"

"No." And the door was firmly closed.

They stepped down to the street. "Where do we go from here?" Gotthilf wondered.

Byron looked around with narrowed eyes. "C'mon. And think of a question you can ask." Gotthilf followed him over to an old man sitting on a step, one hand on a cane and another holding his pipe. The up-timer nodded his head to the old man. "Good afternoon, *Grossvater*. I am Lieutenant Chieske, and this is Herr Hoch."

"Fuchs," the old man grunted around the stem of his pipe.

"Herr Fuchs, we are searching for one . . ." Byron turned to Gotthilf, who fumbled the paper out of his pocket. "Lubbold Vogler."

Herr Fuchs took the pipe from his mouth and spat expressively.

"Does he live there?" Byron pointed to the house they had just left.

"Nay."

"Did he live there?"

"Aye."

"Do you know where he went?"

"Nay."

"Did he have some small children?"

The old man finally showed some expression, as his mouth tightened. "Aye."

Byron looked to Gotthilf. He had been smiling at the sight of Byron meeting someone even stingier with words than the up-timer, but now realized he was supposed to ask something. "Um ... er ... when did he leave?" He was gratified when Byron nodded in approval.

Herr Fuchs thought for a moment. "Three years ago."

"Did he say where he was going when he left?"

"Nay." They waited a moment, but the old man said nothing more.

"Thank you for your time." Byron held out his hand for Herr Fuchs to shake. "You've been very helpful."

They turned to leave, and the old man took the pipe from his mouth again. "If you find him, tell him I remember he still owes me twenty pfennig. And give him a lick from me for the way he beat those children." He clenched his teeth around the pipe stem again and gave them a firm nod, which they returned.

"Well," Byron breathed. "Well, well, well, well, well." Gotthilf looked up to him as he tried to keep up with the up-timer's long strides. "I do believe we've found our man."

"Found?"

"Well, so to speak. It appears we have a name for him, which is more than we had. Now we just need to truly find him."

"And how do we do that?"

"We go back to the street tomorrow and talk to Willi. One way or another, we'll find Herr Vogler through him." Gotthilf watched as Byron's face turned cold again; colder even than the other day. "And then we'll have a little talk."

The ice in Byron's voice caused the down-timer to shiver.

Gotthilf couldn't decide if Lieutenant Chieske looked preoccupied in the early morning light, or if he was just sleepy.

"Do you have a gun?" Byron asked.

"The musket belongs to the city."

"No." Byron shook his head. "I meant a handgun; a pistol."

"I have a pistol," Gotthilf replied. "One of the new percussion cap revolvers from Suhl."

"A Hockenjoss and Klott?"

Gotthilf nodded.

"Got it with you?"

Byron held out his hand. Gotthilf, with mingled pride and embarrassment, pulled the pistol from his pocket and handed it to him. He watched as the up-timer handled it. The young man took a great deal of pride in his new pistol, although he thought it a bit plain. It still bothered him, however, that he had been forced to settle for the silver-chased model with bone handles. His father had made it very clear that their family was not named among the *Hoch-Adel*, so there would be no gilded toys.

"A good weapon." Byron handed it back. "A little too pretty for my taste, though." Gotthilf was unable to keep his astonishment at the up-timer's reaction from his face. Byron laughed, producing by what seemed sleight of hand a weapon from underneath his jacket. "Now this is what I would call a good pistol. None of that fancy work on it that has to be kept polished and clean."

Gotthilf stared at the pistol. It wasn't pretty. It was all metal, and looked like a slab with no decorative work on it. No gold or silver chasing, no carved ivory or woodwork. Just pure function—to shoot, perhaps to kill. A chill ran down his spine at the sight of it.

"Keep yours with you all the time now." Byron made his disappear again. "And Gotthilf," Byron started to turn away, "make sure it's loaded."

Erna watched as Willi tried to argue with Uncle.

"But Uncle . . ."

"No, I said! You will not go out, not with those . . . those . . . spies looking for you."

"But . . ." Willi started.

"No!" A slap knocked Willi against the wall, where he slid to the floor. "Now do as I say."

Uncle looked at the huddled boy for a long moment, then turned away and left the room. Free to move without the glare of Uncle's gaze being on her, Erna hurried to Willi's side and helped him sit up.

"Are you all right?" She pulled his head around to see where he had been hit. Willi's ear was a bright red, so that must have been where the slap landed. "Are you all right, Willi?" she whispered.

Willi tried to stand, then folded up again. "'M dizzy," he murmured.

Erna helped over to their corner and covered him with their blankets after he laid down. She crouched by his head. "Willi?"

"Mmm?"

"Willi, don't you try to talk to Uncle for a while. He's . . . something's not going right for him. I heard men yelling in the back of the house a couple of nights ago. It woke me up. The back door slammed, then he came into our room and stood by the front door for the longest time."

She shivered, remembering what the light from the other room had revealed. "Willi . . . Willi, he had a gun. A pistol."

"Why would Uncle have a gun?" Willi slurred.

"I don't know," Erna replied, still whispering. "But he does. And it scares me."

"Mmm."

A long moment of quiet passed.

"Willi?" There was no response. Erna checked to see if he was breathing. He was, so she guessed he'd gone to sleep or passed out. She wiggled around, then sat with her arms around her knees, waiting until Uncle told her to go do her work.

She hadn't been able to tell Willi the most important part. After Willi had been knocked to the floor, Uncle had stared at him, cold and hard. Then he'd put his hand in his pocket and started to take out his gun, only to stop and, after a moment, slide it back in.

That scared Erna more than anything.

The space outside the bakery was empty. They loitered in the area until well past the time that they had seen Willi before. Gotthilf watched as Byron's lips tightened in frustration.

A large woman appeared in the doorway of the bakery, looking up the street. Byron elbowed Gotthilf. "Come on." She looked to them with a frown as they approached.

"Your pardon, Frau . . ." Byron began.

"Frau Kreszentia Traugottin. And you are?"

Byron introduced them as city officials looking into various irregularities. "I see that the boy is not here today."

The woman's frown turned thunderous. "You're not looking to harass Willi, are you?"

"No, no, indeed not," Byron soothed. "We want to talk to him because we think he knows something that will help us. And we want to make sure he's being taken care of. It bothers us that a child that young is begging in the streets."

Gotthilf watched as Byron's conversation with Frau Kreszentia—"call me Zenzi"—elicited the information that no, she didn't know where Willi lived; no, she didn't know anything about an uncle; yes, the last few months he had been here almost every day; and yes, he always came from one direction, often with another youngster leading him.

The conversation drew to a close. "*Bide,*" Frau Zenzi said as she stepped back into the bakery. She returned a moment later with two rolls, to hand one to each of them. "You find my Willi, you make sure he is all right, you tell him his place is still here. Yes?"

They assured her they would do exactly that and took their leave. Munching on his roll, Gotthilf looked back to see her standing in the door of the bakery, looking after them.

Gotthilf swallowed the last of his roll. "For someone who doesn't like to talk," he commented to Byron, "you certainly are proficient at it."

Byron paused in licking his fingers. "Just because I can do it doesn't mean I want to." He finished the finger licking, and continued, "And you'd better have been paying attention, because you're going to start doing all the talking and question asking soon." Gotthilf stared at the up-timer with wide eyes. Byron returned a grin. "Yep. Count on it. You'll talk; I'll just stand around and look threatening."

"Ha." Still strolling down the street, Gotthilf looked up and stiffened. "Byron." He tried very hard not to shout or act excited. "Isn't that the boy who pulled Willi away from us?"

Byron directed a casual glance that direction. "Yep. Now look away." They did so. "The trick is to not stare at the person, but to look that way just often enough to keep him in sight. Except in this case I think it's a her."

"What?" Gotthilf absorbed another surprise. "Are you sure?"

"Yeah. I've been around girls in pants all my life, so to me they're not the automatic disguise for a girl they are for you down-timers." That was the first time Gotthilf could remember Byron using that term. He noted in passing that it was used in a neutral manner. "Girls move differently than boys, even that young. And if you look at her hands, from what I remember they're slenderer than a boy's usually are. So, I think that's a girl." Gotthilf absorbed that as well.

There was a moment of silence.

"Gotthilf?"

"Aye?"

"What's she doing out here? I mean, it looks like she's sound and healthy. She ought to be in school, right? Or in some kind of service?"

"Yes. She should definitely not be out on the street in boy's clothes." Gotthilf was starting to understand what Byron had meant about looking for things that didn't fit the pattern.

"So," Byron hissed, "we have two weirdnesses now—a boy begging who shouldn't be, and a girl dressed in boy clothes who is . . ."

At that exact moment they both saw the girl snatch a kerchief from the pocket of a man she bumped into. She was so fast they barely caught a flash of it before it was stuffed inside her jacket.

Gotthilf saw that Byron's face had gone very grim as he muttered a string of words in up-time English. Gotthilf didn't recognize the words, but he recognized the tone. If some of them weren't blasphemous, he'd eat his hat. "Okay," Byron said after he had to stop for breath, "that's the third strike. Now I really, really want to talk to Uncle."

"So do we take the girl now?" That was Gotthilf's instinctive reaction, but he'd been with Byron enough by now to realize that might not be the best thing to do.

"No." Byron shook his head. "No, I'm starting to get a bad feeling about this. I want you to hustle back and get Captain Reilly and at least a couple more guys, either army or city watch, I don't care, as long as they've got pistols. No muskets. You get there and back as fast as you can. If Bill wants to know what's going on, you just say I said to get here now." Gotthilf opened his mouth. "Go!"

Gotthilf went.

☆   ☆   ☆

It was over half an hour before Gotthilf arrived back at Byron's side, accompanied by Bill Reilly, two of the city watch and another up-timer. Completing the crew was Otto Gericke, who had been talking to Bill when Gotthilf had burst into his office, panting and wheezing from his run.

Byron met them back up the street, waving them to the side of a house on the west side.

"Is she still here?" Gotthilf asked.

"What's up?" Bill was matter of fact as the men gathered around.

"Possible Faginy racket. Got a girl in boy's clothes working as a dip down the street. Pretty sure she's got a mule—think I've got him pegged. We think the same bunch had a blind kid out here begging a few days ago. Girl came and pulled him away, nobody's seen him since."

Bill pulled at his chin. "So, what do you want to do?"

"Follow the girl home. Both she and the boy mentioned someone named 'Uncle.'"

"Ah. You think he's the Fagin?"

"Best guess."

"What is this 'Faginy'?" Gericke asked. Gotthilf listened closely as Captain Reilly described a plan to teach children to perform criminal acts for the gain of those who taught them. He also explained that a "dip" was a pickpocket and a "mule" was someone who would take stolen goods from the "dip," reducing the risk that the pickpocket would be caught with them.

"This 'Uncle' is the man who would do this?" Gericke was frowning. The captain nodded. "I want this man."

"So do we, Master Gericke. So do we." Reilly turned back to Byron. "So, what's the plan, Lieutenant?"

"Gotthilf and I go first. The rest of you follow at least a half block behind, in more than one group. Once we find the place, we figure out what to do next."

"I am a magistrate," Gericke said. "You will be under my authority."

Byron's smile was sharp-edged. "Thank you, sir. That will make things easier."

So it was that Gotthilf found himself once more at Lieutenant Chieske's side, walking down the street with the girl barely in sight ahead of them. The late afternoon shadows were unfolding, and she disappeared and reappeared as she moved in and out of them.

Unfortunately, her route was not straight. Turning the third corner, Byron muttered, "Man, I wish we had radios." Gotthilf was confused again—a state that was all too familiar the past few days of working with the up-timer. Byron caught his expression. "No, I don't mean the crystal radios, I mean . . . oh, forget it, I'll explain later. Might as well be wishing for cars, while I'm at it."

After they passed the next lane that crossed the street, Byron started limping. Gotthilf slowed to keep pace. "No, you keep going," the up-timer said. "I've decided I want to talk to the guy following us, so this is my excuse for dropping back. You keep her in sight and I'll catch up in a few minutes."

True to his word, before long Byron slid back into place beside Gotthilf, who looked over at him. "So?"

"Bill saw me dropping back, so he moved up as well. We took the guy down a few minutes ago. He was her mule, all right; he had that cloth we saw her snitch. He's not talking right now, but the boys have him tied up and are bringing him along."

Just then the girl veered toward a house that looked to have burned. Roof beams were visible and charred. Gotthilf wouldn't have thought there was anyone there, but she just tripped up the steps and opened the front door. It closed behind her before they could react.

Erna was back. Willi sat up from where he was lying in the corner. He felt some better. She was talking to Uncle about Möritz and some things he was bringing. Willi wasn't sure what that was about. But he was very glad that Erna was back. He stood and moved toward the sound of her voice. Maybe she could come talk to him now. "Erna?" he called.

The others closed up with them. Lieutenant Chieske conferred with Captain Reilly and the burgomeister for a brief moment. Gotthilf watched as the captain sent the other men to surround the house.

Byron turned back to Gotthilf. "You ready? Got your pistol?"

Gotthilf swallowed, nodding as he pulled the pistol from his belt.

"Okay. Burgomeister Gericke is wearing his magistrate hat at the moment, and he really wants to have a conversation with Uncle.

You and I will be the first in the door. We're hoping this guy won't cause trouble. Fagins usually don't. It's petty crime they're in, not enough to take big risks for."

Byron pulled his own pistol. "But we're going in prepared. Stay with me, follow my lead, and watch my back. Whichever way I go after I clear the door, you go the other. Got it?"

Gotthilf was poised on his toes as they stepped up to the door, gun before him, breathing rapidly. He felt as if his vision had narrowed to a circle just in front of him. Byron raised his hand to knock on the door.

"Uncle! Uncle!" That was Fritz, shouting as he crashed through the back of the house. "City watch and up-timers outside. They have Möritz, and they're surrounding the house."

There were thunderous knocks on the door. A loud voice called from outside, "City watch! Open up in the name of Magistrate Gericke!"

Willi recognized the voice. "Byron." He was perplexed as to why the up-timers had come here.

He had spoken loud enough for Uncle to hear. "You," Uncle hissed. "This is all your fault."

Willi heard a loud click.

"No," Erna screamed. Willi felt her push him.

There was a loud *bang*. Willi was knocked to the floor.

Byron threw the door open at the sound of the shot. Gotthilf followed him into the house, stepping to the right of the door because the up-timer had stepped to the left. His horrified gaze was greeted by Willi lying on the floor, with the girl they had been following sprawled across him. A dark crimson splotch across the front of her jacket was widening as he watched. Gotthilf tore his eyes from that sight to focus on the man who Byron's pistol was pointed at with unwavering aim.

"Drop the gun." Byron's voice was like the chill of a blizzard. Gotthilf could almost feel snow in the air. Belatedly, he brought his own pistol to bear on the man standing against the far wall. "No one else needs to get hurt."

The man's laugh was high-pitched, almost manic. "And what will you do with me if I do? What would be my fate?"

"Lubbold Vogler, we arrest you on the charges of theft, attempted theft, aiding and abetting theft, receiving stolen property, contributing to the delinquency of a child, and murder." Gotthilf marveled at how matter of fact Byron's voice sounded.

"Ah, all very impressive, although I'm not sure those are all crimes under Magdeburg law. Still, the last could be troublesome." The other—Vogler, since he didn't reject the name—gave a slight bow over the pocket pistol that was a twin to the one Gotthilf held. A wisp of smoke curled up from the barrel, but Gotthilf could see that the hammer was cocked again.

Watching the man's eyes, Gotthilf was very uneasy. He couldn't read Vogler's thoughts, but he knew they were racing, because the eyes were shifting frequently, like a wild animal looking for a way out of a trap.

Byron took a slow step to his left. Gotthilf took a step to the right.

"Drop the gun, Vogler." Byron's voice was even and cold.

"I think . . . *not!*"

Boom!

Almost everyone in the room flinched at the loud report of Byron's pistol, a sound that left more than one set of ears ringing. Vogler, however, did not flinch.

Vogler jerked against the wall behind him, down which he slid until he sat slumped against the wall, legs outstretched and head lolling like nothing so much as a rag doll tossed haphazardly across the room. But rag dolls don't have pistols fall from their lax hands, and rag dolls don't have crimson blood flowing from holes in their chests and don't leave large bloody smears on walls.

Byron gestured toward the large boy in the back of the room who was trying to sneak out. Gotthilf pointed his pistol in that general direction and the boy froze, trying to emulate a statue. Meanwhile, Byron slid Vogler's pistol away from the corpse with the toe of his shoe.

There was a sound in the door. Gotthilf glimpsed Captain Reilly out of the corner of his eye.

"All over," Byron said. "Have someone take the big one into custody. He looks to be about the same age as the mule, so he may be an accomplice as well. The little ones are all pretty much victims, I think. They should be held together until someone can make arrangements for them."

The next few minutes were bustling, as watchmen and up-timers came in and collected the children. Gotthilf put his pistol away after the largest was tied and hauled out.

Burgomeister Gericke walked in after the flurry of activity was over. "So, you killed him, Lieutenant Chieske."

"Yes, sir," Byron responded.

"I would have preferred him alive, Lieutenant."

"So would I, sir. But he had already killed a child and was trying to shoot me. I had no choice."

Gericke's eyes turned and bored into Gotthilf's. "Do you agree with the Lieutenant's assessment, Watchman Hoch?"

Gotthilf swallowed, stiffened, and stuttered, "Ye . . . Yes, Herr Magistrate. It happened as Lieutenant Chieske described it."

The burgomeister's eyes shifted again. "Do you have any contrary comment, Captain Reilly?"

"No, sir. From what we could hear outside, it sounded like it went down the way they describe it."

Gericke paused for a moment, sighed, and nodded. "I agree. The death of the child is ruled a felonious murder on the part of Lubbold Vogler, committed for reasons unknown. The death of Lubbold Vogler is ruled justified self-defense on the part of Lieutenant Byron Chieske after said Vogler attempted to kill him." He looked older, for some reason.

The two up-timer officers relaxed from their stiff positions, with almost identical expressions of relief crossing their faces. The burgomeister shook all their hands, including Gotthilf's, then left the death house.

"Well, your first case solved," Bill Reilly started to comment, when a sound arose from behind them. They turned to see the body of the girl moving.

Willi roused slowly, head aching from the second knock of the day. He tried to move, but someone was lying on top of him. He heard people talking, but it was all blurry to him. "Get off," he whispered, but the person didn't move. He pulled his hands out and started pushing. With some difficulty, he managed to free himself enough to sit up.

The other person's head was on his lap now. He put his hand on it, feeling it, looking with his fingers to see if it was someone he knew. The face was small, thin, with a bump in the nose; a familiar face, it was.

"Erna." He reached down and shook her shoulder.

"Erna." She rolled limply and his hand slipped, to land in something warm and sticky.

"Erna!" He brought his fingers to his nose. The smell of blood filled his nostrils. Something was wrong. Something was very wrong. What had happened? His thoughts were reeling.

Steps sounded in the room. He felt Erna lifted off him, while other hands picked him up.

"Willi?"

"Byron?" Willi was confused. The last thing he remembered, he was home. How did Byron get here? "What happened to Erna?"

"Willi . . ." He felt the man shake his head. "Willi, Erna is dead."

The cold bubble in his chest burst, filling him with shock and grief. The screams followed.

Night had fallen some time ago. Gotthilf felt himself sagging where he stood, watching the final discussions between Captain Reilly, Lieutenant Chieske, Burgomeister Gericke, Frau Zenzi and her husband, and the senior pastor of Magdeburg.

An amazing number of things had occurred in relatively short order. Not long after the burgomeister left, wagons had appeared: one for the corpses and one for the children found cowering in the house. The two larger children, Fritz and Möritz, classified as thugs from the testimony of the smaller ones, were tied up and made to march behind the wagons. The captain and the burgomeister intended to question them some more. They wanted to get to the bottom of Vogler's Faginy scheme, in the hopes that this was the only one.

Willi, once he was worn out from the screaming, would have nothing to do with the wagon. He kept breaking out in sobs for Erna. Byron was the only one the boy would talk to, so Byron carried him all the way back. He was sleeping now, rolled up in a blanket in the back of the children's wagon.

The conference broke up. The burgomeister and pastor walked off together. Byron stopped at the children's wagon for a moment with Frau Zenzi. Willi sat up rubbing his eyes, listening to the words from the grown-ups. He began crying again, quietly, a child's sobbing.

Captain Reilly came to Gotthilf. "Big day, huh?"

Gotthilf nodded.

"I'll be honest with you. I never expected to find anything like this, especially since we're just getting started. The burgomeister and I were talking about it; it just doesn't make sense for this guy to have a gun. That's several weeks' income to a petty crook. Doesn't make sense. There's something going on, here. We need to keep digging." He placed his hand on Gotthilf's shoulder. "This will be big news, you know. You and Lieutenant Chieske should get commendations of some sort for this."

Willi finally nodded and Frau Zenzi folded him in her arms. Gotthilf watched as she nodded to Byron over the boy's head. Byron stepped back, looked around with weariness evident in every motion, then started down the street.

Gotthilf nodded again as he watched Byron. "Where is the lieutenant going?"

Reilly looked at Byron's receding back. "I suspect he's going to get a drink somewhere." He returned his gaze to Gotthilf. "You're his partner. Go with him. It's always hard on a cop when he shoots someone, and he needs you to be with him on this just as much as he has the last few days. If he doesn't want to talk, don't try to make conversation. Just sit with him." The captain gave Gotthilf a small push on the shoulder. "Go on. We'll talk to you tomorrow."

Gotthilf received a sidelong glance from Byron acknowledging his presence when he fell into place beside the up-timer, but no words were said. The statue was back, Gotthilf decided.

Weary himself, Gotthilf trudged alongside until Byron turned in at a tavern. He looked up to see they were entering the Green Horse. That was all right with him. A stool pulled up to a horse watering trough would have satisfied him at this point.

Byron walked up to the bar. "Ale. Two. Large." He spun a coin on the bar top, received the two steins and walked over to an empty table in a dark corner, where he sat with his back to the wall. Gotthilf sat with him and applied himself to his stein.

They were on the third refill when Byron began talking. He began by pulling his pistol out and laying it on the table.

"There it is. The M1911A1 .45 automatic. Like most pistols, designed for one thing and one thing only: to kill people. It does a good job.

"I was supposed to join the sheriff's reserve. I was going to order a Glock, but then the Ring of Fire happened. So, here I am with Jonni's Grandad's old .45 that he brought back from World War II. It still works great. But I sure didn't expect to have it use it for real so soon."

Byron's face was getting red, Gotthilf noticed.

"I had the drop on him. All he had to do was put the gun down. That's all he had to do. He'd have stayed alive for a while, anyway. All he could see was his way."

"The man murdered a child, Byron," Gotthilf responded. His voice was quiet. "And all but in front of a magistrate. He would have been hanged within the next day." Byron shook his head. "Put the gun away, Byron." Gotthilf pushed it with a finger. "Put it up before someone notices."

"Right."

It was the fourth refill before Byron spoke again.

"I failed, Gotthilf. I screwed up royally. Gonna turn in my badge and go back to shipping supplies."

"You didn't fail, Byron."

"Two people are dead because of my mistakes. I failed."

"You did nothing wrong. Vogler killed the girl, then committed suicide by trying to kill you. You did the best you could."

"Then why's that girl dead? Huh? You want to explain that to me?" Byron was genuinely angry, Gotthilf saw. A hot anger, this was, unlike the cold anger he had seen a couple of days ago.

"Sometimes evil wins, Byron."

"You're barely old enough to grow a beard." Byron's voice was thick with sarcasm. "What do you know about evil?"

Gotthilf felt anger of his own rise within him. "Four years ago Tilly's soldiers destroyed this city . . . my city . . . my home. My house and the houses of thousands of others were burned to ashes. Bodies were everywhere. Don't talk to me about evil—I've seen the results first hand. I know about the evil men can do. And sometimes evil wins. But what was it you said to me—that protecting my city from theft and murder and rape, not by soldiers but by those who were just stronger and more vicious was a goal worthy of a man?"

Taken aback, Byron nodded.

"So, we lost this battle. Does that mean we stop fighting the war?"

Byron looked at Gotthilf, and after a moment gave another firm nod. "You'll do, Gotthilf. You'll do. And you're right."

Toward the bottom of that stein, Byron said, "None so blind as those who will not see. Vogler just didn't see, is all."

"Is that from the Bible, too?" Gotthilf thought it sounded scriptural.

"Nope. But according to my friend Lenny Washaw, it was written by a Bible scholar; guy by the name of Matthew Henry, I think. But it's true enough, man—it's true enough."

"Yes." Gotthilf just agreed with Byron.

Byron turned and faced Gotthilf. For all the ale he had been drinking, he appeared to be stone cold sober.

"This is why we do the job, man. This is why we will go back out on the streets tomorrow—to make sure that something like this—Does. Not. Happen. Again. Not on my watch."

"Not on our watch." Sometime during the day, when he wasn't paying attention, something had changed. Gotthilf now understood why Byron was so serious about their work. It surprised him a little, but he did understand it. And after watching a girl's life ebb away because of the greed and anger of one evil man—not even an enemy, but a resident of Magdeburg—he agreed.

Byron was turning his stein in circles on the table. After a few moments, he looked over at Gotthilf with a sly grin. "So, you going to tell me what Gotthilf means?"

Gotthilf had to think for a moment as to what the English would be. "Means God's Help."

"Does it now?" Byron laughed. "Well, that's probably appropriate, my friend. I suspect we'll need a lot of that help in the future—partner."

Gotthilf returned a smile of his own as he warmed inside. "I agree—partner."

On the Matter of D'Artagnan

Bradley H. Sinor

"Charlton Heston or Tim Curry?" mused Cardinal Richelieu.

Since there was no one else in the room, the chief minister to His Majesty Louis XIII of France was speaking for his own benefit.

Richelieu sat in a large chair behind the huge desk that dominated the room serving as his office. Two candelabra provided more than enough light for him to work. He brought out a pair of small boxes from one of the desk drawers, and put them next to a glass of wine he had poured earlier.

He found himself having to squint slightly to study the boxes. His eyes were good, for a man his age, but not as good as they had been more than a decade before, when Armand Jean du Plessis had first been created a cardinal-prince of the Roman Catholic Church.

The printing on the boxes was in English, a language he had only a smattering of, but it was the pictures on them that really interested him. They were not paintings, but rather what were called photographs, just another in a seemingly unending stream of new terms he had learned since the Americans and the town of Grantville had appeared on the scene.

Richelieu had long been an admirer of art; photographs, however, were far different than any paintings that he had ever seen. They showed what really was, not an artist's interpretation.

The photographs were scenes from "movies." As best he understood them, movies were like plays, only they could be watched over and over again—not repeat performances, but the same one, with no differences.

These two movies were of special interest to Richelieu. They were the same basic story, entitled *The Three Musketeers,* but each used different performers, and had been made several decades apart. Viewing them was an impossibility, since he had neither the machine to do it—or the power to run it if he had the machine. So, his agents in Grantville had also supplied very detailed summaries of the plots.

True, the movies did exaggerate events—not to mention playing rather fast and loose with actual facts, as had the book, by someone named Dumas. They even included a supposed relationship between Queen Anne and the English Duke of Buckingham.

Richelieu, himself, was a character in the story. It certainly didn't hurt his ego to know that he would be remembered nearly four hundred years in the future, not just in the history books but apparently as part of popular culture.

That he found himself portrayed as a villain and schemer didn't bother him one bit. A fact of life he had learned a long time ago was that whether or not someone came off as a villain or a hero depended on who was telling the story.

Something about the picture of Curry reminded Richelieu of himself, back when he had first come to the church. It was, perhaps, the gleam in the man's eye, which gave an almost predatory, animal look to the man's face. On the other hand, the older man, Heston, with his hands steepled in front of him, projected the quiet dignified look that Richelieu fancied for himself.

"Yes, I think Heston is more me."

"Excuse me, Your Eminence." Richelieu looked toward the door where one of his secretaries, Monsignor Henri Ryan, had appeared. The young man held several thick folios under one arm.

"Yes, Henri?"

"I have just received word that the Italian delegation will be here within the hour." Henri placed the documents he carried in front of Richelieu. "These are the reports on the things they want to discuss with you."

The younger priest stared for a moment at the two movie boxes lying on the desk. His distaste for them was rather obvious. Richelieu made a mental note to have a long talk with Henri about learning to conceal his feelings on some subjects, whether it was the Americans or the Spanish or whatever. That was one of a wide variety of skills Henri needed to develop.

"Very well, let me refresh my memories of these matters, and then bring them in when they arrive."

"Of course, sir." Henri started to leave, but stopped a few steps from the door and turned back toward the desk. "Also, that man, Montaine, arrived, a short time ago, saying he needed to see you."

Richelieu cocked his head slightly. Montaine was not due to report for at least a week. His unexpected appearance suggested that he came bearing news.

Of course, the Italian matter was also pressing.

"Very well. Have him wait in the smaller library. If he is hungry, have the kitchen prepare something. I shouldn't be more than an hour or two at the most. Did he say what he needed to speak to me about?"

"Yes, Your Eminence. He said it was on the matter of D'Artagnan."

Charles D'Artagnan stared out the window. It was an hour after sunrise and the narrow street below was already filled with people; there were food vendors, merchants, barbers, craftsman and their customers. A woman screaming at a man in a greasy apron, who was selling meat pies of some kind, caught his attention.

The exchange continued for a few minutes, with invectives flying between the two. The verbal combat only stopped when the woman handed several coins across and the vendor passed her back several of the meat pies. The two parted with smiles and wishes for the best of the day.

D'Artagnan felt something small and furry rub against the side of his hand. He looked down to the window ledge and found himself confronting a tiger-striped kitten who was very vehemently demanding attention.

He reached down and gently picked up the animal. The kitten was not happy with this idea, preferring to be petted rather than held, and struggled to escape his grip even as he began to stroke the animal's temples and then under its chin. The response came quickly, and the kitten stretched out, offering its neck for more attention, showing its approval with some very loud purring.

"Like that do you, little one?"

"I must say, you certainly have a way with animals, my dear Charles." A dark-haired woman clothed only in a sheet stretched out on the bed that filled much of the room. She had raised herself up on one elbow and leaned across the impression in the mattress that, until several minutes before, D'Artagnan had filled.

He smiled. "I have had a bit of experience with the wilder creatures of the world."

"Do you think you can bring out the animal in me?" Charlotte Blackson asked, laughing.

"I'll do what I can," he said, and walked back to the bed.

He set the kitten down on a side table, much to the chagrin of the animal. The cat reached out to try to drag his hand back, but D'Artagnan ignored the protests, intent on a different goal now.

He reached over and gently ran his finger along the edge of Charlotte's chin. The gesture brought a purr to her lips and a very inviting smile.

Charlotte Blackson was a beautiful woman. Her husband, a Musketeer, had been killed in the war. While not rich, he had left her well off. Charlotte had, in turn, taken her inheritance and shrewdly parlayed it into much, much more. Now, six years later, she was the proprietor of a dozen businesses and a partner in several more. She had even begun to move into some of the minor social circles of Paris. D'Artagnan had met her a few months before when he had stopped a thief intent on making off with her purse. In spite of the fact that she was more than a decade older than he, D'Artagnan soon found himself enamored of her.

"Yes, you do have a way with animals." Charlotte reached up and wrapped her arms around him. The sheet fell away, its edge dropping over the end table and trapping the kitten for a few moments.

"I try," he said as she plastered her lips against his.

"So what do you have for me, Montaine?" asked Richelieu.

Montaine was a small man, dressed in shades of brown, with a face that, other than having an immaculate pencil thin moustache, was not unique in any way whatsoever. Two minutes after they had seen him, few people could describe the man; most failed to even notice his presence, which had often proved a major advantage.

He stopped a half dozen steps in front of the cardinal's desk. Montaine never approached any closer than that; it was as if there was a line on the floor that he could not, or perhaps would not, cross.

Richelieu had employed Montaine for nearly four years, but actually knew very little about the man, other than the fact that he was loyal to France, i.e., Richelieu, and he had been remarkably effective in the various tasks that were set for him.

"I have located the man you are seeking. His name is actually Charles de Gatz-Casthenese. His mother's family was named D'Artagnan. He is from Lupiac, but he was raised in Gascony and came to Paris just over a year ago. He has been calling himself simply Charles D'Artagnan. He has not made a secret of who he is, but has not gone out of the way to make it known either."

"Indeed," Richelieu prompted.

Montaine nodded. "He attempted to get into the Musketeers, but was turned down, I believe because of his lack of military experience. However, he was able to secure an appointment with the Royal Guard."

"Continue."

"From the reports I have seen he has proved to be quite the gifted swordsman. He also turns out to not only to be good with his sword, but he knows when to fight and when to walk away. I suspect his superiors have an eye on him for eventual promotion."

"What of the other three men I asked you to find?"

"Oh, yes. I'm afraid I have bad news in that area. I could find no trace of anyone by the name of Athos, Porthos or Aramis currently serving in the Musketeers. From the way they were described in that book you gave me, I should have been able to find them, or at least someone who had heard of them. It's really a pity; the story makes them seem the sort of fellows I would have liked. However, I have found some very young men, barely in their teens. Issac de Porteau, Henri d' Aramitz and Armand de Sillegue d'Athos d'Auteville. I suspect they may have been the ones that this Dumas fellow modeled his characters on. They are all relatives, to one degree or another, of the commander of the musketeers, Monsieur de Tourvelle. So I did not inquire too extensively. I can, should you require more information on them."

"Unnecessary." De Tourvelle was a man that Richelieu knew of, quite well. He bore watching and could be either friend or foe to the cardinal, depending on the needs of the moment.

Perhaps it was true that the Athos, Porthos and Aramis of the movies and the book might not exist. It was entirely possible that those three were indeed simply characters who had been invented for the purposes of these entertainments. However, that did not mean they might not eventually still be of use to him.

"Have you actually met this D'Artagnan?"

"No, Your Eminence. I didn't feel that wise at this time. I have learned enough about him to know that this young Gascon is someone that you might do well to be wary of. He would not be easy to control and could end up being very much of a loose cannon."

Richelieu had come to trust Montaine's opinions. But he had also learned that there were times when you wanted someone who was not easily controlled, so this young man might suit him quite well. "Very well. Bring him to me, but do it quietly. I do not want the world to know of my interest in this man. Not quite yet."

"That might prove difficult. If it were a formal summons he would come, of that I have no doubt. However, D'Artagnan seems to have an agenda of his own and I do not see him allying with others, even you, sir," said Montaine.

Richelieu meditated for a few moments on the man's words, then took a single sheet of paper and began to write on it, adding a large daub of hot sealing wax to the bottom of the page into which he placed not only his official church seal but that of the chief minister of France.

"You must wait until the chance offers itself and bring him to me. If he is indeed as stubborn as you suggest you may have to *persuade* him." Richelieu passed the paper to Montaine. "This may be of assistance. I will trust in your discretion about when and how to use it."

D'Artagnan stood quietly in the doorway of an abandoned storefront. This was not the best part of town. From the look of the grime on the windows and the rust on the shutters, this place could have been shut up for decades. *That* suited D'Artagnan's needs perfectly.

From here he had a clear view of the Flying Pig, a tavern just down the block, and few would be able to see him, even if they were standing directly in front of him. A covered lantern sat at his feet. To add to his camouflage, D'Artagnan had left his uniform in the wardrobe at Charlotte's home. Tonight was not a night to be known as a Royal Guardsman.

No, tonight was a night for personal matters.

The Flying Pig was a low dive at its best. At its worst, it was a dump. The clientele asked no questions and only demanded to be left alone to muddle their dark thoughts in cheap wine and nearly tasteless ale.

D'Artagnan had gone into the Flying Pig twice, two times more than he would have wished. The smell inside the building reminded him of a charnel house or a battlefield long after the fighting was over, when the crows held forth. It was not a place that, even in the darkest of moods, he would willingly seek out.

Yet the Flying Pig fit the man he was seeking like a glove.

D'Artagnan had watched his quarry enter the tavern. Since there was no back door, D'Artagnan settled back and waited. At just past ten o'clock the tavern door opened and two men emerged. Both were short and round, their clothes the color of sand stained dark after a rainstorm. Neither man was steady on his feet. It seemed a miracle that they both didn't end up face down in the mud.

They stopped, for a moment, almost directly in front of his hiding place, then moved on. One of them began to sing, very badly.

D'Artagnan came up behind them in a few steps, grabbed both and slammed them hard against each other. Then he dragged them backwards, kicking the door of the abandoned shop open and pulling them inside. By the time the door had swung shut he had both of his prisoners on the floor.

The whole incident hadn't taken even thirty seconds.

Hand on the hilt of his sword, D'Artagnan waited to see if the attack had caught anyone's attention. One minute, then a second one, passed and there were no cries of alarm.

He recovered his lantern and opened it to look down at them. One was barely breathing, and would not be waking up anytime soon. But the other, the one that D'Artagnan wanted, surprised him. The man had actually begun to snore. This wasn't what he had expected, though the man fairly reeked of cheap wine and ale, which explained it.

D'Artagnan grabbed him by the lapels of his threadbare coat and shook him hard. "Wake up, you scum-sucking piece of filth."

There was no response at first. "If its money you're wanting," the man said finally, "then you're too late. What few coins I had have been sent to keep company with their cousins in the tavern keeper's cashbox."

D'Artagnan snorted. "I sincerely doubt that you have ever had enough money to interest me."

"What do you want from me, then?"

"I want your memory." D'Artagnan shook him again, then, while the man was still rattled, dropped him and held the lantern up close to his face. "I know who you are, Andre Marro. I know that you were once seneschal to the family LeVlanc, as your father and grandfather had been before you. It is for that reason that I've come looking for you, that I want your memory."

At the mention of his name Marro's eyes shot open. If it were possible, his face went paler than it had been.

"I . . . I . . . I . . ."

"Don't deny it. That will only make things worse. I know all about what happened to the LeVlancs and why it happened. You do as well, since you were there. I've tracked down the other servants who survived the purge. They didn't know the name of the man that the LeVlancs trusted to organize the whole thing, but they all agreed on one point. *You* knew who it was."

Marro groaned. D'Artagnan slapped him twice. Finally he muttered a name, a name that D'Artagnan recognized.

"If you have lied to me, I will find you, no matter where you run or hide."

Marro curled into a ball and tried to shrink into the floor. D'Artagnan walked away and slammed the door.

D'Artagnan came awake with a start and pulled himself up almost completely out of bed before he was fully aware. He struggled for each breath, every one coming as a hard won victory while cold, clammy beads of sweat rolled down his face.

Images cascaded though his mind: blood, the edges of swords, screams, the smell of burnt gunpowder, all rolling over and over and over. Intermixed with them was a single face, one that brought him a feeling of warmth, yet cut into the very fiber of his being.

"Charles, what is the matter?" Charlotte's voice was a distant sound for him.

"I'll be all right," he gasped. "Everything is all right."

"Right. You have nightmares like this all the time." Charlotte pulled the covers up around his shoulders to warm him, and her arms wrapped tightly to hold it in place.

"This will pass." He knew the reason for the dream; the reason had followed him for more than twenty years. "It is not the first time I have had to face demons in my dreams."

"I don't understand."

D'Artagnan drew the blanket tighter around himself but let his arm slide out to put around Charlotte. "It's complicated," he said, finally. "I must face someone, someone I have been searching for a long time. I know where he is, but I have never been able to find him with no one else around."

"Who is this person?"

When he told her, Charlotte's reaction was not what D'Artagnan expected.

"I think I might be able to help, my dearest," she said with the hint of a smile.

Charlotte giggled. "Please, Monsieur, is this the act of a gentleman?"

"I hardly think a gentleman is what you want right now." The man who had been nuzzling her neck for the last few minutes laughed.

They were standing in a garden to one side of the Hotel Transylvania, where a ball had been going on for many hours. Charlotte wasn't even certain who was throwing this ball; she had the feeling that a great many of the guests felt the same way though most would sooner die than admit it.

Manuel Zarubin had been standing near one of the windows when Charlotte spotted him. He was not openly circulating among the guests, but remained in one place, letting others come to him. It had taken nearly an hour for Charlotte to gain his attention and finally lead him into the darkness of the garden.

"It would all depend on what the gentleman in question might be offering. So what are you offering, my good sir?" Charlotte drew her words out so each one was a breathy echo.

Zarubin was fully twenty years her senior, but still muscled like a soldier. His neatly trimmed beard was streaked with grey, but in a manner that made him seem exotic rather than ancient. A few streaks of graying hair had snaked out from beneath the perfectly coiffed wig he wore.

"Perhaps I can show you." He pushed her back into the shadowed area between two large trees. His hands moved quickly into the opening presented by her cleavage; the staves of her corset screamed as they were pushed out of shape.

"Sir, I beg you, do not do that. I am, after all, a lady." Charlotte tried to pull back. Her action threw her up against the fork in a tree just behind them, lodging her where she could not move.

"You are no lady, tart," Zarubin said, pushing his hand farther down.

"My good sir, I believe that lady said she was not interested in what you had in mind." D'Artagnan moved toward the couple from behind a gazebo, where he had been waiting.

Zarubin twisted his head, his face showing surprise and anger at being interrupted. "Begone, sir! This is none of your affair."

"On that matter—" D'Artagnan laughed. "—I would say that you are definitely wrong. This is most definitely my affair."

He grabbed Zarubin and yanked him away from Charlotte. That the man managed to stay on his feet was a surprise, though his wig did go flying off onto the ground.

"You are a dead man, assassin." The Spaniard's voice was quiet and cold.

"We all die, sometime. Perhaps it is my time, perhaps not. Personally, I would put money on my walking away from here alive."

Zarubin pulled a rather fancily decorated sword from the sheath at his side. "Then you would lose your money, just as you are going to lose your life. I suggest, instead of boasting, that you put steel into your hand."

"My name is D'Artagnan," he said, and brought his own weapon free. "Prepare to die."

Zarubin made the first blow with a driving lunge meant to end the fight immediately. D'Artagnan parried the thrust and responded with several of his own.

"Enjoy this, dear Charlotte." Zarubin didn't take his eyes off his opponent. "You obviously know this young upstart. I hope you had a chance to say goodbye to him. Once I am finished with him, we can resume our little tête-à-tête."

D'Artagnan said nothing. He struck for Zarubin's chest with three quick jabs, which the man parried with ease, his battle hardened reflexes obvious with every move. As he parried Zarubin's counter strikes, D'Artagnan stepped to one side, his foot hit an uneven patch of ground and he went down, his sword slipping out of his grasp and out of reach.

"Now you are mine." Zarubin closed the distance, looming over his foe, intent on finishing the fight as quickly as possible.

D'Artagnan's dagger came into his hand as he rolled to one side. Striking blindly, D'Artagnan drove the blade hard into Zarubin's chest. The man trembled for a heartbeat and then he fell, the light fading from his eyes.

"Fight, don't talk," D'Artagnan muttered.

"Monsieur, do not move, or we will be forced to shoot!"

The command came from two men in Musketeer's uniforms with pistols in their hands. They had come from the direction of the hotel. Others were coming behind them to find the source of the disturbance.

"Charles, would you please settle this whole matter," said someone from behind D'Artagnan.

Startled, he turned to see a small man, dressed in brown, who was stroking his thin moustache as he spoke, walk forward from behind a statue of the Greek god Prometheus.

"I must say, it is rather cold out here and I think that Mademoiselle Blackson would definitely like us to escort her home," said the stranger.

The small man stood looming over D'Artagnan for a moment, just staring at him, before he offered him his hand. Once D'Artagnan was back on his feet, the newcomer's small fingers slid into the pocket on the right side of D'Artagnan's vest; producing a small folded sheet of paper, one that D'Artagnan knew for certain had not been there earlier.

"There are times, my old friend, when you get so centered on your task I suspect that you would lose your way in your own home." The little man turned to the Musketeers and offered the paper. "I believe that you will find that my friend had a full and proper warrant for what he did this evening."

☆ ☆ ☆

"The bearer has done what he has done by my order and for the good of the state," intoned D'Artagnan as he stared at Cardinal Richelieu.

The cleric said nothing, just cocked his head slightly and waited. D'Artagnan wasn't sure just what he had expected to happen. From the moment his blade had plunged into Manuel Zarubin, he had expected to wind up in the Bastille, not standing in front of the king's chief minister.

"I know what is on that warrant, young man, since I wrote it," Richelieu said finally.

Once the Musketeers had read the warrant, D'Artagnan and his companions had been released. After escorting Charlotte home, the small man, who refused to even give his name, led him to Richelieu.

That the cardinal had been awake and working in his office fit his reputation for having a hand in everything that happened in Paris and France every minute of the day and night.

"Then I suppose I have you to thank for my freedom, Your Eminence?"

"Indeed, you do," Richelieu agreed. "And how do you propose to repay me for that favor?"

"What would you call fair payment? You seem to have some interest in me. This fellow," he gestured toward Montaine, "obviously works for you, and, I would guess has been following me for some time."

"That he does, Charles de Gatz-Casthenese." Richelieu smiled. "Don't look so surprised, I know who you are. The question is what I do with you. You have obviously been planning the death of Señor Zarubin for some time. So let me ask you the next question. Why?"

D'Artagnan didn't know whether to smile or be worried at this latest turn of events. "Justice, Your Eminence. Justice."

"I thought the king and I were the dispensers of justice in the realm."

"You are, but sometimes that task falls into the hands of others. In the case of Zarubin, it fell to me. I had no choice in the matter. If you will recall, the year before he was murdered, Henry IV, our current king's father, was the victim of another assassination attempt.

"Most of the conspirators were captured and executed, as they should have been, but not the man who organized it. My father was killed while still searching for the ringleader. My mother was convinced that he must have gotten too close on the trail of the villain and was murdered for it. I have searched for most of my life to find out who that was. Three weeks ago I found out that it was Zarubin."

"You were duty bound to avenge the attack on his late majesty?" Richelieu steepled his fingers.

"Duty bound, yes, but not for that reason. If you will recall, the king was unhurt. I have known all my life that for my father's soul to rest there must be justice. It was a matter of the honor of my family."

Richelieu was silent for some time. "There will be consequences for his death, political problems that I really did not need at this time."

"I regret nothing that I have done. I am prepared to accept whatever penalty I have earned for my action."

Richelieu pulled a folded sheet of paper out of his desk. It bore both his personal seal and the seal of his office. It had obviously been prepared some time ago. He passed it to D'Artagnan.

He could feel his jaw hanging open as he read the document. "I do not understand, Your Eminence."

"What is there to understand? That is a commission as a lieutenant in my personal guard. If you accept this, know that while your loyalty must always be to myself—and that means to France—I will, from time to time, call on you, for shall we say, special duties."

The man in brown chuckled. "Do you think Dumas would approve, Your Eminence?"

"Dumas?" asked D'Artagnan, but Richelieu waved the question away. "What of the consequences for the death of Zarubin?" he continued. "If I recall your statement not minutes ago, you said that you didn't need the political problems that might come from it."

"True, but there are ways to turn them to the advantage of France." Richelieu's smile was cold. "That is where a statesman can be as deadly as a swordsman. As for you, Charles D'Artagnan, I feel that *your* skills can be of use to me, and in turn to France, in these most unsettled times."

"How did you know of me?" asked D'Artagnan.

Richelieu hesitated for a moment and then smiled. "Let us say that you came to my attention because of a man named Charlton Heston."

D'Artagnan shook his head. "I have never heard of this person."

"It is highly unlikely and completely unnecessary that you have. Perhaps one day I may explain who he is." Richelieu took a bag of coins and tossed them toward D'Artagnan. "Consider this an enlistment bonus."

"Why do I have a feeling that my life has just become quite interesting?"

"Because it has," said Montaine. "Personally, I think that a celebration is in order." D'Artagnan had almost forgotten the little man's presence.

"It is late, gentlemen and I am tired. I will leave the celebrations to you young men." Richelieu turned and left the room.

"I, for one, could use a drink," said the small man to D'Artagnan. "I also know an excellent tavern not a stone's throw from here."

"Lead on. I think I am going to need several drinks," said D'Artagnan. "By the way, it occurs to me that you still have not told me your name. I have no idea who you are."

He grinned and flamboyantly traced the line of his moustache. "I have many names. Why don't you call me Aramis?"

A Filthy Story

Aamund Breivik

Daniel Pedersson cursed and swung the entrenching tool again. It went *splat* instead of *crack*, again, and he cursed some more. Not that swearing helped; he was already covered in filthy sewage slush beyond all imagination. The supply depot's jury-rigged sewer system had worked fine all summer, but now the outlet had frozen solid and the sewage had backed up all the way to the officers' latrines. Removing the blockage was a horribly filthy job, but this was the Swedish Army. There was always someone who could do with some "disciplinary measures." Ah well. Daniel had been punished before, and he probably would be again.

Not that he was entirely innocent of this current mess either, but he couldn't help feeling that it ought to be procurement officer Paal Nilsson-Loo down here clearing it up instead of him. They weren't even supposed to have a supply depot here, never mind sewers. So what if he'd helped construct this dodgy plumbing in the first place? Or that he and some other enlisted men had been a little too enthusiastic when they found the sewage was blocked, and the enlisted men's latrines were *upstream* of the officers'?

Nilsson-Loo had been ordered to set up a small Swedish Army procurement office for the Grantville area. The Swedes were buying so many goods and services from the booming industry there that they needed someone to sign contracts and inspect the goods, to ensure the crown always got its money's worth. He made a decent living, more than decent in fact, by skimming what he saw as his rightful share off every single deal. A bit more than what the crown might think he was entitled to, but he kept the witnesses quiet by sharing some of his questionable income with his subordinates.

Like when he decided he liked the up-time-style indoor plumbing so much that he had his men lay pipes from their fancy new latrines out to a nearby drainage ditch. Not just his own shiny porcelain throne, but the men's too, since he didn't want to smell their waste if he could help it. Now it had all gone wrong, and the Grantville authorities had gotten wind of their unauthorized plumbing. They'd declared it all to be the Swedish Army's problem, after repeatedly using the phrase "code violation." Along with other, less polite English words and phrases which Daniel could now add to his vocabulary. Other new additions were "septic tank" and "leach field." Nilsson-Loo had therefore declared it must be Daniel's problem, for not doing the job right in the first place. So while Daniel was down here in an overflowing ditch, Nilsson-Loo was probably off spending his "skimmings" on women. Or on something else Daniel didn't want to know about; there were rumors, and he worried that his boss might stain the Army's reputation one day.

Before he could employ his new skills in language and septic engineering, he had to remove all the effluent from the drainage ditch and deposit it in a more permanent location so it couldn't run off downstream to pollute the waterways. This was backbreaking, boring, seemingly endless work and he'd been at it alone all day. There had been some commotion earlier, but nobody had bothered to tell him what was going on and he couldn't leave his work to find out.

He'd just about finished hacking the frozen sewage into slush and dirty ice cubes, when a sour-looking military policeman arrived escorting a surprisingly cheery person who was carrying a number of buckets. Surprising, that is, for someone about to wade waist-deep in raw sewage with frozen crusty bits on top. Vague recognition kicked in.

"Hey, aren't you one of those ski-troop heroes? What are you doing here on punishment detail?"

The man answered something unintelligible: *"Eig e skilaupar, jau, meinn neigu noukon hjelte"* it sounded like. "Say again?"

"Sorry," the man answered. "I'll speak German instead. I've gotten used to my Swedish friends understanding me, but they've had some time to learn. My name is Torjer Lien, and I'm a skier but no hero." He grinned. "I'm here for offending a supply officer."

"Why? And what's so funny about it?"

"Well, the reason isn't funny." Torjer's face darkened, all merriness gone. "It started when the ski troops were asked to test a new piece of equipment, a 'sleeping bag' made to an up-time pattern and with up-time-style zippers." Torjer spoke while he worked, filling two buckets with filth and handing two more to Daniel. "The 'prototype' we were shown looked good, and when we let a recruit use it for a week it didn't rip or break or anything. That's how we test new equipment—if it's recruit-proof then it's probably strong enough for general issue. We told them it was a great idea, if they would only make them big enough that we could actually use them while wearing all our winter clothes and equipment. The prototype was a bit tight when you put your rifle and everything inside, like we sometimes do to thaw out frozen locks and water bottles."

They carried the buckets over to a hand cart for transport uphill to a large pit. It was going to be some punishment, as there must surely be a hundred more bucketfuls to scoop up and remove.

"Our boss, Captain Virenius, ordered a full platoon set of sleeping bags just like the prototype except a bit wider. What we got—what the supply officer gave our captain—was bags the same too-small size as the prototype and with a thinner, finer-looking type of zipper. The supply officer claimed these were newer, better zippers than the one on the prototype."

The two men continued filling and emptying buckets of unimaginable filth. "We didn't know the zippers were bad—he'd charged the army for a larger version with deluxe extra-strong zippers, and only bought the standard size with cheaper zippers. Zippers designed for ladies' dresses!" Torjer shook his head, and continued to work.

"So out we went, on an exercise to test our new tactics and equipment against friendly 'enemy' units who'd be looking for us, and if we were spotted they'd fire blanks at us. All pretty harmless, but nobody wants to lose a battle even if it isn't for real. So we decided to be serious about it, you know, moving quickly and making cold camp. Just the sort of job for up-time-style sleeping bags, if only the bloody zippers had worked." Torjer spat and cursed for a few minutes in unintelligible Norwegian, apparently without repeating himself.

"The first few nights were great. I had a good, thick reindeer pelt underneath my warm, cozy sleeping bag and I slept like a baby. Except for when that clumsy son-of-a-taxman Ante stumbled in the alarm line and woke me half an hour before it was my turn on stag. The fifth night, however, we were pretty close to the 'enemy' and everyone was a bit on edge. So when our mess kits began to rattle during dog watch, we all burst from our sleeping bags and ran to our defensive positions. I don't think anyone noticed at the time, but nearly all of us tore those lady-fashion zippers open without using the little pull tab thingy. Nobody had told us that would destroy the zippers."

Daniel felt confused. "Back up a little. Mess kits? What made them rattle?"

"We use them for an alarm system," Torjer explained. "You tie a long piece of string to a bunch of tin pots or whatever will make noise, like a couple of mess kits tied together. Run the string out to the sentry post, and he can alert those in the tent without leaving his post. But that's not the point.

"There was a terrific noise, with the alarm string being jerked so hard it nearly took the whole tent down. We thought all hell was breaking loose, and stormed out into the darkness. Some fool opened fire, and the others followed suit. Including me, no less a fool than anyone. But at least I only reloaded once before I realized that we were shooting at shadows."

They were making progress on removing the slushy, near-frozen waste, but somehow that only made it worse. The effluent was now running in fits and starts, bringing fresh and rather more odorous waste their way. They had forgotten about all the sewage standing under pressure in the blocked pipes, and with the blockage removed there was something like a volcanic eruption. At least the fresh stuff wasn't freezing.

"It turned out that the sentry hadn't pulled the alarm string, and neither had any other man. It was a deer—a stupid, insomniac deer that went a-walking right between the sentry and the tent. It tripped in the string, and scared the crap out of us."

Daniel couldn't quite bring himself to laugh in his present circumstances, but he was still curious. "And what did the deer have to do with your offending the supply officer?" he asked.

"Nothing much, but the zippers did. They would have failed sooner or later, so it didn't matter if the alarm was raised for a deer or for the whole Danish Army. We had opened fire, announcing our presence to the whole county, so we had to leave. Fast."

Torjer shook his head. "Breaking camp quickly in near pitch darkness and running like the devil himself was after us. That's a recipe for disaster, even in the best of times. And then the weather changed; it turned first wet and then cold. Our skis were soon caked with ice, which isn't nearly as slippery on snow as you might expect. Not when the snow is wet and sticky. Our uniforms were soaked with icy water, which then froze like a suit of ice armor. After a few hours I noticed young Nils Larsson was getting even more clumsy on skis than usual, but when I asked him he claimed to be fine."

Torjer slipped on something unmentionable, landed in something worse, and after an exceptionally long bout of swearing he seemed to have forgotten the story.

"And was he? Fine, that is?" probed Daniel.

"Huh? Oh, him. No, he bloody wasn't. The damned fool had taken his boots off in the tent. Well, you're supposed to do that, but you're also supposed to remember where you put your woolly socks. When that whole deer incident went down he was in too much of a hurry to find both socks, so when we set off skiing he only wore one. Frostbite on three toes, he had. He also had hypothermia, which is why he didn't notice the frostbite. Did you go to that lecture on hypothermia and frostbite, when the up-timers held first aid instruction?"

Daniel nodded. "Yeah, they told us the extremi-somethings get cold first and then when the brain begins to cool you get stupid."

"The 'extremities' you mean," Torjer corrected. "That's your fingers and toes, and other things that stick out. Like your privates. Remember what else they said?"

Daniel gulped, wide-eyed: "If you get bad frostbite, they have to cut it off. Really, the . . . ?"

Torjer nodded sagely. "Yes, that part too if it's really bad."

Some time later, the two men were about to haul the last cart over to the pit when Torjer's hand slipped and he fell face first on the frozen ground. The sudden additional load made Daniel lose his grip, too, and the cart went backwards into the ditch.

"There's even shit on the drawbars," Torjer muttered.

They eventually finished up and walked towards the warm showers, a wonderful invention even if it wasn't quite as social as a communal tub. Waddled to the showers, rather, trying to move without touching their filth-soaked and half-frozen clothes.

Warming up, Torjer picked up the story again. "Now, if someone gets hypothermia near civilization you simply throw him in a hot tub and thaw him out. But when you're in the middle of nowhere and all your gear is wet, you stick him in a sleeping bag and crawl in with him to share some body warmth. Personal privacy be damned."

"Yes, I remember," said Daniel. "That's what they told us at that lecture."

"And that's what mountain men like me have always known," replied Torjer, "only we've always used furs and blankets instead of sleeping bags. Problem was our no-good, stinking sleeping bags were too small even for one man, and the bedeviled zippers didn't work so we couldn't put two bags together to make a large one. In the end we put poor frozen-toes into the only bag that still had a functional zipper. Which saved his life, but meant I had to sleep in a bag that couldn't be closed properly." More profanity followed.

"Look, he had to amputate a toe but he'll be fine otherwise. No longer fit for winter duty, but he'll live. Me, on the other hand, I nearly froze my balls off. The zipper would sort of close, but every time I fell asleep it would open again. Right over my privates, dammit. And me out of my pants, as they were soaking wet and I had to get warm somehow and maybe I wasn't thinking too clearly myself, being cold and all. Remember what I said about extremities? I came *this* close to freezing my manhood off! Because of a bleeding lady-fashion zipper and that filching, cost-cutting supply officer!"

Torjer was clearly working up a temper, and Daniel had to concentrate on not laughing. It might be bad for his health to annoy Torjer, he decided. "So you set out for revenge. I guess I can understand that"

"I sure did," Torjer continued. "Or I tried to as soon as I learned it was this Nilsson-Loo fellow's fault. I skied all the way here in anger, not even stopping for a change of clothes. I took my axe and ran to his office, thinking I'd chop a couple of his toes off or something. Or maybe an ear. I'm not choosy." His mood seemed to brighten. "But while we'd been on patrol, this shit had been happening to the sewers and nobody had thought to tell me.

"This guy's an officer, right? And the officers' latrines had backed up, spilling right over and running onto his office floor. So there I come, charging in unprepared, and I slip on the filth and lose my axe. Right at his crotch, it went! He'll have to wee sitting down from now on, and it was an accident! A genuine, beautiful, honest-to-god accident with plenty of witnesses. I'd have been hanged if I'd neutered him on purpose, but they can't punish me for an accident!"

When they were done laughing, Daniel remembered. "Then why are you here, if they can't punish you?"

"For laughing! Insolence, they call it!"

So they laughed some more.

The Treasure Hunters

Karen Bergstrahl

March 2000

The librarian stamped the book and handed it across the desk. "This is a grown-up book, Mikey. It came all the way from a library in Richmond and you can only have one renewal on it. It *must* be back by April sixteenth."

Michael Arthur Tyler grabbed the book before she could change her mind and quickly muttered, "Thank you." He didn't want her phoning his mother with a complaint about his manners. Momma might tell him to return the book and leave "grown-up" books until he was older. Just because he was small everybody thought he was still a little kid. No matter how he stretched, he stood barely 4'9" in his sneakers. Small, thin, and with an unruly mass of sandy colored hair that flopped over his eyes, he was pegged by people who didn't know him at eight or nine at most. Lots of folks who did know him still thought he was only ten.

Michael was afraid he would be this small forever. Nanna had told him that his father had been small until he was fifteen and then had started to grow. She always said that he would grow too, but Michael wasn't sure he believed her. He didn't know if he could stand another year of being the smallest boy in class.

Once outside the library, Michael shuffled down the sidewalk. His feet absently kicked at rocks in the universal manner of fourteen-year-old boys. His thoughts were far away in place and time. Tucked securely under his arm was his prize, a copy of *The Lost Tomb*. The book promised secrets of a new Egyptian tomb—the biggest ever found.

"Hey, Dweebie!" Danny Colburn yelled. "Whatcha got there? Didn't your momma teach you to share?" Danny and his twin, Shawn, appeared from around the corner. "Look, Shawn, Dweebie's got a book! Does it have pretty pictures, Dweebie?" The two boys loomed over him. Shawn snatched at Michael's book while Danny made a couple of mock swings at Michael's head. The twins were big. They stood almost six feet tall and were the same age as Michael. Since the third grade the twins been the biggest kids in class. Since the fourth grade, Michael had been their favorite target.

"Maybe it's got real words—really small and simple words. See Spot run. Run, Spot, run!" Shawn guffawed.

"Naw, gotta be pictures—puppies and kitties. Here, gimme that book, Dweeb!" Danny shoved Michael into Shawn's arms and yanked the book away. Shawn pushed Michael hard, forcing him to his knees. Michael made a futile grab for his book before Shawn slammed him face-first into the sidewalk.

"Aw, Dweebie. This can't be for you—it's all small print. Maybe it would be good kindling . . ."

"Give my book back!" wailed Michael. Panic made his voice squeak.

"Hey, Dweebie." Shawn shoved Michael back down with his size twelve shoe. "I didn't tell you to move. Did you tell him he could move, Danny?"

"Naw, Stop wiggling, Worm, or we'll stomp you . . ." Danny threatened.

Michael, his face squashed against the sidewalk, fought tears. The twins usually were satisfied with giving him a black eye and a bloody nose but they had torn up his books before. This was a library book. The last time the twins had torn up a library book all of his allowance and savings hadn't been enough to pay for it. His dad had to make up the rest. Dad had walked Michael down to the library with the money and complained about the cost of the book the whole way there and back. When they got home he'd taken his belt to Michael and warned him, "That better be the last time I have to cough up money for one of your weird books, boy, or your hide will be black and blue for a year. Why'd ya want such a dumb book anyway? For Gods sake, Mikey, grow up and stop reading such useless shit."

What would happen if the twins tore this one up? If he fought back maybe they would just beat him up and forget about his book. He tensed, ready to roll over and grab for Shawn's foot when a loud shout echoed down the street.

"Daniel! Shawn! Get away from Michael *right now*!" Mr. Reading, the elementary school principal was striding toward the boys. He looked furious. "How many times have you two been told to leave him alone? I'm going to have another talk with your parents." Mr. Reading grabbed both boys and shook them. He looked down and asked, "Are you okay, Mikey?" When Michael scrambled to his feet and nodded, Mr. Reading took the book from Danny's oversized paw and inspected it. "Obviously this belongs to Mikey, not you two louts. Here, son." When Mr. Reading turned away to hand the book to Michael the twins took off at a run. "I'll be calling your parents!" he yelled.

"Umm, thanks, Mr. Reading." Michael said in a small voice. He peered around wildly. Bad enough that the twins had nearly ripped up his book and given him another beating, but this! The school principal rescuing him was almost too much. If he was lucky none of the other kids had seen.

"Still interested in archeology, eh, Mikey?" Mr. Reading asked.

"Yessir. "

"Good, good. It's an interesting career. Do you have any ideas on what you want to dig up?"

"Yeah . . . See, there's this new tomb in the Valley of the Kings— that's what this book is about." Michael politely showed the book to Mr. Reading.

"So you're reading up on the new discovery. That's good scholarship. Keep learning and you'll do well in college. Its good to have high goals, Mikey." Mr. Reading smiled and put his hand on Michael's shoulder. "You keep studying hard and you'll make it. Now, I'd like to hear more about this new tomb."

"Yes sir. See, the pharaoh Rameses, that's Rameses the Second, had something like a hundred sons . . ." Michael's mind raced. If he gave a good enough answer maybe Mr. Reading would be satisfied and leave before anyone saw them together. ". . . and this tomb—they call it KV5—well, it's where all those sons got buried." Unfortunately Mr. Reading showed no signs of leaving. Instead he walked beside Michael, asking questions about archeology.

Michael tucked his book under his arm and walked and talked automatically. Inside he wailed at the unfairness of it all. By tomorrow morning every kid in school was going to know Mr. Reading had walked him home. Like he was a kindergartner! When they came to his house, Michael's heart sank further. His father was home early. He could hear him yelling at his mother. With a quick "goodbye" flung at Mr. Reading, Michael fled inside and upstairs to hide his "weird" book.

Spring 1632

Michael leaned on the hoe and eyed the garden patch with satisfaction. Not even Nanna or Gramps would find anything to complain about. He'd turned over the soil, carefully mixing in just the right amount of compost the way Gramps had shown him. He and Gramps had made a chicken wire composting enclosure last fall and filled it with raked up old leaves and cut grass. Over the winter it had turned into nice black compost, just like Nanna said it would. All his rows were straight and evenly spaced. Each had a neatly lettered sign telling what was growing there. Three stake and wire trellises were ready for training the peas and a couple of old tomato cages stood guard at the far end. Gramps had built the fence up high enough to keep deer out. Butch wandered over from his patch of shade and sniffed at the corn sign.

"Leave it be, Butch. Don't you go digging in here or Gramps'll make a rug out of your mangy hide," Michael warned the dog while he scratched the mutt's ears. "Your job's keeping the raccoons and possums out of the garden." He had to lean over to pet the dog, a sign that he was growing taller. Last fall he didn't have to lean over to scratch Butch's back. "Hey, Butch, look at this!" Michael pushed up his sleeve and flexed his arm and eyed the resulting small bulge with glee. "I'm getting muscles!"

Butch panted companionably and wandered back to his shade without voicing an opinion on either the "no digging" rule or Michael's new biceps.

"Hey, Mike! We're going down to the fairgrounds. Want to come along?" Joe Matowski called out. Jon Sizemore and Willy Lutz stood beside him outside the garden gate. "They're having a team roping practice. Annette's dad is going to be there and she said they're looking for somebody to work the gates."

"Yeah, yeah! Wait 'til I tell Mom I'm going with you." Michael grinned at his friends and raced for the back door. If Annette O'Reilly was going to be at the team roping, it was likely that her cousin Jo Ann Manning would be there, too. Jo Ann hadn't giggled when he gave his report on archaeology in class. The other kids whispered, giggled, and squirmed in their seats but Jo Ann sat still and listened. She had asked a couple of smart questions and smiled when he answered them.

The boys trudged back up the road, tired, dirty, and happy. The outing had been a success—they had gotten to move the steers in and out of the pens.

"What are you going to do this summer, Mike?" Joe asked.

"Don't know. I've got to keep the garden going and Gramps said he wants me to help out at the restaurant." Michael sighed and tossed a rock.

"That doesn't sound too bad. My folks want me to start Latin class over the summer. Pop's got this idea that I should go to that university in Jena." It was Joe's turn to chuck a couple of rocks.

"I've got a job at the Kudzu Werke. If it works out I might get apprenticed," Jon crowed, throwing a good-sized rock a long way down the road.

"Cool! How about you, Willy?" Michael asked.

"School *und* . . . and more school. English and Latin. I am to prepare for the university, also." A pair of rocks whipped out in quick succession from Willy's hands.

"Bummer." Michael sent three rocks after Willy's.

"Yeah, bummer." Joe also got three rocks off but dropped the fourth.

Jon grinned and rapidly tossed four rocks after Joe's.

August 1632

"Troy is right where Homer said it was," Michael pontificated. He knelt on the floor and reached under his bed. "Schliemann used the description in the *Iliad* to find it. But he got a surprise when he dug up Troy. There wasn't just one city. He found eleven cities, each built on top of the previous one." Michael pulled out a fat, dusty notebook. "It's all in here. Maps, articles, pictures, and all sorts of stuff. You can copy what you need."

"Wow! Thanks, Mike! This should make our report a lot better than any of the others. Right, Willy?" Joe Matowski grinned at the other boy.

"*Ja, ja.* But we must change the picture titles to Latin," Willy pointed out, flipping through the notebook. He stopped suddenly, his eyes big. "*Ist* . . . is this gold?"

Michael scooted over and peered over Willy's shoulder. "Yeah, oh, yeah. That's 'Priam's Treasure.' Schliemann found it. The woman wearing it in this picture is his wife, Sophia. She was a Greek he met while looking for Troy."

"Gee, I thought you said archaeologists weren't treasure hunters," Joe complained. "You said archaeologists were interested in old pots and things."

"Well, Schliemann wasn't really an archaeologist. He was a rich guy trying to prove that Troy really did exist. Because he didn't know how to do archaeology, he dug great big trenches completely through Troy. The real archaeologists who came later hated him for doing that."

"But he found this gold?" Joe thumped the picture. "What did he do with it?"

"Yeah, he found it." Michael replied. "I think he gave it to some museum in Berlin 'cause it was supposed to have been destroyed during World War II."

"Supposed to?" Joe asked, his voice showing his interest. Willy also stared at Michael in fascination.

"Everybody thought so until a couple of years ago—ah, about 1996 or so." Michael flipped to the back of the notebook and showed them a newspaper clipping. "Turns out that the Russians stole it and hid it."

"Cool. This is great, Willy." Joe grinned at his friends. "We get all these neat pictures and a treasure, too!" Joe read a bit of the clipping then said, "Says here that Schliemann found Troy in 1871. Does that mean that the treasure is still there now?"

"Guess so . . . yeah, it would be." Michael nodded and slowly smiled. The thought of an undisturbed Troy appealed to him.

"So maybe we ought to go dig it up."

Michael thought for a minute, then shook his head. "No, what I want to do is get there first and do a real archaeological dig. Just digging for the treasure would mean destroying Troy again. The Treasure of Priam was buried really deep. We'd be digging for years. Besides, there are other treasures, bigger treasures that aren't buried under an entire hill."

"Come on! What treasures?"

Michael dove back under his bed and pulled out two more notebooks. "The first is the Atocha. It's a real big Spanish treasure galleon that sank in shallow water off Florida. It had tons of gold, silver, emeralds, everything."

"Wow! Way cool!" Joe flipped rapidly through the second notebook. Willy reached over and stopped him at one picture showing a bare-chested man with many gold chains draped over his neck and shoulders.

"So much gold. Where is Florida?" asked Willy.

Joe sat back suddenly and shut the notebook. "It's in America," he said, his voice flat and defeated. "Halfway around the world from here. It's also under water and we don't have any scuba gear."

Michael nodded. "Yeah, and even if we had dive gear we don't know how to use it. Well, Troy's on land but its not very close, either."

"What's in the other notebook?" Joe eyed the third notebook, the fattest of all. "Another underwater treasure?"

"Nope. This one's King Tut's Tomb. It's on land, but it's in Egypt." Michael sighed and opened the notebook. There on the first page, in rich color, was the golden sarcophagus of the boy pharaoh, Tutankhamen.

October 1632

"Wilhelm, come in, come in. See who is here!" Willy's mother called excitedly. "Your Uncle Johannes has come, all the way from Hamburg!"

Willy carefully kept his face expressionless and looked at his father. Uncle Johannes' visits were exciting—filled with tales of the far off places he'd gone and the strange sights he'd seen. But Willy knew how much his father detested Uncle Johannes. Hermann Lutz sat glowering across the table from his brother-in-law. Inwardly Willy groaned. Uncle Johannes's visits meant trouble.

"What a little scholar you've become!" Johannes Fraze smiled warmly at his nephew. "You'll be a professor the next time I see you. A big, important professor with a solemn stare and clusters of students clamoring for your favor. You will be much too important and much too busy to see your poor old uncle."

Willy shook his head. He could feel his ears getting warm and knew he was blushing at his uncle's teasing. "No, Uncle Johannes, I'll never be too important to see you. I'm not really much of a scholar so I'll never be a professor."

"Come now, boy! I seem to always find you reading some textbook or another."

Willy looked up, startled. "This isn't a textbook, Uncle Johannes. I borrowed it from another boy in school to practice reading English."

"There you are! You've learned to speak and read English like one of these Americans. And you're learning Latin, which is the language of scholars. These are not minor accomplishments, my boy. If you don't wish to be a professor, then you can be a merchant. Merchants need to know languages, too."

"How many languages do you know, Uncle Johannes?" His uncle sometimes claimed to be a merchant but Willy's father never believed his claims. Smuggler, thief, or cheat Uncle Johannes might be, but not a merchant. Willy's mother always defended her brother vigorously, attributing Johannes's lack of money to robbers and dishonest merchants who didn't pay him for his goods.

"Oh, several—my Polish is very good, so is my Spanish. I can make my way through France without trouble and I've enough Italian to get by on. But English I've never learned. Here, tell me what it says under this picture."

"It says," Willy did a quick translation in his head, "that it is a picture of Herr Howard Carter in front of the tomb of Tutankhamen."

"Amazing! You say these pictures are called *photographs*?"

Willy nodded.

"All these up-time things are very interesting. Do you know if any of the up-timers are teaching the making of photographs?"

"No, but the teachers at the high school would know."

"Ah! I think I must ask them about this and other things. There are opportunities here for a merchant." Uncle Johannes stroked his chin. "You say that they have classes to teach English? Classes that anyone can attend?"

"Yes, they have them at the high school. Some are in the evenings so people can work and still go to them."

"I think this might be an excellent time for me to learn English. There are good profits to be made in English goods . . ." Uncle Johannes's face was solemn but his eyes held a glitter and kept darting to the pictures in Michael Tyler's notebook.

February 1634

Johannes Fraze hummed cheerfully and carefully but quickly packed his belongings. All the other members of the household were away and he wanted to be gone before any of them returned. He neatly wrapped the all-important notebook in a piece of up-time plastic and slipped it into an oiled leather sack and closed it. The resulting package he placed in the bottom of an up-time rucksack he had bought from one of the neighbors. On top of the book went a heavy purse that clinked. Johannes grinned. His year in Grantville had been rewarding in many ways. Several months ago he had slipped one of the color pictures out of the notebook. With that in hand he had made the rounds of down-timers—gullible down-timers.

He chuckled over how easy it had been.

"Herr Arndt, I come to you because I know I can trust you. I have found an opportunity for great wealth. In the library while reading to practice my English I stumbled across records of a statue. It has not yet been found and dug out of its Italian hillside. Such a statue! Solid gold! Here, look at this photograph." One look and the mark was hooked. Arndt had been so eager he hadn't even allowed Johannes to finish his pitch.

"If only I had more money. How much did you say it weighed? Oh, all that gold! Just think of it! We'll all be rich!" Reichard Arndt gibbered. The man's eyes never left the picture while Johannes explained how many shares his money had bought.

Johannes firmly pried the photograph of King Tutankhamen's golden mask out of the man's reluctant hands. When he had Arndt's attention, he explained, "I must insist that you keep this a complete secret. You cannot tell anyone, not your wife, or your sons, or your best friends."

"But why not? Klaus Lumpe and Heinrich Neumann are good men. They deserve to be rich, too!"

Johannes hid a grin. "Ah, so. Let me think about them. The secret must be kept lest other, less honorable men, find the statue first. Should I deem your friends trustworthy enough, you still must swear not to talk about it even between yourselves. It will take time to get all the necessary equipment together. More time will be needed to travel to Italy and locate the hill where the statue is buried. No one else can know what we plan until then or they might beat us to the statue."

And so it had gone time and time again with the carefully selected marks. The quick pitch, their names scribbled on a notepad with other names, and their cash in hand and each sworn to secrecy. Or at least until the previous night at the Gardens.

"Going to look for King Tut's tomb?" an amused voice asked. Johannes quickly turned the photograph over and slid it into his pocket before he replied.

"King Tut? Is that whose statue it is? A true work of art. Do you know who the artist was who made such a beautiful piece?" Johannes kept his face straight and any nervousness out of his voice. Up-timers were tricky to deal with. Some appeared to know little; others had more information rattling around in their heads than a gaggle of university professors.

"Some Egyptian, I guess," said the up-timer. "That coffin was made a long time ago. Well before Jesus' time. It sure is pretty. Strange folks, those Egyptians. All that gold wasted on a coffin."

"Remember the exhibit that came around?" a second up-timer stood beside the first. "My granny took us kids up to Pittsburgh to see it. We stood in line for a couple of hours, but it was worth it. Man, they had some pretty stuff! Set me to thinking about heading to Egypt to find me another king's tomb. I remember how disappointed I was when I found out that a lot of the gold stuff was actually carved wood covered in gold leaf."

"Yeah, that's right." The first up-timer laughed. " We studied the pharaohs in school. A lot of us dreamed of treasure hunting. If you're interested in knowing more about that coffin, you should check up at the school. There's bound to be a book on it. Come on, Ol' I'll Pay You Back Tuesday, this is Tuesday and I want some beer." The first up-timer grabbed his companion's arm and both headed off toward the bar.

Johannes sat and sipped his beer. His thoughts were racing frantically but he knew he didn't dare let anyone see how upset he was. Several of his marks were seated close by. Johannes hoped none of them had heard the up-timers. He considered what to do. These up-timers didn't appear to be suspicious of his intentions nor did they appear interested. Still, it wouldn't do to trust appearances too far. Now might be a good time to move on. In truth, there weren't too many marks left in Grantville. This had been a good swindle, a very good swindle. His purse was heavy and his "partners" were expecting him to depart for Italy. He needed a story for his sister and her family—no, best just leave a vague note.

Glancing around the room he'd shared with his nephew, Johannes contemplated some of the other rewards he'd gained in exchange for the longest stretch of honest work he had ever done. His sister refused to charge him rent and only accepted a pittance to cover his food so he had honestly earned money in his pocket. Even Hermann had stopped glowering and warmed up enough to grant that Johannes might just have had a long and terrible run of luck. It would be weeks before either of them realized how he had gulled them. Another package, as thick if not as carefully wrapped, contained a wealth of up-time materials he could peddle across Europe. The photo he'd used around Grantville rested in his purse, waiting to be brought out again with the plea "if I only had a few florins we could recover it." The world was full of gullible people who were dazzled by pretty pictures and stories of easy riches. He'd sold fake treasure maps and saints' relics all across the land for years. This time he had a *real* treasure map.

He gave a last look around and knelt down to feel under the bed. There had been a couple of other notebooks under there from time to time. Wilhelm had shown a surprising lack of trust in his uncle after he'd caught Johannes going through the one about a Spanish galleon. Cursing under his breath, Johannes got up and straightened his clothes. There were many things he would miss—indoor plumbing, efficient heating, soft beds, and so on. He wouldn't miss his nephew's sharp eyes. Johannes found himself debating about making one last call on Hilda. Oh-so-willing Hilda who thought they were engaged to be married. Her charms included an extremely gullible father who had borrowed money on his business to fund the treasure hunt. Of course, he and all the other "investors" thought the treasure was a solid gold Roman statue buried in Italy...Johannes chuckled. That had been his best idea.

He might go to Italy, after all. Italy was also full of gullible people, not a few of them quite rich. Italy had many charms—its weather for one, and the fact that it was far from the armies blundering about Germany.

After a check of the closet he shrugged into his coat, hoisted the rucksack and stole out the door.

April 1634, Naples

"Johannes!" the voice cut through the noises of the crowded market. "Johannes! It is you! How long has it been?"

Johannes found himself facing a familiar man, one Jakob Witterwald.

"Ah, Jakob. So you have managed to stay out of jail?"

"Yes, yes. So have you, I see. Come, old friend. There is an inn down here with the best beer." In a lower voice Jakob added, "They have a room where two old friends can talk alone."

Smiling, Johannes motioned for Jakob to lead the way. They walked to the inn, Jakob chattering on about his relatives, the weather, the price of tobacco, and other meaningless things. Once they were settled in the inn's back room Jakob became serious.

"The last that I heard, you were headed to that place—Grantville. The town full of demons, wizards, witches, and all manner of magic."

"Old news, Jakob. Old news. I did go to Grantville. There wasn't a single wizard or demon in sight. In fact, I spent all of last year there."

"Ah! No demons or wizards. No magic, either?" Jakob sounded

wistful. "I've been working a neat little scam based on 'Grantville Magic.' Tell me about the place and I'll have some nice hooks for my scam."

"You would do well to drop it. Too many people know the truth about Grantville's 'wizards.' Unless you stick to backward villages, that will trip you up." Johannes shook his head. "There is no money to be made in such places."

"No . . . true." Jakob shrugged. "Tell me about Grantville anyway. You *are* looking prosperous. Whatever scam you've been running is profitable."

Johannes grinned. "Would you believe that I spent my time in Grantville doing honest work?" He lit his pipe and began to talk.

Well into the evening Johannes pulled out the photo of the mask of King Tutankhamun. Jakob's eyes glittered. Once the up-time notebook was unwrapped and the rest of the pictures displayed Jakob was hooked. He leafed carefully through, asking Johannes to translate, asking questions.

Johannes considered his luck. Jakob had contacts in places Johannes didn't. The two of them had run several successful swindles together. Given the right clothes Witterwald made a convincing professor. There was a certain noble Italian with more wealth than brains . . .

"Why are you just conning for pocket change?" Jakob suddenly asked. "There is a king's ransom in gold sitting in this tomb. Sitting there, waiting for someone to come along and take it."

The thought stunned Johannes for a moment. He shook his head, answering cautiously. "Do you have any idea how heavy a solid gold coffin is? Or how difficult it would be to move it?"

"Certainly. But it could be melted down. Gold bars are heavy but easier to manage." Witterwald thumped his finger on a picture of several small gold items. "These pieces alone would pay for the trip."

"But Egypt is closed to outsiders." The pictures appeared to dance in the candlelight, beckoning to Johannes.

"When has such a prohibition stopped either of us? I know a man, a Muslim, a wealthy merchant."

There was little doubt Jakob did know such a man. There wasn't a port in the Mediterranean that Jakob hadn't sailed into.

"Will he help us? Say for ten percent?"

"We split the rest evenly?"

"I get fifty percent. You get forty and your Muslim friend gets ten. I discovered this. I researched it and I spent the time learning enough English to understand what is in the notebook. Without my work, you would have nothing."

Witterwald looked mulish for a moment. He sighed, shook his head and replied. "Granted. You get fifty percent. I agree. You have the knowledge to find this tomb and that is worth half. I'll take forty percent. Ali gets ten percent. Done?"

"Done."

The inn by the docks was dim, dingy, and smelled of rotten fish mixed with tobacco smoke. A lack of windows and the few lamps did little to relieve the dimness. The smells exuded from the clothes and bodies of the men siting around smoking, drinking, and gossiping. Johannes thought it wasn't the worst inn he had seen, but it came close. This place didn't seem to fit with Jakob's description of the man they were to meet here, either. Ali El-Rahman was supposedly a wealthy merchant and a Muslim. Both made him a most unlikely client of this inn.

The man Jakob finally greeted didn't look like a wealthy merchant. He did look like an Arab with his dusky skin, dark hair, and close-cropped beard tracing his jaw line. The dirty, tattered clothing didn't fit a wealthy Arab merchant's dress. The man was as thin as a starving dog. Most merchants, especially the wealthy ones, looked far from starving. Johannes grinned. Ali El-Rahman probably was an Arab but Johannes would bet his last florin the man was no more a respectable merchant than Jakob or himself. All the better! Johannes understood rogues.

A little silver got the three "merchants" the use of a back room. With a flourish Johannes produced the up-time notebook and the picture of King Tut's coffin. In the flurry of speech that followed El-Rahman proved to speak acceptable Spanish. That was good. Johannes didn't want to be forced to depend upon anyone, not even an old acquaintance like Jakob, for translations.

In minutes a deal was struck. Ali would arrange passage on a Greek ship bound for Alexandria. "The Greeks hate Turks," Ali explained. "The Greeks won't care if we're all good Muslims or infidels. In Alexandria, the bey uses Turkish troops for customs and to stop infidels from landing. Even if the Greek sailors suspect you two aren't Arabs, they won't tell the Turks."

Summer 1634, Alexandria

The air was breathlessly hot but Johannes and Jakob sat shut up in the small ship's cabin, not daring to go out on deck. Turkish patrols regularly swept the docks, collecting taxes and tributes and looking for illegal activities and unauthorized infidels. If caught the best they could expect was to be fined and shipped out. At worst they might be sold as slaves. On their last stop they'd learned that anyone claiming to be an up-timer would automatically be put to death if found anywhere within the Ottoman Empire. The idea that the local powers might consider possession of up-time materials the same as claiming to be an up-timer worried Johannes.

Johannes and Jakob had let their beards grow on the voyage and both were sunburned enough to pass for Arabs at a distance. Unfortunately, the only words either knew in Arabic were "Inshallah"—hardly enough to stand up to an interrogation. Ali had been unexpectedly reluctant to teach them anything more.

Ali had explained that while Egypt was divided into twenty-four districts, each overseen by a Mameluke bey, the sheikh al Balad was the most powerful of the beys and should be able to ease their way. The Arab was off the ship seeking out the sheikh's men to present the requisite bribes. Johannes wondered about Ali and the bribes. The more Jakob swore Ali was trustworthy, the more Johannes wondered.

Johannes had been forced to reconsider the group's financial resources in light of all the bribes that would have to be paid out. He hoped what they had would be enough to pay for a boat to take them up the Nile and leave enough for the bribes they would need when they found the tomb.

Fall 1634

They had come so far—and now this! The very rocks seemed to mock them. Dry brown stones rested on more dry brown stones along the narrow and twisting little valleys. The lifeless valleys all twisted away from the river. Each had little side branches, equally lifeless, twisting off endlessly. Everywhere the cliffs were riven in wild patterns of cracks. The sun made the shadows darker by contrast. Here, away from the river, even a trace of green was missing.

Johannes wiped sweat from his face on the sleeve of his filthy galabiya. In Alexandria, there had been many men in European dress. Ali had explained that some infidel merchants and such were allowed within the city. He had warned them that they needed to visit a market and find local clothing before leaving the city. Johannes demurred, concerned about the lightness of his purse.

Ali's advice had proved correct immediately outside the city. Their European clothes stood out and attracted unwanted attention from every quarter. Coming across three Egyptian peasants, Ali had offered a pair of copper coins and the natives cheerfully stripped off their dirty robes. The Egyptians offered their loin cloths for another copper coin, but even Ali couldn't bring himself to take up that offer. He had given them a copper for their tattered and filthy turbans.

Johannes sat on a large rock and stared at the barren hillsides. Jakob was wandering in circles, staring up at the lifeless cliffs and cursing. Ali simply sat silently in a sliver of shade from a boulder. Johannes wondered if this valley, the fourth they had looked at, was the right one. It had all been there, buried in the up-timer notebook. Several clippings commented on the barrenness and that many of the tombs had been nearly invisible, hidden among cracks and fissures. It was the pictures, the photographs, that had fooled him. All those neat and tidy up-time roads and cleared tomb entrances with staircases and large signs. He'd known not to expect the signs or paved roads. Yet those pictures had beguiled him into ignoring the words.

All of it was in the notebook he had stolen and so carefully carried all this way. The maps in the notebook made it look simple. But now, here in the actual place, Johannes realized the difference between the photographs, maps made in the twentieth century and the reality of seventeen-century Egypt. On the maps it was so easy—"This is the tomb of Rameses II and here is the tomb of King Tutankhamen." But the neat little dot on the map didn't help him much. Was the Rameses tomb on the slope just in front of him, or under that pile of rocks to his left? Or was it down the way where Jakob was pacing? Or was it in a completely different valley? The maps didn't show enough details. The photographs were no better. Nothing in them matched what was here.

They might not even be in the right place along the Nile. The ruins across the river should be the temples of Luxor, but he wasn't certain. Giza had been the last place he had been able to match the notebook's information with seventeenth-century Egypt. Except—the pyramids looked different. With the help of one article he finally figured out that the difference was the lack of large holes in one pyramid. Somebody had blown huge holes in the side of it before the photographs were taken.

Despite the year he had spent in Grantville learning English, Johannes found it difficult to understand many things in the notebook. He realized that, except for the small section on the pyramids, the notebook held little information about the rest of Egypt. Most of the clippings and articles focused on the Valley of the Kings and King Tutankhamen's tomb.

Nothing in the notebook warned him that Egypt was full of ruins. All the way up the river, they had seen ruins. None matched the photographs in the notebook. Nor did the notebook have anything to say about all the towns' names being different. One page did show a map with the village and town names as they had been in Roman times and what they were called in the twentieth century. Once past Giza, the names didn't match either set.

Discouraged, they pressed on, grimly searching each major ruin for clues. A week ago, wandering amongst the ruins on the east side of the river, Johannes had found a section of wall that seemed to match one of the pictures labeled "Temple of Luxor." But they could not be certain it really was. Here, unlike at the pyramids, the ruins were in worse shape than the pictures showed.

Frustrated, Johannes had gone over the entire notebook again. He had even re-read the handwritten list stuffed in the back pocket. It was a list of things needed for an expedition to the Valley of the Kings. Carefully written in pencil, it listed shovels, tents, canteens, a compass, and such. Three different hands had written it; the only one he could read easily was his nephew Wilhelm's. Boys they might be, but one of them was pretty sharp for at the bottom was the entry "Money for bribes." Of more use to him were several pages stuck between the photographs and clippings. These pages were Wilhelm's notes in a mixture of German and English. A note stuck behind the section on Luxor had the telltale line "the temples were rebuilt . . ."

So here they were, highly detailed maps in hand, but not

knowing where they were. If the ruins across the river were the Luxor temples then the Valley of the Kings should be found here, directly across the river. If they could figure out which of the featureless wadis was the Valley of the Kings and if they could find the right tomb in the valley, then the maps should make sense . . .

"There are a couple of openings, Johannes. There's one just over there and another there," Jakob shouted, hope tingeing his voice.

The three men scrambled up the loose scree and into a low, dark entrance. Johannes grinned, his heart racing. It was a tomb entrance! The rock around them had been carved out. If they could identify which one it was the map should at least tell them if the Rameses tomb was to the east or west of it. The three men lit candles and crawled into the darkness. Half an hour later, filthy and exhausted, they crawled out. It was a tomb, a tomb filled almost to the roof with sand and rocks and having not a single painting to match with the pictures. After a rest the trio tackled the other tomb. This one, higher on the slope, wasn't so full of debris and there were some paintings visible. Carefully Johannes compared the photographs with what he could see by candlelight. Again nothing matched.

Johannes brushed the dust gently with his fingertips. "Here, Jakob, hold the candle closer. Careful you don't drip wax on the photograph again!"

"Hey! Look there!" Jakob yelped in Johannes's ear. "These figures match!"

"And," Johannes sighed, "the rest don't."

"So it isn't the right tomb?" Jakob didn't bother to hide his disappointment.

"Maybe not . . . I think it might be the name of a relative." Brushing past the other man, Johannes crawled toward the tomb's entrance. In a little patch of sunlight, he flipped through the notebook, searching for a half-remembered picture. He found it and peered at it and then read the paragraph below it. Hope soared in him and he re-read the relevant passage. A noise from outside in the wadi barely registered. He crawled back to the painted wall.

"Look, Jakob. These people match this photograph. That one is the pharaoh and this is his queen." His voice rose with his hopes. "This is the queen's tomb, not the king's. That's why the cartouche doesn't match. We're in the Valley of the Queens!"

"So now we can find this King Tut's tomb and all that gold?" Jakob was grinning widely.

"Yes . . . that tomb is in another valley but now . . . now I can find the right valley. Put out the candle. We don't have many and we need to save them." Jakob complied, plunging the two men and the tomb into twilight relieved only by the light coming from the entrance. Without a word, Jakob began crawling toward that square of light.

Johannes eyed his companion thoughtfully. How far could he trust Jakob? They had known each other for years and run scams together without problems. Still . . . Lately Jakob had become very friendly with Ali. They often had their heads together, talking softly. Jakob claimed Ali was teaching him Arabic, but Johannes wondered. He was positive that neither Jakob nor Ali had any knowledge of English. The notebook was useless to either of them. However, once Johannes had identified the marker tombs and located the area where King Tut's tomb entrance was buried, the notebook would become irrelevant. Until then, he suspected his life might depend upon their inability to read the notebook.

Back in Alexandria he and Jakob had discussed when and how to end their partnership with Ali once the treasure was in hand. Neither of them saw any need to waste any share of the treasure on the Arab. Having seen the reality of Egypt, Johannes had revised his plans several times. They needed Ali and his Arabic language skills to get back to Alexandria. Perhaps it would be best to allow Ali to get on the ship with them. Accidents at sea were easily accomplished and left no inconvenient bodies. Johannes now wondered if Ali and Jakob were planning an accident for himself.

Perhaps he should sound out Ali. Jakob's strong back would be helpful in digging out King Tut's tomb. Helpful, but not absolutely necessary . . . And there were all these handy tombs in which to hide the body.

Jakob momentarily blocked the light exiting the tomb. He yelled something unintelligible but Johannes paid no attention. He was deep in thoughts of double-cross.

Crawling from the darkness into the bright sunlight blinded

Johannes. When hands grabbed his arms, he thought Jakob and Ali had decided to put their own murder plan into action. His vision cleared enough to let him see the wadi floor below the tomb.

Ali and Jakob were on their knees, each held by two large men. Ali was pleading frantically. Jakob had the look of a stunned ox. A number of riders surrounded them. The riders, Johannes realized with dread, were Sheikh al Balad's Turks.

The pair of large Turks holding his arms threw Johannes down the slope. Skidding on his back, he struggled to stop his slide. If he could evade the men waiting below and make it to that other tomb . . .

Another pair of Turks grabbed him, hustled him the rest of the way down the slope and slammed him to his knees. Someone grabbed Johannes's hair and yanked his head up so that he looked into the face of a richly-dressed man mounted on a magnificent white horse. Something slithered down the scree and the white horse danced and kicked at it. Michael Tyler's notebook broke open and the pages flew about. Several of the Turks' horses shied at the flurry of paper. The Turks' leader curbed his horse's restiveness easily, never taking his eyes off Johannes.

Three Turks scrambled about, grabbing the loose pages. One of them carried the notebook and rescued pages to the leader with the air of a man handling filth. The leader looked away from Johannes briefly. He flicked several pages with his whip. He snarled something at the man holding the notebook. The notebook dropped and the Turk soldier kicked it away. He knelt and scrubbed his hands with sand.

The Turk's leader said a few words and the others replied with a shout of "Inshallah!"

Ali burst into a loud wavering wail.

The Turks' leader smiled down at Johannes and gestured. Johannes's head was shoved forward, his ragged turban pulled off and dropped in front of him.

The last words Johannes heard, enunciated clearly in Spanish, were "You are infidels. We do not tolerate infidels."

Bathing with Coal

Russ Rittgers

Fall 1633

"Barnabas Kitchner! Wake up! It's Tuesday morning and you have to buy wood for the bathhouse fire."

The thirty-eight year old man rolled over in bed and opened one eye. His wife, Margarete Lutsch, was already dressed and standing in the doorway with her hands on her hips.

Tuesday. People bathed on Saturday and Tuesday in this town of a thousand souls. Saturdays were regimented about who bathed and when. Mothers with young children bathed first. Then old women. Then teenage girls and single women. Single and old men, and then married couples. But today was Tuesday and in this town that meant first come, first served, no separation of ages or sexes. Each day had a completely different social atmosphere which served the community.

The early risers wanted a warm bath, no matter what the season. The late bathers, especially in summer, didn't mind cool water as long as it was halfway clean.

And oh, dear God, did they have clean water. The large reservoir for the baths had to be refilled at least three times every Saturday. Trip after trip, hauling water a hundred yards from their river near the Elbe, back and forth. The small consolation was that he didn't have to personally haul it all. The bad news was that his helpers, Lucas and Peter, lived with their parents and had to be lightly shepherded. Everyone in town had some kind of a useful job, including those who were not as smart or clever as others. Bigger towns and cities had pumps but using Lucas and Peter to haul water was far cheaper and gave them regular employment.

"But it's not even daylight yet! Nobody's going to be at the bathhouse." His feeble protest fell on deaf ears. As usual.

"Get up! You know Augustin Ramminger will be there even before the water is hot enough for you to finish filling the bathing tank. Now get moving!"

Yes, he did know. Augustin had been Barnabas' rival for Margarete's hand ten years earlier. Not infrequently Barnabas asked himself what Augustin would have done in his situation and decided that was why he was now Margarete's husband.

Barnabas had been footloose and fancy free sixteen years ago, the third son of a Lutheran pastor who had no inclination to follow in his father's footsteps or scholastic ambitions beyond his city's gymnasium. So he was without regular gainful employment when he arrived in town. Margarete was good-looking and full-bodied, the daughter of the only bathhouse operator in town. When Barnabas was hired by her father to service its water and fires, he thought himself incredibly lucky. Not only would he have regular employment but he would be in contact with the object of his affections on a daily basis.

One thing led to another and her father—being wise enough not to object—agreed to their marriage ten years ago. The only surviving child of Papa Lutsch, Margarete inherited the bathhouse along with the family home three years later. And in arguments never let him forget where the source of his livelihood originated.

Barnabas sat up in the bed, sighed and scratched his head. There was only the slightest hint of light outside their window.

"Good morning, Barnabas. I've already set aside your usual order of wood." Titus Erlingen pointed towards a stacked pile. He gave a sigh. "But I'm going to have to charge you more. Because of all the construction in Magdeburg, prices for wood, even firewood such as I provide, are going sky-high."

"How much higher?" Barnabas twisted a lock of his graying hair. Margarete was going to give him fits if it was much above what it had been last Saturday morning. Her father had taught her how to manage the bathhouse and one of those skills was bookkeeping.

Titus grimaced. "Ten percent higher today than it was the other day. Heaven only knows when the prices will come down again."

"Ten percent! That's robbery, pure and simple! Why don't you just get out your knife and slit my purse?"

The wood-seller raised his eyebrows in innocence and shrugged. "You know I wouldn't charge you that much if I didn't have to. As it is, I'm barely covering my own costs. I'm having to go farther and farther afield to find firewood, so much of it having been burnt or otherwise destroyed by the imperial forces or the Swedish Army. Every stick of this firewood had to be purchased from its owner, or from a village's allocations."

Barnabas had no idea of where Titus acquired his firewood but had his own suspicions. For one thing Titus was here every Tuesday and Saturday morning, which meant he couldn't have gone that far, not out and back with his lone horse pulling the cart. For another, Titus was simply too well-fleshed. Barnabas suspected that Titus knew of an abandoned farming village and just gathered it himself without payment.

That said, in the fifteen years Barnabas had been buying, Titus never charged more than his competition.

He tried not to moan. "Five percent. I have to be able to tell my wife that I didn't pay the price you first quoted."

Titus shook his head. "Nine percent. Because we've been dealing with each other so long."

Barnabas hesitated. He might be able to get Titus down to seven but he doubted it. Titus looked entirely too unhappy even quoting the nine percent.

"Eight percent, all dry wood and you have a deal."

"Done. You can check each piece yourself."

Barnabas always split some of the new wood into kindling after he filled the stone heating tank. It also gave him something to do while he thought about how to tell Margarete about the price increase.

"Will I have to wait long?" Augustin asked, leaning at the open doorway, a towel over his shoulder. The still unmarried Augustin had done well in the past dozen years. He'd gone from being Barnabas' equal, a gymnasium graduate, to something of a dandy, working as the town's bookkeeper. Barnabas didn't envy him his position or money. He didn't hate Augustin either, but there was no love lost, mostly because he still flirted with Margarete. All Barnabas knew was that there'd never been any gossip with real substance.

Barnabas opened the stopcock on the side of the heating tank and tested the water. "Fifteen minutes, no more."

"Quite all right. I'll just go back to the entrance and talk with your lovely wife." He turned gracefully and walked back towards the front of the bathhouse where Margarete would be waiting at the entrance for early bathers. She enjoyed his company entirely . too much. Barnabas growled, thinking about it.

Years ago he would have seethed with indignation for an hour, but now he simply returned to his work.

The bathhouse wasn't large as such things go. Not halfway comparable to the one in the city he came from. No, this bathing tank was only a dozen feet across with room for no more than several bathers at the outer rim. On Saturdays there would be a line of waiting bathers, but on Tuesdays most of his hot water didn't go into the bathing tank.

Tuesday was when the townswomen did their laundry. Barnabas took each woman's bucket, filled it and received a token in return. Margarete sold the tokens while she took bathhouse entrance fees. A simple enough process but one which drove Barnabas crazy on those occasions when Margarete had been ill.

Katerine Paffenburg handed him her bucket. "How are you today, Barnabas?"

Barnabas placed it on the stand and opened the stopcock. "Not bad, not bad, Katerine. How's your husband? I hear he's back to working as a regular crewman on the river."

The sturdy woman gave Barnabas a grudging smile. "Yes. He's transporting coal downriver to Magdeburg. They need tons of it every day."

He gave a sour grunt. "Tons of coal and the prices of firewood are going up every time I buy. Too bad I can't . . ." He stopped, his mind racing faster than he could put together coherent speech. If Magdeburg was using tons of coal every day, then either the city was richer than Croesus or . . . coal was dirt cheap.

"Well, I for one wouldn't want to use coal at home." Katerine sniffed. "Willi brought home a sack of it last week and threw several chunks into our fireplace while I was out. Our entire house stank by the time I got home! I tell you, I gave him a piece of my mind!" Her red face was pinched in memory of her anger.

"Umm, I think I heard about that. Hadn't heard the details though." In this town, everyone knew almost everything about their neighbors, whether it happened outside or inside the walls of their home. Katerine was not known as a mild, submissive wife who had nothing but adoration for her husband. She'd given him much more than her opinion.

On this occasion, she chased Willi out of the house and down the street, screeching and hitting him with her broom every third or fourth step. Gossips of both sexes had a gleeful field day and last Saturday the bathhouse was filled with reports of the incident.

Barnabas gave Katerine an appreciative smile as he handed her the bucket of steaming water. "Well, now I'll know not to do that myself."

The day went smoothly. Barnabas only had to drain and replace the bath tank water once. The heating tank, on the other hand, had to be topped off frequently.

"What are you thinking about?" Margarete asked as they sat facing the fire after supper that evening. "You're normally complaining about your back or how slow Lucas and Peter refilled the reservoir."

He gave a sigh. "Like I told you, the price of firewood went up again. I think it will keep going up as long as they're building in Magdeburg."

"Well, I think Titus is overcharging. I've looked at the records and we've never, ever paid that much, except when Tilly's army was nearby, seizing all the available firewood for their own fires. Well, and during the middle of winter. But it's certainly not that now."

Barnabas shook his head. "Same or better price than the other woodsellers. I checked. What we need to do is change over to coal. I hear it burns hotter and is cheaper."

Margarete disagreed. "And it stinks. This bathhouse has been in my family for over a hundred years and we've always used wood. Besides, where would we get coal? Our customers would smell of coal fumes when they finished their baths. Surely you heard about Katerine and Willi the other day."

He rubbed his tired eyes. "Okay, you tell me. How much money did we make today, what with having to pay more for firewood?"

His wife's lips tightened into a pucker. "Not nearly enough."

"I'm going to Magdeburg to find out how to use coal to make hot water."

"Lignite," Willi, Katerine Paffenburg's husband, told him Monday morning, taking a rest from poling as the barge floated down the Elbe. "That's what we're hauling. Not the best kind of coal. That's anthracite. Almost as hard as rock and black as pitch. This isn't as hard and doesn't burn as hot, but for most purposes it's good enough. There are boats coming from elsewhere bringing anthracite to Magdeburg."

As soon as the boat docked in Magdeburg, the boatmen began shoveling coal as fast as they could onto the waiting carts. Barnabas jumped off and ran to talk to the first teamster whose cart was nearly full.

"Yeah, I'll take you to where I take this but you'd be better off to run over to the building over there." He pointed to a series of tall brick smokestacks belching a dark brown smoke.

"Heating water?" the foreman asked over the din of men shoveling coal into fiery openings behind him. "That's all we do here. See those fires? Inside the firebox, just past the fire is a cluster of water-filled tubes. Water flows from a feed water tank through the tubes. Gets boiling hot and powers its machine through steam pressure."

"No, no, that's not what I meant," Barnabas broke in, uncomfortably aware that the boat would soon be empty and, as his fare, he had to help pole it back upriver. "I operate a bathhouse. How hard would it be to heat water using coal?"

"Easy as pie. Same operation, but you don't need to keep it under pressure. You'll have to be careful to fill the feed water tank before firing the furnace. That's number one. You'll probably want cast iron tubes for a more efficient transfer of heat. Never, never let them go dry with a fire under them. Number two, you'll want a smoke stack. Not as high as these because you're not going to do that much volume. But high enough to be taller than any chimney in town. That way the wind will blow the smoke away from town. Otherwise you're going to have a lot of unhappy neighbors. They won't like the smell of coal smoke, anyway, but that's the price you have to pay."

"Right. Thanks. I really have to leave. What's your name?"

"Krupp. Andreas Krupp. I'm from Essen but didn't want to be a gunsmith."

"Cast iron water tubes in the furnace and a tall chimney?" Margarete repeated. "That has to be expensive. Very expensive. We simply don't have the money."

"What if we got a loan?"

"Papa always said never to take out loans because it gives the lender power over you."

"Well, I guess we could raise the price of the baths and the water. Or did Papa Lutsch have something against that?"

His wife thought for a few moments. "No, not really. But we'd practically have to double our prices at a minimum. As it is, we charge two pfennigs per bucket. Add a third and you've increased the price by half again. We'd have the same problem with baths. I don't know what people would do but it wouldn't be nice. Probably riot." The corner of her mouth turned in a way that told him she really wasn't worried.

"Margarete, honey, wait. Could we increase the one and not the other?"

She shook her head and then reconsidered. "Bathing, yes, we could do that but not the hot water. Women would simply start a fire earlier in the day. Baths are a luxury, a social gathering and a necessity. No one wants to smell bad. Yes, we could raise that price."

"But that wouldn't solve our problem," Barnabas persisted. "The price of firewood is going up and up. So we'd have to keep raising our prices. Why not take out a loan and just pay that? It's bound to be cheaper to operate."

Margarete gave her head a quick, determined shake. "No. And that's the end of it. Interest rates are far too high. What would happen if we defaulted because of war or a plague? I'd lose the bathhouse, that's what would happen." Barnabas noted it was only she who would lose something.

"Here's an idea. If we said we were putting in a new, improved heating system, wouldn't they pay more for that?"

"Ha! How many years have you been living here? As long as the old system works, they'll stay with it."

"Okay, let's assume we raise the prices enough to cover the cost of the firewood. Everyone knows its price is going up anyway. How long can we continue to raise prices before people stop coming every Saturday and just wash off at home with water they've heated?"

His wife frowned. Then clenched her teeth. Then shook her head and sighed. "A little over a year. Maybe more. Even after construction is finished, Magdeburg's going to need a lot of firewood. The land where they'd been getting their firewood was cleared during the six months of its siege."

Barnabas' mind was made up. "I had hardly any time in Magdeburg before the boat was leaving. This time I'll stay overnight and take the boat back Friday."

"To put in a smokestack won't be cheap but you can get some of new brick at a much lower cost than ever before," Paul Detleff, the first journeyman mason Barnabas ran into, told him. "I know the master mason who owns the best kilns in the city. Caspar Maurer. It's not firebrick, but you only need that for the firebox. Which you'll have to rebuild because no way will a firebox built for wood survive the high temperatures of coal. He can supply the firebrick as well."

In his small office at the mason's hall a short while later, Caspar Maurer gave Barnabas an intense look and then a wry smile. "All this for a small town bathhouse?"

"Yes, Herr Master Mason," replied Barnabas stiffly. "I like wood. I enjoy the smell of wood, but it's getting too expensive. My wife tells me—she keeps the books—that at the way prices are rising, despite owning the bathhouse, we'll be out of business in a year even if we raise our prices. The people just won't pay enough to cover the costs and give us a living. So we'll have to borrow money for the new furnace, boiler and the smokestack. But what choice do we have?"

Caspar had given him an inscrutable twist of the mouth when he mentioned that his wife kept the books. "I know of a bank that makes such loans for small businesses. Reasonable rates. Okay, let's assume you keep the same size bathing tank but replace your stone heating tank and firebox." He paused. "You might want to reconsider how many days you heat your water for bathing. Presuming you have some margin of profit each time. Helps pay off the loan faster. How many gallons does your current heating tank hold?" He scratched out a grid on a piece of paper.

"Master Maurer learned the Grantville advanced mathematics," Paul told him as they walked away with a preliminary estimate for the new construction. "He was already a master mason but taught himself more about using mathematics to determine, among other things, precisely how to draw the smoke from a fireplace all the time, not just most of the time. As you may appreciate, coal smoke is much better far up in the air than down where you're breathing.

"This coming winter the apprentice and journeymen masons here in Magdeburg will be attending classes on physics and mathematics and how to apply them to our work." The young man gave Barnabas a bright smile. "I plan to study as hard as I can so Master Maurer will hire me."

They arrived at another small office a few minutes later. The bell on the door rang as they entered and several heads lifted from the papers being worked on. "Is Catherine Menz around?"

A red-headed woman in her mid-twenties whose dimensions could only be called statuesque came out of a doorway a few moments later. "Did I hear my name called? Oh, hello, Paul."

"Fraulein Menz, this is Barnabas Kitchner. He and his wife own a small bathhouse in a town upriver. They want to upgrade their heating plant."

Catherine gave him a doubtful look and sighed. "No doubt Caspar wrote the estimate. Otherwise you wouldn't be here. Now run along and play. I'll talk with Herr Kitchner."

"*Jawohl*, former chairwoman Menz." Paul bowed deeply to Catherine's obvious exasperation. She made a comic half-hearted swing at the back of his head and he was gone.

"Paul only made journeyman this year," Catherine explained. Which didn't explain anything about the content of his remark. "Come. Sit and tell me about your operation."

Within minutes Barnabas found himself telling Catherine all about the bathhouse, his wife and his town. She was the pleasant kind of woman men liked chatting with. Not only was she willing to listen with genuine interest but she also kept asking him intelligent questions.

"How much do you know about the Committees of Correspondence, the CoCs?" she asked with a warm smile. When Barnabas shook his head, she went on. "They're primarily social and political organizations, set up to protect the rights of ordinary working people. Among other things, this one provides loans to small and start-up businesses."

Barnabas tried not to squirm in his chair. "I don't get into politics and I don't really want to join any organizations."

Catherine gave a charming smile that warmed the inside of his chest. "You don't have to. One of the founding directors of this bank made it more than clear that our real business was not to make loans but to make money. So we make loans to reliable people with small businesses. Based on what you've told me, you and your wife fit that category. Naturally there will be an appraisal and several documents you and your wife will have to sign, but right now I don't see a problem, especially with Caspar being in charge of the construction."

"The master mason, Fraulein Menz?"

"My future husband. Someday. After certain legal impediments have been removed. But yes."

Suddenly, and for the first time, Barnabas completely understood the term "covet" and why it was prohibited in the Ten Commandments.

"So tell me more about this red-headed hussy you met in Magdeburg," Margarete demanded after Barnabas returned from his two-day trip. He had not been able to remove his enthusiasm for Catherine from his report.

"Nothing much more to tell. That was the first and last time I saw her during my visit. Less than an hour. She's just . . . a really nice person who knows how to listen. When she wants," he added with haste. "I told her all about you and the town."

His wife gave him a baleful glare. "So I'm not a nice person who doesn't know how to listen?"

"No, not at all. You're my wife," he babbled, desperately trying to escape what he knew would be a disaster.

"So the only reason I'm acceptable is because I'm married to you? Is that it?" she raged, coming to her feet and hurling aside Caspar Maurer's estimate.

Barnabas had learned through years of frustration and bitter experience that the only way to survive when she was in this kind of a mood was to first say he was sorry, apologizing for anything he might have said. Second, to leave. There was a nice tavern not far away from where they lived. But he couldn't leave before she'd had her say.

"Being out of town the past two days, you couldn't have heard the big news." The tavern keeper grinned as he handed a mug of beer to Barnabas. "Ursula Futter, the burgermeister's widowed daughter, is going to get married again." He paused.

"Who's the poor ba . . . uh, lucky fellow?" Barnabas asked, taking a large swig.

"Augustin Ramminger." Beer sprayed from Barnabas' nose and mouth.

"You bastard!" Barnabas was both choking and laughing. "You timed that deliberately!"

Johann could hardly disagree, as hard as he was whooping with laughter.

Once he regained his composure, he said, "From what I heard today, they've been seeing one another regularly—in his office—for the past year or more. Yesterday her father and another man entered and caught them doing more than just kissing. Just what exactly they were doing depends on who you talk to. The marriage contract hasn't been written and the banns haven't been read, but it'll happen, sure as the sun rises in the east."

Barnabas was still chortling. Ursula Futter had certain less than desirable traits in common with Katerine Paffenburg. Dear Augustin. Oh, dear, dear Augustin, who after so many years of flirting with Margarete and others, was about to enter the dangerous world of matrimony. Dangerous to him, at any rate.

Barnabas took another deep swallow of beer and leaned forward over the bar. "I guess it's either marry her or leave town. When the burgermeister dies she'll have some inherited money and property to add to what she got from old Carl Wetter. She was his second wife and he had four children from his first. All she got was a widow's portion. But that's far more than Augustin would have if he left town."

Johann lifted his eyebrows and gave a sly smile. "Wasn't Augustin always flirting with your wife at the bathhouse? Wasn't he another suitor for her hand back in the day?"

Feeling all was right with the world, Barnabas responded with a broad grin. "Sure. But she and her father both knew that if he'd married her, one of his first acts after Papa Lutsch died would be to try to sell the bathhouse. If there's one thing that she'll never do, it's sell the bathhouse. So flirting, yes, but I knew that's all it'd ever be," he lied. "It kept her feeling young and desirable, so why not?"

He finished his beer and put the mug on the bar. "I think I'll go home. Margarete will surely be in need of some deep consolation, losing Augustin so suddenly and in such a tragic fashion." No wonder she'd been so . . . testy this evening. He gave Johann a big evil grin. "Somehow I don't think he'll be allowed to flirt with her any more."

Barnabas stopped outside the door to their house and took a deep breath. Then lifted the latch. Margarete was waiting in her usual chair near the fire. "You heard, didn't you?" Her voice was dry and cold.

The corner of his mouth wrinkled. "It's a small town. News that exciting doesn't stay secret for more than a day." He brought his chair next to hers, where she sat with her hands together in her lap. He put his hand over hers. "How do you feel?"

"I . . . knew. Oh, not any details but I knew he was close to someone. His . . . attitude was subtly different. More assured. You wouldn't have noticed. But any woman he'd been flirting with for years would." She sighed and then made a deep frown. "You must find all this very funny."

He gave her a sympathetic smile and squeezed her hand a squeeze. "Partly." He gave a small chuckle. "The part about him. Not about you. Frankly, I thought he had better taste." His voice took a sarcastic turn. "Ursula Futter?"

Margarete turned towards him and the corner of her mouth turned up. Her eyebrows raised and she chuckled.

Encouraged, Barnabas turned toward his wife and put a second hand on hers. He looked at her. "Flirting with you meant to me that he recognized the same beauty I saw in you when we first met."

"Huh!" She grunted and eyed him scornfully. "Trying to get around me. You're trying to get me to agree to build that new water heating system, aren't you?"

"Oh, uh, well, not exactly. I mean, uh, no. Not at all."

"Won't work, Barnabas. You can't tell me you hadn't thought about it a moment before you walked in through the door," she said. "I'm not going to agree just because you make a few compliments."

Barnabas' face drooped. "You won't?"

Margarete shook her head as if in sadness. "Some women are so anxious to get a compliment that they'll agree to anything afterwards. I'm not like that. Not at all."

She took a deep breath. "On the other hand, I had two days to think about what you wanted to do. I looked over the books and made some estimates based on what we've been experiencing. I decided that if you came home with proof that the project was possible and we could afford it, I'd approve."

Barnabas stared at her for a moment. "Then you approve?" he asked weakly. His face brightened and he grinned in relief. "You do approve!"

She gripped his hands and smiled at him. "Yes. Now I want to hear all the compliments you were prepared to shower upon me. I warn you, though, that I may not wait until you finish before banking the fire and blowing out the candle."

He stroked the line of her jaw a moment later. "You know, I never would have stayed in this town if I hadn't desperately needed a bath the day I walked in. Your mother took my coin and you walked out of the bath house looking like Venus arising out of the sea, your towel covering..."

Lessons in Astronomy

Peter Hobson

"Your Eminence, I'm fluent in Latin, German and Italian. My French is passable. My Greek is a little weak and I've forgotten most of the smattering of Hebrew the seminary inflicted on me." Father Scheiner knew he shouldn't be taking that tone with a prince of the church, but it was just so frustrating. So much knowledge locked away behind the wall of up-timer English. "And now I've got to learn English? Why can't you people speak a reasonable language? Or, at least write in a reasonable language?"

"I'm sorry, Father Scheiner," Cardinal Lawrence Mazzare replied. "If we'd known we were coming, we'd have been better prepared."

Christopher Scheiner noted the gentle reproof in the cardinal's tone, and the reminder that he probably failed to realize he had given. Cardinal Mazzare wasn't just a prince of the church. He was a prince of the church who had been put in his position by the hand of God. Yet none of that really penetrated Father Scheiner's frustration with the situation. He picked up a book and flipped through it. "This is supposed to be a basic astronomy text for the beginning student. I can't even understand most of these pictures. What is this Hertzsprung-Russell Diagram supposed to tell me? I can guess that luminosity, from the Latin *lumen,* is brightness, but what is a spectral class?"

"Don't ask me. There's nine planets and a bunch of stars and that's about all I know."

"Nine planets?" Scheiner shook his head in dismay. "What can you tell me about the extra three?"

"The seventh one is Uranus. The name causes some unfunny jokes you'll appreciate when your English is better. The others are Neptune and Pluto."

"Uranus. That's the Latin form of Ouranos, the Greek god of the sky. It's a reasonable name for a planet, I suppose." Scheiner paused. "But how do they know it's there? Diligent men have been looking at the sky for millennia, how was it missed?"

"Father, I can't answer that question," Mazzare said. "However, in the next week or so Johnnie Farrell will be coming from Grantville. He's been an amateur astronomer for years and has a really good, up-time telescope. Hopefully, he can answer all your questions."

"Father Scheiner, there's an up-time man with a large box who says he's supposed to see you."

"Thank you, Herr Reichter. Please ask him to come in."

A small, rather stout man in his early sixties walked into the room. "Hi, there. You must be Father Scheiner. I'm Johnnie Farrell and this here's my telescope. I'll be happy to tell you what I can about astronomy."

"I'm pleased to meet you, Herr Farrell." Scheiner walked over and shook Farrell's hand. "I have so many questions and my English is not good enough to get them from the books."

"Well, I've got plenty of books and magazines to show you." Farrell beamed. "I can explain a lot that's in them and probably figure out the rest since I've been reading astronomy books for most of my life. I think I know something about it.

"But first let me show you an indispensable tool for any astronomer." Farrell lifted the box onto a table, snapped several clasps, and opened the lid. "This is a Schmidt-Cassegrain eight-inch reflector with an equatorial mount and go-to. Just point this baby at three stars and it'll show you thirty-thousand other celestial objects just by pressing a few buttons."

"I'm sorry, Herr Farrell. I didn't understand any of that."

Farrell sighed. "I guess I'll have to start with the basics. This is a reflector telescope. It uses mirrors to collect the light."

"An astronomer in Rome, Father Zucchi, devised a telescope that uses a mirror, but I have not seen one before. It does look rather strange. I think of telescopes as being long and thin, not short and wide."

Farrell stroked his telescope fondly. "Okay, let me explain how this one works . . ."

Father Scheiner listened to the explanation and found himself growing more confused. Mirrors, computers, the go-to . . . it all required more explanation "I think I understand how a telescope uses mirrors but it does not look like what I think of a telescope looks like."

"Okay, Father, let's discuss telescopes. There's two main types . . ."

More explanation, until he felt his head must be spinning. Light waves then photons, spherical aberration. "Just a minute, Herr Farrell, wave lengths of light? Light is a wave? And what is a photon?"

"Look, we'll get into the nature of light in a little while. Let's not get sidetracked. I'm still explaining telescopes." Farrell continued with more unfamiliar terms and explanations.

Scheiner could feel himself moving from puzzlement to frustration. "I thought you said that light came in waves. Now you say light is particles?"

"Father, light's complicated. Sometimes it acts as a particle, sometimes it's a wave. I don't really understand how it works. A guy named Maxwell described light in four equations. Trouble is, those equations are calculus, which I don't know. Let's just stick with telescopes. I know telescopes. Anyway, what we got here is a Schmidt-Cassegrain, which is a different type of reflector. When the light enters the telescope, it goes through a corrector lens which fixes the spherical aberration."

Scheiner interrupted. "So the light goes into this lens here . . ."

Farrell seemed to be getting as frustrated as Scheiner was. "Hey, Father, don't touch the lens. This telescope is the only one of its kind in the world and it's irreplaceable. It'll take probably decades before technology is up to duplicating it. We'll have to baby this 'scope, which means no touching the glass. I'll let you use it, but I'm going to supervise you all the time."

"If we use this tonight, can you show me Uranus?"

"I'll just drop my drawers and show it to you now." Farrell blushed. "Oops, sorry, Father. I shouldn't be so crude."

Scheiner couldn't hide the grin. "I now understand something that Cardinal Mazzare told me recently. I really want to see the planet Uranus. Can you show it to me tonight?"

"Sorry, Father, but I can't. I don't know where it is and the go-to doesn't either."

This was even more confusing. "I thought you said that one could just press some buttons and the telescope would point to several thousand different objects."

Farrell blushed again. "Sure, sure, fixed objects, no problem. You want to look at stars, galaxies, nebulas, things that don't move, the go-to can find 'em. But for moving stuff, like planets and comets, the go-to doesn't work. It needs to know what the time and date is for those and I can't tell it what the date is. Yeah, I know that it's May 15, 1635, but that doesn't help. The go-to won't use any dates before January 1, 1990."

Scheiner pondered for a moment. "Can you give me any data on Uranus's orbit? Perhaps we can calculate its position."

"I've got lots of old copies of *Astronomy* and *Sky & Telescope* magazines, I'm sure they'll give the right ascension and declination of Uranus for various dates. But those dates will be almost four hundred years in the future. What good will that do?"

More unfamiliar terms. Scheiner did his best not to snap his question. "What, pray tell, is right ascension and declination? Or rather, since I can guess they're parts of a system of positioning, what is the basis for the system?"

"They're celestial longitude and latitude, with celestial north being near Polaris and the prime meridian in Aries. I have the details in my books. But I don't know how to calculate orbits. I don't know the math."

"Fortunately, Herr Farrell, I do know the . . . math. I have the Rudolphine Tables and the rest of Kepler's work on planetary orbits. If you can get me the data, I can do the calculations." Feeling that he was back on familiar ground, Scheiner moved to a chair and waved Farrell to another. "Tell me, what do you know about astronomy? Not the telescope or the go-to. Real astronomy."

Farrell sat and shook his head. "I'm not a real astronomer, just a guy who enjoys looking at stars. I've read some books and magazines, but I'm not any kind of scientist. You've just shown me that I know less about light than I thought I did. I know the words but I don't really know what the words mean. You're the hot-shot astronomer and scientific advisor to the cardinal. History will remember you as an astronomer. History won't remember me at all."

"Herr Farrell, why do you look at stars if they do not tell you anything?"

"But they do tell me things. They tell me the universe is immense and beautiful and that God created it."

"You remind me that I am not only an astronomer but also a priest. You are right, that is a good reason for looking at the stars. My friend, let us learn about God's universe together." Scheiner rose and extended his hand. He was pleased when Farrell extended his own.

"What a beautiful night for observing." Father Scheiner had just reached the observation position they'd been using.

"Yes, it's a gorgeous night. Nice and warm and not a cloud in the sky."

Scheiner smiled. "Herr Farrell, in the past month you have shown me many interesting things. Now I would like to show you something. Please position the telescope at the right ascension and declination I have written on this card."

Farrell made the adjustments and waited for Scheiner to take a look. Instead, Father Scheiner stood aside and motioned for him to look first. He looked through the eyepiece. "I see a disk among all the pinpoints of light."

"Congratulations, Herr Farrell. You are the first person to see the planet Uranus. Perhaps history will remember you as the discoverer of the seventh planet."

Wish Book

Gorg Huff and Paula Goodlett

"Gary Jordan!"

Gary Jordan Burke flinched. He almost always flinched when Joyce got to screeching. It was an automatic response to her high-pitched, overly loud voice. *You'd think the woman thought everyone was deaf.*

"Gary Jordan!"

"Yes, dear?"

"Go downtown and get some more paper scrap. We're nearly out."

"Yes, dear." Gary suppressed a sigh. Still, he'd best get downtown and do as Joyce wanted. If he didn't she'd get into his garage again, looking for non-glossy paper. She mostly left the glossy stuff alone, but any thin sheet of print was in danger around Joyce. Of course, so were ear drums.

Gary spent a lot of time in the garage. He almost had to, considering how crowded the house seemed. Heck, Joyce and her screech were a crowd all by themselves, but add in visits from kids, grandkids and assorted relatives—well, the place was a madhouse half the time.

"A man can't hear himself think around here." It had been bad enough, back before the Ring of Fire. It had gotten three . . . no, six . . . no, twelve . . . well, a whole lot worse since then. Mom and Dad were living with them now, since they'd sold their house when they ran out of money. That was bad enough. But the worst was Aunt Muriel. Oh, Lord . . . Aunt Muriel.

The woman never, ever quit talking. Talking in the same kind of screech Joyce had. Even so, she did pay rent. Which was more than Mom and Dad did. Mom and Dad just assumed they'd be welcome until their dying days. Which they were, really. It was just that money was so damned tight. And feeding everyone wasn't getting any cheaper. And Gary really, really didn't like thinking about the property taxes and the way they were probably going to go up.

So, going out after paper scraps wasn't all that much of a chore. Well, it was, but it was worth it to get away from the screeching and protect what was left of the reading material in the house. Which, come to think of it, was mostly what people had used just before the paper scraps. He remembered old stories about the Sears and Roebuck catalog, back before it became the Sears catalog. How people would go to the outhouse and use the Wish Book twice. *Now, that's recycling.*

Gary froze. The Wish Book. They called it the Wish Book and everyone in America had one. Almost, anyway. Now that he was thinking along those lines, he remembered other stories told about the Wish Book; people ordering whole houses out of it and life-saving things. Teachers teaching children to read using it. *Talk about advertising penetration.* He'd been trying to figure a way to make some more money for a long time. And now he thought he'd found one. The big problem was that he didn't have a lot of money to put into the idea. Which meant he needed to talk to Mom and Dad. And Muriel.

"So, I don't see any reason to wait, Aunt Muriel. In fact, we shouldn't wait. Somebody else might beat us to the punch if we do."

Muriel watched him squirm for a few moments. It had to have been hard for him to do this. Gary Jordan was a proud man, one who'd done well by Joyce. But times were hard and getting harder, at least in this household. Too many people, not enough income to support them all. "I'll do it. And I'll get your parents to invest, too. It'd be downright foolish to sit on what they got for the house, planning to leave it to you and Duncan when they croak. It'd make a lot better sense to put it into the business. Instead of the Sears and Roebuck catalog, why couldn't it be the Burke catalog? Running a mail order business out of the garage ought to work."

☆   ☆   ☆

Well, that meant the garage would be lost as a quiet haven,
Gary knew. But he needed to do something. So he'd have to
sacrifice. Who wasn't, these days?

"First thing we need is a catalog."

Muriel shook her head. "First thing we need is some inventory.
We ought to be able to buy in bulk and get a discount. And then
we need an engraver, to do the pictures to go in the catalog. Then
we get it printed up and sent out."

"But there are already such things," Ursula Reifsniderin said.
"There are seed catalogs and catalogs of other things as well."
Ursula was a refugee who had needed a place to stay. She acted
as primary translator for the family as well as general help and
instructor in the German language and German ways. She was
still learning English, but was learning it a lot faster than they
were learning German.

"You mean they already have the Sears catalog?" Gary asked.

"I don't know about this Sears. I don't know that word, but
merchants have listings of their products they send out."

That got them into a discussion of what would make their
catalog unique, which led to a discussion of what had made it
unique in the original time line. It took some working out and
some research. What they finally determined was that it was a
combination of things. The Sears catalog had been a general merchandise catalog with a lot of products, which made it distinct
from the more specialized catalogs. It had also been published
in a time when transport had gotten much cheaper. Which made
Gary and Muriel nervous, but pleased Ursula because the same
thing was happening around the Ring of Fire with the new roads
and the railroads getting started.

Their first catalog was a simple thing. Not very big at all. Not
too fancy, either.

But it was an actual book, well, booklet, bound with thread and
it did work. In some ways, it worked too well. Orders poured in
from as far away as Jena. More than they had the stock to fill.
Which caused its own problems, including letters of apology and
refunds when requested. Each of which cost them money. And
some of the suppliers jacked up the price for products they had
already ordered. They ended up selling some stuff at below cost
because of that. In spite of all the headaches, they made a profit

that first year. Not as large a profit as they'd have liked, but still a profit.

Muriel kept the books. The woman was a whiz with numbers and she had all day free, unlike Gary and Joyce. They kept their day jobs. Had to keep body and soul, together, after all. Mom and Dad helped, too. Most of their inventory was small stuff, so no one had any trouble lifting the various items and packing them up.

The hardest part of it all was reading the handwriting on the orders. Ursula Reifsniderin was a treasure. She was the one who took the packed up orders to the post, using the red wagon that had been around since the kids were little.

Ursula looked in the mirror and grimaced. She wasn't fond of her face. She had survived some rough times in her life and they had left marks. Grantville had been her salvation and the Burkes her blessing. She remembered a line, she couldn't remember where she had read it or heard it, but when she thought of Burkes it always came to mind, *"Who is your family? The ones who put you out or the ones who took you in?"* The Burkes were her family now and the Ring of Fire her fatherland. In general, it was a good family and a good fatherland.

She abandoned the fruitless examination of the mirror and set to work. They needed a bigger cart than the little red wagon.

"Look, Papa."

Johan stopped what he was doing and straightened up, grabbing at his back when he felt a twinge. "Yes, Anna? What is it now? And have you finished your chores? Picked up the bread, as your mother asked?"

Papa's back hurt a lot. Anna repressed some concern about that. It did tend to make him a bit irritable. "Papa, look at this. A man dropped a whole stack of them in the village. I've been reading it. It says here that you can order all these things from Grantville. I think Mama would love one of these." Anna pointed to the drawing.

Her papa grunted and took the book. He began flipping through it. The words "Pain Relief" caught his attention. "Dr. Gribbleflotz' Little Blue Pills of Happiness. Says here they're good for all matter of ache and pain."

"The little box is pretty, too." Anna hesitated. "It couldn't hurt to try them, could it?"

"Perhaps not. And you're right. Your mama would like that."

"I don't believe it for a minute," Hans said. "All of it is too cheap. It must be a scam."

"It came from Grantville," Freidrich pointed out. "And Pastor Schultz says they do things differently there. He's even been there."

"The whole village knows that." Hans' voice was full of scorn. "Like you could not know that, the way the man talks about it." He flipped another page. "Hm. Ursel would like that."

"Mama, Mama!"

Adele flinched at the shrill shout. *Children. You just can't keep them quiet.* "Shh, child, shh. Not so loud please. What is it?"

"It was so exciting, Mama. An up-timer came through the village. In one of their pick-up trucks. And he had a box of these. Then he gave me one. Look."

Adele shook her head even as she reached for the pamphlet her son held out. "Child, child, child. Your curiosity is going to get you in all sorts of trouble one of these days." She began flipping through the pages, looking at the drawings. "Oh. Papa would like one of those, don't you think?"

"What about the 1633 catalog?" Joyce asked. She and Gary were in bed watching TV, just like before the Ring of Fire. Of course, the movies were all reruns and the news was about broken armies, new business, and, of course, the weather and what the little ice age meant to their future.

"What about it?" Gary mumbled, not really paying attention. She could tell. Sometimes it seemed the only way she could get his attention was to screech.

This time she used an elbow to the ribs. "How are we going to handle it? Last year we bought the stuff in advance and ran out a lot. We need a better system."

"Oww. What sort of better system?"

"I don't know, but we have to come up with something. I'm not sending out any more 'Sorry, but that product is out of stock' letters if I can avoid it." She gave him a look. "Aside from what it does to our profits, it hurts our reputation."

☆   ☆   ☆

"Joycie is dead right about that," Pop Burke said. He always had been pretty partial to Joyce. "We took their money, then we had to give it back. It cost us to do that. What we really need is a way to do Collect on Delivery, like they did back in the old days. Didn't do that much anymore, not even up-time. Everyone was using credit cards and checks."

"I don't know if we can work that part out," Gary admitted. "Maybe we can. What we'll have to do, though . . . I think, maybe . . . is get the suppliers more involved, get them to give us better discounts for one thing. Freight costs . . . man alive, those are terrible. But we need guaranteed stock, no more of this 'oh, we're out of that.' And, considering how well we did do, I think a bigger, better catalog will help a lot."

Muriel nodded. "That last one was pretty plain. I bet it got lost in the mail half the time. We need a better cover, something that stands out. Color if we could get it."

"Whoo hee." Pop chuckled. "And pretty girls modeling underwear?"

Mom swatted his arm. "You old coot."

"Hey!" Pop rubbed his arm. "I don't see why not. They did that, even back in the old days."

"I don't see why there shouldn't be pretty girls. And good-looking guys, for that matter," Joyce said. "Whatever it takes to sell stuff. And we've got some good products. Life-saving products, even, now that they've figured out the household fire extinguisher. Adolph Schmidt's gold-plated flatware ought to sell like hotcakes, too. We ought to be able to double the pages this time."

"Me? To model?" Ursula's hand flew to her face. "Oh, no. Not me."

"Herr Gruber will leave that out, Ursula." Joyce smiled. "Back up-time they airbrushed out all sorts of defects. I mean, you'll never convince me that they didn't airbrush the *Playboy* bunnies right, left, up-side-down and sideways. You're the right size and the right build. We'll put your hair up pretty and get you a real nice outfit. That won't matter."

"But . . ."

"It's keep it in the family, or we have to hire someone else. And the more we can keep it in the family, the more money we get to keep."

Ursula reluctantly agreed. Joyce had the right of it there, as much as she hated to admit it.

"I'm sorry, Herr Kruger. But unless you can guarantee a supply of your vise grips at a consistent price, they won't be in the Wish Book this year." Gary Jordan Burke was learning to play hard ball, or at least he was trying. Herr Kruger was one of the people who had jacked up prices last year, which left them selling his product for less than they paid for it. It hadn't been entirely his fault; he had had to put on extra people to fulfill the demand. On the other hand, he wasn't the one that had taken the loss.

"But you won't guarantee to buy them. That is hardly fair."

"You're right. But having your product in our book is very good advertising." Gary shrugged. "It's your choice."

"No, Herr Schmidt, it's not about the flatware." Joyce smiled at the rather beefy down-timer. "We would like to include the Higgins Sewing Machine in our Wish Book. The way it would work is we would forward orders received to you, then receive a commission on sales you made through our Book."

"How much of a commission were you thinking about?" It went on from there and took several weeks to work out all the details. Of course, Gary and Joyce were working out the same issues on other products at the same time. It depended on the product and the company as to how things worked. Sometimes they bought stock outright, sometimes they acted as agent for other companies. Sometimes their agreements were exclusive, sometimes not.

"Oh, I really like this section." Muriel flipped through the pages of the 1633 Burke catalog. "That was clever, naming each section that way."

"Working Man Blues for the overalls is cute, I suppose." Mom sniffed. "But I'm not at all sure about that Mail-Order Bride section."

Pop cackled. "Keep your wife as happy as a new bride." Then he snorted. "But that sure didn't work the time I bought you a new vacuum, if I remember right."

Mom threw him a look. "You old coot. That was our twentieth wedding anniversary. You coulda made some kind of effort."

☆   ☆   ☆

"Mail-Order Bride?" The caption brought Paulus Sandler to a brief halt, then he saw the rest of it. "Keep your wife as happy as a new bride. Ha! As though that can happen." He started to toss the book back on the table, then caught sight of the cover. "Hmm."

He looked at it again, then flipped through it a bit more. "Hmm." He looked at the cover again.

"See something you like?" Albrecht Pfister asked. The other men around the table laughed. Paulus looked over at Albrecht, who was suppressing a grin and not doing a good job of it. Paulus had been a widower for two years now. His partners had each tried to find him a new wife amongst their relatives, but Paulus wasn't impressed with the results. He knew they wanted him to remarry. He even realized that they probably had a point. Maria had been the joy of his life. He still felt it when he thought of her and probably always would. He looked back at the book and Albrecht spoke again. "Think you ought to send off for that one, do you?"

"They're not selling the woman, you idiots. They're selling the things she shows. You know that as well as I do. Besides, I doubt she's real. Or, if real, I doubt she looks like that."

"Dare you to write and find out." Albrecht took a sip of beer. "You never know. It came from that Grantville place. I hear they're strange there."

That put a slight damper on the conversation. Everyone had heard they were strange there and more. By now everyone had met several people who had visited the place and seen the wonders. What they were concerned about was how those wonders would affect them. Paulus and his partners were in the shipping business. They owned, between them, half a dozen barges, and owned or had a agreements with dozens of inns and mule teams for the shipment and storage of goods. They had heard of the railroads but they were far away . . . at least for now.

The drawing of the woman was a topic of conversation time and time again. After a week, Paulus gave up. "All right, all right. I'll write the letter and order the woman. But you know she isn't real."

Paulus knew she wasn't real. He knew this wouldn't happen, that he wouldn't receive a bride in the mail. But she sure was pretty.

Perhaps, if she was real, just maybe she would write to him. But she wouldn't be real, not looking like that. It was impossible. Real women didn't look like that.

"Because I can order it cheaper than we can go there." Johan Weisel shook his head. "To travel to Grantville would be too expensive. To order this, even with the freight charges, I can afford."

Barbara Weisel hid a smile. She'd been pretty sure that was the right approach. First she'd started by asking that they make the trip to Grantville and see the sights. She'd known all along that wouldn't happen. But enough display of unhappiness had gotten her what she really wanted. She would be the first woman in the village to have gold-plated flatware. Wouldn't Maria be envious?

The Gerber Bargain Book came out about three months after the 1633 Burke Wish Book. Gerber had copied their idea and there was absolutely nothing they could do about it. A lot of their nonexclusive suppliers had their ads directly copied in his book.

No one was sure how he had gotten the print plates. Perhaps he hadn't; perhaps all he had done was use their book as a model. That's what Herr Gruber, the engraver, insisted. There were, he said, little differences in the Gerber book and the Wish Book. They actually talked to a lawyer about suing Gerber, but the lawyer told them it probably wouldn't do any good because the guy was based in Halle. Even if they won, the suit was likely to cost more than it would gain them. No one was sure what it would do to sales but they were all worried.

Johan groaned and stretched. "My pills, dear. Please."

Barbara nodded. She was happy that Johan had discovered the Blue Pills of Happiness. He was much less grumpy these days. She had used them a time or two herself, when the monthly cramps got out of hand.

All in all, she thought that many people in the village were a good bit less grumpy these days. Even her mother, who took the pills for the constant toothaches she suffered. "It's getting to be time to order more. But I think we should try the ones from the Bargain Book. They're cheaper."

"I'd be afraid they wouldn't work as well. Let's stick to the Gribbleflotz brand . . . just in case."

"Those are in the Bargain Book, too."

"But we know the ones from the Wish Book work."

Barbara shrugged. "As you wish. And your trousers are worn to the weft again. How about you try a pair of torberts?"

Ursula sighed. There were order forms in the Wish Book that made it easier to tell what was being ordered, in spite of which a lot of people put their orders in letters. People just didn't follow instructions. Still she had a job to do. She opened the letter and quickly realized that there was, in this case, a good reason for not using the order form.

Dear Sirs,

I would have used the order form but the item that captured my interest possessed neither order number or price. This is entirely understandable, for the young lady displayed on the cover and in your Mail Order Bride Section is clearly a pearl beyond price. Capture my interest, did I say? Nay, more. The kindly sparkle of her eyes, the clever wit of her smile, hold me an entranced prisoner even now.

I am not a fool, good sirs, though I know I must sound one. Such a one cannot exist in our poor earthly world. Not unless an angel from heaven snuck to earth in the fabled Ring of Fire. No, it must be the work of a latter day Michelangelo or Leonardo Da Vinci, who has, in turning from uncouth men to lovely ladies, put Michelangelo's David to blushing shame. And in his model found a smile that causes the famed Mona Lisa to raise her hand to hide the smile that, until now, men so remarked upon.

Still, even the greatest artist must needs have inspiration to work from. And the inspiration for these works of art must have been more than a mere physical model. Clearly the artist has managed to capture a bit of the beauty of the model's soul. Nor, I know, can such a thing be bought. It must instead be won. Did I but live in an earlier age, I would don armor and seek out a dragon to slay or perhaps take up my lute and compose ballads by the score.

But we do not live in such times and my singing causes children to flee in fear, convinced, no doubt, that some horrible monster approaches. I am but a man of accounts. A merchant, who even now kicks himself for not having the wit to offer my customers such a compilation of products to be ordered with such ease. So, while I would willingly and happily order all of the items in the Mail Order Bride section of your Wish Book—did I have such a bride as the one you show to gift them with. Alas, the one that would make the others worthwhile is unavailable. But, on the infinitesimal chance that I am wrong . . . that there is such a paragon of the womanly virtues as the pictures display . . . How might she be contacted?

Yours Most Sincerely,
Paulus Sandler

Ursula sat frozen in her chair, staring at the letter, unsure whether to laugh or cry. Clearly the letter was intended to offer the writer up for friendly ridicule for the amusement of the reader. But she was sure that there was a touch of genuine desire hidden in its lines. There was a loneliness in it that she recognized as her own. A loneliness that didn't really expect to find easing. It was that realization that tipped the balance in favor of tears, for she could almost—but not quite—believe that she could ease that loneliness and her own into the bargain. And the certainty that she couldn't weighed on her with a weight she couldn't bear. Tears filled her eyes, a little for the letter but mostly for the knowledge that she would live and die alone. Leaving the letter where it lay, she got up and ran from the room.

"What was that all about?" Gary asked.

Joyce was quicker. She went to Ursula's desk and looked for what some cretin could have written that would upset the normally unflappable young woman to the point of tears. Ready to give the cretin a piece of her mind, she of course saw the letter immediately. And began to read. Gary shortly was reading over her shoulder.

"What's the big deal?" Gary asked, just like a man. "So the guy was over the top. Why not just trash it if she didn't want to answer it."

Joyce slammed him with an elbow to the ribs. "Don't be more of a jerk than you have to, Gary. The problem is she does want to answer it."

Gary stepped out of range because he knew he was about to earn another elbow. "So why not answer it?"

Joyce didn't answer, she just looked at him and sighed. "Stay here. And don't say a word about this to Ursula. Ever! I'm going to talk to her."

Ursula was crying in her pillow when she heard the knocking and realized that she had run out of the room. Embarrassment fought grief and won, at least for the moment. She wiped her eyes and went to open the door. When she saw the letter in Joyce's hand, a new embarrassment added its weight to grief and the tears came again.

"I knew I shouldn't have agreed. I knew it."

"Honey, it's a beautiful letter. It's kind of like the man really wants to know you. He sounds very sweet." Joyce pointed to the phrase "children run screaming in fear." "You've got to like a guy who can put himself down like that."

Ursula blinked back tears. "And now I have to tell this perfectly nice man that I am not what he thinks. I knew Herr Gruber was doing wrong, making me too pretty. No one has ever offered me marriage. My family didn't even want to look at me, not after . . . Mama cried every time she looked at my face. That is why I left. I could bear it no longer."

Joyce patted her shoulder. "You are too that pretty. Why, if we were back up-time, they could fix that in a heartbeat."

"But we are not." Ursula stood, then wiped her eyes. "We are not."

> *Dear Sir,*
>
> *I regret that I must decline your kind offer. It is quite true that nothing was added to that drawing, that I will attest to. But I'm afraid something was left out of it. I feel that it would not be to your advantage, or mine, to correspond.*
>
> *I thank you for the letter you sent and will treasure it.*
>
> *U.R.*

Ursula considered and worked on her response for a week. Even though Joyce had offered to write it, she felt that she must. After at least fifty starts and stops, she finally decided that short and simple was best. But she couldn't resist letting Paulus Sandler know that she did treasure his letter.

"She writes a beautiful hand," Albrecht pointed out. "I wonder what she means, 'something was left out of it.'"

"Pox marks, I'd bet."

"Fat as a house, maybe?"

"No teeth?"

Paulus read the letter again. Something about it spoke to him. But he didn't know what. "I suppose we'll never know. I told you there would be something like this." Even as he blustered, he tried to hide his disappointment.

"Business is slow," Albrecht said. "You could go see. Don't even have to give your name. Just go and look."

"Bah! Pointless."

"Well, there's always my niece, Anna."

Paulus flinched. Anna was, in his opinion, a shrew and as close to witless as he had ever seen.

"Then you ought to go. Every man should travel now and again." *Here, fishy, fishy.*

"Pointless, I say."

"Dare you. Besides, we need someone to have a look at those railroads and see if we can get shipping contracts from Grantville. We got some from that Simpson fellow in Magdeburg."

"We don't have much in the way of connections in southern Germany. We always thought they weren't needed."

"True enough, before the Ring of Fire happened. Now I'm not so sure. It's been a couple of years and they're still there. Even getting bigger. I really do think it's time we started paying attention, don't you?"

The suppliers, some of them, were doing it again, in spite of the contracts. "Unavoidable delays." "We're sorry, but there are just so many hours in a day and we're working our fingers to the bone as it is." It was even true. Of course, some of the stuff they were working their fingers to the bone making was going to Halle to the Gerber warehouse. Gerber's advantage was that he had more startup money. He could make bulk orders, put them in his warehouse in Halle and have them ready for the orders to come in.

"I'm getting worried about this," Joyce said. "This is the fifth 'out of stock' letter I've had to write this week. If this keeps up, it's going to ruin our reputation."

"It's going to ruin us entirely. Waiting for those products is costing us money. And we're still getting orders from last year's Wish Book at last year's prices." Muriel was getting worried. When they had decided to seriously expand the Wish Book for 1633, they had put up the house as collateral for a large loan. They had gone with a truly monstrous print run, fifteen thousand copies and hired extra people. All of which would have been fine if they had or could get enough product to support their orders.

At seven months after the publication of the 1633 Wish books they had filled sixty-three thousand orders and had just under twenty thousand waiting, at an average of three point seven items per order. Mostly small ticket items: measuring cups and spoons, scales, even fabric tape measures, were selling faster than they could be produced. So they had a fair-sized staff that was mostly sitting on its hands waiting for the manufacturers to deliver the product so that they could package it and ship it. And they couldn't let their people go; they had become like family. Instead, she had missed the last two payments on the house. The worry was affecting her temper, which was none too even to begin with.

Paulus Sandler couldn't quite believe what he was seeing. The Wish Book came from here? A small, inconspicuous building, off the main streets of Grantville? There was no warehouse. There was barely room for a person to turn around in the crowded space. How could this possibly be the headquarters of the Wish Book?

He stopped staring in the window, squared his shoulders and tapped at the door. In the few hours he'd been here, he'd already learned to call this kind of building a "garage." It appeared that many of these garages had been converted to living spaces or workshops for various manufactories.

"Come in!"

Paulus flinched. The voice was very high-pitched and screechy. Perhaps that was what U.R. meant when she said that something had been left out. He cracked open the door. "Hello?"

"Come on in. I'm in the back."

Paulus made his way around a stack of barrels. "Ah?"

"What can I help you with?" The woman who spoke was very old, but her eyes behind the thick spectacles were bright. "Were you looking for Gary or Joyce?"

"Ah . . . no." Paulus held out the letter he had received. "I am looking for the person who wrote this."

Muriel looked at the letter. She knew all about it, of course. You couldn't keep a secret in the Burke household. "You the man that wrote?" He wasn't a bad looking man, she thought. A bit beefy, maybe, but nice looking.

"Yes. And I could not help myself. I must know what got left out of the picture. I simply must."

Muriel picked up a copy of the Wish Book and pointed to the cover. Then, with a finger nail, she indicated a scar on the beautiful face. "Ursula has a scar here. A bad one, caused by one of the men who attacked her. But that isn't the worst scar she carries. The worst one is the scar she carries in her heart."

"Ah." Paulus stopped.

"So tell me, buster. Does that change things for you? She's not quite what the picture shows. But she's really a lot more than it shows, too. I've never met a more caring person, up-time or down. And as they say, beauty is only skin deep."

"How am I supposed to know that?" Paulus complained. "I have never met the woman. I don't know how things would go between us even if she looked exactly like the picture. What's she like? Will she find me an old, fat man?" Paulus wasn't fat but he was solidly built and not overly tall. Nor was he a doddering oldster, though there was some gray in his blond hair and lines of care on his face. He looked like what he was, a middle-aged, fairly prosperous merchant. But he knew that to the callow youth he had been, he would look an old man. "Does her smile in the picture there reflect her laugh or is it the artist's grace? Does she laugh with joy or at another's pain?"

He shook his head, unable to really explain what had brought him here "It's true that I came about the girl, but I knew it was probably a fool's errand even as I made the trip. I have no desire to hurt the girl nor any great desire to be hurt myself. The excuse I gave myself was that I was really coming to look over your business. Perhaps it's best we leave it at that for now?"

"Oh no! Gerber's already killing us. Now you want to jump in."

Paulus laughed. "Not necessarily. It's more curiosity than anything else. Is Gerber really hurting you that much? From what I hear back home, you seem to have plenty of customers."

"That's not the problem. It's the suppliers." And from there they went into a detailed discussion of what the business was doing and how it was working. That's what Ursula found Muriel and the stranger talking about over an hour later.

As she usually did around strangers, Ursula stood with the good side of her face toward anyone she didn't know well. This sometimes took some maneuvering, but to Muriel it seemed that it was almost second nature by now. "I'm back, Muriel. Shopping done and the day's packages delivered to the post. The new cart makes that job much easier."

Muriel smiled. "We're pretty much done for the day, then. And I'm tired. Ursula, this is—"

She stopped abruptly because Paulus cut her off. "Albrecht Pfitzer, at your service." He bowed. "Frau, ah, Muriel, rather, has been telling me about you."

Muriel kept herself from flinching. She could understand that Paulus might not want to embarrass Ursula, but she was pretty sure he was making a big mistake. "Albrecht is going to have supper with us, Ursula. He's got some very good ideas about how we could expand the business and I want to pick his brain a bit longer. We'll need to tell Joyce to set another place at the table."

Albrecht was a very nice man, Ursula thought. He hadn't visibly flinched when he saw the scar she bore and had kept up dinner conversation very well. He'd also borne up under the noise level, which was something that Gary didn't always manage very well. Ursula knew that Joyce, Mom Burke, and Muriel couldn't help the pitch of their voices. It did make for piercing conversation, though.

Paulus thought about the Burkes and Ursula all during the walk back to the Higgins Hotel. The Wish Book had been a good idea, one that was clearly working and that had a lot of profit potential. But, as good-hearted and kind as the Burkes were, none of them had a head for business. They'd done reasonably well, even so. What they didn't have was the capital to grow. And he knew, from talking to Muriel, that they were in serious danger of going under. It was a case of too much success, too soon, compounded by the problems with their suppliers.

He, though, had capital. And business sense. And it was clear that Ursula was a part of the Burke family, an important part. He doubted that she would look kindly on him taking over if she thought it would damage her adopted family.

And, now that he thought about it, keeping his real identity a secret might have been a mistake. It had been a spur of the moment thing, an unthoughtout attempt to save them both embarrassment. It had suddenly occurred to him that maybe her letter had simply been a kind way of telling him she wasn't interested. He had never thought that before and nothing Muriel had said supported the notion. It was seeing her face. The unscarred side of her face. She had looked like the pictures. Just like the pictures. What could such a woman see in him? Now he faced another problem. How would Ursula feel when she discovered his deception? Having Ursula think he was dishonest would not make him happy, he acknowledged. She was beautiful in spirit and that spirit called to him. Probably he should have admitted who he was immediately.

Of course, if he helped the Burkes out of their troubles, surely that would make her look kindly upon him. Perhaps even enough that she would forgive him the deception.

He worried at the problem most of the night, even as tired as he was.

Paulus Sandler wasn't the only one worried. All through dinner, Muriel had worried. First, that he had involved her in his lie. Then about why he lied. Was it to save Ursula embarrassment or had he decided as soon as he saw her that he wasn't interested? That actually seemed to make more sense, though he hadn't acted uninterested in Ursula. If he was going to fade away, it might be best if Ursula never found out that Paulus Sandler had come to visit. That led her to worrying if perhaps he hadn't come here about Ursula at all and was just here to scope out their business. For all she knew he worked for Gerber. Finally after dinner she talked to Joyce and Gary about it. Then they started worrying.

"No, I don't think it was all a scam to get a look at how we operate." Gary grinned. "He was looking at Ursula all night and it wasn't the scar he was looking at."

Joyce glared. "Gary Jordan, you are a dog."

Gary grinned. "*Arf, arf.* But I'm your dog, darlin'. Point is, he was interested. Of course, he could be interested in both. There are guys who are interested in more than one thing." He pointed at his chest with his thumb, waited a beat for Joyce's disbelieving snort, then said, "I've met some."

"So what do we do? Drag him back down here and make him fess up?" Joyce asked. "He's going to have to sooner or later—and the longer he waits, the worse it's going to be for everyone."

Gary had been thinking about that. "I think the first thing to do is for me to go down there and have the 'what are your intentions' talk."

"Gary, Ursula's a grownup." It was clear from Joyce's tone she wasn't entirely convinced.

"I know she is, but she's also family, or close enough, and she's been hurt. I don't want to see her hurt again."

"So, if you're satisfied with his intentions, you're going to drag him back here to face the music?"

"I'm not sure. On the one hand, he surely deserves it. On the other hand, it seems like a great way to screw up any hope of them working things out. Ursula is liable to say something because she's pissed. He's liable to say something because he's trying to cover his ass. It might be better if he's not handy to pound on when Ursula gets the news."

Joyce shook her head. "Won't work. If he's not here, Ursula's going to feel like it's because he can't stand to look at her. I know it doesn't make sense, but that's how she's going to feel. Anyway, she's going to figure that the whole different name thing was just a way for him to wimp out. She's going to be hurt and if he's not here to explain himself, that's just going to nail it down."

"What are your intentions toward Ursula?" Gary felt like an idiot saying that but he couldn't think of another way to put it. Nor was he sure how he would answer if Paulus Sandler asked him what business it was of Gary's.

Instead, Paulus seemed relieved. "I thought it was too late . . ." Paulus trailed off, clearly looking for the right words and not finding them.

"Okay." Gary sighed. "Let's go get some breakfast and you can tell me about it."

The tower, if you could call it that, of the Higgins Hotel wasn't finished yet so the restaurant was still located on the second floor of the middle building. But it was pretty darn fancy anyway. Which didn't seem to bother Paulus at all.

They sat down to scrambled eggs, bacon and pancakes while the merchant told his story. After he had gone through it all and explained why the sudden name change, Gary agreed that he was in some trouble. "The good news is you get to figure out what the dog house is like early."

"That news doesn't seem all that good to me."

"Well, you earned it and you know it." Gary grinned.

"You wouldn't sort of, well, explain the situation to Ursula?"

"Nope. I thought about it. But Joyce doesn't think it would be that good an idea. She figures if you don't show, then Ursula will think it's because you can't stand to look at her."

"That makes no sense!"

"Since when have women ever made sense?"

"But Ursula is clearly a pleasant and reasonable young woman. Surely . . ."

"Ursula got cut up and and assaulted eight years ago and the people of her village blamed her for 'inviting' it. A bunch of sickos blaming the victim, if you ask me. Anyway, from what we can gather, she was pretty vain about her looks before that and probably something of a tease. She figured she had lost everything. Which was what the SOB apparently had in mind. Now she figures she's the next best thing to the hunchback of Notre Dame. I know it's not that bad, you know it's not that bad. There's no convincing Ursula, though. You've seen how she hides that side of her face."

"Is that how it happened?"

"Well, that's how we've put it together from the odd comment she's made and a couple of crying jags when she'd had a bit too much wine. Point is, if you're not there to tell her different, she's going to figure that it's because you can't stand to look at her. And that, my friend, means you're going to have to be the one to tell her you were lying about your name." By now Paulus was acting like a ten-year-old who knew he was caught and was trying to figure out a way to get out of 'fessing up. Figuratively speaking, Gary grabbed him by the ear and dragged him home.

Judging honestly, Gary felt that Paulus held his own fairly well. Of course, it was Ursula who had most of the ammunition. The results were not deep passionate love. It was way too soon for that. Some pictures in a magazine, one letter each way. One dinner when one of the pair hadn't even known who the other was. And one "how could you do such a thing?" It was more like an armed truce. Paulus had not lived up to Ursula's expectations; he was on notice that he was on thin ice and he'd already cracked it.

At the same time, Paulus had stood up there at the end and let Ursula know that she could well win a Pyrrhic victory and run him off, and was getting very close to doing so. Yes, he had blown it. People sometimes do. No, he didn't find the scar much of an issue, not nearly so much as the "holier than thou" attitude. No, he wasn't going to run screaming because her face wasn't perfect, but neither was he a lap dog for anyone. Not even her. Looking at Ursula's face, Gary figured she was rather pleased with that last.

"So how do we keep him here long enough for something to grow?" Joyce asked after the fighters had retreated to their respective corners to get ready for the next round. That is, Ursula went to her room and Paulus went back to the Higgins Hotel.

"Do we want to?" Gary asked.

"Gary Jordan!" Joyce screeched.

"Well." Gary defended himself as best he could. "We don't really know all that much about him. We know he's a merchant, a friendly guy and he wrote a funny letter. But that's about it. He could be the next thing to a con man for all we know."

"So find out!" Joyce commanded.

What Gary found out over the next few days, first from Paulus himself, then from some of the commercial interests that were now based in Grantville, was that Paulus was generally considered honest enough, if a bit hard-nosed, in matters of business. That he was a fairly successful wholesaler of everything from pig iron to pepper. The way they decided to keep him around, even before they had confirmation for most of this, was to see if they could get him to help with organizing their business.

"Transportation." Paulus sighed. "The problem, Ursula, or the biggest problem, is transportation." He took a big drink of his beer. "The railroad will help. It will help more than I would have imagined possible before seeing it. But it will be months before it reaches Halle, and longer still before it reaches Magdeburg. And it's running at close to capacity now. What that means is that something like seventy percent of your sales have been within natural-gas-car range of Grantville or the railroads. That's a corridor about twenty miles wide on either side of the railroad in which you have unbelievably cheap transport. After you get out of that pocket, the cost of transport goes way up—to the point that it cancels out the advantage you have in mass production. It works the other way, too.

"Getting the raw materials up here costs a lot more if they aren't local. Look at the prices of your goods. Where the raw materials come through Hamburg, the cost of your goods is four to ten times higher than if the raw materials are found locally. What happens when your competitors have factories and warehouses in Magdeburg and yours are still here? Even with the railroad, they will be able to undercut your prices. You have to plan for the future."

"Is the river really that much cheaper than the railroad?" Ursula asked. "I mean, once the railroads reach Halle and Magdeburg?"

"It can be and it will be. Don't forget that by the time the railroad reaches Halle, it won't be competing with the little barges we have now. We'll build big barges with engines on them, maybe steam or, perhaps, internal combustion. We're still working that out. But my partners and I will have big barges built in Magdeburg before the rail line hits Halle. We'll be able to ship a hundred tons for what it costs us now to ship ten. And we'll have those hundreds of tons to ship, too, because of the industries that are starting up in Magdeburg and all along the Elbe."

Ursula was a bit worried. This particular batch of beer was pretty powerful. Apparently the local brewers were getting ready for the harvest celebrations. She'd determined that the last thing she wanted to do was get falling-down drunk in front of Paulus. Falling down might not be so bad. It was the drunk part she didn't much want. "But this is their home, Paulus. Many of the up-timers, especially the older ones, are afraid to leave Grantville."

Paulus burped. "Mark my words, my lovely, mark my words. It won't be that long until all the modern conveniences are available everywhere. Think about it. I come here and stay at the Higgins

Hotel. I get up in the morning, walk to my own little bath house right there in my room. Get hot water with the turning of a knob. What do you think I'm going to do when I get home? The plumbing is coming. Well, for the wealthy. You can already buy a generator for the electric. There's no reason not to locate the business in a more optimum location."

Ursula grinned. Paulus had been doing a lot of talking with Huddy Colburn and picked up quite a bit of his vocabulary.

He swept his hand in the air, gesturing at the full room. "Every one of these people who wants to make money needs to consider the transportation. It will never be economically viable to have the mail order business located in such an inconvenient location. Well, the business offices can stay here. But not the warehouses and the shipping. What we need to do is convince Gary Jordan and Joyce. And Muriel. And Mom and Pop Burke." He grinned a bit blearily. "The old coot and the old hen. They don't all have to move. Muriel should probably stay here and it might be better for Mom and Pop Burke. Grantville does have the best medical facilities in the world.

"I've been reading, too. We need a parcel service like they had up-time. You Pee Ess, they called it.

"Might be possible, too. All the independent couriers . . . like that Martin over there . . ." Paulus paused. "Hm. I need to talk to Martin, I think. He'll have contacts." Then he shook his head. "That's for the future. Right now, what about us?"

He must be a bit drunk, Ursula thought. He was usually much more reticent. "What about us?"

"You still mad at me?"

Ursula took a sip of beer to delay answering. "Not really, I suppose." Their relationship had smoothed considerably in the last month. Perhaps it was time. "I'm not sure I ever really was. I was . . ." She touched the scar. "I was . . . afraid. Afraid that I would be alone forever. And then your letter came. And I thought maybe . . . but then . . ."

"I was afraid, too. Afraid I had destroyed what could have been."

Paulus had spent a lot of time with a new book in the last month. It had been written by some of the professional research-ers who worked in the national library. It was a translation of management and organizational techniques developed up-time. Quite a bit of it was stuff Paulus already knew from experience, but it was organized and boiled down. Looked at in the light of Paulus' experience and "Business Management 101," the problem with the Burkes' business was that they were running it like a corner shop. They didn't have flow charts or much in the way of organizational structure. They weren't looking at who their suppliers were or, really, who their customers were. They weren't looking at what parts of the operation cost what, or seeing where things could be improved.

Paulus grimaced a bit. A lot of that could be applied to his own business as well. He and his partners had a great deal of experience. Between them they knew their business inside out, but not in a very organized way. Right now, he was a bit scared for his own fortune and his partners. It was unlikely that they would go out of business, but they could be hurt by the changes that were radiating out from the Ring of Fire. They were shippers of goods, mostly transshipers. They shipped quite a bit by barge up and down the Elbe and the Rhine, but they also had contracts with inns throughout northern and central Germany. They ran several mule trains carrying wine, cloth and all sorts of other goods. And one of the problems facing them was the change in the transportation picture. What was going to happen to the muleskinners when the railroad came? What would happen to their business as the muleskinners were affected?

While he had been building business flow charts for the Burkes, he'd also been building them for himself and his partners. Partly because he had an entirely different sort of merger on his mind, he started noticing the merger potential between the Burke's business and his. What he and his partners had was a distribution network, seventeenth-century style. What the Burkes had was access to the suppliers of up-time goods and a really good marketing idea that was already being copied. He started drawing new boxes and new lines, combining the two companies into one larger company, using each to add to the other to fill in missing pieces.

It was really just an exercise. Neither his partners nor the Burkes were likely to agree to it. His partners because they could copy the parts that the Burkes did readily enough. They hadn't yet because they mostly dealt in bulk goods. The Burkes because—like a lot of the up-timers—they seemed to want to keep control of everything in their own hands. At the same time, he did have a responsibility to his partners. The way things were looking, they were going to lose a lot of their trade over the next few years to the railroads.

"So you see, I really must be getting back. Albrecht, the real Albrecht, has written, asking for more details."

Ursula nodded. She and Paulus were walking through Grantville, her to do the shopping, Paulus just to keep her company and because he wanted to pick up some things he'd ordered. "You've been a lot of help. Even Gary says so. I did speak to him of the transportation problems. He is unsure."

"Ah. Here we are." Paulus put his hand on her waist and guided her through the door of Eberhart Leather. "I'm to pick up the briefcases today. Which will be much more professional-looking than a canvas tote."

Ursula giggled. "The mark of a businessman is his fancy leather briefcase. Gary is going to start calling you a 'suit.'"

The counterman, having recognized Paulus, brought out the four briefcases he'd ordered. He'd had the initials of his partners applied to each. "Most excellent," Paulus said. "Most excellent. Wrap those up, please, but I will take this one now." He started transferring the load of file folders out of the tote, but he was a bit clumsy with it. One folder fell, spreading the contents over the floor.

It had to be that folder. Paulus reached for the organization chart, but it was too late. Ursula had already picked it up.

She looked up from it, face flushed. "Just what kind of merger are you planning, Herr Sandler? I don't recall . . ."

"Please don't be upset." He hesitated a moment. "I'm not really planning much of anything yet. It's more of a possibility than a plan."

"It looks pretty detailed to me."

"Yes, detailed, but not probable. What I haven't been able to figure out is the key to the whole thing . . . how to get anyone to agree to it." The clerk was looking at them, so, leaving Ursula in possession of the flow chart, Paulus took her arm and led her out of the shop.

"What do you mean?" Ursula waited till they were in the street to ask. One of the things that had impressed him about her was that she noticed things.

"Let's find a place where we can sit and talk." Paulus looked up and down the street for someplace fairly private.

A few minutes later, Ursula was seated in a corner of a café, waiting to hear Paulus' explanation. She hoped it would be a good one because she didn't really want to believe that he was going to try to steal the Wish Book from the Burkes.

"How many of the businesses in Grantville are now run by down-timers?" Paulus asked.

Ursula gave him a look but answered anyway, figuring this was part of the explanation. *It had better be.* "I don't know the exact numbers, but quite a few."

"Neither do I," Paulus acknowledged. "But I have noticed that a lot of them seem to have a certain amount of resentment attached to it, even when the up-timer gets rich off the deal . . . which a lot of them have."

Ursula nodded and waited.

"A lot of up-timers seem to think that just because they are from the future they know how to run a business. Well, they don't. You've heard the horror stories; I know you have. Even the up-timers have, though they don't seem to be listening all that well."

"If they're that bad, why are you carrying around up-time style management flow charts?" She held up the document in question.

"The up-timer management strategies in the business books that came back with the Ring of Fire are often brilliant and mostly useful. But most up-timers don't seem to have read the books." Paulus grinned at her and she had to acknowledge the truth of his words with a nod.

"It takes more than just the books, anyway," Paulus said. "It takes experience to understand what the books mean and most up-timers don't have it. I doubt if there are fifty up-timers who ran a business before the Ring of Fire. It's a different world view."

"Okay. So the up-timers aren't the world's greatest business people. What does that have to do with what you said before?"

"That's less the problem than the fact that most of them don't seem to realize it. What do you think the Burkes would say if I offered to take over?"

Ursula grinned. "I'm not entirely sure, but I think you might be surprised." She knew that the pressures of running the business weren't doing good things for the Burkes. That they weren't all that happy with the way things were going. "Is that what you have in mind? To take over the Wish Book and make us all rich?"

"Sort of. I have partners too, you know. I have a responsibility to them." Paulus hesitated then burst out. "The truth is, if it weren't for you, I wouldn't be considering a merger at all. And even if the Burkes agreed, I doubt if my partners would."

"Why not?" Ursula tried to keep her voice level in spite of the sudden realization that he cared a great deal for her. She had come to know Paulus and one thing she was sure of was how important doing the best job he could was to him.

"Because they don't have that much to offer. The concept of the Wish Book, which, as Gerber has shown, we don't need to pay for. A little good will, but not that much. I know what my partners are going to say. 'Sounds like a great idea. What do we need the up-timers for?' Unfortunately, I don't have a good answer for that question."

Ursula cocked her head to the side. "You're not as smart as I thought you were. You know what? I have a good answer for that question."

"What?"

"Knowledge. Not business knowledge. General knowledge. Look, a few months back someone wanted us to sell an electric belt that was a cure for everything from the black death to back pain. Could an electric belt do that?"

"Well, from your voice I guess not." Then he grinned. "But if I had just seen a proposal for such a product, I would have no way of knowing."

"Joyce took one look at it and laughed. The idea that electricity could cure a disease was ridiculous to her. On the other hand, the magnetic stand that lets another magnet float above it? I would never have believed that if I hadn't seen it with my own eyes. I would have thrown that one out. But it does work. It's not good for all that much, I grant, but it's a very impressive knickknack and we've had a lot of letters about how much people love playing with them. There have been a lot of things like that over the last couple of years. They know a lot about what works, stuff that makes no sense to us and would take years to pick up on. That's their value. That's what they have that makes including them in the deal a good idea."

☆   ☆   ☆

Paulus tried to keep his nervousness from showing. "Let me start with my business. My partners and I own several river barges and part ownership in some inns, as well as a piece of several mule trains. It's partly what your up-timer books would call a distributed network transport system. Say a load of iron comes in through Hamburg. A merchant there will buy part of the load, then sell it to foundries and smithies. Then he will contact us and tell us how much he wants to go where. We'll agree on a price a timetable, then we'll send it by barge up river or by mule train, east or west. To an inn, where the shipment will be split and then sent by other barges and or mule trains to different destinations, or wait in a back room in an inn until there is transport available to ship it where it needs to go. We only own a few of the steps in the chain, but we have standing agreements with a lot of others. Sometimes we're carrying their stuff, sometimes they are carrying ours. Once in a while, we work out who's been carrying more of whose cargo and pay each other to keep everything pretty much balanced. Scheduling isn't quite catch-as-catch-can, but it's not all that precise, either. It's a fairly slow way of getting your goods from one place to another. On the other hand, it's quite a bit cheaper than hiring a mule train to take your cargo where you want it in one shot."

Joyce and Gary looked at each other. The way that tied in to the Wish Book business was obvious. "Why did you tell us you were a merchant?"

"Because I am?"

"But why didn't you tell us that you were in transportation?"

"Oh. It didn't occur to me for a while that my business and your business had much to do with each other. You see, we don't ship to Mr. Smith on Baker's Lane or Mrs. Jones on Market Street. We ship to Smith and Sons Fine Blacksmiths or to Jones' Tailor Shop."

"You don't do retail?" Muriel asked "Why not?"

"I have been asking myself that same question since I looked at the open spaces in your business flow chart and compared them to the boxes in ours. One reason, I think, is that the guilds wouldn't approve. Have you noticed how much of your sales are to small villages instead of towns?"

"Most people live in villages."

"True enough, but the money is concentrated in the towns. Most towns have rules limiting the import of goods that are already manufactured by the guilds in that town. So, ready-made boot sales are limited to villages where there isn't a shoemakers guild. A battery or crystal set or record player, you can sell most anywhere. Ready-made pants are likely to be blocked. Not always, by the way. If you send it by post, it will mostly get by. What they are really after is someone bringing in a cart load of shoes to sell in town. That might change, though, if more people start using the Wish Book, the Bargain Book or the others that are sure to follow."

Paulus watched their faces. "Anyway, that's why I wasn't thinking in terms of a connection between your business and mine. We don't generally do retail. Then a few days ago I happened to have projections from your business and mine on the table at the same time and suddenly saw the connection. It seemed like we could fill in a lot of the holes in your organizational chart and that you could expand our business. What it didn't seem like was something that either you or my partners would agree too. I went ahead and did the work-up as practice. A way of learning to use what I found in the books. Then Ursula saw it and convinced me that you at least might consider it."

Paulus then launched into a detailed plan of how it would work. He answered questions about how their business would change and be helped by his. When the questions came back to the workings of his business, he said, "You should come with me and see how it works." He wondered if they'd go for it, frankly. While quite a number of up-timers had gone off to other places, a far larger number seemed to be planted in Granville to stay.

Sure enough, they were surprised by the idea. "Ah . . . we'll have to think about it," Gary said. "We hadn't . . ."

Ursula kept quiet. In her own opinion, as good as they'd been to her, up-timers were a bit soft. And very attached to their luxuries.

"We did used to camp," Gary pointed out. "Not much difference, sanitation wise."

"I always hated it," Joyce grumbled. "Always, always, always. Go out in the hot, go out in the cold, pee in the woods . . . hated it."

"Joyce." Muriel glared. "You are such a wuss."

"Am not, either," Joyce screeched.

"Are so," Mom Burke screeched back. "You'd never have made it through the Depression. You're only fifty-five. I'd go, only I'm way too old. And the arthritis has me down too bad."

"Oh, yadda yadda yadda. Do we get the 'walked to school in the snow' lecture now?" Joyce slumped into her recliner. "I didn't say I wouldn't go, people. And there's more than the potty issue, you know. Wasn't that long ago we got attacked, remember? I can't help it. I'm nervous about leaving Grantville."

"You ain't no spring chicken, either." Muriel grinned. "If you don't want to go, I will. What the heck. I'm seventy-four. How many adventures can I expect?"

Joyce snickered. "I can see it now. You on a horse."

"You're a wuss, Joyce."

Ursula went to her room. They were all wusses, she thought. That didn't mean she didn't care about them. But they really were wusses.

Joyce, Gary, Muriel, Ursula and Paulus stepped off the barge in Lauenburg and looked around.

"Sure is a busy place," Gary mumbled.

It was. The barges were lined up, waiting to unload and new piers were being built to accommodate them. Men with carts trudged to and from various warehouses; the taverns were full to overflowing.

Paulus' expression was one of satisfaction. "Yes. And getting busier. Come, please."

"We don't really need them," Albrecht pointed out. "Yes, it was a good idea. I can agree with that. But we don't really need them."

"Yes, we do need them." He explained about the knowledge they all had. "They will keep us from accepting a reasonable sounding impossibility and let us consider impossible sounding things that do work. They also have connections in Grantville that will make dealing there and with up-timers in general easier." *Besides*, he thought, *I need Ursula. And with Ursula comes the Burkes.*

Muriel spoke up. "Reputation is important in retail. It affects sales and can even affect whether we are allowed to sell in towns. Heck fire, the arguments the guilds usually use to justify blocking imports is quality." Then she discussed the patent medicines that used to be sold in their world, and were sold even now all over Germany. Nasty stuff that did no good, but only made things worse. "We can prevent a lot of those mistakes. There will still be some, but if we can keep the number low enough, we can maintain a reputation for quality that will make keeping us out harder and harder as the years go by."

Albrecht was watching Paulus. Suddenly he grinned. "Acquired a bit more family than you thought you would, looks like. All right. I'll go along. But I want some use of those connections. I want my son to go to Grantville, to help there. And my daughter. To put her to school."

"I'm sure it can be worked out," Paulus said. "They have a saying, these people. 'Love conquers all.'"

"They're crazy."

"Yep." Muriel agreed with a smile. "We sure are."

O For A Muse of Fire

Jay Robison

O for a muse of fire, that would ascend
The brightest heaven of invention!
—Shakespeare, *Henry V*

Andreas Gryphius, born Greif, waited outside the door to Amber
Higham's office. He knew he hadn't done anything wrong, knew
that that was not why the high school's drama teacher wanted to
talk to him, but Andreas always felt a kind of nervousness when
he had to deal with authority. He was also nervous because he
was hoping for a teaching position at the high school, and was
afraid that he was about to find out whether he'd gotten one.

The door opened and Markus Schneider strode out, nodding a greeting as he left. Behind Markus, and lingering ever so
slightly when she saw Andreas, was Antje Becker. Markus was
Andreas' age, eighteen, Antje a year younger, and they all knew
each other through the high school's RTT—radio, television and
theater—program. It didn't take long after the Ring of Fire for
Janice Ambler and Amber Higham to realize how vital television
and radio would be for information and entertainment. It wasn't
enough to have performers and presenters. There would always be
a surplus of people who wanted to perform. But any production,
be it for radio, stage or television, would need camera operators, electricians, sound technicians, grips and more. Janice and
Amber decided to start a joint radio-television-theater program

that focused on giving interested students practical experience in the technical side of production. The result was a program for both the radio and television stations, *Beyond Our Control*, a sketch comedy series produced and performed almost entirely by students. Andreas had become the head writer, Markus the chief director of photography and Antje was in charge of sound.

Andreas was starting to branch out. Writing comedy sketches had become less satisfying over the last few months, especially after he'd written a radio play based on an up-time movie, *My Man Godfrey*, which cast a mix of local professionals and members of the high school drama club. Keeping the movie's basic romantic comedy and farce intact, Andreas came up with *Unser Herr Gottfried*, which he considered more suitable for a mass audience beyond the Ring of Fire. It proved quite popular, and Andreas hoped he could parlay his success into the teaching career he longed for, a secure position that would allow him to continue writing his plays and poems and hopefully attract a wealthy patron.

Amber stuck her head out into the hall. "Come on in."

Andreas made himself comfortable in the chair in front of the teacher's desk, but his nervousness must have shown. "Relax," Amber said. "I'm not sending you to detention."

"I had not thought so, Frau Higham. Do you have an answer for me?"

"I do. And I'm hoping you'll see the answer as a positive thing."

Andreas' heart dropped into his stomach. Amber confirmed his dread: He was not going to be hired to teach.

"Andreas, you're better off writing full-time. Teaching's wonderful, so's tutoring, but I know you. You won't be happy doing either of those things because they'll get in the way of your true passion. You'll resent the demands a teaching career will make on you, and you'll take that out on your students, your family and yourself. I've seen too many friends go down that road to want that for you."

"You teach, Frau Higham. And you seem quite happy."

"I do, and I am," Amber said. "But I acted for a long time first. I fed that passion, and over time it became a passion to teach others the craft. But you're not in that place, Andreas."

This was little comfort. "But there's my family's position to think of," Andreas said while trying to hold back tears of disappointment. "My stepfather has never objected to my writing, but he thinks I must find a respectable position to support myself and a future family if I wish to have one. He is not wrong in this."

Amber smiled, a little sadly. "I know we up-timers seem way too eager to flout tradition. But trust me on this one, Andreas. You will be nothing to no one if you go through life miserable and unfulfilled. I don't care what century you grew up in."

"Yes, Frau Higham. I will give thought to your words."

"I know it's scary, but it's time to spread your wings. And I promise I'll do anything I can to help you."

Andreas felt numb as he walked home. Orphaned by the war, he'd traveled west from his native Silesia, sent by his stepfather, Pastor Michael Eder. Andreas found himself in the mysterious new town of Grantville around the time of the Croat raid, traveling there with a group of young nobles and their tutor on a grand tour. The idea was not only for Andreas to get a life education, but also to learn from the tutor, one of the most respected in Danzig. At the tutor's suggestion and with his stepfather's blessing, Andreas stayed in Grantville to take advantage of the high school and its near-university level of education while his traveling companions moved on to Austria and Italy.

Except for one traveling companion. Andreas opened the door to his tiny efficiency apartment. He found his roommate, Paddy, tamping a fresh batch of marijuana into his long-stemmed clay pipe.

Paddy was an orphan too although, unlike Andreas, Paddy had never known his parents. Before Paddy came to Grantville, he didn't even have so much as a last name—he adopted "Antrim" (after the Irish county of his birth) when he arrived—but he did have a quick wit and a likable nature. He also had a beautiful voice, which he could use to imitate nearly anyone after hearing them speak for just a few moments, and when telling his stories, he created different voices for each character. And though he couldn't read ("Never got the knack," he was fond of saying), Paddy could memorize entire stretches of text if someone read passages to him just once or twice. Andreas was often quite surprised to hear his friend spout back scenes he himself had muttered half-aloud while writing.

As Paddy liked to say, all of those gifts were God's attempt to make up for the fact that he'd been born a dwarf and spectacularly ugly. He'd spent his early years in an Irish orphanage. When he was little more than a boy, Paddy was sold to a petty French nobleman who'd wanted a court dwarf. Paddy fully expected to remain in France the rest of his life, but he found himself being traded from court to court, finally landing in Danzig. One of the young noblemen in Andreas' party had brought Paddy along to provide amusement.

The dwarf decided he was staying in Grantville with Andreas and was pleasantly surprised when the local authorities agreed he had a right to do so. Pastor Eder sent his stepson enough for a small room, and Andreas had insisted Paddy move in with him. As Andreas pointed out, it wasn't as if Paddy took up a great deal of space. The money Paddy brought in as a storyteller at the Thuringen Gardens and other places around Grantville helped with the rent and food. Telling stories to the children at St. Veronica's paid for the marijuana that treated Paddy's chronic pain.

The dwarf looked up when Andreas closed the door. "Laddie, you look like someone spit in your porridge."

Andreas watched his friend light his pipe and inhale deeply. "Is the pain bad today, Paddy?"

"Not for much longer. I got to the Medical Exchange early enough to get some Stone Free. 'The stickiest of the icky.'" Paddy said the last phrase in a dead-on impersonation of Tom Stone. Others had started growing the "wonder weed" to keep up with demand for a reliable painkiller that was cheaper than Dr. Phil's Little Blue Pills, but everyone acknowledged that the best stuff came from Tom Stone's greenhouses at Lothlorien Farbenwerke, for which the dyer would take no money.

Paddy exhaled and gave Andreas a stern look. "I'm touched by your concern, lad, but you're changing the subject."

"I'm not going to be teaching this fall. Frau Higham told me I need to keep writing. She said I wouldn't be happy otherwise."

"Frau Higham is a wise woman. You should listen to her."

"But how can I write without a patron? And how can I get a patron without a reputation? If I'd been accepted to teach writing or drama I could have built that, but now . . ."

"Lad." Paddy said the word this time as a command. "You have a reputation. Your work has already reached more people than most established playwrights. What about your work with the school's television company? Or your radio play?" Paddy slid off his chair and drew himself up to his full height—all four feet of it. "I'll not abide you giving in to pity. The opportunities are there if you'll see them."

Joost van den Vondel sat in the Inn of the Maddened Queen, lost in thought. Anyone looking at the chessboard would see at once that those thoughts had absolutely nothing to do with the game Joost was supposed to be playing. He moved his bishop. His opponent, a thin woman his own age, shook her head before he could take his hand off the piece.

Reconsidering, Joost moved his rook instead. Another head shake. When moving his king brought no head shake, he settled on that move. One of the advantages of playing his wife in chess was that she was a pretty lenient opponent, at least with him.

Mayken De Wolff, Frau van den Vondel, studied her next move. She'd never played maddened queen chess before coming to Grantville not quite a year ago, but she was a natural. Joost, on the other hand, was an atrocious player, no matter what rules he was playing under. He only played because he enjoyed spending time with his wife.

Mayken would never be the picture of health, Joost knew. She was a thin young woman when they met, and giving birth to four children had not been the best thing for her. When they fled Amsterdam just ahead of the Spanish siege, he was sure he was going to lose her. He'd hated being apart from her, spending most of his time in Krefeld with their two surviving children, minding the business, while Mayken lived in Grantville and took advantage of the miraculous medical cures the up-timers had brought with them. Mayken's skill at chess was proof of her ability to look ahead and consider the consequences of many different actions. Joost had missed that, but having her with him wasn't worth her life.

In the end, Mayken's generosity bought Joost three more moves. When she called "checkmate," one of the spectators called out a number. He'd taken bets on how many moves Frau van den Vondel would need to checkmate Herr van den Vondel. Vince Masaniello shouted in triumph.

"You see?" he said to a young German named Felix who was getting chess tutoring. "That's how not to play. If Frau van den Vondel would permit me, I'd like to give her a real challenge."

Mayken was willing. One of the inn's servants brought Joost a coffee and a radio. He and Mayken met regularly for a chess game and conversation when he was in Grantville on business. It was a way for them to connect on days when Joost was busy. When Mayken accepted a challenge from one of the other patrons, Joost ordered a coffee and a radio (the up-timers referred to it as a "walkman"). The Inn of the Maddened Queen kept several of these wonderful personal radios to rent so that if nonplaying guests wanted to listen to music or the Voice of America they could do so without disturbing anyone else. It gave Joost a chance to get lost in thought and get in touch with his muse.

Joost van den Vondel was in the silk business. He was also a dramatist and poet, a very good one. And he was fascinated with the mass communications the up-timers had brought with them. Their "television station," WVOA, reached an audience in the thousands, larger than the audience the largest theater could hold. The Voice of America radio station, which had the disadvantage, in Joost's mind, of not being accompanied by pictures, reached many times more people than the television station did. Joost had resolved to investigate these strange inventions more fully on his current trip.

He slipped the headphones over his ears, expecting to hear music. That's what VOA usually played this time of day. Instead Joost heard: "By popular demand, Voice of America is proud to present *Unser Herr Gottfried*, starring Helmut Schickele, Maria Bauerin, Patrick Antrim and the Not Ready for Prime Time Players. This program has been prerecorded."

What followed was a pleasant and cleverly written farce. It wasn't terribly original, but the writer knew what he was doing and had potential. Someone worth knowing, and if Joost was correct about the writer's age, worth mentoring. The credits after the production mentioned the writer as Andreas Gryphius. Joost decided he should meet him as soon as his schedule allowed.

The Sternbock Coffee House was the preferred gathering place for Grantville's art community, such as it was. Most aspiring writers, painters and performers were moving to Magdeburg to seek their fortunes. Even so, Theophilus Mendes wasn't lacking for customers, who came to drink powerful and robust Greek coffee, eat Helena Mendes' delicious baklava and talk music and literature. Regulars also came to listen to poetry readings or musical performances and to doodle on the coffee house walls. Theophilus had heard of an eatery in the up-time city of Chicago that allowed people to write and draw on the walls, and he thought it was a wonderful idea. Theo's sons Arcadios and Constantinos, who got stuck with white-washing the coffee house walls every few months, were rather less enthusiastic.

Andreas and Markus sat looking glum. Antje sat looking exasperated with both of them. Wall doodling was the farthest thing from their minds. Paddy and his friend Martha sat sipping coffee and nibbling on pastry.

"You both knew you couldn't keep working with the RTT program forever. You graduate, you move on. That's the rule," Antje said.

"That's easy for you to say, Antje," Markus groused. "You didn't get 'the talk.'" Turning to Andreas, Markus asked, "Did she tell you to spread your wings?"

Andreas nodded. "It's not so much having to move on," he said. "It's having to explain to my stepfather that being a dramatist for radio or television is a respectable career for the son of an archdeacon and the stepson of a pastor."

"You worry a bit too much about respectability, lad." Paddy flexed the grasper he carried with him at all times for emphasis. One of the apprentices at Kudzu Werke had made it as experiment in mechanics and given it to Paddy when it proved useful in helping the dwarf grab things he couldn't reach on his own.

The plain-looking young woman sitting next to Paddy nodded her agreement. "Andreas, you did such a good job writing *Unser Herr Gottfried*. All my friends love it. You should write another story like that one." Martha Schacht worked as an aide at St. Veronica's School where Paddy sometimes went to tell stories to the children.

Andreas shrugged. "Thanks, Martha. I could write another play, but where will I find a patron?"

"Maybe we need to attract a patron," said Antje. "Produce something on our own and play it in front of potential sponsors. Like the Grantville Ballet did with *Bad Bad Brillo*."

Andreas immediately saw that this was a good idea. It wasn't as if it would cost him much in time to write a one-act play that could then be easily recorded. The problem, as he saw it, was that with a few exceptions, the nobility—at least the ones with all the money—stuck fiercely to their traditions. They might well prefer to patronize a traditional stage company. He mentioned this.

Markus smiled a bit smugly. "You're stuck in the past, Andy my friend. The plays and programs that run on VOA or the TV station all have business patrons. Advertising, the up-timers call it. I've read all about it in books that Frau Ambler loaned me. Many of the up-timers' greatest writers launched their careers this way, on shows with business patrons. Writers like Serling and Chayefsky."

Andreas was familiar with Rod Serling and Paddy Chayefsky, even if their work wasn't entirely to his taste. Watching Janice Ambler's precious recorded episodes of *Playhouse 90* and *The U.S. Steel Hour* had been part of his education as a writer once he enrolled in the RTT program. He began to see where Markus was heading and was intrigued enough to ignore Markus' use of his hated nickname "Andy."

"What you're saying," Andreas said slowly, "is that we should film our own television play as a proposal for something like *Playhouse 90*. An anthology program, I believe it would be called."

"Exactly so."

"But . . . don't look at me that way, Markus Schneider!" Antje had rounded on the aspiring director, who was giving her a very dirty look. He didn't like being contradicted.

Undeterred, Antje continued: "We should consider doing a radio program instead. It would be much less expensive."

"Nonsense," Markus said. "Television is the way of the future. It's here to stay, and it won't be any problem to film a program right here in Grantville. Everything that we need is here."

"But how will you edit it?"

"Jabe McDougal hasn't had any problem editing his videos for the TV station. I can buy his equipment or rent it."

Markus ignored Antje as she enumerated the numerous flaws in his argument, beginning with the fact that it was highly unlikely that Jabe McDougal would entrust his precious camera and computer to anyone not intimately familiar with its use. Markus was basically a good person, but Andreas knew that as the son of a newly rich local merchant, he sometimes thought he could leap any hurdle by paying the right person enough money. Most of the time he was right. However, Andreas doubted money would impress someone dating the daughter of a painter to two reigning kings.

Even as Andreas listened to Antje's counterarguments for radio over television, he couldn't help but be seduced by Markus' vision. He'd wanted to write for theater ever since he could remember, after reading the great tragedies of Euripides and Aeschylus, the comedies of Aristophanes and Terence and the poetry of Seneca. And wasn't theater a visual art? The VOA reached many people, it was true, thanks to the reach of the strange lightnings that carried it and the fact that the "crystal radio sets" needed to turn the lightnings back into sound were affordable to all but the most desperately poor people. But you couldn't see the radio. Andreas loved the television and loved that it could transport him to different times and places—as any good playwright in any time could do, given the right stage.

"I'll do it, Markus. I'll write something for you to film."

Joost wiped his mouth with a cloth napkin and heaved a contented sigh. The Willard Hotel was a pricy place for a business lunch—even by Grantville standards—but it was quieter than the Thuringen Gardens and it was easier to reserve a private dining room at the Willard. One only had to make a reservation weeks in advance, rather than months.

As one server cleared away plates and another poured small glasses of dessert wine, Adolf Aaler—Dolf—sat his up-time briefcase on the table and opened it, handing copies of reports to Joost and Mayken. Dolf was a young man, in his early twenties, the middle son of Joost's business partner Adalbert Aalèr in the Rheinlander Silk and Fine Linen Company. Normally, Dolf's older brother Dieter would be expected to inherit the business from Adalbert, but everyone acknowledged Dolf's uncommon talent and foresight. Shy Dieter was far happier with his nose buried in a ledger than meeting with customers.

Joost could hardly believe that it had been just over a year since he and Mayken had fled Amsterdam. He remembered all too well when Rebecca Stearns and her small diplomatic party had arrived from France full of dire warnings of the impending betrayal of the Dutch Republic at the hands of Cardinal Richlieu. Unfortunately, Rebecca had only her instincts, which were not enough to convince the Dutch ruling elite of approaching disaster.

Joost had been among the very few who had taken Mrs. Stearns' warning seriously. He hadn't known Balthazar Abrabanel personally, but it was impossible to be a person of any standing in Amsterdam and not know the Jewish doctor's reputation. And Joost also knew Balthazar's daughter had inherited her father's intellectual gifts in full measure. If she warned of French betrayal, it wasn't merely to advance her country's anti-French agenda, and Joost would not wait for a signed declaration of war from Richlieu before believing her. Overriding Mayken's objections, he packed up what he could of his family's silk business, liquidated the rest for whatever he could get and left Amsterdam at the first opportunity.

Krefeld, in County Moers, was the logical refuge for them. The van den Vondels were Mennonites, and several Mennonite families had already found refuge there. A hasty letter sent ahead of them paved the way for a partnership with Adalbert Aaler. Adalbert had been just another linen weaver when a small group of fellow Mennonites came to him seeking refuge. They were experienced weavers of silk and velvet, and Adalbert saw the chance to not only do a good deed, but also to be the only person dealing in silk in the area.

Unfortunately, because Adalbert could not match the quality or quantity of silks from Venice and the East, his business balanced on a knife's edge of survival. He had just enough local custom to keep him in business. Joost's capital was a welcome infusion, but it didn't solve the business's basic problem. Joost wanted a solid return on his investment, and Adalbert wanted to leave a prosperous business to his sons and grandchildren.

Ultimately, it was Dolf who found a way out, at a meeting Adalbert had called shortly after Joost bought into the business. Krefeld had its own Committee of Correspondence, which maintained a discreet presence in the shadow of the archbishop of Cologne, the town's nominal ruler. The local Mennonite community, thanks to Mike Stearns' willingness to grant their co-religionists asylum, dominated the Krefeld-Uerdingen CoC and the local committee worked as hard at distributing the practical business knowledge the up-timers had brought with them as it did their new political philosophies.

"The up-timers have a saying for our situation," Dolf said. "When life hands you lemons, make lemonade."

"What's a lemon?" asked Adalbert.

"An exotic fruit with a sour taste," Dolf replied. "But it can be made into lemonade, a very tasty drink many of the up-timers favor. The basic point is that with the right thinking, something that's a weakness can be turned into a strength. Our weakness is that our silk, while very durable, isn't of the quality favored by the wealthy and the nobility for their clothes—unless their fortunes have fallen—and we would hardly want to advertise that fact."

"So what do you suggest?" At the time Joost hadn't been able to see where Dolf was heading.

The young man tossed a bound folio into the middle of the table. Adalbert picked it up and began to thumb through it.

"This folio was specially prepared for me by my friends in the Grantville Committee of Correspondence. The industries and knowledge the up-timers have brought with them require silk for a multitude of uses. Let the Adel preen about in their Venetian silks and pay outrageously for the privilege. We will sell silk for insulation, armaments and motors. Industry. We can establish ourselves in this market and then let everyone else try to catch up with us!"

Dolf's arguments had carried the day, and he turned out to be entirely correct. As Joost saw as he looked over the latest sales figures, he was well on his way to becoming independently wealthy. He nodded approvingly.

"We're making even more money than I thought we would this trip. It definitely justifies opening a permanent office here, even if there weren't other concerns." Dolf nodded to Mayken. "It will be good to have you here to represent us full-time, Joost, and the space with the apartments over it was a real find. And this is even with your continued soft-heartedness where the Grantville Ballet Company is concerned."

Joost chuckled. "Dolf, the day you admit that outfitting the Ballet Company has more than paid for itself is the day I begin to wonder about your sanity." Joost, over the mild objections of the Aaler family, had insisted on supplying Bitty Matowski's ballet company with silk for its costumes at cost, something that had helped build local good will and had fostered contacts with local notables—many of whom were investors in the sorts of industries Rheinlander Silk served. "What about that other matter I'd asked you to look into?"

"Ah, yes, young Herr Gryphius." Dolph slid a scrap of paper over to Joost with an address on it. "The young man's room doesn't have a telephone. I'm also told he frequents the Sternbock Coffee House."

"Very good. Thank you, Dolf. For everything."

It was a couple of weeks before Joost could follow up on contacting young Gryphius. Meetings with clients, taking orders and personally delivering an order of silk to Bitty Matowski occupied his time. Finally, though, he managed to have a few hours free on a weekday afternoon.

He found Andreas by himself in a corner table at the Sternbock Coffeehouse, lost in thought, surrounded by crumpled pieces of paper and empty demitasses. The young man was red-eyed and jittery; clearly, he'd been working hard and sleeping little.

And he was lost in thought. Young Gryphius didn't even hear Joost walk up to him and was very surprised to see the Dutchman standing in front of him.

"Herr Greif?" Joost decided to address the young man by his birth name rather than his nom de plume.

Andreas stood up in a hurry, scattering paper and knocking over an ink bottle—fortunately empty. "Yes. Sorry. I'm afraid you have me at a loss, Herr . . ."

"Vondel. Joost van den Vondel."

"Of course. From Rheinlander Silks, right? You make good costumes, Herr van den Vondel. Very durable material, Frau Matowski says."

Joost nodded, pleased. "You've had occasion to work with the ballet company, then?"

"Not much. I've passed on interesting-looking librettos from time to time, but not much more."

"In any event, Herr Greif, it's not regarding librettos or silk costumes. I wished to talk about your writing. It's quite good, and I feel I may be able to offer you some small opportunity to hone your craft and further your career."

Andreas shuffled the papers spread out in front of him, tapping them together in a neat pile. He began laughing hysterically for a minute or two, then looked at van den Vondel. Joost wondered if his writer was taking leave of his senses. After a minute, Andreas wiped his eyes.

"I apologize. My father and stepfather often said that God has a sense of humor. I think this proves it." Andreas signaled a young man acting as waiter for the establishment.

"Do you care for coffee, Herr van den Vondel? Or perhaps pastry? Frau Mendes is a most talented pastry maker."

If Andreas could count how much sleep he'd gotten over the last week or so, he suspected he could count the hours on one hand. Maybe two, but he was certain he wouldn't need to take off his shoes and socks.

Markus Schneider—Sartorius, these days—was a very good director of photography, probably the best, when it came to using up-time video equipment. He'd always been fond of sketching, and when the Schneider family came into money, they arranged for Markus to take lessons in painting. His talent in that area would not be great enough to allow him to be more than a skilled hobbyist, but it taught him how compose scenes so they would fit into a frame. Behind the lens of a camera, the mediocre would-be painter became a genius DP.

Unfortunately, Markus knew this, and it fed his considerable ego. Andreas had been utterly unable to convince his director to leave the writing to him. Andreas had had a pleasant little one-act comedy, modeled on the work of his beloved Terence, that he'd been working on. It would have been ideal for their "pilot," as Antje called it. Simple story, small cast, and it would take—at most—only two or three simple sets.

Alas, "simple" had no place in Markus' grand vision. At first the changes Markus suggested made sense, along with some ideas Antje contributed. Antje's ideas continued to make sense, but at some point Markus had . . . what was that phrase one of his up-time classmates used? "Jumped the shark," that was it. Andreas was still not entirely clear about the origins of that phrase and had only a vague idea of what a shark was, but it felt correct to his writer's instincts. In the beginning, he'd rather liked this little piece, trifle though it was, but the more drafts he produced, the more he hated it. He couldn't even remember what it was he'd liked about this piece in the first place. He'd walk away from this project if he could, but too many people were depending on him. He had his duty.

The interruption by Herr van den Vondel was most welcome. After introducing himself, the Dutchman wasted little time in getting to the point.

"I heard the play you wrote on the radio, Herr Greif," van

den Vondel said. "It was quite good. You have much potential, I believe."

"I thank you, *mein Herr*. I know your company's reputation as a supporter of the arts."

The Dutchman chuckled. "God has blessed me with two gifts, young sir. He has blessed me with a modest talent for business and a talent for writing. Which may be as modest as my talents in business, but my desire to write poetry and drama is far greater than the desire to succeed in business."

Andreas thought about this for a moment. "How do you reconcile those two desires?"

"With the knowledge that business success funds my artistic endeavors. Which is why you find me here today, young sir."

Van den Vondel accepted tea and baklava from Arcadios Mendes and continued. "I am relocating to Grantville, partly to better represent Rheinlander Silk's many interests here, but mostly to pursue patronage of the arts. I find I have the resources to fund a small drama company, and the . . . I believe the up-timers call it 'mass media' . . . offers great opportunities to present work to a very wide audience indeed. I am told by my business contacts here that this technology will only spread further in the coming years, and I find that the first to grasp a new opportunity may capitalize best upon it, even in the face of inevitable competition. In any event, Herr Greif, I believe I would like to engage your services as a writer, and I seek your counsel as to how to proceed."

Andreas knew an opening when he saw one. He told Herr van den Vondel of the video production he was working on with Markus, Antje and a few others from the high school RTT program. Van den Vondel even commiserated with him over the endless rewrites.

"It's not that bad," Andreas said, though he didn't sound convincing even to himself. "So far Markus' father has been willing to fund us."

Two bells tolled out across Grantville. The up-timers had had to accommodate themselves to laxer standards of time-keeping than they'd been used to, but bells still rang out on the hour during the daytime. Joost looked up in surprise and a little alarm. He handed Andreas a card.

"I'm afraid I must take my leave, as I have business this afternoon. Please contact me when your video production is complete. I would be most eager to see it. I have the feeling the two of us will be able to help each other a great deal."

With every meeting of the main creative team, Andreas, Markus and Antje's planned television pilot spiraled out of control. Matters came to a head just a few nights after Andreas met Joost van den Vondel.

It began with Markus suggesting—very forcefully—yet more changes in the story, which invariably involved more sets, actors and complicated shots. He showed them the new estimated budget for the production. Andreas couldn't believe the total. Antje was livid.

"You mean your father is going to agree to just give us all this money?" Lukas Schneider was well-known as a shrewd businessman—and not someone inclined to be overly indulgent, proud as he was of his son's talents.

"Er . . . no," said Markus. "But I figure we can chip in the difference."

Antje spluttered with rage. Andreas said, in a weak voice, "Markus, I don't have any money. The allowance I get barely pays food and my share of the rent. And Antje's family aren't poor, but there's no way she can contribute what you expect to come up with."

"Well, she'll have to. I'm willing to let you off the hook, Andy, because you've been working damn hard. But it's time for some people around here to start pulling their weight."

That remark earned Markus "Sartorius," would-be genius of television, a hard slap across the face. Antje stormed out, slamming the door so hard the windows rattled. Markus shook his head and managed a look of regret that was almost sincere.

"Now, Andy. I need to talk to you about the part you wrote for your friend Paddy. I'm not sure his character still works."

Andreas didn't manage quite a spectacular exit as Antje, though he was willing to bet he was just as angry. Maybe angrier. For over two weeks now, he'd hated this project more and more and wanted out, but he didn't want to let anyone down. But nothing was worth betraying Paddy. The Irishman was his best friend, like a brother to him. Damaging that relationship was something Andreas couldn't do.

Paddy was still awake by the time Andreas got home.

"Antje told me what happened. Thank you, lad," he said.

"For what?" Outside of mourning his parents, he doubted he'd ever felt worse.

"For doin' what's right. I would've understood, but I'm glad you didn't throw me over."

Andreas managed a wry smile. "Don't flatter yourself. I just felt that prick needed someone to stand up to him." Paddy laughed. "Seriously, though. I don't know what I'll do. I don't know what I'll tell Herr van den Vondel."

"Come up with something. I know you've got it in you, lad."

"I told Markus he could do whatever he wanted with the story I gave him, as long as he put a pseudonym in place of my name in the credits."

Paddy nodded. "It's probably for the best. But before you decide anything rash, Fraulein Becker left some things for you."

Paddy pointed to a stack of compact discs, mostly homemade, with a scrawled note on top saying "Listen to these." Andreas looked through them: *The Best of Stan Freberg, The Goon Show, The Shadow, War of the Worlds,* and many other titles. All classics of radio, many of which had been played as programming on VOA. Andreas listened to them all, and when he woke up the next morning, he was inspired for the first time in weeks.

About a month after Joost van den Vondel met with Andreas Gryphius, Joost received an invitation, cosigned by Andreas and "Markus Sartorius"—presumably the young man Markus Schneider with whom Gryphius had been working previously.

Joost knew all about the split between Andreas and Markus, though Andreas had been close-lipped about what he was working on. Joost had taken time to speak with Janice Ambler and had gotten most of the story from her. She said that the "runaway production" had a long and honored history up-time, mostly in something called "the movies," though Joost was unclear on how "the movies" differed from what was called television. Nevertheless, he understood completely. He'd heard of more than one entertainment whose costs had spiraled out of control.

Now, though, he'd see the results. Theophilus Mendes had agreed to host the presentation for Joost and a few local businessmen and potential patrons at the Sternbock. Markus would present his production, followed by Andreas and his "Grantville Radio

Theater." Mayken was delighted at the prospect and decided to make an evening of it. Her new friends had told her she needed a "date night" with her husband—whatever that was.

There was already a small crowd at the Sternbock when he and Mayken arrived. Joost knew most of the people there. They were local businessmen, mostly down-timers, and a few minor nobles. Exactly the sort of people who would be most interested in gaining prestige through art patronage. Markus Schneider, with a pretty young woman on his arm, mixed enthusiastically with the attendees. Joost recognized the girl as a local actress, one who'd been compared—unfavorably—to Els Engel. Looking around for Andreas, Joost found him standing in a corner of the coffeehouse, nervously conferring with his dwarf friend and a couple of others. Before Joost could go speak with him, it was time for the evening's program to begin.

Markus Schneider, Markus Sartorius as he called himself, introduced his production and wheeled out a television with a small box attached to it. Inserting a cartridge into the box, he pressed a button. The television flared to life and Theophilus Mendes dimmed the lights in the coffee house.

Andreas had been half-anticipating and half-dreading Markus's pilot. The credits certainly looked good, touting "A Markus Sartorius Production," though Andreas had to suppress a laugh when his chosen pseudonym, "Cordwainer Bird" (he'd gotten that name from Janice Ambler), flashed on the screen.

What followed was a train wreck, if a fascinating one. Outside of televised stage plays and a few documentary-style news pieces by Jabe McDougal and a couple of others, no one had attempted a video production on the scale Markus was aiming for. And it was clear that whatever his talents, Markus had aimed too high.

The sets looked horrible, the sound was uneven and the editing was clumsy. Andreas had resolutely avoided seeking any news of the production, trying to distance himself as far from it as possible. He'd heard rumors, though, that the sets had been rushed, and when Jabe McDougal had declined to sell, or even rent, his digital camcorder and editing software, Markus had had to make do with other equipment. Finding video cameras wasn't a problem. There were a number of them that, though obsolete at the time of the Ring of Fire, still worked perfectly well. The editing rig was the real problem. Markus had had to improvise a video editing setup, and the results showed. When the pilot television episode finished a half an hour after it started, there was polite applause.

Now it was their turn. Antje set the small radio with the CD deck on a table and plugged it in. Andreas indicated to Theophilus to keep the lights dim. Paddy stepped up and, with a neat sleight-of-hand trick, produced a phosphorus stick between his fingers. He struck it. The flare and flame seemed bright in the dim light.

"O for a muse of fire," began the Irish actor in his rich voice, reciting Shakespeare's (or the earl of Oxford's, if one preferred) appeal to the power of imagination that began *Henry V*.

"Think when we talk of horses, that you see them printing their proud hoofs i' the receiving earth; for 'tis your thoughts that now must deck our kings, carry them here and there; jumping o'er times, turning the accomplishment of many years into an hourglass." Paddy bowed, and Antje hit "play" on the CD player.

What they'd produced certainly wasn't Shakespeare. When Andreas and Antje were desperate for an idea they could produce quickly but still do well, it was Martha Schacht who suggested continuing the story of the movie *Metropolis*. Fritz Lang's silent opus was a popular movie on WVOA, both because it was a German production and because its themes of class struggle and noblesse oblige played well in the seventeenth century. Less than a day later, Andreas had produced a draft for a fifteen-minute radio script continuing the story of Joh Frederson and his lady love, the saintly Maria, in the vast city of Metropolis. They kept it simple, and Paddy did almost all the voices. Antje worked on the editing until nearly the last minute, but they were all satisfied with the result.

Their audience was satisfied, too. Andreas and his fledgling radio theater company received very warm and enthusiastic applause. Enough of the businessmen present were interested in sponsoring the *Metropolis* series that he was confident it would launch, assuming Voice of America agreed to air it.

Only after the crowd began breaking up did Joost come up to him, shaking his hand and giving him a friendly clap on the back. He shook Paddy's hand as well.

"Well done, young Herr Gryphius, well done indeed. I understand why people love television, but you and your actors painted a real picture with just words and sounds. I would be honored to be patron of your company—if you would be my head writer."

If Andreas managed to stammer out his agreement, he couldn't remember it. He must have because Joost looked pleased and shook his hand again.

"It seems you have advertising sponsors for your *Metropolis* series," Joost continued. "But I would also want a program exclusively presented by Rheinlander Silk and Fine Linen. Perhaps it could be one of these 'anthology programs' Frau Ambler told me of. And of course, we will have to find a better name for this company."

"As patron, Herr van den Vondel, the honor of naming the company is yours."

"Yes it is, husband," Mayken said. Andreas and Paddy watched as she thought for a moment. "I rather like the sound of 'The Firemuse Radio Dramatic Company' myself."

That did sound good, thought Andreas. Speech still hadn't returned to him, though, and all he could do was nod.

"Excellent." Joost beamed. "We should get the first episode of both shows on the air as quickly as we can. Do you have any ideas for the debut of the *Rheinlander Silk Hour*?"

Speech at last returned. He'd been thinking about this very thing quite a bit.

"Herr van den Vondel, there is an up-time farce that would probably be quite suitable. A young nobleman and a Moorish vagabond find their stations in life interchanged through the offices of two capricious and malign princes. The two men gain revenge against the evil princes in a most humorous way."

"Sounds interesting, Herr Gryphius. Let us discuss it further. I've been thinking of a play about the fallen angel Lucifer. Perhaps it might be best to start with lighter fare."

They talked for hours into the night. The first thing they agreed on was that the debut episode of *The Rheinlander Silk and Fine Linen Hour* would need a catchier title than "Trading Places." Frau van den Vondel had an excellent title suggestion, and production soon began on the anthology show's first episode: "Die Gluecksritter."

Pilgrimage of Grace

Virginia DeMarce

"They're not taking what happened in Suhl last January out on Johnny Lee's family because they can't. His dad's been dead for thirty years. His mother wasn't from around here to start with and she moved back to Ohio after a while. Mary Fern—that's his sister, you probably never met her—married one of the Collins boys after she graduated from college and last I heard, they were living in Michigan. You could ask Sandra, I suppose, or Gayleen or Robyn or Samantha, where Ricky and Mary Fern were living, but I don't see what good it would do. It wouldn't bring her back to Grantville to take some of the heat off Kamala."

Cora Ennis plopped five cups of coffee down on the table at the City Hall Café and Coffee House, which had only had "and Coffee House" added since the Nasi family had succeeded in importing coffee beans, while she talked. Before the Ring of Fire, it had been a plain sandwich shop. "But anyway, I think it's a shame. Johnny Lee Horton wasn't the most popular teacher at the high school. Maybe he was the least popular one, but he wasn't the worst one. He made the kids learn the stuff, and he commuted to Fairmont State for years to get his master's in math education, all at his own expense. If you ask me, they should have left him at the school teaching. But they wanted to assign him to Greg Ferrara's 'Manhattan Project' and that meant he had to go into the army, and they couldn't get along, Greg and Johnny Lee, which anyone who knew the two of them could have told Mike Stearns ahead of time."

"Cora," Ned Paxton started a little reproachfully.

The interruption wasn't enough to stop her. "But by then he was in the army and the army, even our little army that we've put together since the Ring of Fire, is like that story they taught us in school about the kid who stuck his hand in a jar and picked up so many marbles he couldn't get it out again, but was too stubborn to let go of some of them and his hand rotted off or some such. I knew there was a moral to that story. Maybe that's why it was in the book in the first place. So instead of discharging Johnny Lee, Frank Jackson sent him off to Suhl to pretend to be a soldier, which certainly wasn't any of Kamala's doing."

She turned her head toward P.H. Johnson. "And that's what I was talking about to start with, Henry. I know you covered up what those boys were doing to Shaun at the pool on Memorial Day weekend. Don't blame you for wanting to avoid publicity. No point in making a bad situation worse. They were just kids themselves, and at least you and your JROTC put a stop to that." Cora wiped a little coffee that she had spilled on her hand off on the towel she was wearing as an apron.

Victor Saluzzo picked up the pitcher of milk and poured until his cup was thoroughly whitened. "I got here late. Can you go back to the beginning?"

Cora tossed her head. "I've got other tables to serve. The rest of them can tell you. Let Henry do it." She stalked off.

Saluzzo raised his eyebrows, looking at P.H. Johnson. "There's another brush fire?"

Before Johnson could answer, Kyle Fleming shook his head. "No more than there's been for the last six months. We've been getting an earful from Cora this afternoon because Anse Hatfield was Henry's son-in-law and I'm chairman of the math department, I guess. Though once Johnny Lee quit to work on development, he wasn't my responsibility any longer, and I hardly know his wife. She's a nurse, not a teacher. Lori says that she's pleasant enough, but she must be around twenty years younger than we are, Lori and I. It's not as if we ever socialized with them, and she never had anything in common with Karyn Sue."

Saluzzo nodded in agreement. Kyle and Lori Fleming's only child had barely scraped through high school. They hadn't even tried sending the girl to college. Not that it kept her from being a loving daughter and a devoted wife and mother. Or a good aide at Heather Beckworth's day care center. Karyn Sue was just a little . . . dim . . . and everyone who had ever taught her knew it. Even in Lake Wobegon, Karyn Sue wouldn't have managed to be "above average."

He thought for a moment. "Kamala was in the class between John and Joe. They'd have known her, if they hadn't been left up-time. Kay's three or four years too old; Jim and Vicki are way too young."

Leota Grover picked up her cup. "Our kids were too young for us to really get to know her, too. Susan was the same year as her little brother Jimmy. Plus, they're both up-time, like John and Joe. Kamala wasn't a problem student, though. Far from it. Finished high school; worked her way through college, got married, had a couple of kids. No problems, aside from the fact that her family resented a little bit that she went all the way through college. RN to Celina's CNA. Well, they resented a lot that Johnny Lee made a big deal about having a master's degree. He sure was a blowhard. That's hardly something we can dispose of, though."

"It's not her family that's the problem," Fleming said. "Except, I guess, that their attitude isn't helping."

"Super-patriots, according to Cora," Ned Paxton said. "The rest of the Dunns. Jimmy's in the army and Jerry Hilton feels guilty that because he's an operator at the waste water plant, he's 'essential' and wasn't included when Mike Stearns made his call for 'every able-bodied man who can be spared.'"

Saluzzo looked across the table. "What was Cora talking about, Henry? In regard to Memorial Day?"

P.H. Johnson banged his cane on the floor. "You know what happened in Suhl back in January. Horton was there as the NUS military liaison to the Swedish garrison that wasn't quite supposed to be in the city. The Swedes had put it there before Suhl joined the NUS, with 'protracted' negotiations for its removal. What that meant was that it was still there, months after it should have been gone. What Pat, my son, said to Anse about him was that Horton was dumber than Bruno Felder, the German captain of the mercenaries who made up the Swedish garrison, and a hothead. But not lazy, which was actually too bad, considering the way things were there. He was constantly quarreling with the locals, especially with the Suhl militia captain, and usually over things that didn't really matter.

"Ivarsson, the Swedish lieutenant who went along, told Anse that the Swedes hadn't authorized Felder's actions. In confidence, Anse told me that Ivarsson promised that the Swedes would stand aside, whatever he and Noelle Murphy did under the extraordinary powers that Stearns had sent with her, and wouldn't think of criticizing after the fact. And they haven't.

"Horton got involved, along with that Pomeranian captain von Dantz who had been attached to Anse's group by the Swedish commander in Grantville. They wanted to make a fancy statement by attacking the gun makers who were trading with the enemy. Noelle said they had to defend the gun manufacturers because there aren't actually laws against it in this day and age. And, hell, my son Pat is a partner with one of the gun makers who were doing it. So Horton and von Dantz and Felder's mercenaries attacked. Anse and his posse and the gun makers and their *Jaeger* fought back. Horton got himself killed in the street fight. Yelling that he was the 'ranking American' in Suhl and saying that maybe Noelle's papers were forged."

He decided not to include something else that Anse had told him. That Anse had specifically told one of Blumroder's *Jaeger* that if shooting started, he wanted Horton dead. Right here and now, that would be a complicating factor. He thought the only people who knew that were Anse and the *Jaeger*, Noelle Murphy, Frank Jackson, Mike Stearns, and himself. And he wasn't supposed to know.

"Well, the army decided to present the incident in Suhl as a mutiny against duly constituted authority, so that's how it went into the papers here. Nobody's ever told Kamala anything different, as far as I know, and all she's done is sort of try to hunker down and keep on doing her job. That Memorial Day thing. Friday afternoon, I had my JROTC out drilling on the field by the community center when we saw some activity over by the pool. They'd filled it, but it wasn't going to open until Sunday. I thought it was just a bunch of kids and figured I'd let it go when we heard somebody yelling for help. When we got over there, seven or eight boys from the middle school had Shaun Horton—the kid's only six years old, for God's sake—stripped down to his underwear and were trying to make him 'walk the plank' off the high diving board into the pool. Jeering about mutineers and how to treat them. Too many pirate movies."

He nodded at Ned Paxton. "We handled it though the school, and have all the boys in summer school on disciplinary probation, with supervised community service. Ned, Archie Clinter, me, and the families. The boys involved are going to know better than to try any stunt like it again. I told my JROTC group to keep their mouths shut, but I guess someone has said something, since Cora knows. And once Cora knows something, the whole town does."

"The kids know," Kyle Fleming said. "The kids at the middle school, at least. Karyn Sue's boy told me about it a couple of weeks ago. He's in the same class as a couple of the offenders. Eleven- and twelve-year-olds."

Paxton sipped his coffee. "I wasn't happy with that, but as far as I know, it was the worst. There's nothing else going on that the police could do anything about. Little jabs about Johnny Lee. Mouth darts tossed toward Kamala at work at the extended care center. Toward the kids in school and out of school."

"Especially out of school, now," Leota Grover said. "And a lot of it's still in that middle school age group. Cora's all riled up because Shae's quit Girl Scouts. She's thirteen and has been in since she was a Brownie. She was going to be the Brownie leader's assistant next fall, but a couple of the mothers objected. Bad influence on the kiddies to have a traitor's daughter in a position of responsibility. You know the drill."

Victor nodded. "Evangeline Walker said something to Viola. Lolly Aossey is really upset about Shae. She's been preaching that 'Be a sister to every Girl Scout' is part of the Girl Scout Law, just as a starting point. But since both Lolly and Christie Penzey are leading the geology field camp again, there's precious little they can do over the rest of summer."

Leota grinned. "Plus, Jim and Lolly just found out that Lolly's in for a lovely few months of non-stop morning-noon-and-night sickness. Susannah Shipley dropped the diagnosis on them last week."

"She's *not*?" Cora was wandering by with refills. "At *her* age!"

"So much for keeping it under wraps for a couple more months." Victor Saluzzo's tone was very dry. "But as for Shae, I hadn't realized that there was anything more to it than a little tempest in a teapot with the Scouts. Maybe someone ought to talk to Archie Clinter again."

Fleming snorted. "The real problem is that it's not dying down.

If anything, it's escalating, and has been for six months. It's gotten bad enough that Alice Clements talked to Price Ellis. Families are worrying whether Johnny Lee's wife should be kept on as head nurse at Prichard's. God, what the hell do they expect her to do? Poison the old ladies? Kamala's worked there at the extended care center since before the Ring of Fire. She started the same year Johnny Lee took the job at the high school. She didn't want to be driving to Fairmont, much less Morgantown, and working shifts, with kids at home. Ellis gives her a pretty regular, reliable, schedule. And just where do they think that he can pluck another registered nurse from? Out of thin air?"

Leota Grover laid her cards down on the table. "Isn't there anything you can do, Frank, to make people be kinder to Kamala and the kids? Just a little more . . . gracious . . . I guess?"

He shook his head. "Hell, it's not that I don't give a shit. But there's other stuff involved."

"Which you're not going to tell me about, because I'm not in the army. Got it. Don't think you're getting off scot-free, though. I'm going to send Henry to talk to you."

Frank Jackson leaned back in his chair. "The shittiest part of it is that if I'd been there, I'd have probably had more sympathy with what Horton and von Dantz were doing than with what Anse and Noelle did. The guns that Blumroder and his cohorts—our noble fellow-citizens of the New United States in its constituent city of Suhl—have sold to high bidders who aren't us will most likely be used to shoot holes in our soldiers one of these days."

Frank stood up, his hands crossed behind his back. "But in spite of that. I'm the general of this piss-poor army, and the worst thing that I can do is not back up civilian control. Not back up the rule of law. The fact is that according to the laws, Blumroder could do what he did."

P.H. Johnson nodded. "I know. Even my own son Pat was looking the other way. He said as much in one of his letters to me."

Frank started pacing. "Mike authorized Anse and Noelle. They did what they had to. Horton and von Dantz were being a couple of cowboys leading a lynch mob, the way Anse saw it. A real nasty lynch mob. Not to mention that Horton had pretty much just sat on his hands until von Dantz got to Suhl, so he was probably letting himself be used. As far as the army is concerned, Horton was killed while resisting lawful orders and that's got to be an end to it. I'm not going to have my guys, when they get into a shooting situation, worrying about whether I'm going to back them up. Or not back them up."

"Where does this get us?"

"I'm not going to make some sort of mealy-mouthed announcement that says, 'It wasn't all black and white. There were at least ten different shades of gray and Johnny Lee Horton was somewhere in the middle.' When you get right down to it, he resisted lawful orders, he was shot while leading a mutiny, and the New United States has its first traitor. There's not a damn thing I can do to soften what Kamala and her kids are going through. Not without making things worse for the country."

"So, in the long run, according to Johnson, Frank sees it as unavoidable collateral damage." Kyle Fleming put his knife down on his plate. "Not that those are words that Frank would use."

Karyn Sue looked at her father. "What *do* those words mean, Daddy?"

Lori thought a moment. She had thirty-five years of experience in interpreting the verbal universe to her daughter. "Those words say that sometimes when you do what you have to do, somebody else gets hurt. A bystander. Somebody on the sidelines. And you can't help it."

Karyn Sue frowned. "Mr. Jackson isn't going to do anything?"

Kyle nodded. "That's right."

"No," Karyn Sue said. "That's wrong. Shae and Shaun aren't even grown up. Shaun used to come to Toddler Haven for day care, after Johnny Lee and Kamala moved back to Grantville. He was in my group for two years before he started kindergarten. Do you know what I think?"

"What?" Lori asked.

"I think that people are just being plain mean. And you're all letting them get away with it. It I let the kids in my group get away with picking on someone like that, Heather would fire me. I know she would. And she'd be right to do it."

"The sickest part of it all," Ned Paxton said the next day, "is that they're both right. Frank and Karyn Sue."

P.H. Johnson nodded. "And there's not a damned thing that we can do."

Cora plopped five cups of coffee down on the table. "Except that you haven't heard what Karyn Sue did. This morning."

Kyle Fleming looked at her. Warily.

Cora grinned. "She marched every single kid in her Toddler Haven group over to Prichard's Extended Care, all holding hands like a row of little ducklings as they paraded down the street, and asked the receptionist to call Kamala down to the lobby. And then she had every single one of the kids hug her."

Victor Saluzzo started to smile.

"While Karyn Sue told every adult standing around, in plain and simple words, that it was because people were being mean to Mrs. Horton."

Saluzzo's smile faded.

"Not that most people are likely to take what she did seriously." Cora looked at Kyle Fleming a little apologetically.

"I know," he sighed. "They can always claim that Karyn Sue didn't understand because she's . . . like that old Christmas song Granny used to sing in the days before we all got politically correct. 'Johnny wants a pair of skates, Susy wants a dolly. Nellie wants a story book; she thinks dolls are folly. As for me, my little brain isn't very bright. Choose for me, old Santa Claus, what you think is right.' The gossips aren't likely to take Karyn Sue's notion of what's right very seriously. I'm sure her intentions were good, but maybe she's just made things worse."

"I just wanted to thank you." Kamala Horton stared at the phone. She'd been crying for two hours before she managed to get her voice enough under control to pick it up and call Karyn Sue McDougal. "But . . . but I don't think you ought to do it again. Gary's in the army and you don't want to be getting your husband in trouble. I know he's up at the oil field in Wietze and you might think that's far enough away, but . . . Karyn Sue, honey, the head guy up at the oil field is Quentin Underwood. I don't think that he'd be very . . . understanding . . . if he got it into his head that Gary was a sympathizer to what Johnny Lee did. Or something like that."

There was a pause at the other end of the line. Then, "It doesn't have anything to do with Gary. Or with what Johnny Lee did. It's about the way people are treating you and Shae and Shaun."

Kamala bit her upper lip. "Talk to your mom and dad, Karyn Sue. You don't want people to start treating Michael and Allyson the way they're treating Shae and Shaun. Believe me on this. You don't want them to do that."

"I don't think that they would. Do you?"

Kamala didn't know quite what to answer. Then she decided that she had to be honest. "Yeah, I do. Right now, I do think they would."

Karyn Sue laughed. "Boy, do you ever need another hug."

"Yeah," Kamala said. "I could use one. Believe me. And thanks again. But ... maybe you had better just stay out of it. That's as fair as I can be to you. To Gary and your kids. And your folks. I don't want to make things worse by sucking other people—good people—down into my troubles."

"It's not as if I have a choice," Kamala said to Alice Clements. "Up-time, if something like this happened, I could move. Get a recommendation from Price, take the kids, and find a job in some other town. Some other state, where nobody would ever have heard about it. But the way things are, with the Ring of Fire, I'm stuck in Grantville. Even if they do get this medical school in Jena going, nobody's invited me to be part of it, and what's the point in going to Jena. The NUS Army has people there, too. I expect that they'd be sure to let everyone know about Johnny Lee." She laughed a little. "So we'd be in the same kind of situation, just without modern plumbing. I guess I'm just grateful that Price isn't going to fire me. And if you're the one who persuaded him not to—which has to have been hard for you to do, with Jack volunteering to go back into the navy and go all the way up to Wismar to pilot one of those boats—I owe you a lot of thanks."

"Maybe it will die down over time."

Kamala shook her head. "I'm not counting on it. Everybody pretty much knows that the king of Sweden is winding up to a shooting war with the League of Ostend this fall. That'll mean patriotism and heroism and everything of the sort. People in town who aren't heroes and aren't ever going to be heroes will take it out by coming down on Shae and Shaun."

"And on you."

"Well, on me, too. But I'm the adult here." Kamala picked up a pen from the blotting pad on Alice's desk and twisted it in her fingers. "Since you're the business manager here at Prichard, I'll warn you now. Fair and square. If things ever develop in such a way that someone does offer me a real job out of town, someplace where there aren't any NUS soldiers to badmouth us, I'll take it. Plumbing or not. So fast you won't even see the blur as I go by. And it won't matter much to me who makes the offer."

Twenty-eight Men

Mark Huston

January 1635

The cold wind cut through to the very core of the men as they walked to the entrance of the mine. It was dark, well before dawn, in the dead time of the night. The cold was complete, a January cold, dry, harsh and sharp. Soon they would be down in the dark and warmth of the mine. Deitrich, the shift foreman, still smiled at the incongruity of the whole thing. They were going into a mine that had been started over three hundred years in the future, and abandoned because it wasn't profitable enough. Abandoned with a large amount of the equipment in place. The power, phones, ventilation equipment, even some of the low electric carts were still there. It was almost if they were placed there for the men to pick up and start the operation again. Of course, many things were missing, or so the up-timers said. But there was much that they could use. So they did.

The mine was a dangerous place, but Deitrich always felt safe there. Even after the up-timer training about the dangers, it seemed a much safer place than the front of a tercio. There he could take a musket ball or a pike at almost any time, and it was far beyond his control. "No," he often said, "the mine is a much safer place." There he had some control over what happened. There were procedures for safety and rescue techniques, and equipment that was designed to provide them with the ability to survive in the worst of conditions. He spent ten days in a special mine safety school before he was even allowed to be on the job site. Deitrich often said that his job under the ground was a warm and safe place to be. It was secure. Snug somehow. That confidence, many said, had made him a natural foreman in the mine. Some said that he was too confident.

Twenty-eight men went down in the mine that late January night.

As part of their training, the new miners had visited a local park and the "Memorial." The memorial was an imposing black granite pillar, twenty feet high, and was inscribed with the names of seventy-eight men who had died in the "Consolidated Coal Number Nine Mine Disaster." The incident had happened back up-time. The trainees were brought to the natural glen that nestled in a small valley, a short distance out of town. There were many carefully planted trees in a small meadow that was now groomed by a flock of sheep. The monument itself was imposing, almost frightening from some angles. From others, it was gentle, stepping back in two places as it reached for the sky. It was most gentle at the top, where there was a cross carved into the face, in a style that looked strange to most down-timer eyes. The clean outlines and the perfectly formed hole in the center of the cross drew their eyes skyward to the top of the monument, away from the seventy-eight names carved into the face. The hole represented loss, a black hole, aching to be filled by those no longer there. Along with the names carved into the front face, there were words calling the ground beneath their feet a cemetery. It was considered hallowed ground.

The miner who trained them spoke of unity and brotherhood. He sounded like a priest as far as Deitrich was concerned. They were told that many famous up-time leaders had been to this place to pay homage, and that it was still used even today as a memorial by families who had lost a father or a grandfather in the explosion. The down-timers brought there became hushed, picking up on the somber mood of their usually jovial up-time partners. This was a holy place for the up-timers, and the rare display of public and universal piety surprised many of the old-hand down-timers. It had struck Deitrich as an unusual mood for the up-timers, especially in public.

It was shift change at the mine, and Deitrich met briefly with his counterpart, the afternoon shift foreman, Johan Gruber. The previous shift had noticed slightly elevated levels of methane near the working face. It was well below the danger level but Johann had duly noted it on his safety report. This wasn't unusual. The Ring of Fire had lifted a three-mile sphere of twentieth-century West Virginia back in time, and its active geology of coal and gas along with it. Methane is common, and there were clear procedures for dealing with it. As well, on a night when the weather was cold and the atmospheric pressure was low, methane tended to outgas at a higher rate.

Not something to worry about, thought Deitrich. *We have training to deal with an increase in elevated methane. Simply clear the area and wait for the ventilation system to do its job.*

The ventilation system was a giant fan. Deitrich had seen it as part of his training. An up-timer and several down-timers were assigned to keep it running day and night. Without the fan operating, the methane would seep out of the surrounding coal and rock and could build up to dangerous levels and cause an explosion. The fan drew fresh air into the mine through the same shaft where the lift moved men and equipment in and out. It was expelled at another shaft, where the coal was hoisted out. The fan was driven by an electric motor that was five hundred horsepower. Deitrich had seen five hundred live horses at once before. When the fan was turned on, he believed that every one of them had been somehow harnessed in the large metal housing. That fan pulled air through the mine with a tremendous amount of volume and pressure, turning the passageways into large pathways for the air. Concrete block barriers were installed through the mine to guide the air to the areas where men were working and along escape routes. Behind the barriers didn't matter, since nobody was working there. As long as those barriers were in good condition and the fan kept running, the methane wasn't something to seriously worry about.

This mine had started as a "room and pillar" mine, Deitrich recalled. That style of mining was practiced back up-time, with up-time technology. Over the past two years the up-time equipment had begun to fail, and old techniques had to be rediscovered. Instead of a conveyer belt, they now used mining carts pulled by mules. Instead of the roof bolts that had supported the up-time mine roof, they now used timber for support, and carpenters and timber men to put in the supports. It was a hybrid operation, but always it was tested so that it would be safe, always safe.

As Deitrich was turning away, Johann called to him. "One more thing, Deitrich. Do you know where your crew is working tonight?"

Deitrich looked at Johann and shrugged. "Of course I do. I inspected it yesterday."

Johann smiled. "You are near the old mine, the one with the monument we visited. Some of the bodies of the men are still in it. Also, it's near the Ring of Fire border. This will be the last shift working in that section. We don't want to get too close to either of those things. The seams and roof are unstable, the engineer tells us, and the old mine may be flooded."

Deitrich shrugged again. "How close are we supposed to be to the other mine? Wasn't that mine massive and went on for miles?"

Johann counted off the hazards on his fingers. "Yeah. Watch out for methane, unstable ribs and roof, and be on the lookout for ghosts under the ground. There were bodies left in that mine up-time, don't forget. They just sealed it up." He was holding up three fingers.

Deitrich also held up three fingers. "I always watch the roof and the ribs—" He dropped one finger, leaving two. "I always watch for methane—" He dropped the second finger, leaving the middle one extended to Johann. "And that's what I think of your ghosts!" Both men grinned, and moved away with a wave, one going home, and the other to work underground.

Their up-time hard hats were now fitted with the old-time carbide acetylene flame lamps. The warm light shone off of the black walls. They were in the Pittsburgh seam, a ten-foot thick layer of coal. That seam had been mined back up-time for a hundred years, and the up-timers had developed amazing ways of bringing it out of the ground, in quantities that were astounding to Deitrich. With the mining machines, conveyors, and the automated processes, the up-time miners could move more coal in a day than Deitrich and his crews could move in a week.

As he walked, Deitrich kept scanning the ceiling, what the miners called the "roof," and the walls, which they called the "ribs." In the older, up-time part of the mine, he didn't worry about the ceiling coming down. They used technology to drive long bolts into the rock to hold it together above their heads. The bolts worked well. When he got to the part of the mine that had been worked since 1631, he always paid more attention. There the roof and, occasionally, the ribs were supported by wood beams and planks, the same way a down-time mine would be, with wooden beams and supports overhead. It had worked for them well in the last couple of years, and they had only lost three men to falls of the roof.

He was always listening to the mine. Deitrich joked that he could almost hear her talking to him. As their mining activity expanded, they eventually reached the edge of the Ring of Fire. The closer to the edge of the ring, the more unstable the rock became. They could hear the rock above them "working" more and more the closer to the border they mined.

The men soon reached the point where they were to part for their different tasks.

"Ernst. Take your crew to the end wall at the far east end. Pay attention to your methane monitor. Get the machinery up and running. I'll be back to check on you when I'm done with these guys. You know where you are going?"

"Ya. West face, cuts twenty-two and twenty-three. Build stopping, remove tracks, secure equipment, get ready to stop operations. Close to Ring Wall. Test for the methane and make sure the ventilation is good. Okay." Ernst nodded and smiled. He was nearly fifty, one of the oldest men on the crew, but strong and steady. He had been one of Deitrich's men when they were with Wallenstein back in '31. He knew Ernst, and knew that he understood.

"The rest of you guys are with me. Ernst, give me your carpenters, you won't need 'em for a while."

"Okay, Deitrich. See you later."

The men began to move to their assigned areas. By the time they started to work, they would be more than a mile apart. Deitrich's crew was mostly apprentices. Young electricians, carpenters, general maintenance men, and miners who still wore the red hard hat that signified that they had been in the mine for less than six months. They began their short hike to the east side of the mine. The west side of the mine, where Ernst and his crew would be working, had initially been mined before it was abandoned back up-time. The east side had not been developed as much. As mining activity ended at the edge of the Ring of Fire, they were stopping mining in that direction, and turning the mine around to the east. Deitrich and his crew were going to begin preliminary work to prepare the area: pull power lines, prepare the floors to accept the relocated rail lines, and perform general preparation and safety inspections. Good work for the apprentices to learn, and he could check nearly everything they did before it would be put into critical service. Ernst and his crew were shutting down the mining operation at the west end, and preparing to relocate the operations to the east side. There would be no actual mining this shift, only maintenance and prepratory work.

As Dietrich and his crew headed to the east side of the mine, they passed a large device with cables coming in and out of it in the mine passage.

"Hey, Zing!" One of the red hats with the carbide lamp turned to him. Zing was a little guy, only on his second trip out of the classroom and into the mine. His real name was Zingerle, but the up-time instructor had called him Zing. His nickname also reflected his attitude, as he occasionally overcompensated for his small height with excess bravado. Deitrich knew this. Knew that it could be good to be brave, but bad to be foolhardy. "What is in that big box with the wires? You electricians keep quiet; he should know the answer."

Zing nodded. "That's easy. It's a suction breaker." Several men laughed, most of them electricians. "What? That's what it is," he said defiantly, turning to his fellow classmates. "It's a switch for the high voltage electricity that's used on the machines and battery chargers. It's called a suction breaker. It needs that because of the high voltage can jump, so it uses suction to open and close."

The group laughed, but abruptly stopped when Deitrich asked the next question. Deitrich's tone wasn't conducive to humor.

"Metzinger. What is that thing? Zing is close, but not right."

The apprentice electrician smiled. "It's a vacuum breaker. Almost everything he said is sort of right. Sort of. But it does disconnect power inby from here. Normally in an up-time mine there are more of them, but we have what we have."

Deitrich aimed the light from his carbide cap light on to Metzinger's lean face. "Good. But you're an electrician, you should know." He raised his voice to make his point. "What Metzinger does with that box is life or death for our little Zing." He shone his light on Zing. "Isn't that right, Zing?" Deitrich asked the question in the voice that he had used as a soldier. It was a voice than held men in place in the face of a musket volley or a pike charge. Unlike most, Zing straightened instead of cowered and answered in a brave, if somewhat tense, voice.

"Yes, sir."

Deitrich glowered. "What is inby?" Several cap lights now illuminated Zing's face, as more heads turned to watch the exchange. There were a few suppressed snickers. Deitrich's eyes hardened.

"We learned that our first day . . . ummm . . . inby is toward the working face—where the actual mining is done."

"And outby?"

"Just the opposite."

"So if we're walking toward our new work area, are we inby or outby?"

Zing took a deep breath. More cap lights turned his way. "We're outby." The answer didn't come with a high degree of certainty. He then brightened. "But we're walking inby, toward the east work face."

The cap lights went to Deitrich. He smiled. "Good answer, Zing. Now what is that thing?" He pointed down a passageway that intersected their path at a right angle. Cap lights illuminated it as the passing group glanced down the intersecting passageway. They saw what looked like a concrete block wall.

Zing looked at him in shock.

Deitrich growled. "This keeps you alive too. You should know what it is. Everyone halt!" The knot of men stopped cold with the command. Deitrich walked down the short passageway. "This passage is called a . . ." He looked to Zing to finish the statement.

"Umm. It's a concrete block wall that seals off the passageway?"

"No and no! I asked you what the passageway is called."

"Uhhh. I think it's a crosscut. Sir." The "sir" was added after the fact, with a measurable degree of hope.

"You think?" Deitrich's voice boomed and echoed off into the darkness. "You can't 'think' down here. You've got to know, Zing. Know! Our lives—my life—yours, all of us—depend on one another down here. We cannot have you taking the time to think. Do you know what you are, Zing? You are an unconscious incompetent!" His booming voice went off into the darkness, as confusion over the up-timer phrase bubbled through the little group.

The bellowing continued after a brief pause. "First word. Unconscious. Asleep, unknowing, unaware. Next word. Incompetent. Don't know what you're doing, not adept, inexperienced. In other words, gentlemen, you are all so wet behind the ears that you don't even know enough to ask the right questions to keep from getting killed. What is that wall called, Zing?"

Deitrich watched as Zing clenched his jaw, straightened to his full diminutive height, and looked him in the eye. "That's a seal, sometimes called a 'stopping,' sir. It secures the area against flowing or escaping gas. It's there as a barrier to isolate working parts of the mine from non-working parts of the mine. It also guides the ventilation."

Deitrich suppressed a smile. Zing was doing well. "And if it's made of wood and cloth, and it's temporary, what is it called?"

Zing stood up a little straighter, if that were possible. "A brattice, sir!"

Deitrich looked up at the group, satisfied. He felt a little bit bad about picking on Zing. Zing always reminded him of a terrier with his quick movements, and the way he was small and seemingly fearless. Deitrich had never liked terriers. "By the end of this month, I want to elevate all of you to conscious incompetents. I want you all to wake up and *know* you *don't know anything*, and that almost anything down here could kill you. I want you all to know when you are being safe and to recognize when you are not, before it kills you. Or me, God forbid. If you kill me, I'll come back to haunt you for the rest of your life, so be extra careful. Learn your procedures, learn your safety gear, and take care of your fellow miners. Take care of this mine, and she will take care of you." As he finished, his voice once again echoed off into the surrounding darkness.

"Let's go to work." Deitrich began walking, and the rest followed him, subdued.

Peter was very tired. He was driving one of the old Grantville public works dump trucks, full of sand that had been hand-shoveled out of a dried up bend of the river. It had been two days of back-breaking, cold, hard labor. Much of the sand in the old riverbed was frozen, and breaking it loose with shovels and picks was difficult. He would arrive at the Grantville public works department soon, park the truck, and head home to bed. The sand would be used on the steep roads around Grantville to maintain traction. He was going to make sure next year that they had enough sand so they wouldn't have to dig it in the winter. It was much easier to remove from the riverbank when it wasn't frozen.

Stuffed into the cab with him were the three men who had helped him with the task. They were asleep, but crammed into the cab of the truck this way, they were at least warm. He looked at the dark road ahead of him through the dusty headlights. He knew that the road conditions could change fast, so he tried to drive no faster than his headlights could see ahead. The frozen dirt roads had been easy and not slippery, but the blacktop roads could be treacherous in icy conditions.

Peter had struggled to stay awake most of the way back to town, but now, near the turnoff for the mine, he began to relax. He shifted in his seat, and stretched to relieve the cramps in his back and shoulder. The downhill road was in good shape, with only spots of snow and ice left in the shaded areas where the afternoon sun didn't reach.

As he was stretching, the truck hit a small patch of ice. It caught him unaware, and because he was tired, cramped, and half asleep, he overcompensated when the truck started sliding. The result was that the back end of the truck caught the ice and then lurched toward the shoulder. The whole thing happened in slow motion.

As he violently jerked the wheel back to counter the developing skid, a joint in the steering assembly broke, causing the left side wheel to part from the steering gear. The massive wheel now moved in whatever direction it wanted, and it was generally not in the direction that Peter wanted it to go.

He saw a slope off to the side of the road that led to the river below. All he could see with the headlights was the blackness of the drop-off. He jammed on the brakes and the truck lurched off the side of the road, halted for a brief moment, its nose down the slope and the back wheels still on the shoulder. It then began to slide down the icy slope.

He kept trying to make it go nose first, but there was no real control. He realized he was now only a passenger, with nothing to do but wait until it was over. He yelled at his coworkers to hang on. He was afraid that the truck might roll over, but it stayed upright, going straight down the embankment. The slope wasn't steep and the transition to the frozen creek wasn't as severe as it could have been.

The truck gained speed and hit the bottom of the ditch nose first. The front bounced up, and then slammed down and through the ice in the shallow creek bottom. There was enough momentum still left to carry the truck out the far side of the creek bed and bounce up the other side. The truck began to slow in what appeared to be someone's side yard. Peter had a brief thought that they were going to make it without any major damage when he spotted the power pole dead ahead.

Ernst wasn't happy. "Willie. Get your head out of your ass." He liked many of the up-timer sayings, and that one was his favorite. It wasn't quite as crisp in German as it was in English, but Willie got the idea. Willie was twenty, and the newest member of the crew, having only just recently finished his safety training. He, too, was wearing the red hat of a new miner. He was daydreaming, gazing into the darkness. His coworkers smiled. Willie was newly married, and his wife kept him up very late. It was unusual for down-timers to get married so young, and Ernst didn't approve of this break with custom. He blamed it on the bad influence of the up-timers.

"Willie. Do you hear me? Remove your head from your ass. Pay attention."

Finally Willie looked at Ernst and blinked. Ernst was standing on top of one of the battery-powered carts, which had a coal scoop on the front. When the coal was blasted away from the mine face, the cart acted as a small bulldozer, quickly scooping the coal into the waiting cars, which would be pulled to the exit by mules. It was the typical incongruity of the new and the old, the familiar and the unfamiliar, that his men had become accustomed to.

Ernst was finishing his start-of-shift methane reading. It was less than one half of one percent, well within safety limits. He eased himself off of the heavy battery compartment to the ground. Since methane was lighter than air, he tested it at the roof of the tunnel, where he could smell the fresh cut pine boards that formed parts of the roof of the mine.

"Time to get to work, gentlemen. Let's go. Willie, get the pneumatic hammer drills and the twenty-foot bits, and start to load everything into the coal cars. Next shift will haul it out.

"Schmidt and Fredric, pick up the undercutting equipment on the other face." Those two men grabbed the heavy pneumatic jackhammer that was mounted on a cart horizontally, right at the floor. Normally, they would cut along the floor into the face as far as the highly modified tool would reach. When they blasted the coal out of the face, the undercut would make it easier to control the blast and to recover the broken coal. But tonight they were disassembling it and all of the support equipment that went with the tool, such as the pneumatic lines, braces, and wedges.

"Hans. You are the loader driver tonight; you passed your certification. Back it outby and put it in the next crosscut. I want it out of the way." He turned to the rest of the men. "When that machine finally breaks down, we go back to shoveling coal into the carts by hand, so we're all very careful of it, aren't we, gentlemen?" He smiled, and the rest of the crew responded with a friendly and half-satirical, "Yes, Herr Ernst."

"Very good. Now get to work." The work area erupted with activity. Hans backed the noisy battery-powered hydraulic loader away from the coal face. The noise of the loader could be deafening and only hand motions and signals with their headlamps could be used. They could communicate basic signals by facing their partner and nodding their head in such a way that the light formed a pattern. Ernst found himself once answering a man in the Gardens by using these headlamp signals. It was so natural that the other man immediately understood.

Ernst watched Hans closely and walked with him as he backed the loader down the tunnel. At the crosscut, Hans backed the loader around the corner. He did it rather fast, and looked to be accelerating instead of slowing down. There was silence for a moment as the loader was put into an emergency shut down, but not soon enough. Ernst could hear the heavy impact of splintering wood as the loader began hitting something.

"*Scheiss*," is what Ernst heard from Hans.

Peter's truck hit the wooden power transmission pole squarely in the center of the hulking front bumper. The truck pushed the pole to the ground as if it were a sapling, and drove the top of it into the ground with a hammer blow. Darkness turned abruptly and prematurely to day as the wires hit the ground and the transformer mounted on the pole exploded. The truck continued to slide toward the transformer and its associated fireworks until it finally eased to a halt. It stopped just inches from the transformer. Peter re-fired the truck engine and put it into reverse to back away from the transformer fire. He stopped when there was no more traction; the back wheels now deep in the frozen creek bed.

Peter's three passengers were awake now. Wide-awake. They shielded their eyes from the bright blue light of the burning transformer and saw the sparks from the downed power lines. They all sat transfixed by the display. Peter saw that the transformer and the top of the pole had landed on a piping assembly that he knew to be a natural gas wellhead. This one appeared to have been abandoned, as there wasn't anything connected to it on the surface. Once they began to understand they were uninjured, they began to smile at each other, and then laugh the giddy laugh of surviving a close call.

One of the men opened the passenger door and started to step out. Peter shouted to stay in the truck, but it was too late, and the down-time laborer jumped out and onto the ground. Peter thought for sure the man would be killed with that much voltage flowing around them in the snow and ice. But he soon realized that the wellhead was acting as a grounding rod, pulling all of the high voltage current away from them. They were safe.

Ernst frowned. The small amount of electric lighting they had in the work area had gone out. "Double *Scheiss*," he thought. At least the air compressor, service power, and the large fan ran off of the emergency generator, so they could continue working for a couple of hours when the generator came on.

It grew very quiet.

Ernst wasn't pleased. it was a matter of honor that Ernst's shift was the most productive, and this wasn't shaping up to be a very productive day. He adjusted his carbide light up higher, and strode toward the crosscut where the loader had disappeared.

Stacks Shackelton had bad knees, the kind that hurt just because the weather changed. The kind of knees that had more than one large scar from surgery, and he was always pulling up his pant leg to show them off. Those knees were really hurting tonight. He sat in the control room topside, monitoring the large fan that supplied fresh air to the mine, watching the lift, and manning the emergency phone. His feet were up on the desk, and he was beginning to get comfortable, when the lights went out.

"Awww, crap." He grabbed his radio and stood up, then winced as his knees straightened out. Dawn was beginning to break over the hills. "Hey, Fred and Fred. You copy?"

The radio popped and crackled in his hand for a moment, and he listened to the unusual quiet around him. Without the noise of machinery and the hum of the transformers it was eerily quiet. He chewed on his lip as he waited for the response. Fred and Fred—or, more properly, Fredric and Fredric—were the day shift maintenance electricians. Their job was to pull the manual switches that allowed them to start the massive backup generator and feed power to critical systems. It was something that would happen automatically back up-time, with lots of complex equipment kicking in during a power failure. But they didn't have the complex equipment. They had Fred and Fred.

The radio came alive. "We're on it, Stacks. Gen should start in a minute. Are you ready to accept load?"

While Fred—or was it Fred?—was talking, Stacks began throwing switches in the control room to shut down non-critical equipment and lessen the load on the generator. They were not totally comfortable with the mine operating this way, so the procedure was usually to contact the power plant and see how long they thought they might be down. Usually he got a call if there was a trip at the main plant, so Stacks figured that it might be a downed line. He would call when the generator started, and then call for more maintenance help to start the mine back up when the power came back on.

Stacks smiled. "All set there, Freddy, my boy. You can hit the go button whenever you want to, over."

"We're starting the generator now, hope it starts in this cold. Damn, it's cold out here. Are you warm in your chair, Stacks, you lazy up-timer?"

"Don't you two boys worry 'bout me none. I'm nice and warm in here. You get the generator goin' and you can cuddle up to the big ol' exhaust and warm up just fine." Stacks looked over at the

Franklin stove that kept him relatively comfortable and rubbed his left knee. It was really acting up today.

Ernst surveyed the damage. The loader was still in good shape, but the mine rib and support beams for the roof were knocked askew. Hans was apologizing profusely and was nervous as hell. It seemed he got the brake and the accelerator confused; the other unit he had trained on was slightly different. Ernst took advantage of the nervousness and proceeded to ream Hans up one side and down the other for his carelessness, all the while surveying the damage to the mine ribs and roof support structure. *Dammit,* Ernst thought, *Deitrich grabbed my carpenters. We'll have to fix this next shift.*

The small scooploader weighed close to seven tons, and was driven from a low seat near the middle. It was a low, solid steel, box-shaped piece of machinery with a scoop on the front. Huge batteries powered it and it could load coal at a tremendous rate when handled by an experienced operator. Ernst knew that Hans had just passed his operator test the day before. As the consequences of his rookie error, he would go back to shoveling coal by hand or get to wield one of the vacuum cleaners that sucked up the coal dust. It was a toss up which was the worse job. Ernst finished his colorful lecture, then began looking at the damage. The loader had snapped a brace that held up the roof and torn boards off the ribs of the mine.

The crosscut showed evidence of the rock "working," or moving around and possibly coming loose, so the carpenters had placed planks on the ribs and the roof for safety. Behind them, the concrete block "stopping" wall that separated the non-working—and possibly methane-filled—side of the mine from the ventilated and working side of the mine looked relatively intact. He looked the damage over and decided that it would be good enough for now.

Four or five miners came around the corner of the crosscut to see what was going on and began to walk toward the loader. Ernst heard the noises from the roof first and his heart jumped into his throat. The rock was "working" above them. His hand went up to try to stop the miners coming down the crosscut. Before he could shout a warning, it was too late. The support gave way, and a twenty-foot long single piece of rock fell out of the roof.

The shifting pressures caused the damaged rib to burst, and it added its own two tons of rock, crushing and trapping the men from above and the side. There were no screams when the rock stopped falling. It was silent, and black with dust.

Ernst and Hans had been beyond the fall, past the rib failure, and were helpless to do anything except dive to the floor next to the loader for protection. They helped each other to their feet. The black dust was so thick they couldn't see more than a couple of feet in front of them. Behind them was the block wall; in front of them was the half-filled passageway with their fellow miners buried beneath the heavy rocks. They could hear the shouts of the other miners who had stayed on station.

Ernst answered them. "How many are under there? Who is trapped?" He began a fit of coughing and stopped shouting. He saw some faint light, probably reflections from the other miners' helmets, above the pile of rubble. At least he and Hans were not trapped.

Willy, the youngest miner, answered, "We think there are four or five under there. We're starting to dig."

Ernst stopped coughing and caught his breath. The dust was beginning to settle. He noticed the there was some movement of air and assumed that the ventilation system had finally come back on. That was good. "Get to a phone. Tell them topside we got a fall and we have men trapped under the fall. Run to a phone. Now! The rest of you start digging." He began coughing again. Hans thumped him on the back until he finally stopped.

"Look." Hans pointed. "I think we can crawl over the top. There's room there; we can get over it. Before there's another fall." Ernst nodded and pushed Hans ahead of him. The younger man scrambled over the top of the pile, paused to listen to the rock, and quickly squeezed through the opening above. Ernst could see the hands of his coworkers helping him from the other side.

Ernst started up the pile. The breeze was blowing stronger as he neared the top. His dusty eyes narrowed. *Something isn't right,* he thought. *This isn't blowing in the right direction. It should be blowing in my face, not from behind me. If there's airflow, then the wall must be . . .* Once he was near the top of the pile, he turned to look. The concrete block wall that separated the abandoned and methane-rich part of the mine was damaged in the fall. It was nearly gone; only the two bottom rows of blocks were left.

The breeze he felt was pressure from the abandoned side of the mine rushing into the occupied side of the mine, where his fellow miners now stood. *Scheiss. The ventilation system is still down!* He pulled his methane meter out of his pocket and turned it on.

"Hey, Fred and Fred. Come in, Fred and Fred. C'mon you two sparkies, answer me. Is your radio working or did you two freeze your asses off out there? Where'n hell's my generator?" Shackelton stared at the radio for a moment. "C'mon, you guys. I need that generator soon," he mumbled. He absentmindedly rubbed his knee again, and began to pace slowly. Finally, the radio crackled to life.

"Stacks, we got a problem. This generator lost the heater, and the thing won't start."

"What do you mean, it lost a heater? The thing is a diesel engine, what does it need a heater for?" Stacks looked at his radio again, and held it up to eye level. "Just get that thing running or we'll lose the whole shift and it will take us another shift to reventilate the mine once we get it running. C'mon, guys. We're depending on you."

"A fuse blew for the heaters for the fuel and the oil. The whole thing is as cold as ice. Don't you know anything about a diesel? These don't like to start when the fuel turns to jelly. It don't flow too well. We got the circuit back up, but it's going to take a while to heat up. Why don't you send a couple maintenance guys over with a torch set? We can at least warm up the crankcase faster that way."

Stacks smiled and pushed the transmit button. "Okay. That's one I owe you. Hey, maintenance. Did you copy the request from the sparkies?"

"Ahyep," came the reply. "We was already goin' when we heard there was no power, Boss. You think we're a buncha dummies over here?"

Shackelton made a face at the radio. "Ten-Four" didn't seem like the right thing to say.

Ernst looked at the meter and his heart raced. The meter read five percent. He reached up and snuffed his cap light, plunging the area into darkness. Then he began to scramble over the top of the rock fall, shouting to the men on the other side. "*Scheiss.* Men. Run. Run as fast as you can. Out of the mine. Run!"

"What did you say?"

"What is it, Ernst? We'll come for you. Are you hurt?"

Ernst tried to answer them but the dust choked him. He began coughing, the dust in his lungs burning and making his eyes water, but still he kept scrambling to the other side, hacking out the cry to run away, leave me, run. He was thinking it as loud as he could, trying to make his voice answer to his command, all the while battering, bruising and cutting himself as he scrambled up to the remaining few feet of the opening. *Just a couple more feet.*

He could see the reflections of the flames from the carbide lights through the opening and realized that those lamps might ignite the methane and air mixture that was flowing into the work area. The readings on the meter indicated the percentages were correct. Now four men with flames burning in their cap lights were scrambling up the other side of the pile of rubble, trying to save him. He had no voice to tell them to go back, to snuff the flames of their lamps, or even to pray.

The last face he saw was that of Marcus Schoenfeld. The light from Marcus's carbide lamp reflected off Ernst's own face, softly illuminating Marcus. Ernst remembered how he had helped Marcus at a meaningless skirmish when they were with Wallenstein; he had a scar across his forehead, another on his cheek, and no teeth. Even without teeth, Ernst could tell that Marcus was smiling at him, encouraging him to crawl forward. In his mind, he saw the day of their last battle together; it seemed like only yesterday.

The last thing either of them saw was Ernst reaching for Marcus's cap light, trying to extinguish it to prevent the explosion.

Willy ran toward the phone. It was over three hundred meters away, in a crosscut. He knew the procedures: tell the command shack who you were, where you were and what happened. Don't tell them what was needed; they would decide that. Topside would decide what was needed.

He was running that mantra through his head when he was hit from behind by a full-body blow, with an additional three or four sharp impacts in his back and legs. He was tossed forward violently, like a rag doll. He hit the floor hard and got caught in the tracks that the mules used to pull the coal cars. His shoulder and ribcage were burning with pain and he could smell horseshit.

His hardhat was knocked off and the carbide extinguished. He was dazed, momentarily trying to figure out if he had tripped or been pushed. There was no light. Whatever happened, he had to get to the phone system and tell them topside. When he tried to stand, his ribs moved in ways that they were not supposed to and he fell to his knees. There was something wrong with his fingers.

Willy tried to walk, and then to trot. He fell again, this time smacking his face against the ribs of the mine. The air tasted like dusty coal mixed with his blood. He gathered himself up and tried again, going slowly, feeling his way ahead. He touched something hanging from the wall. A cable for electric power had been strung along the wall. He followed that, using it as a guide, crying from the pain in his shoulder, ribs and face. He realized that he couldn't hear, and could only perceive a loud ringing sound in his ears. He needed to get to a phone. Who, where, and what . . .

Deitrich had his men spread out doing several different tasks. Some were preparing temporary electric power, some were moving supplies into position, and others were readying the temporary barriers that would divert important airflows from the main passages to the work areas.

He noticed that the power had gone out but wasn't overly worried. The area they were in had no permanent power anyway, and they had prepared to work with only cap and hand lights. Later, as the cleanup on the other end was finished, they would begin to move all of the tracks, equipment, and materials to this end and resume mining as before. But he checked his methane meter every couple of minutes. This end of the mine wasn't as active as the other end and he wasn't worried about airflow. The plan said that it was up to him to pull his men out if he thought it was necessary.

Most of the time the power would come back on in a few minutes. This time it had been at least a half hour, and there was still no power. Surely the generator must be started by now. He stared back at the main passageway, looking outby toward the center of the mine and the lift stations, when he felt the air move around him. The movement was odd, not like the fans had restarted, but as if all of the air in the mine had moved at the same time. The air moved forward, and then back. It was unusual.

He felt his ears pop and shook his head. He looked around at the other men. Guys were shaking their heads and blowing their noses, trying to equalize the pressures in their sinuses and looking confused. Deitrich was confused, too.

"What the hell was that, Boss?"

"I got no idea, Metzinger. I never felt that before."

Metzinger made a face. "Wonderful. If you never felt it before, what are we supposed to—"

It was then they felt the bump pulsing through the earth, and it raised some dust from the floor of the mine. The dust stayed in suspension as there was no airflow to sweep it away, and it hung in the air, lowering their visibility. All of the men stopped working and looked at Deitrich. He stared down the passageway and tossed the problem back in forth in his mind. There was a lot of work to do; maybe the bump had something to do with the power outage.

He turned to his men. "Keep working, you guys. I'll tell you when to stop." He paused, turned to Metzinger, and spoke quietly. "The phones have not been strung all the way down here yet. You know where the nearest one is, don't you?"

Metzinger nodded. "Almost all the way back to the lift. It will take me a few minutes. You want me to see if they know anything in the command shack?"

Deitrich nodded back. "I want you back here quick. This better not be a leisurely stroll to the phone. Walk from here slow. I don't want to panic any of the new guys. Go."

Metzinger strolled toward the telephone, but when he rounded the corner, Deitrich heard his footfalls increase their pace. He looked at his pocket watch. *Should know something in fifteen or twenty minutes.*

"Hey, Fred and Fred, come back on the radio. Did you guys hear that bump?"

"Negative, Stacks. Didn't hear anything except this generator trying to start. What did you hear?"

"I heard a . . . felt a . . . like a bump. Like someone dropped somethin' heavy, y'all know what I mean?"

"Control, this is April on the phone shed. You copy?"

"Sure do, sweetheart. C'mon back to me."

"I felt it over here in the phone shed. And stop calling me

sweetheart or I'm gonna tell your wife, and what she'll do to you is far worse than anything I could do." There was a pause. "Sweetie."

Stacks looked at his radio and scowled. This wasn't shaping up to be a good day. "Thanks, April. Anyone else? How 'bout the lift? CC, you copy there, buddy?"

"Yup, I heard it too, barely. Like a truck driving by. Hey, Stacks, you heard anything from the power plant about when we're gonna get some juice?"

"They don't know. Said they think a line is down and they're checking it. If we don't get this generator working within the next half hour, we're gonna have to pull those guys out of there. A half hour is all I got left for time in the safety plan. Can't go beyond the time, no matter what. So how are you doin', Fred and Fred? Are you boys getting close? I *reeely* needs to know soon. Else there are gonna be a lot of pissed off miners having to climb all the way up and out of the mine."

"Sorry, Stacks. It's gonna be another half hour before we can even try it. I got about eight tons of engine block to heat up, or we're gonna destroy the starter motor. Can we get another torch?"

"You bet. Whatever you need. Maintenance, get over there with another torch, anything you got to help. My phone is starting to ring off of the hook. We must not have been the only ones who heard that bump. Just don't blow yourselves up over there."

Stacks swiveled his chair around and picked up the first line that was ringing. "Control Shack, Stacks.... No, we don't know what it was either.... I have no idea.... Yes, calling the police might be a good idea.... Ma'am, I need to keep this line clear for emergencies. No, no. There's no emergency here. I need to keep this line clear. Ma'am, yes ma'am. No, ma'am. Please, I need to go. Goodbye!" He banged the phone down, and it rang immediately. All three lines were lit.

"Shit, this isn't going to be a good day at all. Control shack..."

Willy stumbled in pain and darkness, blinking his eyes and trying to see. He knew that a working phone had a green indicator light on the base of the box. He kept looking for the green light, concentrating, wiping the sweat from his eyes, and focusing on taking another step.

He tried to ignore his growing pain, push it to the back of his mind, but his eyes had nothing to focus on, so his mind went to his injuries and the pain increased. He tried to maintain focus, and gulped some of the dense air around him. He coughed, and his broken ribs tortured him. He fell to his knees, and then struggled to get up.

He pushed off of the rib of the mine, clawing up the side with his good left hand. As he rose, he hit his head on something hard and metallic and he bit his tongue. More blood. He felt the object with his hand and found a telephone box. There was no green light. No light at all. The phone was dead, damaged by the blast.

He found the cable that served the phone and began to follow it. One foot in front of the other, keeping the cable in his hand. It helped to hold the phone cable, as it became his eyes and gave him more to focus on than the pain.

When Metzinger reached the phone, he was walking at a brisk pace and noticed nothing unusual. His crew was less than a quarter-mile behind him and the other work crew more than a mile away, through a labyrinth of tunnels. There were no signs of anything unusual. He picked up the phone and waited for April to answer. He liked talking to April when he had the chance, but it was unusual to do it over the phone.

"Phone shack. Who's this?"

"Hi, April. Wilhelm here. You know Wilhelm Metzinger. Second-year electrician apprentice? I'm at east section one at crosscut six."

"Hello there, Wilhelm. Is Deitrich with you?"

Metzinger frowned. Always Deitrich. The girls just seemed to like him more. He sighed. "*Nein*, he stayed with the others. He sent me to see what was going on. We heard and felt something, and our ears popped. He thought I could handle it on my own."

"That's nice, Wilhelm. I just talked to Stacks and he doesn't know anything either. But he did say that you guys were goin' to have to come out soon 'cause we don't have power. You probably didn't even notice it down there, but the phones have a battery backup so we can still stay in production. They're trying to get the generator working. Apparently it's too cold or something."

"Should we keep working, or should we come out?"

"Give me a minute, Wilhelm. I want to talk to Stacks. He's not answering his phone, so I need to go see him. Just hold on; I'll be back in two shakes."

Wilhelm looked at the phone. How long was two shakes, he wondered. He passed the time looking around in the darkness, adjusting his cap lantern, and finally scraping patterns in the dusty floor, when he heard an unusual noise over the phone line. There was scratching and line static, and then it sounded like labored breathing. Metzinger listened intently. He finally heard a scratchy voice.

"Help . . . this is Willy. Men trapped, west cuts twenty-two, crosscut, roof fall, trapped . . . this is Willy, men trapped, west cuts twenty-two, crosscut, roof fall, trapped."

Metzinger was stunned. "Willy? This is Wilhelm. What is going on? Willy, do you hear me?"

"Wilhelm? Men trapped, west cuts twenty-two, crosscut, roof fall . . ." His voice was getting weaker.

"Stay on the line, Willy. April will be right back. I need to tell Deitrich. Do you hear me? Stay on the line. April will be right back. Willy. You must stay on the line." Metzinger left the phone off of the hook and began to sprint back to Deitrich.

April was beginning to get frustrated as she banged on the door of the control shed. "Goddammit, Stacks, it's cold as hell out here. Open the damn door. Why the hell aren't you answering your phone or radio? You hear me? Open up!"

"Sorry, sweeth—uh, April. I got three phone lines going at once here." She could hear him reach the door, and begin to open it. "Damn thing's froze shut. Gimme a second here, let me—" The door flew inward and April felt the rush of warm air from the shack. It felt very good. She jumped through the door and he closed it behind her.

"Goddammit, Stacks. You need to answer your radio and phone. I talked to Metzinger and he didn't know what was up with the noise. Wants to know if we should pull them out or leave them in."

"How the hell should I know, April? We need to ask Fred and Fred. You answer the phones for a minute, let me get to them on the radio."

She planted her hands on her hips and glared. "Listen, you dummy. I ain't supposed to leave my phones unattended. And you are not a goddam answering service for anyone calling this place from the outside. Let them ring. Find out about the generator and let me know what to do with those guys." She tugged open the door and stomped out into the cold light of morning.

April trotted back to the phone shack. When she got to her post, she was surprised to discover Metzinger was no longer on the line, but she could tell that the phone was off the hook. She called to him several times over the open line and got no answer. She then noticed a background noise that wasn't there before. The signal to noise ratio sounded—well, it didn't sound right. She scratched her head and looked up at the old phone relay board.

"That's odd." She leaned back in her chair, and stared at the panel. "This thing acts like I got more than one phone open here." She pulled her electronic test meter out of the desk drawer. One last check for Wilhelm first.

"Wilhelm, are you out there? Can you hear me? Wilhelm? Dammit, answer me." She put the phone down and began to check resistance readings through the switch circuits.

Deitrich was growing impatient waiting for Wilhelm to return. It had been over twenty minutes since he left and it was taking far too long. He should have been back by now. He pulled his pocket watch out for the third time in five minutes, and then stuffed it back in his pants. Something just felt wrong. The power had gone out before, and the mine never behaved in this way.

Maybe it was all of the new guys that were making him jittery. There. He'd said it. Well, thought it. He was jittery. That thought made him angry. When Metzinger got back he was going to tear him a new asshole for being slow and lazy. Deitrich heard the returning footfalls and took a breath, ready to verbally rip strips of flesh from his hide. Then he saw Metzinger's face and lost all thought of abusing him.

Metzinger gulped for air and leaned on Deitrich for support. He must have run all the way back. Metzinger gasped. "Willy—Ernst, roof fall by the west coalface. That must have been what we heard. Needs help. Men are trapped. We need to get over there."

"Are you sure?"

Metzinger sat down on the floor and nodded, still gasping for air. "Yah. I heard it from Willy. I was on the phone with April, and he picked up. His voice was very faint." By now some of the other miners had come over to listen to the conversation. A canteen of water was pushed in his hand and he drank deeply.

"What's up, Deitrich?" asked one of the apprentices. Several others chimed in. "What's going on? A roof fall? Where was it? What did he say—"

Deitrich growled at the group. "Quiet. Give us some room. You talked to Willy, right? Metzinger nodded. "When you were on the phone with April, right?" Metzinger nodded again. "Where was Willy; did he say what phone he was calling from?"

"West face." Metzinger struggled to his feet. "We gotta help them, Boss. Willy sounded bad."

"Okay." Deitrich thought for a moment then straightened. "Everyone. Listen up. We have a situation. From what we know, there has been a roof fall at the other end of the mine. We're going to see what we can do. Grab any tool and first aid kits you see along the way. We're gonna double-time it over there and see what we can do to help. Everyone. Let's go. Now."

The guys working farther away had trickled to the group and as Deitrich began to turn away, they fell in behind him. Metzinger stood to follow and Deitrich hesitated. "Good job, Wilhelm. Rest for a moment, then catch up to us when you can."

Metzinger looked relieved. "Okay, Boss. I'm getting a hell of a cramp in my legs. Thanks."

Deitrich turned and began to jog. His old rally cry from the battlefield came to mind. "To me, men!" he half growled and half shouted. "To me!"

"This is damn odd." April scratched her nose and looked at the chart. The chart gave resistance readings for the phone wires. Generally, it was accurate. The more wire in a certain direction, the higher the number. The less wire, the lower the number. Her readings indicated that the phone where she talked to Metzinger was off the hook and was at the end of the line for that circuit. That made sense from what she knew. But on the west circuit, according to her chart, there weren't enough phones. One of them was off the hook, and it was like the wire ended at that phone. She knew there were more, at least three beyond that. She scratched her nose again.

The radio on her bench cracked to life. "Hey, April. This is control. You still got Metzinger on the line?" She ignored it for a moment, deep in concentration, and it cracked again. "April, you copy? C'mon, you're not still mad at me are you?"

She snatched the radio off of the bench. "Stand by, Stacks. I think I got a problem here. Can you give me a couple seconds?"

"Sure can, sweetheart."

She didn't even notice that he called her sweetheart again.

Deitrich and his men had run beyond the telephone that Wilhelm had left hanging and past the main lift station. There was a steady rhythm of men breathing hard, and the cap lights flickering. Each light made a bouncing and fluttering U-shape in the darkness. Occasionally, a light would go to the roof, sometimes to the ribs, sometimes to other miners. They ran in silence, an oddly illuminated chain of lights, panting and passing through the passages.

Darkness was briefly pushed out of their path as they ran and then slipped in behind them as they passed. The deeper they went, the darker it seemed to get. There was more dust in the air at this end of the mine, so their dim cap lights pushed less and less of the darkness away. Deitrich was focused on getting there as fast as possible, and he didn't notice it until one of the new men called out.

"Deitrich! Do you smell smoke?"

He slowed and looked hard at the roof of the mine, looking for a visible trace of the smoke. Without the ventilation, it would cling to the roof, instead of mixing like it normally would. It smelled like burning wood. Why would there be a smell of burning wood for a roof fall? He slowed to a walk for a moment. *Maybe something else is going on*? Ahead he saw one of the green lights for the telephone on the wall, and decided to stop there.

It was there they found Willy. He was alive, but in bad shape and unconscious. Deitrich told two of his guys to get him on a stretcher and back to the lift station.

Deitrich stared at the phone for a moment. Something was odd. It was off the hook. He picked up the receiver and held it to his ear. He heard clicking sounds, and a sound like someone moving around a room. He hung it up and re-signaled the phone room.

"Phone shack. Who's this?"

"April, this is Deitrich."

"Deitrich? What the hell is going on down there? I was talking to Metzinger and he just took off and left the phone off the hook back on the west end. This phone was off the hook, now you're on it, and it doesn't appear that there's any phones active inby from you. And did you guys hear that bump down there?"

"One thing at a time. I have an injured miner, and a possible roof fall over by where Ernst is working. It sounds like you don't know about Willy?"

"Willy? No, I don't. What's up with Willy?"

"He's injured. Badly. I'm sending him topside with two men. We found him at the phone. Did you not talk to him? It would have been right after you talked to—wait, April. I need to think." Deitrich pushed his hard hat back on his sweaty forehead and tried to think clearly. He shook his head and made a decision.

"April. I don't know what the hell is going on down here. All I have is that Metzinger said that he heard Willy on the phone and there was a roof fall down there. And now I smell smoke. And we got no goddamn power down here. I'm going to take this crew and head down to the old working face and see if there's something we can do. You let Stacks know what we're up to, and I'll call as soon as I know something."

"Okay, Deitrich. But I know that they were talking about pulling you guys out until we got some power back."

"I'm wasting time talking to you. We're going to help Ernst. I'll let you know if everyone is okay." He hung up the phone and ignored it when it started to ring. He didn't have time to argue with April. Deitrich turned on his heel and began to walk down the passage toward the working face, where he knew that something was wrong. The smell of smoke grew stronger.

After another two hundred meters, they began to notice unusual damage. The seals had been damaged in the cross cuts. The farther they went, the more damage they saw, until they were stepping over blocks and brick that had been blown out into the main passageway. Their pace slowed. The mine was now wide open on this end; all of the careful seals and brattices had been knocked down.

Deitrich began to think that what they were dealing with might be a methane explosion. Or maybe what was referred to as an "ignition," when gas would be coming out of the rock in a particular area and could form a standing flame, like the gas stove in the cafeteria. He had never seen one, but there were films. Normally an explosion would destroy an entire mine, or sector of a mine. But Willy didn't look burned. Willy had said a rock fall. Something wasn't making sense. They were still a ways from the working face when the smoke and dust started to become a visibility problem. Several men were coughing.

Deitrich looked back. "Guys, go ahead and put on your self-rescuers. They should have gone over that in class. If there's excessive carbon monoxide, this little thing—" He held up the belt mounted canister. "—changes the bad air to good." There was a rustling as the men put them on and tested them.

From the back, Zing spoke up. "Deitrich, we're not allowed to use these to fight fires; these are only for rescue, for us. If there's a fire, we're supposed to . . ."

Deitrich turned to him viciously. "Don't quote me rules, god-dammit. Put it on and let's move. And keep an eye out for the injured."

Metzinger was limping badly from the cramp in his legs when he met the two men carrying Willy. Willy had been patched up when they found him, but hastily.

"Put him down, guys. Let me take a look." One of the men handed him a small first aid kit. "*Scheiss*, we need some light." He looked around. "Let's take him to the tool crib over there."

The tool crib was built into one of the cross cuts, and was generally locked. But there were extra carbide lights stored there, along with concrete blocks, mortar, plastic and cloth sheeting for brattices, and spares of all kinds. Even a microwave oven for heating lunches. It took them almost no time to open the gate and set Willy down on a workbench. Metzinger looked around at all the stuff in the tool crib, including the very valuable compressed air hoses for the tools.

He turned his attention to Willy. "I can handle it from here, guys. I think we just need to stop this bleeding and he should be okay. At least I hope so. He was bleeding through the old bandages." He lifted up Willy's shirt and pulled back the soaked bandages, exposing the gash in his chest that ran along the ribs. They could actually see one of the ribs. The two younger men stepped back. Metzinger pulled clean bandages from the kit and began to apply pressure, gently, to the area. Willy stirred and moaned.

"Now that's a good sign. It still hurts. If you guys want to go back and help Deitrich, I can handle this. It will take me an hour to get there at this rate. I think he needs you more than we do. Go on. I got this covered. If we move him any more, we could kill him."

The two apprentices looked at each other and headed after Deitrich. Neither of them looked like they could stand the sight of blood.

Must not be from around here, thought Metzinger.

"I need that goddamn gen-set now. We got a man injured down there and maybe a rock fall. We need the lift and the goddamn fan. We need it ten minutes ago. Do you guys copy?"

"Stacks, we'll give it a try. We've bypassed the safety controls on the generator and we're using a torch on the outside of the fuel line to try and make it flow. There isn't much more we can do that won't blow this—and us—sky-fucking-high." There was a pause. "Do you copy, Stacks?"

Stacks could clearly hear the implied "asshole" at the end of the last transmission. He didn't care. It comforted him. He knew that whatever those guys could do to get power flowing from the generator, they were doing. At their own risk, all for the guys in the mine. He responded. "Ten-four. But don't you guys get hurt. Do what you can, but . . . Well, just do what you can, we're standing by."

Stacks opened the plant safety manual, and reviewed the procedures for an injury. Apply first aid and remove from plant. Call ambulance. If possible, continue production. That was the gist of it. Well, at least the phones had cleared up since that first bump, whatever that was. He dialed the fire department.

An operator with a pronounced German accent picked up. "Emergency services. What is the nature of your emergency?"

"This is Stacks at the mine. I got at least one injured miner down there and we're trying to evacuate him now. We're not sure of the extent of his injuries, but the information I have is that he's hurt pretty bad. We're trying to bring him out now."

"He's still in the mine?"

"Yeah, still down there. We have no power, so it will be a while before we can get him out."

"Do you know the extent of his injuries?"

"No, ma'am."

"Do you know when he will be on the surface?"

"Ummm. Not exactly, no, ma'am. But we're hoping pretty quick. Maybe an hour before we get him out, maybe less." He looked at the radio, hoping it would give him good news.

"Hang on, Stacks, give us a minute."

Stacks sighed as he heard the dispatcher cover the receiver on her end, and ask a muffled question. He looked at his watch. It was only nine in the morning. It seemed that this shift had already been on for twelve hours.

"Stacks, sorry, I'm back. We already have one ambulance out. Can you give us another call when you get closer to bringing him up? We don't want one just sitting there because if something else comes up, we won't be able to handle it."

"Okay. Let me log the call, and you do the same. There's always a safety review after one of these things." Stacks hung up the phone. Sometimes, doing this job, he still felt like he was up-time and everything was normal. It was a comfortable feeling. But he knew it was false. At times like this he realized how deeply in trouble they all were, and how very precarious things could be. He grabbed the radio.

"How 'boutcha, Fred and Fred? Are you gonna flow some electrons pretty quick, or am I gonna have to do it for you?" As soon as he took his finger off of the transmit button, he heard a large bang from the direction of the generator, followed by another, and then quickly followed by two more. The generator caught, stumbled, stumbled again, and started. He heard it stumble again, and imagined the guys scrambling to control it, working the throttle, nursing it until it flattened out into a steady roar. Finally, something was going right. The radio came to life as he sat down, suddenly very tired.

"There's your goddamn electrons. Give us a minute for this thing to stabilize, and we can start putting loads on it. What do you want first?"

"Give me the lift first, then service power, then the fan, and air compressors last. Let me know when you hit the transfer switches, so I know what's coming."

Deitrich and his men had to slow to a walk, sometimes feeling their way inby. The smoke and dust were so thick that visibility wasn't much more than five or six feet. He kept chattering confidently to the men behind him, and they obeyed his orders. Deitrich was a leader, and he knew what he could expect of these kids. And he was asking them for a lot. So far, they had . . .

"Deitrich! Here is someone. Over here! I have found someone." There was a knot of men forming around a shape on the floor of one of the damaged crosscuts. It was one of Ernst's men; Deitrich recognized him, but couldn't remember his name. He wasn't breathing, but he had one of the "rescuers" in his mouth. And he was burned. Deitrich touched him and knew the man was dead. He clenched his jaw, and stood.

"There's nothing we can do for him now. Leave him."

Zing spoke up. "Boss, they tell us in class that we need to let them know topside ASAP when someone is—well, injured. Shouldn't we call for reinforcements from upstairs? They need to know what is happening, don't they?"

Deitrich turned on the young miner. "I'm in command here. I'll do the thinking." As Deitrich turned, he remembered the dead man's name. And his woman. And their son's names. He felt sick to his stomach. He hated indecision. Hated it in him and in others. He looked forward into the smoke, and back toward the safety of the center of the mine and the lift. Then back to the smoke and the dark. Indecision was over.

"If we go out now, there will be no chance for anyone up there to survive. By going in now and searching, there may be a chance we can rescue someone. We're going all the way to the working face, and look for survivors." He looked at the group. "Any questions?" The cap lights shook back and forth and it was quiet.

Deitrich spoke in the lowest voice he could. But the power was unmistakable. "To me, men. To me. Let's go."

"We're closing power to the lift breakers now. I don't want to lose the gen-set, so go easy. Run the cage down slow."

"Thanks. Okay, CC. It's on you, buddy. Send the cage down and see how many get on it, then start hoisting. We need to get these guys out of there and figure out what's going on."

"Stacks, the cage is going down. It will be 'bout three minutes before it gets to the bottom. When they pick up the phone and tell me, I'll haul them up."

"Thanks, CC. Fred, as soon as you can, and the gen-set is

stable, give me service power so they can have some light down there."

"Ten-four, Stacks. You'll have it in a couple of minutes."

Stacks picked up the landline again, this time to call his boss, Larry Masaniello. It was Larry's day off, but he would be upset if someone was hauled away in an ambulance and he wasn't notified.

Deitrich was more and more worried that they wouldn't find any survivors. The closer they got to the working face, the worse the damage. Now they picked their way over debris piles, pieces of timbers, and finally . . . bodies. Whatever happened, some of the guys started to get away. Some of them had their shoes and miners belts blown off, and hard hats were scattered about. There was no doubt that there had been a methane ignition of some sort, and it had been powerful. They finally reached crosscut twenty-two, where Willy had said the roof fall had occurred. A large rock had fallen. He was afraid that all they were going to find was bodies.

"Check by the face, you three guys. See if there was anyone up there. Shout out for survivors, but don't forget to listen. If we don't find anyone alive, we'll head back." As he said that, some of the explosion-proof lighting fixtures winked on. "Looks like we're getting power back. That's good. Hopefully, we'll get some ventilation going and clear this dust . . ."

Deitrich paused.

He saw the layout of the mine in his head. The fan shafts where the air was pulled in and pushed out and all of the carefully-built stopping that had been blown out from the explosion. The fact that the fan was off had kept it from mixing any further, and probably limited the explosion. But if they started the fan now, all that mixing would happen again, on a much larger scale. There were still small fires burning and smoldering all around them.

The dread hit him like a ton of bricks. He swallowed and looked around. *All these kids.* He was going to try to get them out. It was the least he could do.

"Let's go! Everyone! Let's go! Out of the mine! Now! Fast as you can!" He took two steps backward and stumbled over some debris. "Let's go! Run, goddammit, run!" He caught his balance and ran inby, shooing the ones he had told to go to the face in front of him. "Move it! Let's go!" The group began to stumble away from the epicenter and began to run faster as their panic grew. Deitrich recognized it and let the panic have its head. It could only help.

They tripped, fell, cut themselves, got up again and kept running as fast as they could. All the while the panic gripped them, and they ran faster. They picked their way through the debris, trying to go as fast as possible, sometimes stumbling, sometimes falling flat. As one cap light fell, another would help it up and rejoin the other cap lights, bouncing and weaving down the passage. They were grunting and breathing hard, some making noises like children running from a nightmare, as if they were being chased by some terrible monster. There was no speaking, no conversation, only animal noises.

As they ran, the darkness once again closed silently and inevitably behind them.

"Okay, Stacks. Fan breakers are closed. Go ahead and start it."

"Good job, you guys. Here goes. I got a green light, the fan is starting up. How's the generator?"

"We're stable. Go ahead and put the compressors on and we'll be back in business."

"Compressor start . . . and I show a green light for them, too."

"You owe us a beer. You know that, don't you?"

Stacks looked at his radio, sat down and smiled. "Roger that. Beer is on me." He smiled again and called the fire department dispatcher.

The cold light of the January sun had barely begun to light the old Pence house. Marylyn Pence, a widow, had been renting rooms in her home. It was a way she could make ends meet. She was at the stove, boiling water, preparing to make breakfast. She felt the blast first through her feet. From there it traveled through the house, where glassware rattled, and then echoed off of the hills surrounding the valley. She froze as the echoes died away. She'd become a widow when she heard that sound, many years ago.

A baby cried upstairs. Marylyn sat at the kitchen table, pale and shaking. Her boarder—or rather, her boarder's wife—went to quiet the baby. She heard the footsteps upstairs. Soon the baby was quiet. A moment later, mother and child came downstairs. She was beautiful, Marylyn decided. As radiant as the sun that peeked through the window. Marylyn always liked the kitchen and the way the sunlight bathed it at breakfast. She gathered herself. Before she could speak, the German girl greeted her.

"Good morning Mrs. Pence. It will be a lovely, sunny day today. A little bit cold, *ja*?"

"Yes, a bit cold."

"What was that noise that woke the baby? It sounded like a cannon shot!"

Marylyn took a deep breath. "Maria, is your husband in the mine today?"

Peter felt the rumble beneath the ground. They were all out of the truck, standing in the field. They had used the phone at the house to call the police and request the rest of the equipment to pull the truck out of the frozen mess. The sparking had continued, but the transformer had burned itself out.

The rumble grew and the wellhead erupted in a new flame, the hot yellow flame of natural gas. It was hot enough that they raised their hands to protect their faces. The muted colors of the frost-covered creek bottom, where the low winter sun wouldn't reach for hours, were turned into the harsh light of day. The flame shot above the trees, stayed for a moment, and then receded to a height of ten feet or so, and stayed there. The ground shook even more. The cab of the truck was scorched and the heavy vehicle swayed when the ground shook.

Peter looked at his companions. "What in the hell was that?"

Shackelton was knocked out of his chair by the force of the blast. Several windows shattered, letting in the cold air that slapped him in the face. He heard breaking glass and things shifting and falling in the shed. He jumped up, momentarily forgetting his knees, then winced. "What in the God damn Sam Hill was that?"

The booming noise diminished to an eerie quiet. Then, within seconds, all three of his outside lines lit up. He looked at the phones, started to answer one of them, and stopped. He turned away and triggered the master alarm then looked at the phones, and paused again. What the hell could he tell anyone? He didn't know any more than anyone else.

He grabbed his radio. "I want information. What the hell was that? April? Do you have any communication? April? Answer me, goddammit . . ."

The Reverend Doctor Al Green was in the shower when he felt the earth shift and rumble. He had soap all over his face and stood in place, knowing what it was, already seeing the events that would probably transpire over the next few days flash in his mind. He turned, slowly and deliberately, and rinsed off. He took his time. He prayed a little. This was going to be the last solitude that he would have for some time. He prayed for strength, prayed that it wouldn't be what he was certain that it was.

His wife stuck her head into the bathroom. "You hear that?"

Al paused before he answered. "Yes."

"Was that . . . ?"

He sensed that she didn't want to say it any more than he did. As if by not saying it out loud, she would somehow make it not true.

"Yes."

"Shall I start making calls?" She was asking if she should call out the troops of church ladies, who would be the support for the next several days' events. His church, no matter what the religion of the miners, had always been the center for families awaiting news. It would be no different this time. A mining accident wasn't just another industrial accident. In a town where almost everyone was related to someone else, it becomes a far-reaching family tragedy.

"Yes. Please. And give me just a minute, would you?"

He heard her close the door, softly, and move away. The calls would probably begin on their own. He warmed the shower water a bit and stood with his face in the stream, letting the warm water wash his tears away.

The exact location of the point of ignition was never determined. It was probably near the first explosion, but the damage was too severe to tell. When the air and methane mixture was correct, it ignited explosively and began to propagate a shock wave before it, seeking release. This wave picked up the coal dust that was distributed by the first explosion, and it too became fuel. The flame front followed the shock wave.

The wave front caught Deitrich and his crew, still far from any refuge, in the main passage. They barely realized the beast had overtaken them before they were all dead. The flames followed, but they were of no consequence to those men.

Metzinger and Willy were more fortunate. The heavy workbenches protected them somewhat from the massive damage that the others suffered.

As the explosion progressed, its energy began to dissipate. By the time it got to the lift, the majority of the destructive forces had gone. The flame front had stopped well before the lift. Now came the smoke, lots of smoke, from the multiple fires the flame front had started. Those fires consumed fuel and oxygen, leaving carbon monoxide. So as the echoes of the shock wave were reverberating off the hills, the smoke began to flow through the mine, stealing air from wherever it went. The air in the mine was unbreathable in a matter of moments.

The battered pickup truck raced down the blacktop road on the way out of town. The sun was peeking over the ridgeline now, and Larry Masaniello was trying to get to the mine—his mine—as quickly as possible. He could see a plume of black smoke rising behind the ridge. His coal mine. He was the manager.

His heart was pumping much harder than it had in a long time and he felt physically sick. He was afraid that he would throw up if he didn't keep focus. He had always considered himself a coal miner first, and the mine manager second. The idea of a major mine accident on his watch had kept him awake nights ever since he had taken over for Quentin Underwood. His hands were shaking.

He had to be careful. People were on the road, a lot of them, hurrying to get to the mine. He saw miners and their families. Miners carrying gear and women carrying children shuffled out of his way. He kept honking his horn.

He heard the ambulances coming from town behind him, and the fire department. He could tell the sirens apart by sound alone. He kept the window up, even though he wanted to open it wide to let in the cold air. He couldn't look at anyone in the eye and he felt the stares of those who got out of his way. He swallowed hard once again, and took a deep breath.

Finally, the mine was in view. The tall transfer tower for the coal was the first thing he spotted, before the other buildings came in sight. The mine sat at the very bottom of the valley, and the blacktop road was above it, about a third of the way up the ridge.

Originally, the coal had been removed from the mine on conveyors on the other side of the ridge, and came back to this side for processing. Those conveyors had been sliced off by the Ring of Fire, and the coal now came up a different shaft on this side of the ridge. That was where most of the smoke was escaping. The main shaft, which held the elevator, was smoky, but the smoke was not as thick. He felt a little relieved. If that was gone, then the men, and the mine, might be lost entirely. For now, there was hope that some men had escaped the blast.

When the mine was first constructed, it was surrounded by a large cyclone fence topped with barbed wire, but not now. That resource had long since been redirected.

He wished the fence were still here, as there was a knot of people around the mine control shed already. Things would get out of control real soon if somebody didn't take charge. He could see hand-waving and arguing going on as he approached. He swallowed hard again.

He dropped the pickup truck down into second gear and let the engine slow him down. With the busted up exhaust system, the V-8 made an ominous rumbling sound as he rolled up to the small, but rapidly growing, knot of people. It had the effect he desired, as they all turned and looked at him.

He hopped out of the cab and began to give orders. He looked for the biggest men there. "You four men, I need some crowd control now. Keep everyone back from this shed. If they're cold, have them go into the locker rooms or the old guard trailer. You two, keep everyone away from the lift. I don't want anybody trying to do something stupid. Nobody goes into the lift until rescue is here. You women, get inside before you freeze to death. Go to the locker rooms or the trailer." He didn't stop to see if his orders were followed, but strode to the control shed.

Shackelton met him at the door. "I'm damn glad you're here, Boss."

As he closed the door behind him, Larry felt himself shrink, as the bravado of his entrance wore off. He rested his back against the closed door. Shackelton, along with a much older retired miner whose name he couldn't quite remember, looked a little surprised.

Larry took a breath. "What do we know, for sure?"

"For sure? Not too damn much. The mine phones quit working right after that big ass boom."

"Who's on the phones today?"

"April Lafferty. I heard from the guys before, and there was a roof fall of some sort. Deitrich somehow heard about it and he was headed for the workface when we powered everything up. Then there was just that big boom."

"Have you heard from anybody since the explosion?"

"No, sir." Stacks looked at the ground.

"Could anyone have survived? I mean, the goddamn furniture moved in my house, and I'm over two miles from here."

"Anything's possible, Boss."

Larry needed good news. He hung on to the hope that some men had survived the blast. It gave him a focus. He straightened and noticed the other man. Skinny to the point of bony, bald, with a wisp of gray hair on the sides. He looked vaguely familiar, probably from a union meeting somewhere. He wore a work coat of brown canvas, boots, and work pants. "How did you get here so fast?" Larry asked.

The old man smiled a toothless smile. "I only lives 'bout a quarter mile up the blacktop." He waved up the road, beyond the mine. "I was up'n'bout when she went. Took me only coupla minutes or so."

Larry nodded. "Thanks, old timer."

"My pleasure, son. What c'n I do?" Once again he flashed Larry the gummy smile.

"How well do you remember the lift system?"

"I 'magine I kin help. Y'all wan' me to take a look?"

"Yes, sir. I think I'd like that. Who's on the phone system today?"

Shackelton looked at Larry a little funny. "I told ya. April Lafferty."

Larry's stomach took another flop. "Yeah. You did tell me."

The old man looked at Larry. "You can do it, Boss. Hell, after all of the assholes I seen run mines over the years, you got it all covered. Ya will be jus' fine." He looked Larry in the eyes, shuffled to the door, and was gone. Larry saw that more people had gathered outside. He turned to Shackelton. "Did you call the cops?"

The sixty-plus good ol' boy from Kentucky, who would be down there with the men except for his bad knees, simply nodded. "We're gonna need more crowd control." Larry stopped. He could still feel that sick feeling in his stomach. He fought it back. He heard the first ambulance roll up, followed by the fire trucks. He stood up straight once again. "Emergency Response Team?"

Stacks nodded again.

Larry sighed. "Has anyone called Reverend Green? We should get a couple of busses running between here and the church. This may be a while."

"Prime Minister Sterns?" The lieutenant interrupted the meeting in the prime minister's office, causing all of the heads to turn toward him. This was the weekly morning briefing, and everyone who was there was supposed to have all the pertinent information they needed before the meeting started. If it was important enough to interrupt, it was going to be a surprise. And the men in the room didn't like surprises.

"What is it?" Mike's voice was level, his look clear and relaxed.

"Thought you should know, sir. Telegraph report from Grantville says that a very large explosion has occurred."

All of the heads in the room swiveled and focused on Mike Stearns. A dark cloud seemed to come over his face.

There was a pause.

To the men in the room who knew and understood Mike Stearns, his pause spoke volumes. The lieutenant knew that the pause, the—dare he think it—the hesitation, meant the prime minister was caught up in thoughts about Grantville for a moment.

"Do we know how big? What kind? Where in the town was it located?" The questions came hard and fast, a little harder and faster than normal.

The lieutenant swallowed. "We don't have all that information at this time, sir. The telegraph operator was an up-timer. He said it was the mine. There are expected to be casualties, but he told me to tell you it was a maintenance shift, so there were not as many people in the mine as usual."

Mike Stearns turned his head and looked out the window. The lieutenant could not remember a time when he had seen an expression as painful as the one the Prime Minister now wore. The lieutenant heard him mumble, "Like that will make it any easier?"

There was a awkward moment of silence, until Warner Barnes, an up-timer sitting alongside Duke Hermann of Hessen-Rotenberg, the Secretary of State, cleared his voice. "Ummm, Mike. This is Grantville, the mine. We all know how much this means to you. To all of us. Why don't we adjourn for the rest of the day?"

The lieutenant saw Stearns nod slowly, gather himself, and begin to speak. "Thank you, Warner." His head swiveled around to the lieutenant. "Get me a Gustav—no, wait on that. I need to talk to Larry Masaniello first. I'll go there as soon as it is good for him. If they are in the middle of a rescue mission, I'm the last thing they need getting in the way. He needs a chance to do his job. But I need to go there. Put a Gustav on standby."

"Yes, sir." The lieutenant backed out of the very quiet room.

Reverend Green stood in front of the open door of his church, looking out onto the street. The cold morning air stung his face. It felt good. He breathed deeply and surveyed the block. The church was an old one, built in Grantville's heyday, near the turn of the twentieth century. The massive red brick structure sat next to the rectory. The first of the busses from the mine would be along soon. He stood on the steps of the church, in front of the door, watching and waiting.

The church ladies had already set up the meeting hall in the back of the church with food and more was arriving. He could smell some of it all the way up here. Hot casseroles and rolls, pies, dried fruit, someone had heated a ham and brought it. Plenty of water, maybe even some tea and coffee. The smell of coffee in the church made him think back to the time that it wasn't unusual to have coffee. Now it was almost a special occasion. He looked at the ground.

"Some occasion," he thought, "we could live without more of these . . ."

He didn't have to wait long. The first bus was full of down-timers, some he knew and some he had never seen before. It was escorted by a Grantville police car, the officers bundled up against the cold. As people left the bus, he began to welcome them. It was mostly women and children, a few old men. They came to him with vacant stares, glazed and shocked eyes, red with tears and worry.

He silently prayed for more strength and ushered them through the front doors, to the meeting room. Most had not been in his church and stared in amazement at the high ceiling, the organ, and the serene color of the walls. It was warm inside and soon the place would be warm and humid, like too many people in a house at Thanksgiving, when the windows would fog over on the inside. Warm and safe.

"Welcome, welcome, please come in, welcome, go all the way to the back, there's food and drink, welcome, welcome, you'll be safe here, this is for families of all faiths, welcome, there's food in the back . . ."

There were at least forty people. Reverend Green turned to the police officers. "How many are we to expect? How many are in the mine?"

The smaller policeman spoke first. "Father, there are at least three more busloads of people at the mine. Some won't leave, but you should expect at least another one hundred twenty or more. We're making it clear that we're only allowing families of the miners on the busses."

"How many were in the mine? Do we know?"

The second officer answered. "They think twenty-eight. They're putting together the rescue team now; they should go later in the afternoon."

Reverend Green sighed and bowed his head. "Are you going to stay here?"

"Yes, Father," replied the smaller one.

"Good." He looked up at the man. "We're not Catholic here, so please don't call me Father. I'm a Reverend. We're Baptists here."

"Okay, Reverend. You got it." The policeman tossed a small salute his way, and smiled.

Reverend Green went back inside and headed toward the meeting room. They were going to overflow, so he approached one of the senior church ladies. "We'll need more blankets, and we'll need to open up the sanctuary for people. There will be more. How are we set for food?"

"Could use more," said the woman. "We'll do what we can."

"Talk to my wife. She knows who to call at the other churches. We all need to get involved in this one. Twenty-eight is what they say are in the mine. I pray to God some of them make it out." He looked at the clock on the wall. Eleven-thirty in the morning and the first rescue team had not yet gone in for a search. This was going to be a long, long day. He prayed a little, looked up, and then purposefully stepped into the throng of people, arms outstretched, comforting and welcoming.

Soon another bus arrived, then a second, and then a third. The building was nearly to capacity and the food was running low. Within an hour, a group of Catholic ladies, all of them down-timers, a mixed group of Methodists, and a down-timer group of Lutherans had arrived to help out. There were up-timers in the mix, but most of the crowd were down-timers.

It wasn't too much longer before the reporters started to arrive. There were five or six of them out in the street, kept there by the police officers' watchful eyes. One of them managed to talk his way in, but was soon discovered and tossed out unceremoniously by two very large and angry Methodist women, with support from a pair of Catholic church ladies. Pastors, preachers and priests showed up to comfort the waiting families. Social services were there. The place was filled to capacity. All they could do now was wait.

So that's what they did.

Every half hour, Reverend Green would walk around the church, stopping to talk, to tell someone where to get help, how to notify someone who wasn't there, offer support to the visiting clerics, and check in the back to see how all of the church ladies were getting along. He didn't have a lot to worry about. The groups of women were self-organizing. They agreed on shifts to support the Baptist core group, with relief coming from all other quarters. He stuck his head in the back rooms, and observed them for a moment. It was more diverse than it had ever been back up-time. The Protestant denominations were well represented, as well as support from both of the synagogues in town. There was even a fledgling humanist society represented, and those three people were in the back, working hard.

He leaned against the doorframe and took a moment to watch this miracle. This group of people had become a community, far more disparate than any West Virginia town could ever be, and yet it still functioned almost the same way. Good people looking out for good people. He smiled inwardly. After all, isn't that what a community is supposed to be? Come together in times of need, despite differences. Answer to the common threat, defend the common good? Here in the back room of his Baptist church, were people from different times and faiths, together. Side by side at the sinks and the ovens. Hauling out the garbage, cleaning the countertops.

His inward smile turned quietly outward, as he realized that even in the darkest tragedy, there was good.

From that, he took strength.

The leader of the mine rescue team was a coal miner named Hank Jones. He had been part of a rescue team back up-time. In his mid-fifties, he was still in good shape and was still an active coal miner. Experience had taught him that he should expect something like this someday, and knew that he would have to have a team to back him up.

The typical rescue team is five men. Hank had been training with a group of down-timers he personally selected. He'd hoped to be able to give one of the men a team of his own and expand the training, so that there would be a backup. But there hadn't been time to do so. Never enough time.

Hank and the team were ready to go in. Stacks and Larry had wanted to shut down the fans, shut down everything before they went in. Hank knew better, and there was a heated argument about what to do. It was critical to keep the situation underground stable, to not change the conditions and potentially create new hazards. It was a basic rescue team procedure. Hank's job as a team leader—*the* team leader—was to take charge.

He had to assert himself. When the rescue team is called, they *own* the mine and everyone else works for them. Mine owners, maintenance, management, everyone. There were some Swedes from the army, a couple guys that tried to take charge with a national defense posture that Hank also had to squelch. He was in charge. That's what happens when you call out a team.

Normally he wouldn't assert himself that way. He would hang back, learn who everyone was, take opinions, and collaborate. But this one was personal, for him and everyone at the job site. Larry Masaniello was taking it particularly hard and it could be affecting his judgment, Hank decided. But Hank didn't call Larry on it in public. He asked for a meeting off to the side, and focused Larry on supporting Hank. And the families.

"Keep these guys off my back, Larry. Let my team do our job

down there. Keep the army out of this; that's the last thing we need. We brought them into the disaster planning as a courtesy more than anything else. Help me with those assholes. Focus on them and focus on the families. Have you delegated anyone to speak to the families over at the church?"

Larry shook his head. "No. That has to be me." His eyes began to cloud with tears. Hank could see him struggle, and then smile. "Funny, we never picked anyone for that position in the event of an emergency. Sorta like we didn't think it would happen."

Hank grabbed Larry's shoulder. "You know it's bad. I know it's bad. But at least be honest and open with them. Don't give them a lot of hope, but—well, you'll know what to do. Just be the man that you are. It's all you can do."

The five-man team was ready for the job. They had trained and practiced, sometimes on their own time, sometimes by being paid overtime for the long hours extra they put in. They had the best equipment, including the extra-bright battery cap lights and flashlights. But for four of the men, it was their first real rescue mission.

As they approached the lift with the thin wisps of smoke streaming out, Hank spoke. "All right, you guys. Are you ready for this?" He looked each of them in the eye as he looked around the huddle. Each man met his eyes and nodded. Hank looked for uncertainty and saw none. They were going to have to depend on one another to a degree that they had trained for but never actually experienced. Satisfied with their silent answers, he proceeded.

"Step one is to reestablish communications. Since we don't have any more phone wire, we'll have to trace and repair what we find. We have practiced that in our SCBAs. We should be able to splice the wires within two minutes even with the tank and air mask of the SCBAs. That's what we'll do. We think most, if not all, of the men were at the west face. It's the deepest part of the mine and the farthest away. Since we don't have the ability to put down a full borehole, we're having the well-digging truck try to hit that part of the mine. They will be able, maybe, eventually, to get an air sample. If the improvised bits work, and if it digs a straight hole and doesn't miss. We'll take readings for carbon monoxide and methane every one hundred feet of travel, and stay within sight of each other at all times. Nobody gets out of sight, not unless we plan for it, and all members are aware.

"After we get the phones working and after we understand the mine atmosphere, then we can start looking for survivors." Hank realized he swallowed that last word. Survivors. Based on what he saw and what he knew from the past, it was unlikely that there would be any survivors. But the first team in was always a rescue team, seldom a recovery team. And he intended to keep it that way, until he was absolutely sure.

They stepped onto the lift and gave the signal to the operator. They went down slow, taking air quality readings as they descended, not using their SCBAs. It was smoky, but breathable.

The next hours would be painstakingly slow, as they repaired the phones, established communication, and began the advance down the main tunnel.

It was three in the afternoon when Larry pulled his pickup truck in front of the Baptist Church. It was a busy place. He looked over the notes in his hand and steeled himself. With the short days of winter, the daylight was already taking on dusklike appearance, and it gave an unreal diffused glow to the imposing church. What he was about to do was going to be the hardest thing he had ever done in his life, and he wasn't sure he was up for it. He hoped his wife had made it here. He was going to need support for this.

He had nearly made it to the front doors when he was recognized by the reporters, who shouted out his name, and began to fire questions. "Larry . . . Larry . . . Can you tell us how many might have died? . . . What's the body count? They said that there would be no announcements at the mine, and that everything would be announced here. Is that correct? Did anyone survive? Is the search still going on? We're on a deadline here. People have a right to know . . ."

It was the "right to know" that made Larry turn on them. He had told himself he would ignore the press, but that got to him in a way that surprised even him. He turned to the reporters and a small group of curious onlookers. He exploded. "I'm here for the families of the men who are in that mine! Nobody else. They're what's important right now. You wait your turn, you God damn vultures."

There was one reporter in the front who knew his trade and saw an opportunity when it presented itself. He slipped past one of the barricades that had been erected and started in on Larry.

"So there are fatalities. How many? What did they die of? Are you confirming that there are fatalities?"

Larry started to go for him but couldn't move. Reverend Green had opened the doors and five or six pairs of arms were restraining him. He struggled for a moment until he realized he was being restrained and then relaxed.

Reverend Green leaned toward him. "Priorities, Larry. Remember what's important."

Larry looked at Reverend Green. He didn't know the man all that well. Knew who he was, but didn't really know him. His respect for the Baptist minister went way up that afternoon. He nodded.

"He's only doing his job, and it seems he's better at it than his cohorts. Come inside. I've saved a little coffee for you, if you want it. There are a lot of people who have been waiting for you."

Larry wasn't prepared for what he saw when he stepped into the sanctuary of the church. He froze. There were more than three hundred people crammed into a place that was designed for only two hundred. An image from a horror movie, Alfred Hitchcock's *The Birds*, came into his head. The scene where Tippi Hedren was in the attic, and the killer birds were packed into every nook and cranny, all quiet, staring, and ominous.

He tried to swallow but his mouth was dry. There was a pathway being made to the pulpit. He saw his wife Erica there. She was looking at him too, but in admiration. He locked eyes with her, and moved through the crowd. He could do this. Just maybe, he could do this.

After some introductions, and with a chalkboard relocated from the one of the Sunday school rooms, Larry began. The tension in the room was brutal. "First of all," he began, "I want to thank Reverend Green for his hospitality in accommodating all of this. But I understand that there are people supporting this church from all directions and faiths. Every part of this community, old and new, is here. For that, I thank you all. As I go through this, I'm going to stick to the facts, and what I know for sure. But . . ." He paused, trying to find the right words. "I'm not going to pull any punches—I'm going to tell you like it is as we see it. I'll tell you everything I know. But no matter how bad it gets, don't give up hope. We have hope."

He stepped to the chalkboard and drew a line to show the

surface, a vertical tunnel, and then a horizontal tunnel near the bottom of the board. "We know that something happened. We think it was here." He drew an X at the end of the bottom tunnel. "We don't know what. When it happened, there were men working there . . ." He drew a circle around the X. "And over here." From the vertical shaft, he drew another horizontal line in the opposite direction from the first, only much shorter. "And we had men working here." He drew another circle at the end of that tunnel.

"We had men working on tasks at different ends of the mine. The distance from this X to this X, is about one and a half miles. When something happened early this morning here . . ." He pointed to the first X. ". . . the men from here went to help." He pointed to the second X in the smaller tunnel. "The men in this longer tunnel were the more experienced miners. Those in the other end were mostly apprentices with our most senior man.

"Since the explosion we felt, we have not heard from any of them. There was contact shortly before that explosion, but none after. All of the communication in the mine is down due to damage, so we needed to send men inside to see. There are men in there now, and they're setting up communications and trying to move forward. The farther they go, the more damage they're seeing, indicating that whatever happened this morning—the explosion, also happened at this end of the mine." He drew a circle around the end of the longer tunnel. "That's where we think everyone was."

He stopped at that point and looked at the audience. There was a range of reactions, all of them subdued, some of them delayed as translations were made. Several sniffles. But these were a pragmatic lot of people, and the reactions were more stoic than he expected.

"The farther we move into the mine, the worse the smoke. The air quality—the survivability of the air that they can breathe—is diminishing. The rescue team is now wearing what we call SCBAs, or 'self-contained breathing apparatus' because the air in the mine won't sustain life." He paused, letting the statement sink in. There were several sobs as the understanding grew. It was as if nobody wanted to cry out first. Eyes went back to him.

He let the room settle a moment. "That does *not* mean that they're all dead. It just means that we can't breathe the air on the way in. We're attempting to drill a hole from here..." He put an X on the surface above where the miners were. "... to pump in air to this area." He drew a line from the surface down to the end of the long tunnel. "That will take us most of the night, if it works. There's a lot that can go wrong in drilling this hole. We're using equipment that's not designed for this, and it's slow going.

"We're also moving down the tunnel from the elevator to the area where the men may be trapped and unable to communicate. This is being done by the rescue team.

"So far, we have found no one, alive or dead. It will be after sunrise tomorrow that we think we'll have the hole drilled, or the men down to the end of the tunnel." He paused for a moment. "This is hard, I know." He stepped from behind the pulpit, so there wasn't anything between him and the audience. "Members of my family have sat in those pews the same as you, waiting for words, alive or dead. It will take time, and even when we find the dead, it may take time to identify them. We won't announce anything until we're positive. It may be several days. I can take questions for as long as you like and I'll be staying here through the night with you."

The questions went on for many hours, and Larry answered them all. Honestly and to the best of his ability.

He met every person in every family.

He was right. It was the hardest thing he had ever done, or ever would do.

Hank was tired. His men were tired. They were nearing the limits of their endurance and were very close to giving up when they got the news from topside.

The air sample that had been pulled at the far end of the mine, where the well-drilling rig had managed to break in, had shown very high levels of carbon monoxide. Levels that couldn't sustain life even for a little while. Miners had self-rescuers, and additional ones were scattered through the mine and on equipment, so the possibility existed that someone could have been swapping them out over the last thirteen hours, but... But, if the guy had that kind of energy and wherewithal, he would have gotten out by now.

Hank sat by the phone, took off his mask for a moment to grab a slug of water and quickly put it back on. He sat with his back to the ribs, and his hard hat off to cool his head. He motioned at the guys to gather around him. He looked at his watch. They had broken every rule about how long a rescue team should be in a mine. But he had no choice. Dawn of the second day had broken above them, and they had found no bodies, no survivors, and massive destruction. The explosion had blown all of the seals down, along with most of the lighting, vacuum breakers, mining carts. Even all of the mules were dead, over thirty of them in their stalls. The loss was just about total.

Hank was trying to decide if this was a rescue mission or a recovery mission. Recovery meant that they had to leave now, rest, re-equip, and come back to fight the remaining fires and remove the bodies. "One more crosscut, guys, and that's it. We don't want anyone to have to look for us and drag our butts out of here in a body bag. One more crosscut, and we terminate the mission. The far end of the mine does not have a sustainable atmosphere, and we're way past the time when someone could use the self-rescuers to survive. They only last for an hour when new, and all the ones in the mine are a couple of years old." He held out his arm, and one of the team members helped him to his feet. "One more crosscut, and we call it."

The other members of the team looked at each other, and nodded quietly. They fanned out across the tunnel and went deeper into the mine.

The onlookers at the mine scanned the sky when they heard the buzzing sound of an aircraft in flight. They searched the clear and cold morning sky. The direction of the sound couldn't be pinpointed. Most people turned to the north; the rest turned in multiple directions. The aircraft came into view from the northeast and the gathered crowd turned to watch it. The aircraft began a long slow turn around the rising column of smoke. It circled only one time, and then turned toward the landing strip.

A murmur began, wondering who was on the craft. Rumors flew. Guesses were made. Most of the down-timers had no idea who it would be. It was certainly not important, at least for them.

Mike Stearns stared at the column of black smoke rising from the metal structure that made up the entrance of the mine. From his perspective in the air, eight hundred feet above the ground, it looked bad. Very bad. He leaned his forehead against the cold glass canopy as the airplane made the wide turn over the mine. He was aware of the upturned faces pointed in his direction and just as aware when they turned back after identifying the plane, focusing on the reality in front of them. Whoever was flying above them wasn't important, not today. He looked at the smoke again. His breath began to cloud the glass in front of him. He let it obscure his vision. *Is this how a mine owner feels when something like this happens in his mine, under his direction,* he wondered. He had always hoped so, in the past. But he was never sure.

Larry was nudged awake gently by Reverend Green. "Telephone, Larry. They want to talk to you. The mine. It's Stacks."

Larry eased to a standing position and every eye that was awake followed him. When they saw he was moving toward the phone in Reverend Green's office, the people who were already awake woke the others. Larry let his wife stay asleep, closed the office door behind him, and picked up the phone.

"Masaniello."

"Larry, Stacks. The drill got in, we pulled a sample, and it was only eight percent O two. There's no way . . . they took a couple of samples just to be sure. They've been down there too long. We think we need to call it. I have been in touch with Hank and he's going to do one more crosscut, then we'll transition into a recovery mission. But he and his team need to come out, no matter what." Stacks' voice was flat, almost emotionless. It was as if he let any emotion into his voice, he wouldn't be able to control it.

"Thanks, Stacks. You did what you could." Larry hung up the phone and turned to Reverend Green. He simply shook his head.

"You did what you could too, you know."

Larry scoffed. "Did I? I don't think so. There's always something else I could have done, or should have done. Some procedure, some rule about safety. I don't know . . . *something*. I'm responsible for their deaths. Nobody else. My mine, my responsibility."

There was a soft knock on the door and Erica poked her head into the room. "Someone here to see you." She opened the door and Mike Stearns walked in. The look in his eyes mirrored the one in Larry's. Grief and pain. Mike and Erica came in, and closed the door behind them.

Larry looked directly at Stearns. "They're calling it, Mike. They're all dead." Erica came to him and gave him a gentle embrace. Mike just nodded.

Larry looked at the ceiling, tears welling in his eyes. "Mike, I'm a coal miner from a little town in West Virginia. I got no business runnin' a mine. Crew of guys, yeah, maybe, but a whole fucking mine? What was I thinking? Hell, what were you thinking? I wasn't the right guy for this at all. No wonder Quentin Underwood is such a prick all the time. Who could live this way?"

Erica pulled herself closer to him. Reverend Green looked at Mike, and his eyebrows went up, as if to say "Well . . . ?"

Mike took a step forward. "Would it help you to know that I have been anticipating this for over a year?"

They all looked at him with surprise. "What we're doing here isn't trying to make a buck off of the backs of our brother miners, Larry. That's how Quentin thinks. That's all he thinks about. That's how he can do what he can do. He has skills, but no, I dunno—no *humanity*, I guess. He's perfect for this shit, precisely because it doesn't bother him." Mike leaned back against the door. "But you and me, we're different. We're not trying to make a buck. Do you know *what* we're doing, Larry?"

Larry was confused and angry. "We're digging a hole in the ground and killing people for coal."

There was a brief flash of anger in Mike's eyes. "That's right, Larry. But why do we have to do that? Think about it. Why?"

Larry hung his head, and stared at the floor for a moment. He then looked up at Mike, then his wife, and finally Reverend Green. He pointed to the door, and the people gathered outside the office. "I need to talk to them."

Mike nodded, slowly at first, then empathically in a final nod. His wife—"*thank you Lord, for Erica*"—just hugged him.

Reverend Green spoke next. "We'll follow your lead, Larry. You take the pulpit and we'll be behind you. We'll be there."

Larry took a deep breath and let it out. He straightened and headed for the door. When the phone rang, he was caught off guard, and actually jumped a little. Larry stopped as Green answered, "First Baptist." There was a pause. "He's right here." He handed the phone to Larry.

"Masaniello."

"Larry, Stacks." The tone of Stacks' voice wasn't anything like the last call. The emotion was overflowing, and he was close to tears. "We found two guys! We found them alive!" Larry could hear a background of cheers and celebration. "I just got the word from Hank. We're sending down two spare SCBAs and a stretcher team. One of them is pretty bad, but Hank thinks he'll make it! You won't believe it! Metzinger, that clever SOB, was living off of compressed air. He was in the tool crib—and you know that air is piped in there for testing the pneumatic tools—so he set up a compressed air line, a valve, and they got under some plastic sheeting. They've been there for over sixteen hours! They're fucking alive!"

"Thanks, Stacks. What are the names?"

"Wilhelm Metzinger and Willy Huenefelder."

Larry wrote the names on a pad of paper from the desk. "What does Hank say about the rest of them?"

The tone of Stacks voice changed again. "He—Hank, uh." Stacks volume lowered on the phone, somewhat conspiratorially. "Larry, I don't know that I agree. Now that we've found these guys, I think we should keep this a rescue mission, not a recovery. Hank is saying that it should be a recovery from here on out. I don't know, and some of us think that—"

"Stacks, if Hank says it goes to recovery, it goes to recovery. That's his call. That's what he does for us. Does the compressed air go any farther than the crib?"

"No. Metzinger had to rig up something because it was damaged downstream from the tool crib."

"Then there's really no hope, is there, Stacks?"

"No." He heard Stacks half sigh and half sob into the phone.

"Thanks, Stacks. And, Stacks . . . good job."

"Thanks, Boss."

Larry placed the phone back in its cradle, and double checked the two names on his paper. He turned to the others in the office. "They found two of them alive. Metzinger and Huenefelder."

Smiles broke out across the room. Then Mike very quietly asked a question. "And the mission changing to recovery?"

Larry nodded. "Hank called it. One miracle is all we can expect per day, I suppose. This actually makes it harder for the twenty-six other families, doesn't it? And it won't be easy for the other two, either."

Larry straightened with as much resolve as he could muster,

rubbed his face with both hands to clear his eyes, picked up the paper, and strode to the doorway. The others filed out behind him.

It took almost a month of working around the clock to get the mine back in operation. Things were tight for energy supplies over the last part of the winter, but by spring, production had resumed. In the meadow, where the monument stood for the up-time miners who had been killed in the Number 9 Mine disaster, the bodies of twenty-six down-timers were buried. A stone was erected for them, with names and other words carved into the face, in English and German.

They have not died in vain.

These men fought the battle under the ground,
just as others fought it above the ground,
on the sea and in the air.

These men fought for the community and the nation and,
through their sacrifice, helped to bond them together.

We are all in their debt.

An afterword on Dr. Johnson

Eric Flint

For those of you who have the misfortune to be ignorant of the personage of Dr. Samuel Johnson, to whom I referred in my preface, he was a prominent eighteenth-century literary figure. He was born in 1709—the same year as the passage of the Statute of Anne, the first real copyright law in the English-speaking world—and he died in 1784. He was the author of the famous *A Dictionary of the English Language*, many literary works, and was the subject of James Boswell's *Life of Samuel Johnson*, probably the single most famous biography ever written in the English language.

Johnson was also a renowned quipster, and even people who've never heard of him have usually heard some of his wisecracks. Probably the three most famous are:

> *The road to hell is paved with good intentions.*

> *Patriotism is the last refuge of the scoundrel.*

And:

> *Depend upon it, sir, when a man knows he is to be hanged in a fortnight, it concentrates his mind wonderfully.*

Not surprisingly, since he was a writer himself, many of his remarks focus on the writer's craft. Here's one of my personal favorites, since I'm also an editor as well as an author:

> *Your manuscript is both good and original. But the part*
> *that is good is not original, and the part that is original*
> *is not good.*

The best-known of all his quips about being an author, however, is:

> *No man but a blockhead ever wrote, except for money.*

Professional writers love this line—and I am no exception. But
what's really fascinating about it is that it's perhaps the single
most blockhead statement ever made about being a professional
writer.

Why? Because, second only to playing the lottery, the business of writing has got to be the chanciest way to make a living
imaginable. There are a few exceptions, granted, and those are
the authors best known to the public. But, taking the profession
as a whole, it is quite literally true that the average short-order
cook, waitress or hotel maid will earn more at those trades in a
lifetime than the average author will at theirs.

The truth is, I could with far greater accuracy state that *no man
but a blockhead ever wrote, thinking he'd make money.* I do not
know a single writer—and I am no exception—who began writing
because he or she really thought they'd earn a lot of money by
doing so. They did it simply because they had something they
wanted to say. If they could get paid for it, of course, all the
better. But they would have written anyway.

So why do authors love the quip so much? Partly, I'm sure,
because it stiffens our resolution as we sally forth to joust with
tight-fisted publishers. But I think the main reason is that the
wisecrack is our all-purpose shield to fend off the inevitable accu-
sation from many reviewers and some readers that the author is
clearly prostituting himself or herself, forsaking the demands of
The Art of Literature for the sake of filthy lucre.

It can get annoying, sometimes. I once said to a particularly
persistent critic of mine that if he conducted himself in his own
line of work the same way he demanded that I conduct myself
as an author, he'd be fired from his job inside of a week.

Any job.

So it goes. No man but a blockhead ever wrote, thinking
everyone would like his work.

Images

Note from Editor:

There are various images, mostly portraits from the time, which illustrate different aspects of the 1632 universe. In the first issue of the *Grantville Gazette,* I included those with the volume itself. Since that created downloading problems for some people, however, I've separated all the images and they will be maintained and expanded on their own schedule.

If you're interested, you can look at the images and my accompanying commentary at no extra cost. They are set up in the Baen Free Library. You can find them as follows:

1) Go to www.baen.com
2) Select "Free Library" from the blue menu at the top.
3) Once in the Library, select "The Authors" from the yellow menu on the left.
4) Once in "The Authors," select "Eric Flint."
5) Then select "Images from the Grantville Gazette."

Submissions to the Magazine

If anyone is interested in submitting stories or articles for future issues of the *Grantville Gazette,* you are welcome to do so. But you must follow a certain procedure:

1) All stories and articles must first be posted in a conference in Baen's Bar set aside for the purpose, called "1632 Slush." Do *not* send them to me directly, because I won't read them. It's good idea to submit a sketch of your story to the conference first, since people there will likely spot any major problems that you overlooked. That can wind up saving you a lot of wasted work.

You can get to that conference by going to Baen Books' web site www.baen.com. Then select "Baen's Bar." If it's your first visit, you will need to register. (That's quick and easy.) Once you're in the Bar, the three conferences devoted to the 1632 universe are "1632 Slush," "1632 Slush Comments," and "1632 Tech Manual." You should post your sketch, outline or story in "1632 Slush." Any discussion of it should take place in "1632 Slush Comments." The "1632 Tech Manual" is for any general discussion not specifically related to a specific story.

2) Your story/article will then be subjected to discussion and commentary by participants in the 1632 discussion. In essence, it will get chewed on by what amounts to a very large, virtual writers' group.

You do *not* need to wait until you've finished the story to start posting it in "1632 Slush." In fact, it's a good idea not to wait, because you will often find that problems can be spotted early in the game, before you've put all the work into completing the piece.

3) While this is happening, the editor of the *Grantville Gazette,* Paula Goodlett, will be keeping an eye on the discussion. She will alert me whenever a story or article seems to be gaining general approval from the participants in the discussion. There's also an editorial board to which Paula and I belong, which does much the same thing. The other members of the board are Karen Bergstralh, Rick Boatright, and Laura Runkle. In addition, authors who publish regularly in the 1632 setting participate on the board as *ex officio* members. My point is that plenty of people will be looking over the various stories being submitted, so you needn't worry that your story will just get lost in the shuffle.

4) At that point—and *only* at that point—do I take a look at a story or article.

☆   ☆   ☆

I insist that people follow this procedure, for two reasons:

First, as I said, I'm very busy and I just don't have time to read everything submitted until I have some reason to think it's gotten past a certain preliminary screening.

Second, and even more important, the setting and "established canon" in this series is quite extensive by now. If anyone tries to write a story without first taking the time to become familiar with the setting, they will almost invariably write something which—even if it's otherwise well written—I simply can't accept.

In short, the procedure outlined above will save *you* a lot of wasted time and effort also.

One point in particular: I have gotten extremely hardnosed about the way in which people use American characters in their stories (so-called "up-timers"). That's because I began discovering that my small and realistically portrayed coal mining town of 3500 people was being willy-nilly transformed into a "town" with a population of something like 20,000 people—half of whom were Navy SEALs who just happened to be in town at the Ring of Fire, half of whom were rocket scientists (ibid), half of whom were brain surgeons (ibid), half of whom had a personal library the size of the Library of Congress, half of whom . . .

Not to mention the F-16s which "just happened" to be flying through the area, the army convoys (ibid), the trains full of vital industrial supplies (ibid), the FBI agents in hot pursuit of master criminals (ibid), the . . .

NOT A CHANCE. If you want to use an up-time character, you *must* use one of the "authorized" characters. Those are the characters created by Virginia DeMarce using genealogical software and embodied in what is called "the grid."

You can obtain a copy of the grid from the web site which collects and presents the by-now voluminous material concerning the series, www.1632.org. Look on the right for the link to "Virginia's Uptimer Grid." While you're at it, you should also look further down at the links under the title "Authors' Manual."

You will be paid for any story or factual article which is published. The rates that we pay are five cents a word for any story or article. This pay rate is professional, as established by the Science Fiction & Fantasy Writers of America, Inc. In the event a story or article is later selected for inclusion in a paper edition, you will get no further advance but will be entitled to a pro rata share of any royalties earned by the authors from that volume.

Grantville Gazette

An electronic-only magazine of stories and fact articles based on Eric Flint's 1632 "Ring of Fire" universe

The *Grantville Gazette* can be purchased through Baen Books' Webscriptions service at www.baens.com (then select Webscriptions).

Each electronic volume of the *Gazette* can be purchased individually from Webscriptions, or you can purchase them in packages from Webscriptions as follows:

- Volume 1. This volume is free and can be obtained from the Baen Free Library. (Once you're in the Baen web site at www.baen.com, select "Free Library" on the left hand side of the menu at the top. Then, select "The Books" and you'll find *Grantville Gazette Volume 1*.)
- Volumes 2–4, $15.
- Volumes 5–8, $15.
- Volumes 8–10, $15.
- Volumes 1–10, $40. This special offer allows all of our fans to read all of the stories published so far at a bargain rate.
- Volumes 11–13, $15.
- Volumes 14–16, $15.
- Volumes 17–19, $15.
- Volumes 20–22, $15.
- Volumes 23–25, $15. Volume 23 is available, with Volumes 24 and 25 in production.

Or you can subscribe through www.grantvillegazette.com, which is an electronic magazine that publishes six issues per year. The cost for access to the site for one year is $50.00. Downloads are available for each issue, and certain benefits also apply for members of the Ring of Fire club. See www.grantvillegazette.com for more details.